Sweet Hearts

By the Authors

Melissa Brayden

Waiting in the Wings

Heart Block

How Sweet It Is

Soho Loft Romances

Kiss the Girl

Just Three Words

Ready or Not

Rachel Spangler

Learning Curve

Trails Merge

The Long Way Home

LoveLife

Spanish Heart

Does She Love You?

Timeless

Heart Of The Game

Karis Walsh

Harmony

Worth the Risk

Sea Glass Inn

Improvisation

Wingspan

Blindsided

Tacoma Mounted Patrol

Mounting Danger

Mounting Evidence

Sweet Hearts

by

Melissa Brayden

Rachel Spangler

Karis Walsh

2015

SWEET HEARTS

ISBN 13: 978-1-62639-475-9

This Trade Paperback Original Is Published By
Bold Strokes Books, Inc.
P.O. Box 249
Valley Falls, NY 12185

First Edition: December 2015

Credits
Editor: Ruth Sternglantz
Production Design: Stacia Seaman
Cover Design by Sheri (graphicartist2020@hotmail.com)

Contents

Firework

Melissa Brayden

Chapter One

Lucy Danaher was a daydreamer. She always had been, dating back to the first grade when she used to get into trouble for staring out the window at the swirling clouds rather than paying attention during handwriting instruction. As an unfortunate result, she'd never really mastered the cursive *S* and lived in shame.

Simpler times, she thought with a smile as she stared dreamily out her twenty-ninth-floor office window, struck at the way the big fluffy white cloud above the skyline looked soft enough to sleep on. Lucy did that a lot, the staring at work, because the San Diego skyline, the dips and leaps that framed the high-rises, never ceased to transfix her and carry her away from the hustle and bustle of the office.

"Luce, your two o'clock is here," her assistant Trevor said from the doorway of her office. A glance at the planner on her monitor reminded her that she'd agreed to meet with that reporter she'd been playing phone tag with. Something about a feature story and how it came to garner the attention it did. While she had a million things on her plate, she knew it was never wise to turn down a little PR, and better to raise awareness about their industry. Not a lot of people understood the concept of a newswire service, and it was important they took every chance they could get to educate the public. That little feature story the reporter wanted to discuss had been picked up in over twenty-five regional newspapers, all because of the press release they'd put on the wire. It should be an easy interview, and then she'd get back to working with legal on the contract language and figuring out how to convince the Dallas editors to not make so many transmission errors.

"Got it," she said, turning back to Trevor. "Give me a minute to grab some notes, and send him in." She was happy to meet with the guy and toot Global NewsWire's horn a bit. In the end, it just meant more business, and as the CEO of a multi-million-dollar company, that's what she was all about. She checked herself in her compact just to make sure she was presentable, running a hand through her long dark hair to fluff it some. She'd worn it down today and questioned that choice now, especially if there was going to be a photo. She applied a touch of lip gloss and turned at the sound of the door opening, smiling, already in people mode. She was good at people mode, and it had landed her where she was, but she didn't relish it as it related to business. She did, however, relish the salary. GNW took good care of her, making money a distant concern.

"Ms. Danaher?" *Whoa.* She locked eyes with a statuesque blonde whom she was not at all expecting. Wait, hadn't Trevor written down the name Kris? She glanced absently at her computer screen before refocusing on the looker. She wore jeans and a white cotton button-up, untucked, but slim fitting. Straight blond hair fell to her shoulders and sea-green eyes sparkled at Lucy in greeting. This was not the reporter she was expecting to see.

"Call me Lucy." She extended her hand. "And you are?"

"Kristin James of the *Union-Tribune*," the woman said, grasping it. Firm handshake, but not too firm, which meant she knew what she was doing. She had Lucy's attention.

And aha, Kris in her appointment book must, in fact, be Kristin.

The day was looking up. Regardless, she made a mental note to discuss gender-neutral names with Trevor at her next opportunity. Kristin wore a low heel, but Lucy had her pegged at maybe five-seven, a good two inches taller than her. Nothing she couldn't remedy with a strategic heel of her own. "Please sit down. Can I offer you something to drink?"

"No, thank you. I'm fine." Kristin glanced around. "Wow. I love your office. The view is breathtaking. If I worked here, I don't know if I'd ever get any work done."

"It's a struggle I don't always win," Lucy said, following Kristin's gaze to the skyline behind her, understanding Kristin's sentiment more than she realized. "But I wouldn't trade it for the world."

Kristin studied her. “You’re young for a CEO. I was expecting someone, I don’t know, buttoned up and a lot stuffier. A nice surprise.”

Lucy sent Kristin her best smile. “I think that’s a compliment.”

Kristin held her gaze and nodded. “It definitely is.” This was going well. She liked this Kristin. Her interest was piqued on multiple levels.

“What about you? Have you been with the paper long?”

“Not too long, no. I moved to San Diego just last month from a suburb of San Francisco.”

“I love San Francisco. Making friends yet?” Lucy asked.

“Here and there. My biggest learning curve has been navigating your highways. I’m just now starting to really get my bearings.”

“Traffic can be ridiculous, but it’s a great way to come up with a killer grocery list.” Lucy tucked a strand of hair behind her ear and circled back behind her desk. “Please, have a seat.”

Kristin sat in the leather club chair across from Lucy’s desk and held up a digital recorder from her messenger bag. “Do you mind if I record our interaction?”

“Not at all.”

“Great,” Kristin said, smiling. Her eyes really were a remarkably vibrant color, especially against that crisp white shirt. “Shall we get started?”

Lucy made a sweeping motion with her hand and took a seat behind her desk. “By all means.”

Kristin sat back and consulted her notes before raising her gaze and speaking into the recorder. “This is Kristin James interviewing Lucy Danaher of Global NewsWire on the afternoon of May twelfth. Ms. Danaher, GNW recently ran a press release about a young man who rescued a school bus that stalled out on a rural railroad track as a train approached. Since that time the story has inarguably received a great deal of attention in the media.”

“That’s true,” Lucy said, grinning. “Our Des Moines office ran the release, putting it on the wire. A large number of regional papers with high circulation picked up the story and ran it as a prominent feature. We were happy to get it out there in the world, and I think this example shows how far our reach really is at GNW.”

“A feature story the *San Diego Union-Tribune* ran as well.”

“Yes, we were thrilled to see that. The story is not only an exciting one, but quite touching on a basic human level. The gentleman who saved those children"—she referred to the file folder on her desk with the clippings—"Jonathan Ableman, is a true hero. He deserves every bit of attention he receives."

The sides of Kristin's mouth seemed to tug and she sat there for a moment. Given the silence, Lucy wondered if she should expand upon her answer, but Kristin beat her there. "Interesting, the classification of Mr. Ableman as a hero. You're certainly not the only one who thinks so."

Lucy smiled, unsure of the point of the comment. "You disagree?"

"Let me ask you a question first. A newswire service like yours is more or less a wire for hire, correct? People pay you to send out press releases to a much wider audience than they could ever reach on their own, correct?"

"Quite true. Our clients use our services to distribute newsworthy information via press release to global, national, and regional circuits. The client selects a circuit and we send out the release for them. The wire, on the other side of things, is a prominent tool for news organizations gathering stories."

"With your company's name at the bottom of the release."

Lucy sat forward, trying to anticipate what it was this woman was angling at. "Each release is labeled as a GNW transmission when it's sent out, yes."

"In that case, don't you feel a responsibility to make sure that the information you're transmitting is credible?"

Wow. Okay. She took a moment because it felt like she'd walked into something here. "While it's true we keep a watch on the content our clients ask us to transmit, and an editor reads and proofs each release before sending it out, the responsibility to authenticate the information ultimately falls on the client."

"So you pass the buck?"

"No, not at all," Lucy said, making sure to keep her voice calm, even keeled. "But we process thousands of releases during a twenty-four-hour period. We can't fact check each one any more than UPS can go through every package that comes into its warehouse. Plus, each story is sourced at the bottom of the release with the name of the PR firm requesting transmission. We're a delivery service and don't claim to be anything more."

"Thereby you take no responsibility if the public is misinformed based on one of your transmissions?"

"Again, that falls to the client." Honestly, Lucy wasn't sure whether to zig or zag at these purposeful questions and wondered if she shouldn't stop the meeting and refer all of this to legal. But, no, she could handle this woman, and she knew one thing for sure. When she and Emory, her best friend, built this company from the ground up, they'd believed in the work they did and she'd stand by it. She consulted the file in front of her. "In the case of this release, Mr. Ableman was represented by a public relations firm. We transmitted the release containing his story on our Feature Circuit, used by news agencies to pick up human-interest stories."

"And that makes it acceptable? Because it came from a public relations firm?"

"It's acceptable enough to not refuse service."

"I see."

"Are you saying his story is untrue?"

"I am."

The exchange was now clipped and charged with an intensity Lucy hadn't planned on when she agreed to participate in what she thought would be a fluffy accessory piece to the school bus story. This was so not how she envisioned her afternoon. This Kristin woman was a shark in sheep's clothing.

She handed Lucy a file folder that seemed to contain the work of a private investigator. "There was a school bus," Kristin said, pointing at a paragraph on the report. "It did stall out near a railroad track." She held up one finger. "Not exactly *on* one, but close enough to be dangerous. A group of nearby farmers worked together to move the bus to safety, but it seems Mr. Ableman was not one of them. In fact, he's not known to any of the farmers, nor can the school bus driver authenticate ever seeing him there. No one in that town has even heard of the guy, nor do they recognize his photo."

Perfect. Lucy dropped the folder in annoyance. "So he made it all up?"

"It seems he insinuated himself into an existing story and sensationalized it."

Lucy shook her head. "That's horrible."

"It is. What's worse is that hundreds and thousands of citizens across the nation were able to hear his story because Global NewsWire put it into the world as fact."

"We'll issue a retraction," Lucy said quietly.

"I think that might help."

Lucy rubbed her forehead. "So this is an exposé that you're working on, not a feature?"

"I'm writing a piece examining the importance of truth in the stories we pass on in our society or, rather, the lack of importance. A number of national scandals from news anchors to authors fabricating facts have dominated headlines over the last few years. Jonathan Ableman is a local example of a perpetuated untruth."

"I see."

Kristin picked up her recorder. "I think I got everything I need here. Thank you so much for speaking with me today."

Lucy stood. "So you're going to include GNW in this story? Ms. James, we were duped just as much as the rest of the world."

Kristin offered a polite smile and Lucy now wanted to roll her eyes at how beautiful this woman was. The universe's way of playing a mean joke on her, clearly. "I'm just gathering some facts at this point," Kristin said.

"Well, I encourage you to give it some thought before running with it."

"Of course." Kristin nodded courteously. "Enjoy the rest of your afternoon." And then the blonde with the eyes was gone.

"Easy for you to say," Lucy muttered to the empty room. She reached for her cell and called Emory, who was off that day. Two years ago, when Emory met Sarah, the love of her life, she'd made some changes to her lifestyle, and handing Lucy the reins at GNW had been one of them.

"What's up, Luce?" Emory said upon answering.

Lucy swiveled in her chair, dropping the corporate powerhouse persona. "It's been a day. I might die if we can't do drinks. Can we? This is the part where you say yes."

She heard Emory laugh quietly on the other end of the phone. "I think I can swing drinks. Sarah will be with Grace at her gymnastics lesson." When Sarah moved in with Emory, they'd made the decision to raise Sarah's ten-year-old daughter, Grace, together. The kid was a riot. Precocious, quirky, and fun.

"Gymnastics class is perfect," Lucy said. "I love tumblers. Especially drinking from them. You in?"

"Are you planning to be dramatic?"

"I can't promise I won't be, because I am dramatic and did you not just hear me say I had a day? Because I did. I had a *day*, and I'll need appropriate friend support paired with a cocktail of my choosing."

"Those are two things I can do. Meet me at the Lavender Room at six?"

"With bells on. And I'm not kidding. I'm stopping and buying bells. I'll need them to cheer me up. I'm stressed."

"I'd expect nothing less."

❖

It was a quarter to six when Lucy made it home, which meant she would sadly be late for drinks with Emory. Even more tragically, it happened a lot. Something she was working on, though the nature of her high-status job didn't help. When you were in charge, people tended to wait on you without complaint, and she would never want to take advantage of that. Lazy and entitled were two things she did not aspire to be. She fired off an apologetic text to Emory so she wouldn't race over to the bar and made her way into her small beach house and slipped out of her heels, scrunching her toes that were at long last free from the endless day.

Instantly, she heard the click, click, click of tiny paws on the aged hardwood. Her Yorkshire terrier, Bernadette Peters, appeared in tail-wagging greeting. "Why, hello there, you tiny bundle of love." Bernadette Peters licked her face happily, her whole body shaking in excitement because at long last her owner was home. "I missed you too. Let's get you some dinner and a chew toy. What do you say?" Her answer was more shaking, which in Bernadette Peters speak translated to wholehearted agreement.

Lucy strode farther into the two-bedroom beach bungalow she'd come to adore. Her place wasn't big like Emory's beach house half a mile down the shoreline, but it was charming and it was hers. Her favorite spot on the back deck faced out over the water. She'd start her day with a cup of coffee and often end it out there with a nightcap, watching wave after wave roll in from the Pacific.

As soon as BP was fed and fawned over properly, Lucy quickly changed clothes from high-powered CEO to Everygirl about town in dark jeans and a midnight blue V-neck. She topped off her look with a long necklace and fruit punch lip gloss, pulling her hair back on the sides to complete the transformation. With keys in hand, she hopped into her silver Aston Martin and headed to the Lavender Room.

Emory was, of course, already there when she arrived, nursing a Kentucky Mule at a small table. "I got one for you too," she said to Lucy and slid a drink her way.

"You're the nicest to me."

"I am. I'm so glad you noticed."

The Lavender Room was a lesbian bar that knew how to do things right. Upscale in nature, the décor was classy. Through the center of the room stood a square mahogany bar with a row of cream-colored upholstered bar stools along each of its sides. Matching lighting fixtures with cream-colored shades hung from the ceilings, and jazzy piano music played from the bar's speakers.

"I haven't seen you in three days," Lucy said. "What's new? Give me your updates."

Emory, her blond hair pulled into a subtle knot at the back of her neck, considered the question. "Grace wants to start her own talk show for ten-year-olds and has decided to practice interviewing people, which is code for Sarah and me. Today, the pint-sized Barbara Walters delved deep into my childhood and I'm not sure I'm over it."

"She hasn't asked to interview me yet."

"Trust me. The clock is ticking."

"And how's Sarah?"

"Busy, but happy. She's working on a whole list of summer activities for when Grace gets out of school. The word Disney may have been tossed around."

Lucy regarded Emory, amazed at the woman she'd become. "Who would have thought two years ago that Emory Owen would don a pair of mouse ears and sing 'It's a Small World' while riding Dumbo?"

Emory winced. "I'm not sure I'd go that far."

"Well, I have to. It's happening."

Emory laughed and stirred her drink absently. "So what happened to you today? Why all the over-the-top lamenting on the phone?"

"Do you remember the school bus feature that snagged all of that attention four months back?"

"I do."

"The guy made it all up. Or at least made up his part in it."

Emory sat back. "Shit. Seriously?"

"Yeah. And without knowing this, I agreed to talk to a *Union-Trib* reporter about the story and walked blindly into her trap."

"*Her* trap?"

"Yep, Kristin something, whose main goal in life is apparently calling me onto the carpet for running the release."

Emory laughed it off. "That's ridiculous. We're a wire service and not responsible for the journalistic integrity of others. Don't sweat it."

"Trust me. I get that, but the Miss America of news reporters I spoke with this afternoon sees things very differently. This could be some really bad PR, and I hate bad PR."

"I'm sorry, Miss America?"

Lucy sat back in her chair and sighed. "Miss America with an ax to grind is more accurate. Miss America with an evil streak. A vengeful side. There'll probably be a movie about her one day. Wes Craven style."

"1990 would like that reference back."

"Still. You should have seen her, all beautiful and unaffected. Like she was the morality police and I was in major violation and not capable of her divine understanding of journalistic integrity." Emory smiled at her. "What? What are you smiling at?"

"It's just very rare that someone gets to you like this."

Lucy set her drink down in defeat. "Yeah, well, I felt attacked."

"I can see that. But you know what? It's not your fault, nor is it the fault of the company. We had no way of knowing."

"Right? Why couldn't she see that?" She turned her head and followed the progress of a blonde on her way to the bar, pausing because Lucy wasn't sure she was actually seeing what she seemed to be seeing. No way. It couldn't be. What were the odds?

"Luce? You okay over there?"

She turned back to Emory, heat flaring in her chest. "She's here."

"Who's here?"

"Evil reporter. She's here in this room."

"Oh, show her to me! I need to see this woman."

"Don't you dare be obvious, but she's at the bar, looking perfect and superior."

Emory delayed a moment before casually turning her head in the direction of the bar, where Kristin seemed to have taken a seat. "She's pretty. You were right."

Lucy shook her head in warning. "Don't let it fool you."

"And gay apparently."

"We don't know that for sure."

"Well, she's at a well-known gay bar so I'm going to wager the chances are good. I'm quite astute, you know."

Lucy shrugged. "She's fairly new to town. Maybe she's trying to meet people."

"Yeah," Emory said. "Gay people."

"So she's a lesbian," Lucy said to herself, mulling that over. "Well, not entirely shocking. There was some mild flirting before she set out to destroy me and everything I stand for."

Emory held her thumb and forefinger close together. "Maybe a little dramatic again. Why don't you go talk to her?"

"That's the craziest thing you've ever said to me. Should I parasail naked next? Why would I talk to her?"

"Because you're clearly bothered by the whole experience. Maybe," Emory said calmly, "this is your chance to smooth things over."

Damn it. Lucy hated it when Emory made valid points. She took another drink, hoping the alcohol would numb her senses a bit, especially if she was going to face Ms. Kristin James. She set the empty glass on the table. "If I don't return, call for help."

Emory held up her phone. "On it."

Lucy gave her head a little what-the-hell shake and stepped up to the bar alongside Kristin. "Vodka martini," she said to the bartender. "Two olives."

Kristin glanced her way and offered a smile in greeting. "Ms. Danaher."

"Ms. James." Lucy realized her voice sounded cold, aloof, which prompted her to pause, reminding herself that the goal here was to deliver some sort of peace offering. There were olives in her drink. Maybe she could fashion a branch of some sort. "Listen to us," Lucy said lightly. "I thought we'd done away with the formalities. I'll call you Kristin if you'll call me Lucy."

"We should definitely give that a shot."

The bartender placed a martini in front of Lucy and she sipped it lightly. "I haven't seen you in here before. Are you stalking me?"

Kristin nodded. "Desperately. How did you know?"

Lucy smiled. "I can't reveal all my secrets," she said, which earned a polite laugh.

"I come in for a drink after work on occasion," Kristin said, "but only once in a while. It's a nice little spot."

"I think so too," Lucy said. "My friends and I love it." Kristin had a great mouth, kind of pouty and full. She gave herself a mental shake. This was the woman who'd slammed her in her office only a few hours prior. How was it that Lucy was now irrationally captivated by her very attractive lips? The bottom one especially, as it—*stop it.* Sometimes she didn't understand herself.

"About earlier today," Kristin said, swiveling her stool in Lucy's direction. "I hope there are no hard feelings about the interview. You seem like a nice enough person."

That was her, the nicest. "Of course not. And to prove it, let me get your drink."

Kristin held up a hand. "Oh no. I couldn't let you do that."

"But I want to," Lucy said, meeting the green eyes that wouldn't stop. The bartender, having heard their conversation, nodded and accepted Lucy's American Express.

"That's very generous of you," Kristin said, raising her glass. "I don't know a ton of people in town, so when someone does something nice…well, it resonates. So thank you."

"You're welcome," Lucy said. "And now you've met me, so you know one more person."

"This is a valid and encouraging point." And then, "You're welcome to sit."

Aha, an invitation. "Maybe just for a minute, if you don't mind."

"I don't mind at all."

Lucy slid onto the stool next to Kristin's. "Good, because if I'm being honest, I didn't like how we left things at my office. I'm not sure we ever saw eye to eye."

Kristin moved her head side to side as if considering this. "No, perhaps not. But maybe we don't have to agree in order to be friends."

She pushed the comment aside and focused on her goal. "But I was hopeful that I *could* get you to understand."

"Why GNW ran the press release?" Kristin asked.

"Yes. Because, as I said, it's not our job to differentiate."

"I realize that's how you feel, but that kind of outlook doesn't do a lot of people any good. If it weren't for that not-our-fault policy, there wouldn't have been thirty-two erroneously run news stories throwing a literary parade for a bald-faced liar."

"We didn't set out to deceive anyone." Her eyes met Kristin's and she decided to just be honest with her and ask for what she sought. "Please don't include us in this story."

Kristin closed her eyes momentarily. "You want the story killed."

"Not killed. Just for you to leave GNW out of it."

"So that's what this is?" Kristin held up the drink halfheartedly. "Not a token of friendship at all, but a negotiating tactic."

Lucy didn't know what to say to that because voiced out loud, coupled with the dejected look on Kristin's face, her actions now seemed a little low. "No, it was both."

Kristin stood. "I understand. And it's fine. But I should probably get home."

Lucy stood there, feeling not only like she'd dug herself further into a hole with the story, but she also seemed to have hurt Kristin's feelings. Apparently, she had some. Who knew? "Kristin, for what it's worth, I didn't mean to—"

"All is well. Enjoy your night."

Lucy stood there experiencing full-on crash and burn as Kristin left the bar. She headed slowly back to Emory, who smiled up sympathetically. "That didn't look like it went so well."

"That's because it didn't. She hates me," Lucy said, plopping down into the chair like a petulant child.

"Who could hate you?"

"Right?"

"And while I'd love to stay a little longer and list the many attributes that make you amazing, I need to head home and whip something up for dinner."

Lucy sighed. "I figured you'd be out after one drink. It's okay."

While she adored Sarah and Grace more than was even possible, there were times when she missed her friend and the old days when they stayed out late, chatting about life or strategizing about the business. In all honesty, she felt a little lonely as of late.

"Keep your chin up, Luce. Everything will be all right."

"Sung by the Killers on the album *Hot Fuss* in 2004."

Emory shook her head. "How are you able to do that?"

Lucy grinned. "It's a gift. One of many."

Chapter Two

Kristin James hadn't enjoyed her day.

It started with the five pages of notes she'd received from her editor, Dalton, on the preliminary work she'd turned in on the exposé. Then she'd received a call from her landlord that he wouldn't be fixing the dishwasher that continued to leak water onto the kitchen floor of her rental house, followed by the embarrassing exchange at the Lavender Room with that press-release-CEO of all people. But the fact that her Honda Civic wouldn't start once she'd made it to the parking lot of the bar was just about all she could handle.

Instead of curling into the fetal position and surrendering to the universe, a course of action that she had first considered, Kristin sat on the curb outside the bar, waiting on the cab she'd called. That's when she saw the blonde Lucy had been chatting with make her way to a Jaguar convertible and pull out of the parking lot. A girlfriend, perhaps? They *were* at a lesbian bar. The two of them would certainly make a striking couple. Her phone buzzed in her pocket, interrupting her thoughts. Anticipating the cab company, she was surprised to see the readout.

"Hiya, Mom."

"I haven't heard from you in two days."

She smiled and relaxed back onto her hand. "Which isn't a lot of time."

"You've never been a mother."

"True. But I'll try to remember if I ever am one that two days is minimal."

She heard her mother sigh. "How are you doing? Ready to move home yet?"

"Nah, I'm doing okay."

Quite honestly, the "move home" didn't sound like such a crazy suggestion anymore. She missed San Francisco, having lived there her entire life. Her friends, her family, a dating scene she was familiar with. The job at the *Union-Trib* had sounded like an adventure, a chance to do the kind of investigative journalism she wasn't finding at her desk job at *The Chronicle*. But the transition had been hard. She'd met some people at an environmental activist meeting, but they were just acquaintances at this point. A couple of people at work had been friendly enough, but quite honestly, Kristin was lonely and beginning to really feel it.

"And the house? Are you all settled in?"

She took a deep breath and brightened for her mother's benefit. "The house is wonderful." Yep, no puddles of water on the kitchen floor at all. Apparently, she'd need to go dishwasher shopping over the weekend. She pushed forward. "I bought the cutest little curtain for the kitchen window. It looks out over this little side yard." She left out the part about her next-door neighbor leaving his spare car parts all over the ground.

"And you've made friends in the city?"

She nodded to sell herself the lie. "I have. We just met for drinks actually. It's a fun little group. We might be getting together for a movie night this weekend and I was thinking I could pop my special popcorn for them." Tears welled in her eyes at the dishonesty, but she couldn't bear to upset her mother, who worried about her incessantly.

"That sounds like so much fun, sweet girl. You don't know how relieved I am that you're doing so well, and I won't keep you anymore as you're probably with friends. I love you and will talk to you soon."

"Love you too, Mom."

She hung up the phone and sighed, wishing half of what she'd reported to her mother were true. But there was a bright spot in her world—her work. Her mind was already firing after the conversation with Lucy earlier. Kristin believed in her story and was excited to get up each day and work on it. Not to mention, it was a topic that had her captivated. There was certainly a lot of gray underneath the umbrella of truth, to the point that she wasn't sure where the line became firm.

In fact, it now had her examining her own avoidance of the truth in the conversation she'd just had with her mother. It was something to think about and maybe include—lying for the greater good. She did, however, want to examine the topic from all sides. That's the part that got her blood going, as there was something enthralling about compiling information, connecting the dots, and figuring out how it all went together in order to tell the best possible story.

Kristin checked her watch. The cab that was supposed to have picked her up twenty minutes ago was nowhere in sight. She stared across the parking lot and watched as the cars on the exterior street hugged the bend in the road, their headlights sharpening then blurring on the curve.

"Stargazing?" a voice behind her asked.

She glanced over her shoulder and saw Lucy watching her from a few yards away. Perfect, just what she needed. Of course the high-powered CEO who looked like she walked out of a fashion magazine was here to observe her down-and-out moment. "Something like that."

Lucy closed the distance between them until she stood next to Kristin's spot on the curb, peering down at her curiously. "Seriously though, what are you doing sitting on the sidewalk at night?"

Kristin blew out a breath. While she'd really rather not involve Lucy Danaher in the details of her mid-evening plight, there didn't seem to be a way to get her to move on without first supplying her with an explanation. "Because my car won't start and I'm waiting on a cab."

Lucy scratched the spot just above her lip as she thought. It was quirky and cute. Kristin brushed that thought aside as aggressively as it had come on. "This is quite tragic," Lucy said. "I'd be happy to give you a ride. Where do you live?"

Uh-uh. No. "That's a very nice offer, but my cab will be here any minute."

A pause. "Okay, then I'll wait with you." Lucy took a seat on the curb.

"What are you doing?" Kristin asked, eyeing Lucy and her newfound proximity.

"Waiting with you." Lucy glanced around. "I just said that, no?"

"Not necessary."

"It is so. You're an attractive woman alone in a parking lot at night. No good-hearted human would leave you here. Someone could Kristin-nap you."

She studied Lucy. "I see. And that's you? A good-hearted human?" She hadn't meant it as a dig but realized that's how it had sounded by the overly wounded look on Lucy's face.

"You may not realize this, Ms. James, because for whatever reason you've decided you hate me, but I am, in fact, a good person."

She held up a finger. "For the record, I do not hate you."

Lucy scrunched an eye. "Feels like you hate me."

She couldn't help but smile. Lucy, was…amusing, even when she didn't want to find her amusing. And attractive, and she certainly didn't want to find her that. Kristin held up one finger. "Just because we see things differently in regard to the press release doesn't mean I hate you. In fact, it's nothing personal at all. I'm sure you're quite lovely."

"Now we're getting somewhere. Except you did just storm out of the bar an hour ago. We haven't quite dealt with that yet."

Kristin nodded, as she had done that. Her feelings had been hurt and she'd been embarrassed. She now realized that she could have handled it all more in stride. "I apologize for the storming. It's been a long day."

"You can say that again."

"I apologize. It's been a long day."

Lucy stared at her, mystified. "Pause the world. Did you just make a joke?"

Kristin felt the corners of her mouth tug. "A little one."

"Well, color me impressed and willing to admit it. The crackerjack reporter has a humorous side. Who knew?" Kristin raised her hand. "Aha. And confident too."

"That's me."

They stared out at the stationary cars in the parking lot for a few moments, the silence palpable before Lucy finally turned to her. "Okay. We should go now, yeah?"

"Go?"

"Your cab clearly stood you up and I'm going to drive you home." Lucy stood and headed into the parking lot.

Staring after her, Kristin sighed in surrender. "Fine, but your good deed is not going to get me to kill the story."

"Not at all shocking," Lucy said without turning around. "You're rather stubborn."

"Hey! I have conviction. There's a difference."

Lucy passed her an overly sweet smile over the top of a silver Aston Martin. "Sure there is."

Eight minutes later they turned into the Verde Oaks subdivision. Kristin pointed ahead of them. "Take the second right, and it's the second to last house on the left." Lucy pulled into the drive and ducked her head, peering up at the home.

"This is a very cute place with a lovely green door."

Kristin cringed. "Thanks, but don't look too closely. The green door is the best part." Lucy raised a questioning eyebrow. "I was a bit misled in the rental process."

"That should go in your article," Lucy said. "Someone didn't tell the truth."

"You have a point," Kristin said, laughing. She then took in the fact that Lucy was watching her with a curious expression, and she was instantly self-conscious. "What? Do I have something on my face?"

Lucy shook her head almost imperceptibly. "No. It's just, you have a nice laugh is all."

She nodded, meeting Lucy's eyes. "Thanks." Was it just her or had the mood just shifted completely? Because unless she was imagining it, there seemed to be a snap-crackle-pop thing in the air that didn't have much to do with her news article. She opened the door, moving them out of it, focusing on her words and not the flip-flop her traitorous stomach was doing. "I appreciate the ride."

"Anytime," Lucy said. "You'd do it for me, right? You know what? Don't answer that."

Kristin shook her head and smiled. "Good night, Ms. Danaher."

"Ms. James."

Kristin headed into the darkened house and all but collapsed on her sofa, also known as the snuggliest sofa known to man. Big and tan and amazing with navy blue and white striped accent pillows, a gift from her mom.

In the midst of her snuggle, she ruminated over the day's happenings, a practice that was part of her nightly decompressing ritual. There had been the meeting with Dalton, which reminded her she still needed to go over his notes for the story again. Then the less than thrilling conversation with her deadbeat landlord, resulting in four hundred dollars for a new dishwasher. Then there had been her frustrating interactions with Lucy Danaher along with the not so frustrating save-and-rescue. She turned onto her back and stared up at the popcorn ceiling.

Lucy was a puzzling person. That was for sure.

A puzzling person with thick dark hair and Bambi eyes, her brain amended. She smiled at the description, because there didn't seem to be much that was innocent about Lucy Danaher.

❖

The newsroom at the *Union-Trib* was a flurry of activity the following morning as San Diego was in the midst of a pretty big news week. A money-laundering politician, a local and well-liked weatherman caught with a prostitute, and a series of convenience-store robberies had all hit in just the past twenty-four hours. The buzz of chatter infiltrated the room as reporters called to verify facts and secure sources, and editors rushed to fill the news hole. The paper was put to bed at six p.m., which was an earlier deadline than Kristin was used to.

"Hey, James, you have the copy ready from the third Valero knock over?"

Kristin glanced up at Dalton and checked her watch. "I have five minutes."

"Make that three."

She kept her eyes on her monitor and focused on the words, rather than the gray-haired man with the crease between his eyes staring down at her. "I can have it for you in two if you give me a little breathing room. So how 'bout it, huh?"

He held up his hands and backed away. That was the thing about Dalton. He was gruff, but he was good at his job, which meant the notes he'd given her about her story the day prior had been good ones. Streamline. Narrow the focus and keep it simple. They were journalistic basics, but sometimes she needed to hear them.

After a quick proof of the robbery story, she hit the send button and fell dramatically backward into her chair. "Kristin James, out."

Marissa, her colleague one desk over, shook her head. "Now you're just showing off."

Kristin passed her a smile. “A little. You almost done?” She glanced at the clock, noting how little time was left to hit their deadline.

“Watch this.” Marissa leaned her head very close to her monitor and made a show of hitting the send button. “I like to make them sweat.”

Marissa Cruz covered city politics for the paper and Kristin really liked her. They were similar in age and did pretty well together at the inner-office banter. Kristin had her pegged as a potential friend, though it was still a bit early to tell.

“I don’t know about you,” Kristin said, “but I could use a cocktail. Happy hour?” It was the first time she’d invited Marissa anywhere socially, but today seemed like a good enough time for it, as the day literally had not stopped since the moment they’d arrived at work.

“I would love to and we should very soon, but it’s my anniversary and my husband is taking me out. Sitter and everything.”

Kristin smiled. “Aww. Happy anniversary. How many years?”

“Seven, which makes it our wool anniversary. How in the world do you satisfy the wool category when it’s ninety degrees outside?” Marissa shrugged. “So I got him the DVD of Marilyn Monroe in *The Seven Year Itch*.”

“Clever.”

“I thought so. At least I’ll get a laugh out of it.” Marissa slipped her bag onto her shoulder and powered down her computer. “But we’ll get that drink soon, okay?”

“Holding you to it,” Kristin said and watched her coworker head to the elevator.

So she was on her own again tonight. What else was new?

She drove home exhausted, but not exactly looking forward to another night of her, a frozen dinner, and Ryan Seacrest. Not that they weren’t a great trio, but tonight the idea was barely tolerable. She could do some work, but honestly, her brain was fried from the crazy demanding news day. So last minute, Kristin made an executive decision and turned the car around.

The Lavender Room was fairly quiet when she arrived, but then it always seemed to be on weeknights. A small group of women sat around a circular booth directly across from the bar, laughing and seeming to have a good time. She nodded at them as she passed, took a seat at the bar, and smiled at the spiky-haired bartender as she approached.

“Let me guess? A pinot grigio?”

Kristin thought on this briefly. "I think I'm gonna branch out tonight. A glass of the Sterling cab, please."

"Good choice." The bartender nodded and poured, doing that little turn of her wrist that Kristin could never seem to master.

"Very impressive," she said, moving her finger in a circular motion. "The twist at the end."

"It was," said a voice from behind her. "I'll have a glass of the same, extra twist, please." Kristin turned to find Lucy standing there, who held up her hands in defense. "I'm not stalking you, I promise."

She sent her a sideways glance. "Jury is still out on that one."

Lucy took the stool next to Kristin's. "Well, let me know when they decide my fate. Jail's not sounding so bad right now."

"Rough day?"

"You could say that. I really shouldn't even be here. I have contracts to peruse, presentations to prepare, and about fifteen managers who need to meet with me on various topics. But I think I just need a moment to catch my breath. Do you ever have that?"

"I do. It's totally necessary, and you did the right thing." Lucy's hair was pulled into a thick ponytail today, which swirled luxuriously against her white suit jacket. Kristin wondered how one accomplished such a swirl, as she wouldn't have a clue. Her ponytails were much more straightforward. Perhaps *boring* was the better word.

Lucy turned to her. "I didn't ask if I could join you."

Kristin waited for Lucy to say more but she didn't. "This is true."

"I suppose I could leave you to your drink."

"It's an option," Kristin said with a smile.

Lucy raised a shoulder. "I mean, for all I know, you're waiting on someone. A hot date perhaps."

Kristin nodded. "Yep. The hottest. She'll be here any minute now."

"She?"

Kristin glanced around. "Well, we are in a gay club." And then apologetically to Lucy, "Did you miss that?"

"Touché. And no, I definitely didn't miss that." There it was again. That moment of sustained eye contact that sped up her heart rate and left her mouth dry.

"Want to get a table?" Kristin asked.

"So you're asking me on a date already? Wow, you move a little fast for me."

Kristin shook her head. "You're infuriating, you know this?"

"So you *don't* want to go on a date with me?" Lucy was smiling in a way that told Kristin she was enjoying every minute of this. But she was also moderately adorable alongside the infuriating, which was an interesting dynamic. With Lucy, it all blended together.

"Let's start with the table," Kristin said.

"Well, okay. I can get behind this plan." They picked up their drinks and made their way to a nearby cocktail table with a small candle flickering from inside a glass holder. The lighting was dim away from the bar, which added a whole new, calming element to the atmosphere.

"So do you come here a lot?" Lucy asked.

Kristin laughed. "Cue the flirtatious pickup line."

Lucy's jaw dropped. "I would never. You hate me. Known fact."

"See, there you go again. I told you last night. I do not hate you. As in, I don't. There's a lack of hatred at play. We just have a few differences of opinions."

"Right," Lucy said, pointing at her, "the whole journalistic holier-than-thou thing. There's that."

"Hey! Now who's hating?"

"Valid point. Cease-fire?"

Kristin nodded. "Cease-fire."

She studied her drinking companion with interest. "So what's your story, Lucy Danaher?"

"CEO by day, professional Lavender Room stalker by night. Oh, and I adore smoothies and rock and roll." She sipped her wine and met Kristin's gaze. "And now you know everything."

"Smoothies, huh?"

"Strawberry is my favorite. Tell me one thing about you."

"Just one?"

"I figured we should pace ourselves. See how it goes. I'd rather we not break into an enormous fight in a public place, so I'm baby-stepping."

Kristin thought on this. "I like to run. I only get the chance a couple of times a week, but it's an outlet. Do you run?"

"Only if something is chasing me."

Kristin laughed. "Well, it's great for stress. You should try it sometime."

"Okay," Lucy said, nodding. "I'm putting it on the list right after my recreational root canal." The smile relaxed from Lucy's face and she swirled her wineglass.

"Can I ask you a serious question?"

"Fair enough." And then Lucy looked away and smiled.

"What went on in your head just then?" Kristin asked.

"You'll think it's stupid. You're the super-serious type."

Kristin let her mouth fall open. "I am not. Tell me what was funny."

"Fair enough is a great drag-queen name. I collect them. It's a thing."

Now it was Kristin's turn to smile. "I'm sorry. You collect drag-queen names?"

"I do. It's a hobby. You run. I collect drag-queen names. Both are perfectly acceptable pastimes. You had a question?"

"Yes," Kristin said, noticing for the first time a tiny scar just below Lucy's eyebrow. She wondered absently how it had gotten there before forcing herself to focus. "Do I seem unapproachable to you?"

"To me. Yes. You turned the screws on me without warning in our business meeting. I'm right to be a little wary of you."

"No, I don't mean you. I mean the collective you. The larger you. You as in anybody. Do I seem unapproachable to the average person?"

Lucy glanced around and understanding flickered. "You mean to women. Lesbians."

Kristin thought on this, recalling the nights she'd spent alone at this very bar. "Yeah, I guess I do."

Lucy sat back in her chair. "Then yes."

"What? Really? Why?" This so wasn't fair. "I'm friendly enough. I smile. And I'm a genuine person."

"It's none of that," Lucy said, pointing her finger in a circular motion.

Now Kristin was lost. "Well, what is it then? Just tell me what you think it is. Outside of the whole news story disagreement, I mean, that you find off-putting."

Lucy bit her lower lip and seemed to consider how to proceed. It looked really good on her, the lip-biting thing. Kristin wouldn't mind taking in that visual for a little while longer. "It's not off-putting," Lucy finally said. "It's intimidating."

"What is?"

"Well, have you looked in a mirror lately?" Lucy asked and calmly sipped her wine.

Kristin struggled to follow the logic. "Not since this afternoon. Why?"

Lucy rolled her eyes. "Come on. You must know you're gorgeous, and that can be intimidating to…What should we call them? Interested parties of the lesbian variety."

Kristin felt the blush hit her cheeks. "No. That's not it."

"I mean it is. Objectively. And if the two women at the bar who keep glancing over here every few minutes thought you would be halfway interested in them, they'd be over here buying you a drink."

Kristin had never considered such a theory. She knew she was decent enough looking, but the fact that Lucy thought so was new and interesting information. "You think I'm attractive?"

"I didn't exactly say *I* thought that. We were talking about the collective, remember?"

"Oh."

A pause. "Of course I think you're attractive," Lucy said, relenting in a semifrustrated huff. "I have a pulse. God."

Something warmed in Kristin and she smiled. The wine gave her an extra shot of courage. "Do you have a crush on me, Ms. Danaher?"

Lucy shook her head and smiled widely. "No way. You're the one who asked me on the table date, remember? I think it's the other way around. You don't ask people to tables unless you're crushing."

"I did do that, and I'm thinking right about now that it was a good decision."

At Kristin's words, Lucy's smile dimmed and her lips parted. What was it about this woman who could frustrate her one minute and charm her the next? Kristin wasn't sure, but she knew one thing. She wanted to find out.

They killed a second glass and argued over the benefits of the impending warmer weather. "It's awesome," Lucy said. "Pool time, suntans, and barbecues."

Kristin accepted the bill and her credit card from the waiter. "Sunburns, sweat, and tourist season."

"The Fourth of July," Lucy countered.

"Ohh, I do love the Fourth. I can concede on that count. There's something about the fireworks bursting and filling the sky that makes my heart stop."

"Mine too," Lucy said quietly. They smiled at one another. "Thanks for the drinks."

Kristin closed the leather portfolio that contained her credit card slip. "Don't thank me. You're getting it next time."

"Next time?" Lucy asked.

"Yeah, I mean, if there is one then—"

"There will be."

Kristin wasn't sure exactly what was bubbling between them, but whatever it was had her complete and undivided attention. The give and take, the challenges and yields all kept Kristin on her toes, and she loved that.

They walked together to the parking lot and Lucy followed Kristin to her rental car. She'd had her own car towed and would pick it up the following week, once the obscure part it needed arrived at the garage.

"Just want to make sure it starts," Lucy said, smiling from a few feet away. She was partially illuminated by the glow of a nearby street lamp and looking more beautiful than Kristin had ever seen her.

"And if it doesn't?"

"Then I suppose I'll have to rescue you again. Can you believe that?"

"Two rescues? That's a lot."

Lucy shrugged. "Guess I'm just that kind of girl."

Kristin shook her head in wonder. She'd had a fantastic time that night. Probably the best since she'd moved to San Diego. Whether it was the wine or the ups and downs of the conversation, she didn't know, but in that moment, she found herself overwhelmingly attracted to Lucy Danaher. The kind of attraction that made her mouth go dry and her stomach flutter and more than anything she wanted to act on it. "I've never met anyone like you, you know that?"

"I can safely say the same to you," Lucy said, meeting her gaze. Her eyes shone brightly, the blue more deep and intense now. Resisting the pull for reasons she'd examine later, Kristin started her car successfully and Lucy held up a hand in farewell. "Until next time, Ms. James. I had fun with you tonight."

"Me too," Kristin said. "Good night." She offered Lucy a last smile before closing the door and pulling away. Alone in her car, she admitted to herself how desperately she'd wanted to kiss Lucy in that parking lot. Just close the distance between them and do it. The thought alone sent a delicious shiver through her body. But that's when reality flashed. She shouldn't make out with one of her sources. Journalism 101.

But how long had it been since anyone had sparked that kind of reaction in her? She closed her eyes at the red light and took a deep breath. It was probably for the best.

It turned out she was excellent at self-delusion.

Chapter Three

Sarah Matamoros presented Lucy with an oversized cup of coffee that Saturday and sat across from her on the back deck with a cup of her own. "You look thoughtful," Sarah said, studying her.

"Nah, just in one of those moods." Sarah had left her jet-black hair down that day, which allowed it to blow easily with the wind off the nearby water. Lucy sipped from her cup as she watched the waves roll in. The coffee was strong, the way she liked it, and she closed her eyes as it warmed her from the inside. Emory had taken Grace to a movie that afternoon, so she'd stopped by to hang out with Sarah. "Can I ask you a question?"

"Of course," Sarah said. "And you don't need permission first, Luce." Lucy smiled at her. Though Lucy had started out as Emory's friend, she and Sarah had discovered a friendship of their own not long after Sarah and Grace had moved in with Emory. The fact that Lucy's own house was only a five-minute walk down the beach made popping over to their place not only easy, but a frequent occurrence. Over time, it had become clear to Lucy that she really liked Sarah, who was kind, funny, and a wonderful partner to her best friend. In fact, when she thought about the kind of life she wanted for herself one day, Emory and Sarah were the first couple that sprang to mind. They were lucky.

Lucy turned to Sarah. "What did you think of Emory the first time you met her?" Sarah laughed out loud at the question. "What? What's so funny?"

"Well, it wasn't good," Sarah said.

"Really?" Lucy sat up a little taller in her chair, anxious to hear the rest. Sarah had been hired to organize Emory's mother's house after she'd passed away suddenly from a stroke, and from what Lucy knew, they'd fallen for each other rather quickly.

"Really," Sarah said. "I thought she was cold, stuck-up, and bossy."

Lucy scrunched one eye. "Well, she *can* be a little bossy. She has control issues. Well, she did until she met you."

Sarah smiled. "I remember sitting on her mother's back patio with her one night and just being struck by how beyond beautiful she was and then thinking it was a shame she wasn't a nicer person."

Now Lucy was the one laughing. "Why am I just now hearing about this? This is good stuff."

"You never asked."

"Huge mistake. When did it change?"

"Well, after that, she started to let me in a little at a time, and I got to know her. The actual her. It turns out, she wasn't cold and aloof at all. In fact, she was probably the most awesome person I'd ever met."

"Who's the most awesome person you've ever met?" Emory asked, joining them on the deck.

"Some blond woman I live with," Sarah said with a dismissive wave and turned her head upward to Emory for a kiss she was promptly granted. "You're back. How was the movie?"

"Devastating," Emory said. "I feel like my heart's been ripped out and stomped on. Why does she love these sad teenage movies?"

"Because she thrives on overblown emotion in narratives," Sarah explained calmly.

"I get that, but she's putting on beachwear right now to head down the shore with Walter and I'm going to sit here and contemplate my mortality for a few hundred hours."

"Now who's being dramatic?" Lucy asked.

Emory pointed at Lucy. "Valid point. It's clear to me that I spend way too much time with you and Grace. You're rubbing off."

"Finally," Lucy said, raising her fist in victory.

The dog door swished and Walter, the friendliest chocolate retriever that ever lived, appeared and came promptly to Lucy, wagging his tail and waiting patiently for the appropriate attention.

"There's my guy," Lucy said and dipped her face to Walter, who immediately covered her cheek in doggy kisses. She looked up at

Emory. "I was talking to Bernadette Peters and we were thinking that Walter could come live with us now."

"BP did not say that," Sarah countered. "She tolerates Walter at best. Though I suspect it's just an act. I've seen the way she prances around, that little tongue peeking out of her mouth all the time. She plays hard to get, that one. A trollop."

"It's true," Lucy mused, smiling. "I taught her everything I know."

"Lucy!" Grace practically shouted as she emerged from the house. "We just saw the most awesome movie about this girl with cancer and then she meets this boy with cancer and then it gets so sad you wouldn't even believe it."

"I don't know how you bounce back from that so easily," Lucy said.

"It's just make believe, but I love it. I might need to write a book this summer. I like how they affect people."

"I have all the confidence in you," Lucy said sincerely.

Ten-year-old Grace was the spitting image of her mother, about as precocious as a child could be, and just as quirky too. Lucy was one of Grace's regular babysitters and the two of them had racked up a number of adventures together. Space-themed manicures, forts in the living room, and fashion shows starring none other than Walter himself. She never really knew what to do with kids before Grace, but she enjoyed this particular kid, which said a lot.

Grace headed back inside. "I'll be right back."

"Freeze, monster," Sarah said. "You're up to something. I can tell. You've got that Grace-on-a-mission face."

Grace's facial expression switched to instant innocence. "I'm just going to grab the Saran Wrap."

Sarah studied her, as if trying to piece it together. "What do you want Saran Wrap for?"

Grace blinked back at her. "To make Walter a bathing suit."

"Walter doesn't need a bathing suit," Emory said gently. "He loves the water."

"He probably wants one though. Lucy and I always dress him up when you guys go out." As if on cue, Walter passed Lucy an apologetic look. The looks Sarah and Emory passed her were more of the question-mark variety.

In response, she held her thumb and forefinger very close together. "I mean, sometimes," she told them. "Just when he's feeling jaunty."

"Interesting confession," Emory said, eyeing her, and then turned back to Grace. "I vote for swimming sans Saran Wrap."

"Me too," Sarah said. "And we're the parents so we win." Grace sighed audibly in response.

"Come on," Emory said. "I've got my suit on and I'll go in with you guys." With that she unbuttoned her white cotton shirt and revealed the blue bikini top beneath. Sarah's eyes did a quick and appreciative sweep across Emory's body, much to Lucy's amusement. At the knowing grin from Lucy, she blushed.

"Caught," Lucy mouthed to her. Sarah offered up a guilty shrug in response.

"You guys want to join us?" Emory asked. It was only May and she already sported a tan, a perk of living on the beach. If Lucy weren't averse to outdoor exertion, she might actually have one herself.

"I think Lucy and I will stay here," Sarah said. "Continue our chat."

They watched as Emory, Grace, and Walter made their way from the beach house down to the shoreline in a picturesque little line reminiscent of a Norman Rockwell painting.

"So who's the girl?" Sarah asked pointedly, once they were alone.

"There's not a girl. Why do you think that?"

"You're a big liar, I'm thinking, because there is too. You're suddenly interested in talking about relationships and you have this faraway, preoccupied thing happening, which makes me feel quite strongly that there's a girl."

Lucy sat back in her chair in defeat. "There's a girl. At least, I think there is."

"See? I'm all knowing. You guys should just accept this. Who is she?"

"She's this reporter who's planning to include GNW in a news story she's writing about truth and its place in our culture. She's going to use me as an example of how the public can be easily misled by an irresponsible news agency."

"I see why you like her," Sarah deadpanned.

Lucy sat forward, feeling the need to defend Kristin. "I realize that sounds bad, and to be honest, it is. I hate that she's writing this story, but we've spent some time together and there's just something about her that has me…I don't know. Captivated."

Sarah raised an eyebrow. "Captivated is a pretty telling word."

"Isn't it? And it's like when I'm with her, I want to shake her one minute, and make out with her the next. Is that normal?"

"It's hot is what it is," Sarah said, her eyes dancing. "Sounds like you guys have some fiery chemistry."

Lucy nodded. "Chemistry. I think that's what it is. There's this off-the-charts chemistry happening that has me forgetting to breathe sometimes, and I've never really been susceptible to that kind of thing before, you know? Where it's like the allure is in charge and just pulling me along for the ride. There I'll be, staring into her ridiculous green eyes and wondering what it would be like to kiss her because she's smart and beautiful and so over-the-top frustrating, which I think seems to be part of it. The frustrating."

"Oh, I'd say it's definitely part of it. Look how worked up you're getting."

"And I don't do that, right? At least about women."

"I've never seen it."

"Because it doesn't happen. And now you're smiling. Why are you smiling, Sarah?"

"Because I love how clearly out of sorts you are right now. It's awesome."

Lucy shook her head. "I'm not so sure it is."

"Even better. Because I'll tell you the last time I felt that out of sorts."

"When was that?"

Sarah smiled knowingly. "When I met Emory."

❖

Kristin should just go home. Inherently, she knew she should. It had been a whirlwind of a Friday and she could use the alone time to decompress, watch a movie, or just veg on the couch.

But the exit off the highway that would take her to the Lavender Room was just ahead and tempting her in a big way. Unfortunately,

Friday night meant it would be a lot more crowded and the chances that she'd run into Lucy again were also slim. She was probably out with friends having a fabulous time.

Or maybe even on a date.

She shoved that thought aside as it didn't sit well.

As Kristin neared the exit, the what-if section of her brain grew harder to ignore. Maybe she'd just drive by the place, see what might be going on. No biggie there. Drive-bys were totally noncommittal, breezy, even. Plus, the stakes were low. What was the harm?

But when she arrived in the parking lot of the Lavender Room and saw the silver Aston Martin, the stakes shot up a whole hell of a lot. Not a ton of people drove cars like that. In fact, only one that she'd encountered. She checked her reflection in the mirror and applied a bit of strawberry lip gloss, hardly recognizing herself for caring so much about her appearance, apparently another new development.

The place definitely came with a whole separate vibe on the weekend. First of all, there were *lots* of women. That was her first observation. And not club kids either; the crowd seemed to be more established, sets of friends meeting up, celebrating the end of the workweek over drinks. Next, she noticed the loud music and dancing in the room adjacent to the bar, making the place a lot more lively than usual.

"Can I buy you a drink?" It took a moment for Kristin to register that the question had been aimed at her.

"Sure," she said, smiling at the woman. She had short hair, combed to the side, and kind eyes. "I'm Kristin."

"Barrett," the woman said as they made their way to the bar. "What do you do, Kristin?"

"I'm a journalist. What about you?"

"I'm an attorney, actually."

Kristin ordered a white wine spritzer, in the mood for something a little more celebratory and fun. Barrett stuck with beer. She turned to her, now interested. "What kind of law?"

"Environmental mostly."

"Really? I belong to an environmental action group that I joined when I moved here, Green Stuff. Have you heard of it?"

"I have," Barrett said. "You guys do great work."

"We're currently planning a demonstration to draw awareness to the carbon emissions from the utility giant on Claussen Road."

Barrett smiled knowingly. "You mean Slater Energy. Yeah, they're horrible. Shoot me the date and I'll see if I can be there."

Kristin nodded, already excited, and accepted the business card Barrett handed her. "I will do that. We could use all the help we can get."

"I'm glad I met you," Barrett said. "I have some friends over there. Care to join us?"

"I'd love to meet your friends," Kristin said. "I don't know a ton of people in town."

"Well, I can help with that part." She followed Barrett to a well-populated table and instantly recognized the blonde closest to them, though her mind searched for why. "Kristin, this is my friend Emory and her partner, Sarah."

The blonde turned and extended a hand. "Nice to meet you, Kristin," Emory said. And then, "Have we met before?"

"I'm not sure actually, but I wondered the same thing." She went on to say hello to Sarah, who smiled warmly and took her hand.

"And that over there is Mia," Barrett said, "followed by Christi Ann and then Lucy." Kristin made eye contact and waved hello to each new woman until her gaze landed on a pair of very familiar blue eyes. Lucy tilted her head to the side knowingly and smiled.

"Lucy I'm familiar with," she told Barrett.

"You two know each other," Barrett said, gesturing between them.

"We do," Lucy said. "She's planning to malign me in the *Union-Trib*, but I'm working past it."

"She's a bit of a handful," Kristin told Barrett.

"Then you've definitely met Lucy," Barrett said.

"So that's where I've seen you," Emory said, pointing at Kristin. "You're the audacious reporter."

"And you're her date from the other night," Kristin said, pointing back at Emory.

"Not a date," Emory corrected, kissing Sarah's hand. "But yes."

"Right. Of course," Kristin said, bopping her head and motioning to Sarah. "But now I remember why you're familiar."

Barrett found Kristin a chair and she joined their group, learning lots about the women. Emory was apparently the owner of GNW but took a backseat to let Lucy run the place while she pursued life as a painter. Mia and Christi Ann, while fun, didn't seem to have a lot to contribute to the conversation but did offer a few snarky comments. Sarah, however, might have been her favorite. She seemed warm, thoughtful, and fun.

"So what do you think of Lucy?" Sarah asked out of nowhere, as the rest of the table continued to debate whether Pilates was beneficial to one's health or sent from Satan to torture humans.

Kristin chose her words carefully. "I think she's amusing, complex, and kinda stubborn."

"Oh, she is," Sarah said. "Trust me. But Luce is good people. Don't give up on her." It was interesting advice and Kristin wondered what had prompted it. Had Lucy said something about her to Sarah? She stared across the table at Lucy, who was fully an advocate of the Satan theory.

"I'm just saying that when you take exercise and add a hateful contraption, I'm out. It's a method of torture, and I would much prefer to steam luxuriously in a sauna." The comment conjured the image of Lucy in a towel, and Kristin swallowed against her body's response. Lucy must have felt Kristin watching her, as she met her gaze and winked.

Five minutes later when Lucy made her way to the bar for another drink, Kristin waited a few moments before following. "I really like your friends," she said, leaning her forearms on the bar alongside Lucy. "They're a lot of fun."

"Thanks," Lucy said, smiling at her. "I like them too. Barrett is a sweetheart."

"She seems to be."

"How do you guys know each other?"

"We just met tonight actually. She bought me a drink when I arrived."

"Aha. Apparently you're not as unapproachable as you thought." Lucy turned her attention casually to the cocktail menu. "And you're interested?"

"In a cocktail?"

"In Barrett," Lucy said, eyes still on the menu. "You guys would be cute together."

Kristin wasn't sure how she felt about that comment. "Thanks. But it's not Barrett who's invaded my thoughts of late." At her words,

Lucy set the menu down and looked up at her. Her eyes were wide, luminous as they searched Kristin's face. But there was a sparkle in them too and a tugging smile that had Kristin forgetting to breathe. God, this woman was gorgeous, even more so than she remembered.

"How about we get out of here and see some of the city?" Lucy asked.

The change in conversation had Kristin struggling to keep up. "The city?"

"Yeah. I have a feeling there's one part you've yet to see."

"And you're the tour guide?"

Lucy nodded. "Reporting for duty."

Done. Decided. "I should say good night to Barrett and thank her for the drink."

"Okay. How about I meet you at my car in ten so as not to be obvious. I don't want to hurt anyone's feelings."

"I think that's for the best." And then she lowered her voice. "This is all super covert."

"All the more exciting," Lucy said, one eyebrow arched.

❖

They left the windows down as they drove up the steep hills with Bruno Mars singing his fast-paced single from the car radio and their hair blowing in the breeze. Lucy stole a look at Kristin, who hadn't said a whole lot since they'd left the Lavender Room, but she'd placed her open palm out the window and there was a smile on her face that said she was enjoying herself. "Are you going to tell me where we're going?" she asked.

"You'll see soon enough," Lucy said. She wasn't at all sure what to do with the flutters around her heart that seemed to be multiplying in Kristin's presence. "Tell the investigative journalist in you to relax and enjoy the scenery."

"But I am," Kristin said quietly, her gaze never moving from Lucy. So not helping the heart flutters.

Five tension-filled minutes later, and Lucy pulled her car to a stop at the spot she knew to be the most breathtaking of any other spot. From where they sat in the front seat, they could see all of San Diego beneath, the lights of the city twinkling almost as brightly as the stars overhead.

"Oh my," Kristin breathed. "You can see everything at once."

"Exactly. I thought you might like it." But Kristin was on the move and headed out of the car. She walked to the edge of the cliff, which had Lucy's heart hammering away for a whole separate reason as she exited the car herself.

"Whoa, whoa, whoa. Back away from the edge before I'm forced to perform heroic acts to save your life."

Kristin turned back to her in calm amusement. "I'm perfectly safe. I just wanted to see it all. Just look," she said, staring down at the city.

"I am," Lucy said. She retrieved a blanket from the car, laid it across the hood, and slid up and onto it. "It's gorgeous up here, which is why I wanted you to see it. Believe it or not, I come out here by myself sometimes just to clear my head. It's so removed from everything, yet it's all right here at the same time. This is what perspective looks like," she said, gesturing out.

Kristin joined her on the hood of the car. Music still played softly from inside. "You have a lot of layers, Lucy Danaher. Not one who's easy to predict."

"Good." Lucy stole a glance at Kristin and then looked away, intimidated by the pull she felt to her. "I'm glad you haven't got me figured out. Maybe you're wrong about me in that story you're writing."

Kristin smiled. "That story has nothing to do with you and who you are as a human. It's about best practices from a business standpoint."

Lucy sighed. "You realize if we go down this path, we're probably going to argue."

"So let's not," Kristin proposed, sitting up a little straighter. "Let's enjoy this night and this beautiful view for what it is. Because I, for one, am happy to be here with you."

Kristin was close, Lucy realized. Very close.

The outsides of their thighs touched and she was vaguely aware of the faint scent of strawberries. The song on the radio switched and Adele covered an old Garth Brooks favorite, slow and smooth. As they listened in silence, staring out at the city below, Lucy realized it was definitely one of the more romantic settings she'd experienced, and quite simply, it made her notice Kristin all the more.

Kristin's mouth was somewhat heart shaped and full in the most wonderful way. And then there was the dimple on her left cheek. God, that dimple did things to Lucy when it showed up. Ridiculously attractive, she decided, that was Kristin. She was utterly seduced.

"What's going on over there?" Kristin asked quietly.

Lucy shook her head. "You."

"What about me?"

"I'm not supposed to like you."

"I remember. I'm not supposed to like you either."

"Yet the only thing I can concentrate on right now is doing this." She touched Kristin's cheek, slowly leaned in, and kissed her. It was a soft kiss, a tentative brushing of her lips across Kristin's, but that was only the beginning. The warmth she encountered was intoxicating, and being this close to Kristin had her head spinning in the most awesome sense. Lucy's instinct took over and she deepened the kiss, as there was no choice not to. Kristin's mouth began to move against hers, sending a jolt of heat straight through Lucy. She moved her other hand to fully cradle Kristin's face, and then into her thick hair.

Kristin knew what she was doing. That much was clear. She kissed Lucy with skilled precision, like it was the most important thing in the world that she do this properly. And damn it, she totally did, Lucy thought distantly as her limbs went weak.

"What is this thing?" she breathed, pulling her mouth from Kristin's, searching for air. "Because it feels a little crazy."

Kristin's eyes were heavy, unfocused. "Crazy good or crazy bad?" Not waiting for an answer, Kristin leaned in and kissed her some more, which had Lucy grasping the fabric of Kristin's shirt for stability.

"Crazy like I'm a little off the rails."

"Good. Me too," Kristin said.

More kissing. The best kind of kissing. Olympic medal kissing. As their lips clung, Lucy closed her eyes in order to hold it to her for one more moment, it was that good.

Once they broke apart, she stared at Kristin, still holding on to her shirt and reintroducing herself to the concept of air. Once she had some, she blew out a breath. "I feel so much better now."

"Than what?" Kristin asked, curiosity across her face.

"Than every other human who doesn't get to kiss you on top of a car overlooking the city."

Kristin broke into a smile. "That was a very good answer. I really like that answer."

Lucy leaned her back against the windshield and pulled Kristin gently down next to her. The night was chilly and Lucy had left her sweater inside the car. However, there was no way she was moving from this spot. Uh-uh. The fact that Kristin wrapped her arms around Lucy's waist and settled her head against Lucy's shoulder helped the cause immensely, however.

They lay there on top of the car, under the stars, listening to the music with the quiet sounds of nature around them. It felt like uncharted water to Lucy. Kristin wasn't like anyone she'd ever been drawn to before. She didn't fit the profile in the slightest, and maybe that's why it all felt so different.

So intriguing.

So complex.

But then again, Lucy loved a challenge.

Chapter Four

The next day, Lucy set the stack of forms from legal on her coffee table and adjusted Bernadette Peters, who was curled into a ball in her lap. She'd been at it for well over three hours and there was still a second stack staring her down. Yes, sir, it was a thrilling Saturday afternoon in the Danaher household. Who didn't enjoy poring over wordy legal jargon on the weekend with a side of jazz music and a cookie-scented candle? The truth was she'd been putting off approval of the contract language for their international accounts for too long and it was best she just knock it the hell out so she could focus on marketing strategies and leadership development. The jazz and the candle were just incentive to keep her going.

She placed a kiss on BP's tiny head and with a deep sigh went back to work. It was only a few moments before the buzz from her phone invaded the silence. She glanced at the readout, a text from Kristin, and smiled. "It's the girl I kissed last night," she whispered to BP. "She's very pretty, but maddening at the same time. Like you." She turned her focus to her phone and read the text.

Feel like going for a run this afternoon?

She paused and typed back her answer because it was one of the crazier questions she'd been asked. *Um...Have you met me?*

It took a minute for Kristin to reply.

I have. Infuriating. Opinionated. Adorable.

Okay, now that was pretty good, the adorable thing. It had Lucy a little tingly and a tad bit smiley. She stood with her phone and walked the course of her living room as she typed. *I'm a horrible runner. I told you. Tragic.*

The response was quicker this time.

Good thing I'll be there to help you.

Lucy sighed. Running? Really? Was she seriously going to do this? She supposed it *would* make for a nice break in her day. Her eyes were beginning to cross from staring at documents for hours on end. Plus, she'd get to look at Kristin in athletic attire, so there was that upside. She started to type. *Fine. But I have a feeling I'm going to regret this.* She stared at BP, incredulous. "I'm about to go running," she told the dog, who cocked her head in mystification. "I know. It's crazy." Her phone vibrated at an incoming text.

I thought we could run on the beach. Where should we meet?

Lucy glanced out her back window at the sand and surf, smiled, and returned to her phone. *I know the perfect spot.*

❖

Kristin knocked on the big brown door with the wrought-iron design in the window at exactly three p.m., the time she and Lucy had agreed upon. It was several long moments before Lucy appeared, seemingly surprised to see her.

"You're early," she said, opening the door for Kristin to come inside.

"Am not," she said. "I'm right on time."

Lucy thought on this. "I think I often assume that everyone is on Lucy time, you know, late."

She laughed. "Well, welcome to Kristin."

"That sounds like an invitation," Lucy said with a raised eyebrow. "Kidding. I can be bad sometimes. Come inside and see my digs."

Kristin followed Lucy through the small entryway of brown travertine tile. Right off, she caught that the beach bungalow was full of impressive little touches. Crown molding, interesting pieces of art on the wall, and the cool flooring, which morphed to engineered hardwood as they advanced into the living room. "How many bedrooms?" Kristin asked, as she took in the place.

"Two. Not a huge place, but it's mine."

And it was, in fact, very Lucy. Feminine, classy, and attractive. Kristin then shifted her attention as an adorable Yorkshire terrier quickly padded its way in her direction.

"Oh my goodness," she said, kneeling. "You're the cutest thing on the planet." The tiny dog seemed to enjoy the compliment and licked her nose in thanks.

"This is Bernadette Peters. BP for short. Spoiled rotten, but extra snuggly."

"Can't argue with that combo." She looked up at Lucy. "Wouldn't have pegged you for a dog person though."

She lifted a shoulder. "It's my goal to keep you guessing."

"So far, so good," Kristin said, shaking her head and narrowing her gaze.

"Excellent." And then, "I should probably change out of jeans for this running thing we're going to do."

"This running thing? Oh, that descriptor doesn't bode well."

"No, it doesn't. But I'm extra excited to put on my athletic wear that sits lonely in my closet for most of its life. Your outfit is pretty awesome." The comment and the appreciative way she'd said it sent a tiny shiver up Kristin's back. She'd chosen her black midcalf running pants and bright blue tank top, which she thought seemed beach appropriate. "I also love the ponytail. I think I'll follow suit with the expert today," Lucy said as she disappeared around the corner.

Kristin took a seat on the couch and scratched BP's head, prompting her to roll onto her back for more. "Oh, you like that, do you?" BP blinked back from her upside-down position. She missed having a dog.

In a few short moments, Lucy reappeared in a matching black and white workout outfit, a look which included her dark hair pulled into a ponytail, sans the swirl this time.

"Okay. I'm ready. Let's do this before I change my mind." Lucy was already sporting a semi-pout, which forecast an uphill battle ahead of them.

They headed out to the beach, the short jaunt to the water's edge shocking to Kristin. She couldn't imagine how awesome it must be to live this close to the water, to be able to run on the beach each morning or just sip coffee and watch the surf. "God, it's gorgeous out here." And it was. The temperature was warm, but not the uncomfortable kind of warm. The sun had already begun its daily descent, and in a couple of hours they would have a pretty picturesque sunset on their hands, if she had to guess. She turned to Lucy. "So why don't we take it easy and stick with a basic jog." Kristin demonstrated and Lucy fell in beside her.

"Okay, a jog seems harmless." They ran in companionable silence for a few long moments before Lucy turned to her. "How long are we doing this for exactly?"

Kristin passed her a look. "I thought we'd do a mile or two. Nothing major."

"A mile or two?" Lucy practically squeaked.

"Or less," Kristin amended. "We can adjust as needed." They ran for a bit and Kristin felt her muscles begin to lengthen and engage.

"You're one of those people who likes exercise, aren't you? It's not that you do it out of necessity or to stay in shape, you do it because you *like* it. Am I close?"

Kristin smiled as she ran. "I do happen to enjoy it, yes." Out of the corner of her eye, she saw Lucy shake her head in dramatic disdain. Lucy, she was finding, was often dramatic.

"People like you do this to us."

"People like me do what to you?" Kristin tried to keep the smile off of her face.

"You guys invent things like CrossFit and spinning and Pilates and yoga and make them trendy just to torture the rest of us."

"We do do that. We have meetings about it, even. Who told you?"

"Evil meetings. I knew it." Lucy lifted a hand. "Exercise is important, yes, but it should be considered work. We should hate it automatically. And you guys don't. You're also the people who invent things like fat-free sour cream and guilt the world into eating it instead of the fantastic real stuff. I miss the real stuff."

"You're such a victim. I'm sorry."

"I am."

"A cute one though," Kristin said, before sprinting ahead. "Come on, victim. Catch me."

"Hey!" Lucy called out from behind her. But it was only a few playful moments of Kristin jogging backward until Lucy closed the distance. "You're trying to kill me. I thought so before, but now I'm sure of it." She gulped in some air. "Time to turn back?"

Kristin smiled, as they'd barely run half a mile. "Not quite. But I'll make a deal with you. See the boardwalk ahead?"

"I do. It calls to me."

"Great. Well, if you make it to that boardwalk without stopping, I'll buy you an ice-cream cone as a reward."

Lucy's eyebrows shot up. "Really? That's allowed? Mid-exercise dessert? Because I could get behind that little rule shift."

"Definitely. What's the point of running if there's not a little payoff?"

The smile on Lucy's face brightened. "I like the way you think, Little Miss Reporter." And with an extra spring in their step, they covered the half mile to the boardwalk. It turned out Lucy Danaher operated quite nicely on incentive. She filed that away.

With a mint-chocolate-chip cone for Lucy and salted caramel for Kristin, they strolled the Mission Beach Boardwalk. The lively walkway had two lanes, which left plenty of room for the Rollerbladers gliding past, folks lining up for the Ferris wheel, and food vendors galore. The place had a laid back feel to it, very much reminiscent of what Kristin had come to know as the Southern California vibe. It was a great destination to run to. Halfway down the walk, Lucy steered them to a bench that looked perfect for people watching.

"So how'd I do? Are we talking runner hall of fame?" Lucy asked, taking a lick from her cone. It was an awesome visual that sent a shot of something powerful to Kristin's center and downward. *Whoa.*

"Well, you made it here and that's major."

"Right? Now, how are we getting home? Cab?"

Kristin had to laugh at that one. "Very funny."

Lucy shrugged. "I had to try." And then she brushed a stray piece of hair from Kristin's forehead in a move that seemed so natural it was startling.

Kristin thought back to the night before at the overlook. The view of the city. The quiet. The *kissing*. God, the kissing. It might have been the best make-out session of her life, and that was even counting Nadine Duarte, who was two years older than her in high school and blew her mind with an impromptu make-out fest in the locker room while the rest of the class played in a volleyball scrimmage. It was hard to beat an impromptu high school make-out fest, but she and Lucy had done that to a surprising degree.

"Where did your mind go just then?" Lucy asked. "You had the most faraway look."

"I was wondering about you actually." A half truth.

"Moi?"

"Yep. Tell me a little-known fact about you. Aside from the cutthroat CEO thing."

"Well, the cutthroat CEO thing is important."

"Naturally. What else?"

Lucy turned to her, all thoughtful and such. "As in I skipped the third grade?"

"Totally like that. Did you?"

"I did. I was miserable though. All of my friends were still in third grade and I missed them. We had different recesses. It was all terribly heartbreaking."

Kristin raised a finger. "First of all, impressive, smarty-pants."

"Thank you."

"Second of all, you're a major social butterfly, aren't you?"

Lucy considered this. "Friends have always been important to me, yes. And I happen to love a good cocktail party." Kristin enjoyed the way Lucy's eyes sparked with excitement when they touched on a topic she enjoyed. "Now you. Tell me a Kristin fact, and don't hold out on the good stuff. I want to know about that day you were taken downtown for shoplifting."

"You heard about that?"

Lucy turned her head to the side and regarded Kristin out of the corner of her eye. "You so did not get arrested."

Kristin smiled, prompting Lucy to lower her ice-cream cone, which was a shame because Kristin was having a fabulous time watching her eat it. She was already a little familiar with that tongue and enjoyed watching it work.

Lucy gestured at her with what was left of the cone. "I cannot tell if you're messing with me right now. Are you messing with me?"

Kristin gave in. "No shoplifting. But I have been arrested before. Twice actually." With that she got up and headed back down the boardwalk, discarding the little bit that was left of her ice cream so as not to be too full for the run ahead of them. Lucy was hot on her heels.

"Whoa, whoa, whoa. You cannot say something inflammatory like that and then walk away. I'll need details."

"And you shall have them, once we make it to that two-story house in the distance."

Lucy followed her gaze. "This is cruel and unusual punishment, you realize this?" But she was halfway smiling and that was everything.

"Come on, champ. No more complaining." Kristin started the run at a slow place and noticed Lucy fall in stride next to her.

"Calling me champ will get you everywhere, by the way."

"You like that, huh?"

"I do, as I'm the champ."

Kristin laughed. "I'm going to remember this."

They ran in companionable silence with only the sounds of the waves crashing and the distant call of seagulls overhead. Kristin let her mind drift. On their phone conversation, Lucy had invited her to stay for dinner, and while she'd brought a change of clothes, she didn't want to overstay her welcome. But it was fun hanging out with Lucy, seeing her life up close and personal, and that wasn't even taking into consideration the wild attraction.

"Bam," Lucy huffed, pointing. "House in the distance is here. Tell me the prison story."

Kristin passed her a quick glance. "I never said prison. I said jail. They're different."

"Semantics. What was the charge?"

"Unlawful assembly."

"So a protest?"

"Exactly. In San Francisco, there's this energy giant that refuses to use any sort of environmentally safe practices, so the group I belonged to staged a protest."

"And they arrested you for that?"

"When we refused to leave, yeah, they did. But I knew going in I'd be arrested."

"And you did it anyway?" Lucy asked, incredulous.

"Sometimes that's part of drawing more attention to the cause. A few people get arrested and suddenly the local news is a little more interested in covering the story."

"Sure, but to take a personal hit like that."

"Well, it's something I care about. What do you do when something you care about is at stake?"

Lucy thought for a moment. "Throw a charity event or write a check."

"Sounds to me like you don't want to get your hands dirty."

"And it sounds to me like you're being a little judgmental," Lucy fired back.

And there it was again, that push-and-pull that reminded Kristin how very different they were. She took a breath and tried to explain herself. "I just think that when you care about a cause, it's important to do something about it from the ground up. Make your voice heard."

"So you're saying that what I do doesn't matter? That when I donate money, it's meaningless? Because I completely disagree."

"Of course not. It's just a little passive."

"It is not. Passive is sitting on the couch thinking about doing something to contribute."

Kristin nodded. "Okay, that's a valid point."

"I have lots of those. Trust me."

"You're definitely not shy about *arguing* for what you believe in."

"Yeah, well, that's me. The opposite of passive. Speaking of, do you know what's also not passive?" Lucy asked.

"What?"

"Me beating you back to the house." And before Kristin knew it, Lucy was several yards ahead of her in a rather impressive sprint en route to the beach house that was now not that far off. She took a moment to enjoy the view before her competitive side kicked in. Refusing to be beaten, Kristin took off and gained on Lucy steadily. Her longer legs and daily workouts proved advantageous and she overtook Lucy at the last possible second, tossing her hands in the air before collapsing onto the deck.

"You're right. That was not at all passive," she breathed to Lucy, who had fallen onto her back. "But I think the term *champ* now belongs to me."

"Fine. Okay, you win at anything athletic. Let's just stipulate that now."

"Perfect," Kristin said. They lay there a moment to let their breathing even out. "Hey, Lucy?"

"Yeah?"

"Thanks for going running with me."

Lucy flipped onto her stomach and cradled her chin in her hands, looking down at Kristin. "It nearly killed me, but I'm glad we did it.

You get to relax now, however, as this is the portion of the evening when I dazzle you with my culinary prowess."

"Yeah? What are we having?"

"I thought papaya salad, chicken marsala, and potato pancakes. Thoughts?"

"I think it sounds like you win at cooking."

"Finally," Lucy said, smiling. "You don't give in easily."

"That would be because the extent of my cooking ability is the heating up of frozen food."

Lucy's mouth fell open as she pushed herself up. "A crime."

"Admittedly."

Lucy offered Kristin a hand and pulled her up. "How about we take some time to get freshened up and I'll start dinner."

"Great. Do you mind if I grab a quick shower?"

Lucy took a minute with the question. "Um, no. No, of course not. I'll use the one in my room and you can have the guest bathroom."

Kristin didn't want to intrude and the long moment it took Lucy to answer the question made her think that maybe she had. "I don't have to shower."

"Don't be ridiculous," Lucy said. She headed for the house and then opened the door. "If you want to take off your clothes just a few yards away from me, who am I to stop you?"

Kristin felt the heat hit her cheeks instantly, and the tug in her stomach let her know that the comment had registered.

Lucy passed her a victorious smile. "You coming?"

Kristin gave her head a little shake. "On my way."

Lucy stood under the stream of hot water and closed her eyes, trying not to notice how sensitive her skin felt as the water hit and ran down her body. At the same time, she tried to forget that Kristin-of-the-frustrating-and-the-gorgeous was showering just down the hall.

"What am I gonna do with you?" she said to her reflection in the mirror as she toweled off. But she knew one thing. There was a choice laid out in front of her. Kristin was in her home, and they were about to have dinner, and then she could either send her on her way—the safe choice—or let herself wander down a path that could only mean trouble. They had off-the-charts chemistry, no question about it, but there was also the fact that she thought about Kristin a lot, and if they took things further, chances were good that a simple one-night stand would be next to impossible if the week prior had taught her anything. She'd want more, and was that really a path she wanted to go down? "Not fair," she said to the mirror. Lucy had to be practical. She and Kristin had nothing in common and, in fact, saw the world from two entirely different vantage points. Plus, Kristin had a way of sticking with her and infiltrating her thoughts and maybe a few fantasies. It was best not to give her any more power and complicate things further.

Decision made.

Dinner and good night. Easy. Done. They'd enjoy each other's company and adjourn. She needed to save herself from further preoccupation with Kristin James, news reporter, and that meant staying strong.

"Hey," Kristin said when Lucy emerged from her room. She was already sitting on the couch, petting BP and looking fresh faced and amazing in gray shorts and a light purple tank top that had Lucy's mouth watering.

Yeah, totally screwed.

She took a deep breath and forced a smile. "How was the shower?"

"You have A-plus water pressure," Kristin said. "And this dog loves me, I think." To her credit, Bernadette Peters seemed to have picked up on exactly what Lucy had and sat halfway propped up on Kristin's lap as Kristin gently stroked her head. Lucky, lucky dog.

"She definitely seems to," Lucy said, tilting her head and taking in the image. "Why don't you guys hang out and I'll start dinner?"

"Did you hear that?" Kristin said to BP. "We get to hang out and get into trouble."

Lucy shook her head. "I see a very dangerous relationship in the works."

"And which relationship is that?" Kristin asked, smiling.

With an amused shake of her head at the pointed remark, Lucy went to work preparing the meal, tossing on some mellow tunes for the room.

The kitchen and the living room had an open floor plan, which allowed Lucy to watch as Kristin attempted to teach Bernadette Peters to roll over, a task that was akin to convincing Dr. Phil to grow hair. She smiled at the effort, however, and enjoyed the show, which consisted of Kristin turning BP in a tiny slow-motion circle and then cheering for her as if she'd conquered the world.

For the next forty minutes, however, Lucy lost herself in the pans and sauces and tiny little details that made cooking one of her favorite tasks. As she put the finishing touches on the salad, her skin tingled and she found Kristin standing next to her.

"I cannot believe you've done all of this in that short little period of time. It looks amazing."

Lucy smiled up at Kristin over her shoulder. "Thank you. I had fun doing it."

"We had fun too," Kristin said. "Can I show you something?"

"Of course."

With that, Kristin rounded the island into the living room with Lucy following behind her.

"Okay, Miss Bernadette," Kristin said. "This is your big moment." She moved her index finger in a circular motion, and in response, something amazing happened. BP, who was known strictly for long naps and cuddle fests, slowly bowed her head and rolled in a slow, unsteady circle on the ground.

"Oh my God," Lucy said, still not quite believing what she'd just seen. She pointed at her dog. "Did she just roll over on command?"

"She did," Kristin said, scooping up the dog and kissing her face. "Because she's the smartest tiny dog ever."

"You worked at it for like, what? Forty-five minutes?" Lucy asked, trying to understand.

"She's clearly a prodigy."

"Well, who knew?" Lucy asked everyone and no one. Mystification was too mundane a word for what she'd just witnessed. She turned to Kristin.

"Just takes persistence is all. I think that's how I accomplish most feats. Not by talent or know-how. I just keep at it." Kristin tucked a strand of hair behind her ear. It was down now after the shower and the blond seemed brighter than ever.

"Well, you are to be commended. As in awarded some sort of medal of honor. A parade maybe."

Kristin, looking proud of herself in the most adorable way,

shrugged. "You could just kiss me again, because it was beyond awesome the last time."

God, that sentence did something to Lucy. A hit of something powerful shot instantly through her. The earlier plan to sidestep seemed to fly right out the window when she was faced with the real, live Kristin, standing in her living room and smiling like that. It didn't take much thought. Lucy stepped into Kristin's space and cupped her cheek, pulling her the short distance downward. When their lips met, the kiss that resulted was toe curling and zero-to-sixty. Lucy let herself drown in the way Kristin kissed her, all thorough and authoritative. She was aware of Kristin's hands on her lower back and about died when they slipped under her shirt and rested on the bare skin there. The same skin that had been sensitive in the shower just an hour before was now on fire beneath Kristin's touch. As they continued to kiss, Lucy wanted those hands other places.

And *now*.

In just that moment, Kristin pulled her mouth away and Lucy felt the loss. "We should have dinner," Kristin said, straightening the clothes that Lucy had once again grabbed hold of.

"Hmm?" she asked, struggling to make her mind work again.

"Dinner. The one you made for us. We should eat it. Probably." But then they were kissing again and she wasn't sure if it had been her fault or Kristin's, as the edges of reality seemed to have blurred quite a bit. She was aware of the sensations that were storming her system, however, as Kristin's tongue slid into her mouth. She was absently cognizant of the fact that instead of grabbing a fistful of Kristin's shirt, her hands were on the move, moving across Kristin's skin, slowly, deliberately, as if trying to memorize all of her.

"Okay, dinner now. For real," Kristin said, moving out of her touch. "There should be dinner."

Lucy took a moment and nodded. *Dinner. Right. That.* "On it," Lucy said, rounding the island and blowing out a breath. She moved the food onto serving plates, a task that allowed her sensibilities to drift back and the heat she felt to settle into the manageable column.

As she took her spot at the table, Kristin passed her an easy smile. "This looks amazing. Thank you for cooking."

"I'm happy to cook for you. I don't have a ton of company."

"No?" Kristin said, taking a serving of the chicken.

"Mainly Emory and Sarah, who you met. They live just up the beach a bit. The house you made our running goal earlier was theirs."

"Seriously? That must be cool to live so close."

"It is." And while she tried to focus on the conversation, it seemed to be a losing battle. Instead, she noticed the way Kristin tended to move the hair off her forehead if it came remotely close to covering her eye. God, it was sexy, as was how smooth her skin looked, which took Lucy back to how it had *felt* just minutes ago beneath her fingertips. The music that had seemed fun and mellow while she cooked now read sexy and romantic, given their recent interaction. It was coming at her from all angles and Lucy didn't know how much longer she could go on.

"So it turns out the food tastes just as good as it looks," Kristin said quietly, meeting her eyes and holding there. Lucy blinked back.

"Yeah?"

"Mmm-hmm. You're talented. At a lot of things," Kristin said.

"I can be." God, this was cruel. Her body temperature, which had leveled out as she made the final dinner prep, was right back up there in the stratosphere. The aching that had taken up residence within her had moved lower and was also growing harder and harder to ignore. They went back to eating, the tension so thick, Lucy felt it all over. She sipped from her white wine glass and placed it carefully back on the table. A bite of papaya. Exhale. She shifted in her seat uncomfortably.

"Lucy."

She closed her eyes briefly at the use of her name. "Yes?"

Kristin spoke slowly. "While I love what you've prepared, I'm not sure I feel like eating dinner right now after all." It was a simple statement, but Lucy understood its implication clear as day.

"And why is that?" Lucy asked, meeting those expressive eyes.

"Because I'd rather finish what we started not long ago."

Lucy didn't need any more encouragement than that. As she stood, Kristin grabbed her hand and pulled her in. Lucy accepted the invitation and settled herself on Kristin's lap where they met in a clash of lips and tongues that felt so right it was frightening. She combed her fingers through Kristin's hair as they kissed, moving it back from her face as heat enveloped her once again. But it wasn't enough and their pace quickened. She adjusted, straddling Kristin, and slipped her hands beneath her T-shirt as they kissed, moving them up her rib cage to the outside of Kristin's bra where, through fabric, her breasts filled Lucy's hands and she massaged gently, pulling a gasp from Kristin as they kissed. *Hot.*

Her hips pushed against Kristin's stomach as her arousal skyrocketed at the intimacy of the touch. Flames licked through her. She needed more. And fast.

"My bedroom is behind us," Lucy said between kisses.

Kristin pulled her face back far enough to look up at Lucy, her eyes searching. "Does that mean you're taking me there?"

Lucy nodded, her eyes closing as Kristin's hands wandered down the back of her waistband pulling her in more firmly, which was so okay with her it was ridiculous. Unfortunately, their travel to her room meant breaking the contact that she couldn't get enough of.

Wordlessly, she took Kristin's hand and led her the short distance to her bedroom. She flipped on the light and Kristin flipped it off. "Well, okay," Lucy said, just as Kristin's mouth claimed hers, moving them backward. A slash of early moonlight illuminated the room and Lucy understood why Kristin wanted the lights off, as the effect was rather sexy all on its own. While taking it slow sounded like a really nice plan, Lucy didn't feel so inclined. "I want to touch you everywhere," she breathed. With a purposeful unbuttoning and unzipping of Kristin's shorts, Lucy slid her hand inside to explore. The quiet moan the contact elicited only encouraged Lucy, as she stroked purposefully through the warmth, taking pleasure in the way Kristin's breathing had shifted, now shallow and quick. Kristin moved against Lucy's hand in a tantalizing display, searching for more, and while Lucy wanted to give it, there were other things she wanted first.

It was time to lose those clothes. She eased back a step.

Kristin was way ahead of her and pulled the T-shirt over her head, revealing to Lucy the white satin bra that showcased the tops of generous breasts.

"God, you're beautiful," Lucy breathed, drinking in the image.

❖

It was beyond hot the way Lucy's eyes combed her body. Kristin felt that gaze all over, and a sizzle of pleasure moved across her skin.

She hadn't planned on sleeping with Lucy. Technically, this was only a third date, and in Kristin's world, things moved a little slower.

But this was different.

The things Lucy inspired her to feel were new, overwhelming, and insistent and she could no more stop herself from breathing than taking what she so desperately wanted that night. That much had been clear after the spark-loaded kiss before dinner.

Standing before Lucy in her bedroom now couldn't feel more right. Need traveled through her like a thunderbolt, and while she wanted Lucy to finish what she'd started, Kristin had to even things out. She moved to Lucy, claiming that mouth once again, tasting just a hint of sweetness from the wine, as she backed her toward the bed. She broke the kiss and pulled the shirt over Lucy's head and made quick work of her bra. She took a moment with Lucy's breasts on display to her now before dipping her head and kissing one, pulling a nipple into her mouth and swirling her tongue around it. Lucy slid fingers into her hair, holding her in place, which was no problem at all because Kristin was in heaven and getting more turned on by the second. With her arm at the small of Lucy's back, she lowered her onto the bed and took a moment to take off what remained of her own clothes. The moonlight fell across Lucy's face as she watched, her lips parting noticeably as the rest of Kristin was revealed to her. She pushed herself up onto her elbows from where she lay on the bed and lifted her hips as Kristin slid the jeans and panties off her legs.

Kristin was wet and craving release. And though she was beyond ready, she wanted Lucy to join her there first.

On a mission, she started on those legs, newly tanned from the afternoon, and kissed her way up their length, up to Lucy's inner thighs. The attention had Lucy squirming beneath her mouth and moving her hips in these subtle circles that drove Kristin wild. Too soon. She moved up Lucy's body and paid ample attention to each breast, skating her teeth across each nipple. Lucy had the most awesome breasts, and as she explored them further, she slipped a thigh between Lucy's legs and moved it upward, causing Lucy to hitch in a breath. She moved under Kristin in a teasing circle.

"God, you're stunning," Kristin said and focused on Lucy's neck. She ran her tongue across its column, as the pulsing ache from between her legs increased to the point that she thought she might burst. She found Lucy's mouth and drove her tongue inside as Lucy continued to move against her thigh in a thrilling rhythm. That's when hands were on her face and big blue eyes blinked up at her.

"Now," Lucy breathed. "Please."

Kristin nodded, knowing all too well. She parted Lucy's thighs and eased her hips between in a move that had them both moaning in surrender. She pressed against Lucy, who tossed her head against the pillow. As Kristin began to move against her, Lucy matched her thrust for thrust in a dance that pushed Kristin closer and closer to the edge. Urgency swam through her and she buried her face in Lucy's neck as they moved and moved, lost in the climb of sensation. As the dance escalated to a frenzied state, Kristin slipped a hand between them and pushed into her while applying direct pressure with her thumb to Lucy's most sensitive spot. The result was breathtaking, and Lucy cried out and writhed in a display that slammed Kristin in the throat. She didn't have time to dwell, however, because control snapped and she tumbled over and joined Lucy there, the bolt of pleasure speeding through her like a train. She was vaguely aware of sound coming from her mouth as her muscles contracted in a payout more powerful than she'd planned on. She reveled in the waves of pleasure that stormed her system.

When all was said and done, she fell alongside Lucy and lay there, quivering deliciously, staring up at the light patterns across the ceiling, her arm across her forehead. Cognizant thought floated back to her slowly, though her limbs felt liquid and not fully hers.

Lucy pressed against her side and placed a kiss beneath her jaw as they both continued to simply breathe. She wasn't sure how much time went by, but the mood shifted to peaceful, and along with it, they shifted together. Lucy now lay partially on top of her and Kristin had her arm across Lucy's back, holding her close. "Are we still alive?" Lucy asked finally.

"Not sure," Kristin managed. A long pause. "Wherever we are, I like it here."

"Have you ever done that before?" Lucy finally asked, looking down at her.

Kristin smiled. "Had sex? I have, yes."

Lucy poked her ribs and Kristin laughed. "No, crazy. What we just did."

"I think you're going to have to be more specific," Kristin said. "Because a lot of things just happened."

Lucy propped herself up on her elbow and rested her head in her hand before tracing circles on the outside of Kristin's breast. Her voice was quiet when she answered, almost shy. "Come with someone, at the same time. As in, what we just did."

"Oh, *that*," Kristin said, now wildly aware of the sensations those traced circles were causing. She closed her eyes and forced herself to focus on the question. "No, that I have never done."

"Me neither. A first," Lucy said, shifting the tracing to Kristin's stomach. "Do you realize what an amazing body you have?" She placed a slow kiss on Kristin's collarbone.

Kristin swallowed against the onslaught of arousal in response to all the sensual touches. "I don't know how to answer that."

"You don't have to," Lucy said. "I'm just doing a little marveling here." As Lucy's hand drifted lower to her abdomen, she steadied herself, not quite sure how it was that she was so turned on again so soon.

"Yeah, well, the marveling goes both ways," Kristin told her, and God, did it ever. Lucy was everything she imagined she would be and more. Beautiful, sexy, and so responsive in bed it was ridiculous.

"The together thing," Lucy shook her head. "That was beyond anything I've ever…"

"Yeah?"

Lucy pulled back from the careful touches that had Kristin so heated and brushed the hair from Kristin's forehead. It was sweet, the gesture. Tender even. "Mmm-hmm," Lucy said. "I like that we were able to do that together. Have you been with a lot of women?"

"Oh, we're going there? Okay. You make three," Kristin said.

Lucy took a minute with this. "Three. That's it?"

"That's it. How many have you slept with?"

Lucy frowned. "I don't think I know the answer to that question, and in comparison to what you just said, that sounds awful." She fell onto her back in devastation, prompting Kristin to laugh.

"No, it doesn't," she told Lucy. "You're you. I'm me. If we were the same person, that would be totally boring and I wouldn't want to tear your clothes off the way I just did, see? I happen to like how crazy different we are and the clothes-ripping-off thing. Both. So there." That seemed to help. Lucy smiled and slid on top once again. Kristin loved the way they fit together.

"Well, that's good," Lucy said, "because we are, in fact, very different." A kiss.

"We are." Another kiss, deeper, longer this time. "But I don't think we have any chemistry."

"None. Zero," Lucy said, her eyes heavy lidded. She moved until her mouth was very close to Kristin's ear and whispered, "But if you don't mind, I think I need to taste you now." As Lucy crawled down her body, Kristin closed her eyes, her heart jackhammering in her chest because she didn't mind at all.

Chapter Five

Kristin sat back in her desk chair and sighed, halfheartedly clicking off the notes she'd just reviewed from Dalton. She'd sent him the latest draft of her story that morning, with the knowledge that something was missing. The heart and soul of the piece was there, that much she knew, but the communication of ideas was off somehow and she couldn't put her finger on why. While she wanted his feedback, she wasn't sure she was prepared for what he'd had to say.

The short entry in bold print at the bottom of her story was short and to the point.

You're playing it safe. This should be an evocative piece about the paper trail of that school-bus story and its hometown tie-in. Global NewsWire is headquartered in your readers' backyard. You're burying your lede. Why?

She stared at the grooves in her desk and closed her eyes. Though Dalton had a valid point about the GNW angle, a story about a local company was not what she'd set out to write. But then again, maybe that was the *better* story.

God. She shook her head.

The ramifications of writing it could be significant.

This was *Lucy*'s company. Lucy, whom she'd texted with daily but had yet to actually see since their amazing night together the weekend prior. Lucy, who occupied her thoughts on a loop of wonderful. How was she supposed to be objective about this?

Kristin sat there for the better part of an hour working through her thoughts. There was a war waging within her, between her journalistic integrity and the very real feelings she already had for one of her subjects. She shook her head. No. She couldn't think that way. She had to remain objective. Even if it meant hurting the one person she so desperately did not want to hurt. She flipped through her notes and set to organizing, seeing a natural progression of the story start to take shape. Her fingers couldn't type fast enough as she set out on this new course. While she hated to admit Dalton was right, the story practically told itself.

Her phone buzzed, pulling her from her thoughts. An incoming text message from Lucy. She smiled. While they'd tried to make time to see each other after work that week, it simply hadn't been possible given her impending deadline and Lucy's stacked schedule, given that second-quarter earnings releases loomed in the distance.

Lunch tomorrow?

While she wanted nothing more than to spend more time with Lucy, unfortunately, she was busy most of the day. She started to type her response when an idea occurred to her, inspiring a change of direction.

I have plans, but I'm thinking you should come. You up for it? She paused and waited for the response to come in.

Um, sure. What are we doing?

Oh, this was going to be good.

❖

"What are we protesting exactly?" Lucy asked, as they exited the car. She still felt a little skeptical and was unsure why in a million years she'd agreed to this—other than she'd really wanted to see Kristin again.

"Irresponsible environmental practices for the sake of making a buck."

Lucy nodded. "Right. Irresponsible environmentalists are going down today."

"That's the spirit." Kristin gestured to Lucy's attire. "And this casual thing you have going on here is a good look on you. Not a designer label in sight, yet you still rock it."

"Gasp. I think you just took a shot at my daily wardrobe."

Kristin handed Lucy a sign and kissed her cheek. "Never. I

love your wardrobe. It could pay off my school loans and is thereby impressive."

Joking aside, Kristin had instructed her to wear comfortable attire, so she'd selected a worn-in pair of denim capris and her heather pink top. Pink was, after all, a feisty color. She was also quite proud of herself for arriving at Kristin's place on time that morning. One coffee stop later and they'd made it to the plant well in advance of the scheduled meeting time.

As they approached, there was a rather large group of people gathered on the sidewalk in front of the plant labeled Slater Energy. According to Kristin, Slater made a big show of making the public think it was green, when all the while, they were one of the worst polluters in the nation.

"So what will we do exactly?" Lucy asked as they made their way to the group.

"It's a peaceful protest. We'll hold our signs and make it known to the company that there are concerned citizens who are aware of their practices and are not going to stand for it. If we get news attention, that's a bonus."

"Got it. And what is it we want them to do?"

"Well, Slater is notorious for huge carbon dioxide emissions. If they spend the extra money to implement a carbon capture plan, they can significantly decrease those emissions. They just have to see it as a priority."

"And we hope to make them do that?"

"Exactly. Are you a little nervous right now?" Kristin asked.

"Not at all. I'm excited to see you in your element."

"It doesn't get any more real than this," Kristin said with a smile. Her blond hair was pulled back loosely into a clip today, and she wore white shorts and a gray shirt that showed off her awesome skin. If nothing else, Lucy would enjoy the view that morning.

However, something kind of unexpected happened. An hour later, Lucy found herself…into it. The protest was made up of several local organizations pulling together for the cause, and these seemed to be smart, like-minded people, who genuinely cared. She held her sign and chanted *Carbon capture plan!* along with the others and watched as one executive after another filed past into the building, many of them sneering or shaking their heads in disgust at the protesters. She didn't get it. How could they not care? How was that okay?

When the news crews arrived, the mood shifted and the tension between the protestors and the Slater executives seemed to escalate. Two hours in, a spokesperson for the company addressed them and asked the group to disband, but the group leaders had no such intention, a decision that Lucy had to applaud.

As the morning shifted into afternoon, the sun beat down overhead with a newfound ferocity. With summer in full effect, the community coolers were now empty. Kristin turned to her. "There's a convenience store across the street. I'll grab us a couple of waters."

"Great. I'll chant double for you."

Kristin smiled. "You're doing really well with all of this. More than I would have predicted."

Lucy raised an eyebrow. "You underestimate me, Ms. James." But in all honesty, the whole thing had been eye opening for Lucy. While she still stood by the need for charitable donations, it was also clear to her that there was more to be done in the world, and these people all around her were good examples of that. "I'm actually happy to be here."

"I'm glad." Kristin stepped into her space, dropping her tone in flirtation. "We should have dinner tonight. Somewhere nice."

Lucy closed her eyes at the concept. A romantic dinner would be killer after the week she'd had and the physical demands of standing on her feet all day under the hot sun. "I vote yes."

"Perfect. Back with water in a few. You sure you're good here? You could always come with me."

"And who would fight for what is right in your absence? You go. I got this."

"Lucy?"

"Yes?"

"You're really cute right now."

Lucy broke into a smile because the way Kristin was looking at her made her skin tingle in the most wonderful way. "Stop objectifying me so you can start fresh later." She winked at Kristin and went back to her chant.

❖

After scoring a couple of waters and sandwiches from the small deli within the store, Kristin found herself in a rather long line. The guy at the front seemed to have made an Olympic event out of choosing just the right brand of cigarettes. She craned her neck to see what she could do about speeding up this process, but the rule follower in her kept silent and waited her turn. In the meantime, she ruminated over the events of the day. The protest, thus far, had been a successful one, and unless something over-the-top happened in the city, they should score some media time. She imagined they'd break up close to late afternoon, and that would give her and Lucy enough time to head home, freshen up, and change, before coming together again for dinner.

She was picturing something quiet where they could catch up after the week prior, and maybe champagne to celebrate Lucy's first successful protest. Given, it might be her last, but she had to award the woman big-time credit for showing up and being such a great sport. As dramatic a front as Lucy sometimes put up, she seemed game when faced with any sort of challenge, and Kristin found that admirable.

"That'll be twelve dollars and sixty cents," the cashier said and bagged her items. She paid and headed back to the parking lot as a group text message came in from the leader of her environmental group.

Okay, so that was less than ideal. Did everyone make it out of there?

Kristin stood there a moment in an attempt to understand what the message meant, as a string of replies flooded in from various group members.

I'm good. Left after he threw the punch.

Me too.

I'm fine.

Both Beth and I are good.

With fear in her throat, Kristin jumped in her car, at the same time scrolling through her contacts to call Lucy. No answer. She gunned it. As she pulled into the parking lot of the Slater building, the red and blue lights confirmed the worst.

"What happened?" Kristin asked a familiar face from the protest as he and his friend hurried to their own car.

The man turned to her, his expression grim. It was clear he was still hyped up on adrenaline. "Cops showed up and asked us to disperse at the property owner's request. Some folks got riled up. One guy got in the cop's face and that's when they started grabbing people and taking 'em downtown."

Kristin closed her eyes, instantly guilt ridden for not having been there. "I'm looking for my friend. Dark hair, about this tall, wearing a pink shirt." She watched as the final police car drove away.

"The girl in the pink shirt was one of the ones arrested," he said matter-of-factly.

She shook her head. "No, no, no. Please tell me that's not true."

He glanced over at his friend for confirmation.

"Yeah, she was," the friend said. "She was trying to reason with the cops and they took it as a refusal to disperse."

This was so not good. "Okay, thanks," Kristin said. Her mind raced as she drove the fifteen minutes to the police precinct. Guilt reigned. She never should have gotten Lucy mixed up in all this and she certainly shouldn't have left her alone at the protest.

The police station was a bustling mess when she arrived. She patiently waited her turn as her concern grew to panic. The officer who took her question asked her to wait nearby as he tried to learn what he could about the arrested protestors.

An hour passed without word.

Her stomach rumbled, reminding her that she hadn't eaten since breakfast. It didn't matter. A second hour passed. She stared at the haggard faces of the people in the small waiting area. The fluorescent light brought out each furrowed brow, highlighted each tear. Just looking around, she could tell it hadn't been a good day for any of them. Finally, an officer appeared.

"It's been decided that in the matter of the Slater protestors no charges will be filed. If you'll head through that door, you can wait in the hallway for your friends to be released."

Kristin allowed herself to breathe again. *Thank God.* Twenty minutes later, when a group of familiar faces emerged from behind the glass door, she braced herself. She'd be perfectly fine with Lucy yelling at her or giving her the silent treatment. But what if Lucy never wanted to see her again? That one she wouldn't be able to handle. However, the smile Lucy greeted her with was a scenario she wasn't prepared for.

She held up her hands, palms out as Lucy approached. "I am so sorry."

Lucy nodded, took Kristin's hands, and brought them together. "Let's just get out of here."

"Of course." As they walked to the car, day was shifting to night as the pinks and purples swirled in the sky. "Did I mention how sorry I am? Because I can say it again. I am so sorry, Lucy."

Lucy passed her a look over the top of the car. "As in the sorriest?"

"As in. Also, I feel like I should do something to make it up to you, a cash payment, my firstborn, something."

"You're creative. You'll figure it out." Lucy got in the car and Kristin followed her there. "It wasn't that bad actually."

"No?" Kristin asked.

"No. I met a woman named Marge who wanted to know what kind of moisturizer I use. I'm fairly confident Marge could benefit from a helpful moisturizer tip or two, so I offered some insight. It's not a bad day when people compliment your skin."

Kristin couldn't help but smile. She remembered how Lucy's skin felt beneath her fingers, and she was every bit deserving of that compliment. Marge knew what she was talking about. "I suppose skin compliments do go a long way."

"Well, when you're in the slammer," Lucy said as they drove, "little things matter."

Kristin passed her a look of amusement. "So it's the slammer now?"

"The big house, the tank, or yes, the slammer. It's what we insiders call it."

She was being playful now and it was like a giant weight had been lifted off Kristin's shoulders. Lucy didn't want to kill her. She was making jokes, even. "I have to say that I'm super surprised you're taking this so well," Kristin said. "You have every right to want to kill me."

Lucy lifted a shoulder. "I don't see how that benefits me in the long run, the killing. And trust me, I considered it. This is what I keep coming back to. You didn't arrest me and you weren't the guy who got the cops upset by mouthing off. You simply believed in a cause. If nothing else, I have a great story to tell now. Lucy Danaher was arrested today. I should take out a press release at work and up my street cred. I might need a tat."

Kristin laughed. “The socialites would love it.”

“Right? Just think of the corner whispering that would take place at parties. The intimidation factor would be huge. Think they’ll ever insult my canapés again? Not likely.”

Kristin laughed. “Silver lining.”

The conversation lulled. Kristin flipped on the radio and eighties music, her favorite, filled the car.

Lucy turned to her. “Are you rocking out to Cyndi Lauper right now? Is this happening?”

Kristin stopped mid-head-bop. “Yes, because Cyndi gets life.”

“I wonder if she’s ever served time like me.”

“You haven’t served time. You were in a holding cell for three hours.”

“Three hours is an increment of time, Kristin. I’m livin’ the struggle. Now turn up the music so I can sing poorly and celebrate my newfound freedom.”

Kristin did just that, and as the sun set over the water, they drove alongside the beach, singing loudly to “Girls Just Want to Have Fun.” It was summertime, she was with an amazing woman, and life had amazing possibilities.

Chapter Six

Lucy blinked against the sunlight that illuminated her bedroom and lazily made note that morning had arrived. It was Saturday and she had no plans, making it the best kind of morning ever. Her limbs felt heavy, her body felt fluid in the most wonderful way, and the events of the night prior came flooding back to her in all their detailed glory.

Kristin, she thought languidly to herself and then rolled over to find the object of her racy memories asleep next to her. The golden glow of the sunlight touched Kristin's bare shoulders, and Lucy smiled at the sight, and at the recollection of the delicious things they'd done to each other. She placed a kiss on one of those shoulders and snaked an arm around Kristin's waist, moving closer to her. It had been three weeks since the protest, and quite possibly the best three weeks of Lucy's life.

"Good morning," Kristin murmured with a slight smile on her face, though her eyes remained closed. Lucy delicately feathered her fingers into Kristin's hair and moved it off her forehead, then took a moment to watch her sleep, knowing full well it would be a short-lived visual. Her hand drifted lower to Kristin's breast, and with her index finger she circled the nipple. "What are you doing?" Kristin asked, though the smile had grown.

"Just saying good morning back," Lucy said, dipping her head to taste the spot her hand had just explored. She heard Kristin suck in a breath as she pulled the nipple into her mouth. She dropped her hand between Kristin's legs and greeted her properly, loving the murmur of approval she received from Kristin, who shifted against the touch and surrendered as Lucy slid inside.

"God," Kristin breathed, lifting her head from the pillow. Her eyes were open now and she was fully engaged, looking beyond sexy. Kristin in an everyday moment was beautiful, but Kristin fresh-faced and turned on was another level entirely. Zero-to-sixty, Lucy reminded herself, the way it always was with them. It only took a few minutes before Kristin writhed beneath her touch and gripped the sheets as pleasure washed over her in a display Lucy would never get tired of.

As the final shock waves subsided, Lucy claimed her mouth in a tantalizing kiss. "Sorry I woke you. Kinda had to."

Kristin blinked back at her. "You know how to make a morning a memorable one. That's for sure."

"I really like the morning."

"And I like that you like it."

Lucy relaxed back into the bed. She couldn't remember the last time she'd been this happy. While their jobs kept them busy, she and Kristin had begun spending more and more time together in the evenings, and the weekend sleepovers were a definite favorite of hers. They were still very different people and probably always would be. Kristin stuck to her running schedule and would rather stay in and watch a movie together on the couch. Lucy liked to go out on a Saturday night and spent her free time planning parties or charity gatherings with her friends. Kristin attended environmental meetings. Lucy went to the spa. Kristin followed politics. Lucy followed baseball. But underneath it all, Lucy had developed a deep appreciation of their differences. How boring would it be to date someone just like herself? Hadn't that been why she and Emory hadn't worked out, back in the day?

Kristin slipped her hands beneath the hem of the Padres T-shirt Lucy had put on before falling asleep and caressed Lucy's stomach with her thumbs. "Do you know what makes me happy?"

"I don't," Lucy said. "You should tell me."

"Waking up in the morning and remembering that you're here next to me." Kristin gave her head the tiniest shake. "I can't seem to get enough of what that feels like. That little burst of energy I get when I open my eyes and see you."

They were maybe some of Lucy's favorite words ever and she felt the smile break across her face. Honestly, she couldn't agree with the sentiment more. Kristin made life shimmer in a way she'd never experienced before. Talking to her was enthralling, looking at her was mesmerizing, and kissing her was like heaven on Earth.

"Let's just stay in bed for a couple of hours," Kristin said. "What do you say? We can be lazy and adventurous at the same time. Though you've already checked your adventurous box once this morning."

"While I want nothing more than to live in this bed with you, I must take a temporary leave of absence. I require pancakes. Sustenance." And with that, Lucy was up and putting on her robe as Kristin gaped at her. "What?" Lucy asked nonchalantly.

"You can't do that."

"Do what?" She passed Kristin an innocent smile.

"You know exactly what. Ravish my body and then dash out of here before I get to have any fun myself. And Lucy, I really, really want to have fun with you right now."

"You seemed to be having a good time a few minutes ago." Lucy said with a circular point back at the bed. But the way Kristin looked now had her rethinking her plan. All sexy and amazing with tousled hair and pouty lips. "God, look at you." Before she could help it, she climbed back in bed and claimed a final, scorching kiss. The kind that curled her toes and sent the tingling sensations dancing across her skin. "Okay, no more of that or we'll never get pancakes. Chef Lucy needs to report to the kitchen."

"Chef Lucy, stay here and be naughty with me some more. The pancakes can wait."

"They can't either. Pancakes can't be made to wait. They're too important in the scheme of life."

"And the rest of the fun?" Kristin asked with the most adorable puppy-dog eyes.

"After the pancakes, we have all the time in the world to come back here and do…whatever we want."

At that, Kristin perked up considerably. "Okay, now this is a scenario I can get behind."

"We can try it from behind if you want." She winked playfully at Kristin and headed for the stove.

Twenty minutes later, they sat around Lucy's circular kitchen table, enjoying some of the fluffiest pancakes Lucy had ever managed to turn out. "I'm highly impressed with myself right now," Lucy said, examining the substantial height of the bite of pancake on her fork.

"You excel at pancakes, Luce. Gotta hand it to you." Kristin tossed a bite to BP, who inhaled the unexpected treasure and offered Kristin's ankle a lick in appreciation.

"Thanks. And I swear that dog likes you more than she likes me, not that I blame her."

Kristin rested her chin in her hand and smiled at Lucy. "Are you saying you like me, Lucy?"

"I think that is what I'm saying. Yes." The mood was light, but the words sparked something in Lucy and she felt the smile dim on her face. Because she *did* like Kristin. She liked bantering with her. She liked the way Kristin consistently challenged her and didn't always let her get away with things most people did. She loved the long talks they had late at night after making love. She liked the pensive look Kristin got on her face when she was thinking about whatever story she was writing in her head. She loved it all. *Pause, rewind. Deep breath.* How did the word love sneak in there? She wasn't in love with Kristin. They'd known each other less than two months. Love took time. But in a shocking revelation, she did think she could be in the process of *falling* in love with her, and that was a little scary. Something to maybe push aside for examination later.

"Why do you look like you're about to pull the fire alarm?"

She was now aware of the fact that Kristin was studying her. "Hmm?" Lucy asked absently. She hadn't quite rejoined the conversation fully after her world had shifted on its axis moments before. Because, whoa, she was falling in love with this woman. As the seconds ticked by, she grew more and more sure of it.

"I was just asking, a moment ago, how long you were going to hold that bite of pancake half the distance to your mouth. Are you taking a break? Was it maybe a heavy pancake and you can't move it any farther?" Kristin was smiling at her, and that smile did just what it always did, grounded her. It brought her back to the here and now and she remembered another thing she loved about Kristin. She served as an excellent voice of reason.

Lucy inhaled deeply and the terror dissipated. In its place, she found courage. She stared into those eyes the color of the sea and said what was in her heart. "I was just thinking how wonderful you are and how it's hard to believe you weren't a part of my life just a few months ago."

Kristin relaxed back into her chair. "I know. I feel like I've known you for so much longer. Maybe it's because I spend so much time thinking about you when we're apart. I don't like being away from you. Besides our fiery debates and playful chatter, you're also super hot. Speaking of which…"

"Yes?"

"Are we through with the pancakes now? For the love of God, say yes."

The fire in Kristin's eyes gave Lucy a little thrill she felt all over. "We are."

❖

It was dark out and most of the newsroom had headed home for the day, but Kristin had done it. She'd put the finishing touches on her exposé and once she'd hit send, it was on its way to Dalton and then to the cover of the Sunday feature section. She sat back in her chair and let the feeling of accomplishment wash over her. It'd been a long row she'd hoed to get here. The move, the new job, and the intense hours of research and reshaping, had all led to this moment.

She felt like celebrating. Champagne, maybe. And there was only one person she wanted to share this moment with. Given, Lucy didn't love the fact that her company was mentioned in the story, but she surely, by this point, understood that the story was merely an impartial examination of a series of events. Nothing personal. In fact, she seemed to root for Kristin as she worked long hours. That didn't mean Kristin wasn't fighting against the butterflies bouncing around her stomach at the thought of Lucy actually reading the piece.

She called Lucy instead of texting her, simply because she wanted to hear her voice. Whether she would have believed it three months ago or not, Lucy had come to mean everything to Kristin. And while the workweek kept them from spending any sort of appreciable one-on-one time together outside of the occasional quick lunchtime rendezvous, Kristin always seemed to crave more.

"Hey, sexy reporter person," Lucy said upon answering. "Do I get to lay eyes on you tonight or do you have to work?" It was the last day of June and Friday night. Neither of them had work the next day, so of course, they'd get together and enjoy the summer night. Maybe even walk on the beach if Lucy was up for it.

"Oh, eyes will be laid."

"That's all though? Just eyes?" There was a mock sadness in Lucy's voice that made Kristin smile.

"I have a suspicion there might be more. I can't be sure."

"Well, who can? Now come over here and let's watch bad TV and talk about our weeks."

"Sold."

Lucy opened the door to her beach house fifteen minutes later. "Well, that was fast. Come here, because I have missed you this week."

After a leisurely hello kiss that had Kristin walking on air, she held up the bottle she'd brought with her.

"And you have champagne?"

"I'm a ninja today." She placed another kiss on Lucy's amazing lips and followed her inside, tasting strawberry lip gloss, which was most certainly on its way to becoming her favorite taste on the planet. Lucy was more casual than she was, wearing workout shorts and a black tank top. "How do you manage to make a basic tank top look like that on you?"

"I think that's a compliment, which I will accept. Oh, and you'd be proud of me. I stepped over to the dark side and went for a run to Emory's house."

"You ran the five minutes to Emory's house?" Kristin made sure to sound extra shocked for proper ribbing to occur.

"Yes, Miss Pretentious About Running. I did. Though I hated every moment of it, I was glad I'd done it when it was all over."

"I don't know who you are, but I'm really impressed with you right now."

"Is that why there's champagne here? Because you're celebrating my newfound appreciation for running. I'm like blue-ribbon-on-field-day caliber now."

"Whoa. And yes, that is most definitely it. It's here for your running celebration. I also finished my story, so both things."

Lucy broke out into a smile that Kristin felt straight down to her toes. "As in, gone forever? It's done?"

"I turned it in"—Kristin consulted her watch—"half an hour ago."

Lucy stepped into Kristin's space and snaked her arms around Kristin's neck, looking up at her. "You, Kristin James, are one awesome and accomplished human. I'm very, very proud of you. I know you've been working incredibly hard on this story." She leaned in for a slow kiss. "When do I get to read it and bask in your journalistic prowess?"

Kristin knew this moment was coming, and she'd imagined it on more than one occasion. Now that it was here, she felt sick inside. When she'd taken Dalton's advice and made the decision to make Global NewsWire a bigger part of the story, she'd had her reservations. But the fact of the matter was that this was her career she was talking about, and journalistic integrity mattered. That meant she couldn't let her personal life color her point of view when she crafted a story. It had been difficult to push her feelings for Lucy aside and write what she did, but in the end, it had been the right decision. The story needed that hometown anchor featured prominently in the exposition. Lucy was a career-driven woman herself and Kristin was confident she'd get that. At least, she hoped she would.

"You don't have to read it right now," Kristin said, releasing Lucy and turning to unwrap the foil from the bottle. "Let's have a glass." She was delaying the inevitable here.

"Oh, but I want to." Lucy slid onto one of the bar stools facing the island. "I've actually been really curious about how it was coming along but thought I'd stay out of it until you were finished."

Kristin struggled with the cork and considered this. "You didn't have to do that. I would have let you read it."

"And now I know for next time." With a loud pop, the cork flew from the bottle and collided with the ceiling in a festive display. Lucy stared at the ceiling in amusement and then back at Kristin. "You give good cork."

Kristin smiled. "Among other things."

"And you're still stalling." Lucy patted the countertop in front of her. "I'd like my champagne with a side of news story, please."

"Fine. Okay. Coming right up." She placed a glass of champagne in front of Lucy and handed her the laptop, which was open to the story. "Let me say this first. Please try and keep an open mind as you read. The story runs on Sunday but I wanted you to have a chance with it first. So we can discuss it."

Lucy studied her for a moment before nodding solemnly. "Of course." A flicker of concern crossed her features as she turned her attention to the screen.

Kristin took a seat on the couch behind her, giving Lucy space to read. Suddenly all the reasons she'd given herself to write the particular story as she did fell by the wayside as she watched Lucy, who meant the world to her, read back the words. She controlled her breathing to calm her nerves and took note of the fact that time seemed to inch by. Seconds felt like minutes. Minutes felt like hours.

Somewhere along the way, it became clear to Kristin that Lucy had stopped reading. She closed the laptop in front of her, and though Kristin couldn't see her face, she'd gone very still.

"Luce?" she asked quietly.

"Yeah?" But she still hadn't turned around.

"Talk to me. What did you think?"

"I guess I'm a little surprised is all." She finally did turn around then. To say she appeared stricken was an understatement. The color had drained from her face and her eyes appeared haunted, wide. "So I might need a minute." She turned back around, but it wasn't like Kristin could just sit there and do nothing. The look on Lucy's face had about killed her. She was up and circling the island instantly.

"Hey, don't pull away from me right now. What's going through your head? You know this isn't personal."

Lucy stared at the wall and gave her head a slow but subtle shake. "How could it not be? Not only do you mention the company I've worked hard to build from the ground up, but you've made it the crux of your story."

Kristin took a moment to compile her thoughts, because the distant look on Lucy's face made her feel as if she'd been punched in the stomach. "I tethered the story to GNW because its corporate headquarters are in San Diego and it allowed readers a connection to the story."

Lucy stood. "Well, I'm happy I could be that for you. Do you mind if we call it a night early? I'm suddenly not in the mood to socialize." She headed in the direction of her bedroom.

"Luce, please, let's talk about this. If you're angry about the story, say so."

Lucy turned back to her then, her eyes flashing. "How could I not be angry? I've spent the last two and a half months sleeping with a woman that thinks I'm morally bankrupt and a perpetuator of untruths."

"The story doesn't say that. I don't think that."

"Did you or did you not write a news article that begins with a call for truth in our society and then segues into an example where a local company failed to do just that?"

"That's a really harsh way of putting it."

"You used my name, Kristin, and associated me with the act of misleading the public. How are you and I supposed to come back from that?"

"We'll find a way. Let's talk this out. I don't want to fight with you."

"Too late, because I want to fight with you."

Kristin took a seat because the words were coming at her fast and furious and she was struggling with where to go. The way Lucy phrased it made the whole thing sound horrible. And it wasn't that. It was an objective story about a series of events that actually took place. She pinched the bridge of her nose. "I don't understand why you're so shocked by all of this. You knew the moment we met that I was writing this story and had plans to include Global NewsWire. It's not ideal, but it's how things played out. What kind of journalist would I be if I twisted the story to suit my own needs?"

"It's true I knew you were writing the story, but things were different then." Her voice was much quieter now, which Kristin wasn't sure was a good thing. She moved toward Lucy because she needed to be close to her, to let her know that nothing had changed. But Lucy had her hand out.

"Please don't touch me right now. I feel like I've given myself to you in so many ways only to find out that who I am is undervalued. And that is not okay."

Kristin shook her head. "You can stand there and be as mad as you want about the story. I get it, but don't tell me that I don't value you, because you mean more to me than you realize."

"Apparently not."

Kristin backtracked, attempting to see the situation as Lucy did. "So you thought I would drop the whole thing once we started dating? Leave you out of it?"

Lucy crossed her arms, indignant now. "Actually, yeah, I did." The warmth in the way Lucy looked at her was not only gone, but replaced with cold indifference. How was that possible? Something was off here and Kristin wasn't sure what. Then a horrible thought occurred to her and the question left her lips before she could even fully process its meaning.

"Is that what this has all been about?" Kristin asked. Lucy stared back at her, her expression unreadable. Kristin felt a prickle of fear inch up her spine. "Please tell me that wasn't your goal all along, get close to me to get me to kill the story?"

Silence reigned.

But it couldn't be that. It was a ridiculous notion. The moments between them had been too authentic, too tender, to be part of anything manipulative. Lucy wasn't that kind of person and Kristin was sorry she'd even raised the question, understanding how offensive it must have sounded. She held up a hand. "Wait. I should apologize for even suggesting something so—"

"So what?" Lucy asked, raising one shoulder nonchalantly. "What does it matter what my reasons were? It's not like we had a bad time, and now you're running with the story anyway. Oh, well."

Kristin shook her head, wishing she could take it all back. "Stop it. This isn't you."

"It's me in your eyes though, isn't it?" Lucy said pointedly.

"No. God"—Kristin ran a frustrated hand through her hair—"I shouldn't have suggested that what we have is anything but real."

Lucy took a step toward her, her eyes flashing hurt. "No, you shouldn't have. But at least now I know where we stand, what you feel I'm capable of. Lying and deceiving the public, and then faking it with you for months just to keep it all quiet. Yep"—she nodded—"that's me to a T." With a disgusted shake of her head, she was gone.

Numb. That's how Kristin felt as Lucy exited the room, closing her bedroom door with a dignified click. Kristin took a moment before showing herself out. And as she drove home, she relived how her best laid plans had crumbled into something unforeseen and awful. Quite honestly, she didn't know which end was up or how to fix it. Everything she did only seemed to make it worse. The story was one thing, but the accusation she'd hurled at Lucy was another. She wasn't sure there was any way to come back from this, and she struggled to breathe as the hurt slashed through her.

She'd lost Lucy.

It was over.

Chapter Seven

Lucy ignored the knock on her back door. It was going on four in the afternoon and the stupid mechanical staff in *RollerCoaster Tycoon* were, for whatever reason, refusing to fix her bumper cars in a timely manner and that simply wasn't acceptable. If they worked for her in the real world, they'd be fired by now. No exceptions.

The knock was louder now, but as answering the door wouldn't help her theme park, she let it go. The sound of a key in the lock had her rolling her eyes. Really? Five seconds later, Emory stood in front of her looking anything but pleased. "Why are you not answering the door for me?"

She gestured to the screen of her laptop that sat on top of the blanket that sat on top of her lap that was curled up on the sofa in the middle of the afternoon with BP pressed to her side. "*RollerCoaster Tycoon* is being frustrating right now."

"Not a good reason. Trevor called and said you were sick. And since you haven't once called in sick in all the time that I've known you, I thought I'd stop by and make sure you were alive."

"As you can see, I am." She refocused on the screen. "And deeply depressed about the state of my theme park."

"Not good enough," Emory said, circling in front of the sofa. "And, oh my, you're wearing pajama pants in the late afternoon. You're the opposite of a lounger. That's red flag number two. What gives?"

Lucy shook her head. "I don't want to talk about it." And honestly, she didn't. She'd spent the weekend thinking about Kristin and the news story and their interaction Friday night ad nauseam and where had it gotten her? Nowhere good, that was for sure. This breath of fresh air that had walked into her life and made her feel happier than she'd actually thought possible had just told the world that she was ethically questionable, and then accused Lucy of manufacturing their relationship for personal gain. Did it get much worse than that?

"Well, you have to talk about it," Emory said.

"Nope. It's a law that I get to choose."

Emory took a seat on the couch next to Lucy. "There's no law. You just made that up."

"Unimportant detail."

"You found her, I see," Grace said from her still-open back door.

Emory nodded. "I did."

"You brought the tiny person?" Lucy asked, with an exasperated sigh.

"I find she's often helpful," Emory said. "Plus, I'm on after-school duty today."

At Grace's arrival, Bernadette Peters leapt from the couch and scurried to Grace, who was undoubtedly one of her favorite humans.

"Hiya, BP," Grace said. She retrieved a dog treat from the jar on top of the fridge and held it up for the excited pup. When BP saw the treat, she immediately rolled over and looked to Grace expectantly for her reward.

"Whoa," Emory said, pointing at the dog. "When did she learn to do that?"

But it was too late, Lucy felt the tears start.

"Okay, okay. So maybe we've touched on something a little tender. Am I right?"

Lucy nodded and brushed the tears from her cheeks with windshield-wiper hands.

"Did you teach Bernadette Peters to roll over?"

Lucy shook her head. "Kristin taught her."

Emory's mouth made a small *oh*. "I take it you read the story. I tried to message you, but you didn't answer. I take it you and Kristin had an argument?"

"We did. It's over, and suffice it to say it didn't end well."

Emory looked across the room at Grace, who was in the midst of a game of tug-of-war with BP over one of her plush toys. She dropped her voice. "Can you tell me what prompted this?"

Lucy ran her fingers through her hair because she wasn't sure talking about it would help. At the same time, why the hell not? She couldn't feel much worse. "She finished her story and let me read it. I said some things. She said some things. But the fact of the matter is the story is out there. It ran yesterday and it's water under the bridge. The story. Kristin and I. All of it. It's time that I look ahead, and I will do that as soon as I get these stupid maintenance guys to do their job." But honestly, Lucy wasn't sure how to move forward and just forget the past couple of months. The world looked lifeless now in comparison.

"All right. Let's talk this through. The article wasn't great for GNW."

Lucy met her eyes. "Are you kidding? It's catastrophic."

"I wouldn't go that far." Emory took a seat and seemed to organize her thoughts. "I think the article was well written and a fair representation of the series of events. It made me think, which I suppose was her goal."

"How are you not furious?"

Emory lifted a shoulder. "Because in a week, people will have moved on. We know we didn't do anything unscrupulous, and this whole thing comes down to semantics of what a wire service actually is. Do I love that she included us in the story? Of course not. Do I think it's the end of the world? I don't."

Lucy studied her. "You're really taking this in stride, you know that?"

"Would you rather be with a woman who compromises what she believes in?"

"I don't know, maybe."

Emory shook her head. "You wouldn't. I know you."

Lucy tossed her head back against the sofa. "I guess not when you put it that way."

"So you can be together again," Grace called from across the room. Just when you thought she wasn't listening…

"It's more complicated than that, tiny person," Lucy said.

Grace was on her feet and moving into the living room, all calm and cool and ten years old, the way Grace often was. "No, it's not. You like her, so tell her so."

Lucy raised a shoulder. "Just tell her so, huh?"

"Yeah, like that. You could write it in a note, or call her on the phone, or text it to her."

"Who are we texting?" Sarah asked from the back door. Well, it was a full-on party now. The gang was all here. Sarah had their dog, Walter, on a leash and wore workout clothes, damn her. Upon seeing BP, the chocolate retriever let out a little whine, which prompted Sarah to let him off the leash so he could seek out his reluctant friend. Walter tended to think everyone loved him, and secretly BP probably did.

Emory turned to Sarah. "Grace feels Lucy should text Kristin because she really likes her despite the fact that Kristin wrote a story that painted Global NewsWire in not the best light. Lucy still seems to feel that Kristin undervalues her integrity and that's hard to overcome. You follow?"

"I do."

Emory pointed at Sarah. "This is why I'm hot for her."

Sarah kissed Emory hello. "That's the only reason?"

"Well, no, not even close."

"Excellent." Sarah laughed and took a seat next to Lucy. "I read that story last night and despite the GNW tie-in, it's a thoughtful piece. It makes you stop and think about how we look at the world. What details we value."

"I'm sure it was a great story," Lucy said with a wave of her hand, "but has your girlfriend ever publicly maligned you?"

Sarah thought on this. "No. I can't say she has."

"And to be honest, it's not even the story that keeps racing through my mind, it was the insinuation she made questioning the legitimacy of my feelings for her. That I had ulterior motives for being with her."

"Do you think she really feels that way?" Sarah asked.

Lucy lifted her hand and let it drop. "I don't know. She tried to take it back, but how do you put toothpaste back in the tube, you know?" Her throat tightened with emotion, because God, she missed Kristin and it had only been a couple of days.

"I think you owe it to yourself to hear her side of things, have a discussion, and work through it, if possible. Given she's worth it. Is Kristin worth it?"

Lucy shook her head. "I can't see past the hurt right now to answer the question." Sarah and Emory exchanged a look across her. "I totally saw that, by the way. The knowing glance. Don't flaunt your knowing glances at me when I have no one to knowing-glance with."

"Don't know what you're talking about," Emory said. "But I agree with Sarah and think you need to do something radical and have an actual conversation with her. Not an argument, but an exchange. Because you've smiled more in the last few weeks than I can ever remember, and that says something."

Lucy scrunched one eye. "Maybe someday. But I think the result will be the same."

Emory stood. "Step one, talk to the girl. Step two, make sure you're at work tomorrow. I can't have the company going under just because your heart has been smashed to bits. I'll need you to buck up and be the kickass CEO you've always been."

Lucy gasped. "You're cold. The state of my soul demands I build more roller coasters."

"I'm thinking the roller coasters can wait."

Grace came around the couch. "Is Lucy going to the boardwalk with us for the Fourth?"

Emory smiled triumphantly. "Good question. She most definitely is, as it will force her from this house. Plus, Lucy loves the Fourth of July and fireworks."

"Yay!" said Grace, whose excitement had both dogs on their feet in joint celebration. "She always shares her cotton candy with me."

"She's a giver that way," Emory said, and ruffled Lucy's hair.

It wasn't until late that night when Lucy was tucked into bed and listening to the sounds of the waves just outside her window that her phone buzzed, signaling an incoming call. In the dark of her bedroom, she saw the readout and swallowed back the slash of hurt when she saw it was Kristin calling, her photo smiling back at Lucy from the screen. She stared at it for a moment as doubt and need waged a war within her. If she closed her eyes, she could still feel Kristin's warm skin up against hers, the way her hair would tickle Lucy's shoulder.

With a quick exhale, she slid the phone into the off position and tucked it away in her bedside table. With the covers pulled in around her, she closed her eyes against the still-very-raw emotion.

She wasn't ready.

And she couldn't help but wonder if she ever would be.

❖

Kristin surveyed the desolate newsroom and took note of the fact that other than a staff photographer caught up in a game of Solitaire, she was pretty much alone. It was July third and nearly half of the paper's staff had taken off the second portion of the day to gear up for the Fourth's festivities with their families. Given that Kristin didn't exactly have anyone to celebrate with, she focused on her next project, which she was able to handpick after the overwhelmingly positive response to the article.

The readers had responded in droves once the story ran and wanted more thoughtful exposés like this one, and that had the higher-ups asking her for more. She'd immediately pitched a piece on Slater Energy that would juxtapose their claims about green practices with what it was they were actually doing. And wouldn't you know it? She was green-lit just like that.

As she drove home that evening, she thought about Lucy and tried her phone again to no avail. She didn't blame Lucy—she'd probably ignore her calls too.

The truth was, she'd come to matter to Kristin a great deal more in just the short amount of time they'd spent together than any other woman ever had, actually, and that said something about what they had. The knowledge that she'd hurt Lucy in the midst of an already difficult time for them had her not sleeping and racking her brain for a way to fix it all. Kristin knew in her heart that the words weren't true the moment she said them, and she was even more convinced of that now that time had offered perspective. If Lucy needed some space for these few days, she'd give it to her. But one way or another she was determined to apologize and find a way to get back to where they were. It was too important not to.

As she pulled into her driveway, her phone buzzed. Closing her eyes against the hope that Lucy was finally willing to talk to her, she checked the readout. It was from a number she didn't recognize.

How do you feel about fireworks? –Emory Owen

Kristin raised an eyebrow at the question, as it had her full attention.

Chapter Eight

The sun was setting on Mission Beach, and Lucy snagged a wispy blue strand from the cotton-candy baton Grace carried and smiled as the sugar crystals dissolved on her tongue. The Fourth of July celebration was in full swing on the boardwalk and there was a lot to see and do. Live music played from a central bandstand, and nestled in among throngs of food booths selling both the sweet and savory were jewelry vendors, carnival games, airbrush tattoo stations, and of course, street performers galore. It's possible she broke a mime or two's heart in the course of their stroll.

Lucy dropped an arm around Grace's shoulder. "You gonna ride the Giant Dipper?" she asked, pointing up at the roller coaster that snaked up, down, and around.

Grace considered this. "I'm more of a stand and wave sort of kid."

"Since when?" Sarah called from where she and Emory strolled behind them. "What happened to my fearless wild child?"

"Still here, but I'm growing up, Mom. I'm slowing down and taking in life's little moments more."

Lucy raised an eyebrow and turned back to her friends in question.

"She's been watching a lot of *Inside the Actors Studio* lately," Emory informed her. "Lots of getting in touch with her inner self."

"You want to be an actor?" Lucy asked Grace.

"I'm thinking a director. The big idea person," Grace said with a grandiose gesture.

Lucy smiled. "I like it. We should do movie nights."

"When can we start?" Grace asked with big hopeful eyes that looked so close to Sarah's it was scary.

"Next week?"

Grace turned to Sarah, who nodded her approval, before swiveling back to Lucy. "You're on."

Grace was notorious for her various phases, which Lucy found kind of fun. They were only a couple of months out from her chemistry phase, where she'd spent hours on end conducting experiments with the chemistry set she'd received from Emory for Christmas. Sarah had been convinced she'd burn the house down. Lucy smiled at the memory. Having been around to watch their family grow, change, and mature, she found herself envious, and wondering what it must be like.

She sighed as her thoughts, as if programmed to do so, drifted to Kristin, the person who she thought might just be that happily ever after for her. She'd been upset by what she'd read in the story, hurt by Kristin's accusation, but the biggest blow had been the loss of what she thought they'd had. And while she'd missed Kristin desperately for the past few days, at the same time, she honestly didn't know how to proceed after the whole ordeal. Maybe she'd miss her less, as time went on. It helped to lie to herself apparently.

As evening fell in full effect all around them, the crowds seemed to settle in a bit, everyone securing their spots for the fireworks that would occur in just a short amount of time. Excitement hung in the air, almost as if the energy were charged with group-wide anticipation. She smiled at the families who clustered together with picnic baskets on blankets. As her group approached a bench next to the ever-popular funnel-cake booth, Lucy stopped at what, or rather whom, she saw stand as they approached. She shot a questioning look to Emory, who ignored her and moved to Kristin. Lucy took her in. Kristin wore denim shorts and a red tank top that showed off her tan. Her hair was down and caught a subtle curl from being so close to the water. If the sight of Kristin hadn't slashed through her so effortlessly, Lucy would have thought she looked amazing.

"Hey, Kristin," Emory said. "So *funny* running into you here on this very random bench."

Lucy slid Sarah a what-the-hell look, but Sarah simply smiled.

"Happy Fourth," Kristin said to the group with a hesitant smile. Her eyes met Lucy's and it was clear she was nervous.

"Happy Fourth!" Grace said back. "Do you want to watch the fireworks with us? They're soon."

"Thank you, but I don't want to intrude," Kristin said politely. "But I was hoping I might speak to Lucy."

"What a great idea," Emory said, in a perfect example of why Grace would never direct her in any of her future projects.

"Is that okay with you?" Kristin quietly asked her.

Lucy crossed her arms in front of her as she considered the request, finally blowing out a breath. "Sure. I guess we can talk for a few minutes." She looked back at her friends, who looked victorious at what they'd accomplished. "I'll kill you later," she said to them.

"You guys take your time," Sarah said, ignoring the comment. "Text if you want to meet up." And with that, the three of them headed off down the boardwalk and disappeared into the crowd.

"Don't blame them," Kristin said once they were alone. "This is on me. I wanted to see you and just didn't think you'd agree any other way."

"And why did you want to see me?" Lucy asked. It was a stupid question, she was well aware, but it was all she had.

"I miss you, first of all." Kristin attempted a smile that died on her face, making it clear that none of this had been easy for her either. And good, why should it have been? "But mainly, I needed to explain. Can we, maybe, take a walk? Find somewhere a little quieter?"

Lucy nodded and led them through the throngs to the beach, where they'd gone for a run together, once upon a time when things had seemed so promising. They sat on a wooden block that marked the ending of the man-made walkway and looked out at the night as it hovered over the water. It was July, but still sort of chilly in the evenings, and Lucy could tell Kristin felt it. It was her instinct to pull her in and warm her up, an instinct that seemed less than helpful in this particular moment.

They sat there in silence for a few long moments.

"I screwed up," Kristin said finally out to the water. "And not just a little bit." Lucy watched Kristin, in profile to her now, as she continued. Her face was partially lit by the moonlight, and the lights of the boardwalk twinkled just behind her. "I came to San Diego for a job I thought was everything. This was my chance to prove myself as a journalist. You have to understand that I left my home, my friends, my family, and my entire life to advance my career in news, and that means doing things the right way. In the midst of writing that story, I knew I had to tell it the way I would have if there had been no you and me. But I should have prepared you more. Communicated. Walked you through each step, so you weren't blindsided. I guess a part of me was scared of what you'd say."

Lucy nodded. "Understandably."

"And then when everything blew up in my face, I said something stupid." Kristin took her hand. "Sometimes you wonder as you move through life if you'll meet that someone who will change everything. Affect the way you see the world, and make you excited just to wake up and see their face." She turned to Lucy then. "And that's become you."

Lucy's lips parted at the declaration, but she didn't say anything, do anything. She needed to hear the rest.

Kristin turned to face her. "I never should have questioned what we have, and the second I said the words, I knew they were untrue. I know exactly how I feel about you, and God, I won't lose sight of that again."

Lucy was confused, so very confused, but she saw the opening to ask what she desperately needed to know. With her heart hammering away in her chest, she spoke the words. "And how do you feel about me? Please be honest."

There were tears in Kristin's eyes as she attempted to answer. She opened her mouth to speak, and then took a moment, looking down until she found her composure. When those eyes, glistening with tears, met Lucy's, she knew the answer. "I love you," Kristin said. And with the words, she seemed to find strength. "And what I've learned is that love can really screw you up. But once you find it, you can't live without it. I can't live without you, Lucy." Silence hung in the air between them, but with those words Lucy's heart shuddered and swelled. The breaks and cracks came back together.

"Kristin." The words Lucy said next came straight from her hear,=t, and in all honesty the leap was an easy one. "I love you too."

Kristin smiled and touched Lucy's cheek. And they were kissing. That contact steadied what had moments ago seemed so unstable. In that moment, with Kristin's lips on hers, Lucy felt something good, and solid, and wonderful click into place. They didn't have it all figured out and this past week was a glaring example that there would be rough patches ahead and they would have to learn how to navigate them as they went, but sitting here with Kristin now, there was no way she could turn her back on what could be the best thing that ever happened to her. "Love." Lucy repeated, more to herself than to Kristin. "Who would have thought when that pushy reporter walked into my office that there'd be this?"

A firework burst overhead and magnificent colors showered down in a display that had Lucy's breath caught in her throat. As they watched, Kristin slipped her arms around Lucy's waist, and they sank into one another, snuggled up and enjoying the glorious painting of the sky. Lucy closed her eyes at how good it felt to be in Kristin's arms, to feel the warmth of her skin again. And when the finale hit, and the colorful bursts overlapped in an ever-building succession, Kristin's lips found hers and they shared a kiss that served as an unspoken promise.

"Take me home," Lucy murmured against Kristin's lips. "I've missed you."

"You have the best ideas."

Epilogue

Six months later

"What did he say?" Lucy asked from where she lay on Kristin's couch, Bernadette Peters snuggled into a ball on her stomach. Lucy looked adorable, but even that couldn't temper her frustration. Kristin had been on the phone with her landlord for the past twenty minutes and felt like she'd just run in a series of tiny circles.

"He's not going to fix it," she told Lucy, clicking off the call. Her arm fell to her side in defeat. The heater had been broken in her house for the past three days and her deadbeat landlord was apparently on some sort of mission to see how many times he could say no to a tenant request.

"This is like the five hundredth thing he's refused to help you with. He's in violation of the rental agreement. We need to call an attorney," Lucy said, sitting up and gently placing BP on the chair next to her.

Kristin sighed. "Not worth the time. The lease is up in two months and I'll be done with this little-house-that-couldn't forever. I'll just pay for it myself in the meantime."

"You shouldn't have to."

Kristin smiled and slid in next to Lucy on the couch. "I like when you get all riled up. There's this tiny crease that appears on your forehead and it makes me want to make out with you."

Lucy smiled. "Don't patronize me for my crease. It means business."

"See?" She slid her arms around Lucy's waist and leaned into her. "Now that kind of determination is sexy."

"Do you know what I think would be sexy?"

"What's that?" Kristin asked, stealing a kiss.

"If you got the hell out of here and moved out to the beach with us."

Kristin laughed. "Have you seen an opening?"

Lucy sat taller. "Yeah, it's called my room. Though I guess if you moved in, it would be ours."

And that's when Kristin understood that Lucy was serious. "Wait a second. You're asking me to move in?"

At the question, she noticed the dusting of pink that colored Lucy's cheeks, a telltale sign Lucy was nervous. Hell, she was too now. As the flutters hit her stomach at the prospect of such a big step forward in their relationship, she awaited Lucy's response.

"Yeah," Lucy said finally, glancing at the floor and then back at Kristin. "If you think it's too soon, just say so. But I happen to be very much in love with you and would like nothing more than to wake up to those gorgeous green eyes every morning."

Kristin took a minute with the words because they felt so very good that she wanted to luxuriate in them a bit.

"Say something, Kristin," Lucy said and pulled in a breath. Kristin threaded her fingers through Lucy's and answered her with a searing kiss. When they came up for air, Lucy was smiling. "While that was, wow, incredibly attention getting, it wasn't an answer."

"It was," Kristin told her. "Because that's the way I plan to kiss you each and every morning."

Lucy blinked back at her. "Is that a yes?" Kristin nodded and they stared at one another, the weight of what they'd just decided settling. "Whoa."

"This is sorta big," Kristin said.

"And we can't screw it up."

Kristin's mouth fell open. "What if I leave the cap off the toothpaste?"

"Evicted immediately," Lucy said, poking her ribs.

Kristin laughed, and then met Lucy's gaze. "Are you sure this is what you want? You can think it over."

Lucy reached up and took Kristin's face in her hands. "How well do you know me?"

Kristin looked skyward. "Quite well."

"Then you know that I wouldn't ask unless I knew in my heart this was right. So, yeah, I'm sure." Lucy then sent her that sultry, sexy smile. "And in light of this new development, we should maybe celebrate or something."

"Yeah?" Kristin asked, enjoying this idea already. "What did you have in mind?"

"Well, it *is* pretty cold in here"—Lucy raised one shoulder—"no heater and all. We could, maybe, find an alternative way to warm the place up."

"God, I love you," Kristin said.

"Then kiss me. The night is young." Lucy's eyes danced as Kristin closed the distance between them, savoring the anticipation and looking forward to the kiss and everything that would come after.

Readers interested in more from Emory and Sarah can read their romantic journey in Heart Block.

Getting Serious

Rachel Spangler

Chapter One

Hello, everybody," Lisa said a little too loudly into the mic. Her voice reverberated through the speakers and off the wooden floors, but she got everyone's attention. The one hundred plus people in the Pan Am ballroom turned their attention to the head table. The whole place looked like something out of a fairy tale, everyone dressed so beautifully, with golden light reflecting off champagne flutes and dancing across the faces before her.

"For the few of you who don't know me, I'm Lisa Knapp. The program says I'm the maid of honor, but only because Joey wouldn't let me list myself as the maid of ill repute. She should've known better than to entrust me with an honorary role. Honestly, though, you'd think she'd know better than to give me a live microphone by now too."

A few people chuckled, and she settled in. "You see, I've known Joey since we were seven years old. Any illusion of either one of us being maidenly or altogether honorable went out the window in high school."

A group of their hockey buddies at a table in the back offered up a few catcalls.

"No, I kid, I kid. Not about the maiden part. That ship really did sail many years ago, but the honor part didn't dissolve completely until two years ago. You see my friend here"—she looked over at Joey, glowing and dapper in her classic black tux and tie—"Joey knows better than anyone that I'm not above a little dishonorable behavior, because she wouldn't even be here tonight if not for my willingness to bend the rules."

"And thank you for that," Joey said, reaching for the mic, but Lisa quickly stepped farther away.

"Oh no, you don't. I've been here for every moment of your and Elaine's relationship, but these fine people came to the party a little later. They never got to hear all the horny details of how you pined over Elaine from afar. They're all here to celebrate you two. Don't they deserve to hear the whole story?"

She had the audience wrapped around her little finger, and they applauded their encouragement.

"See? The people want to hear the fairy tale, and I give the people what they want. It's my job to tell them in excruciating detail how you fell ass-over-teakettle for your beautiful bride before you ever knew her name." She grinned wickedly and turned her attention back toward the audience. "Really folks, for like a month Joey and I simply referred to Elaine as Her Royal Hotness."

Joey put her hands over her face, but Elaine in her usual way only smiled graciously and lifted her champagne flute.

"She couldn't even figure out a way to talk to her," she continued. "A lesser friend would've left it alone. A lesser friend would've heeded Joey's warnings and rules about not cyberstalking prospective dates, or no hacking into her bank accounts, but I am not a lesser friend."

"So what did you do?" someone finally called out.

"I did what any buddy would do," Lisa said frankly, then paused for dramatic effect. "I called Elaine pretending to be Joey and made a life coach appointment for her!"

Several people in the audience laughed, others looked surprised or even skeptical, but Lisa had their rapt attention and she wasn't about to give it up. "I'm not kidding. I lied to a life coach to help my best friend score a date. I mean, what could've possibly gone wrong with that plan?"

She waited for the laughter to subside before going on.

"Sure, they both threw around words like"—she lifted her fingers to make air quotes as best she could while still holding the mic—"*ethical* and *professional obligations* and *moral responsibility*, but all I heard was blah-blah-blah, because folks, these two women belong together, and while it took them an entire romance novel's worth of drama to figure that out, I knew it instantly. And we're all here tonight to celebrate the fact they have finally added the blessing of the great state of New York to the already long line of people who've been witness to their combined awesomeness."

Everyone clinked their silverware against their glasses and whistled until Joey and Elaine obliged them by giving each other a little kiss. She wasn't sure which one of them blushed more from the attention, yet another sign they were perfectly matched.

"Elaine and Joey," Lisa said, bringing the crowd's attention back to a place where everyone felt more comfortable, on her, "you're perfect for each other. I knew it from the moment I saw you two together, and while I may not have an abundance of honor on my own, I have been truly honored to play the role of comic relief to the epic romance you've shared. I wish you love, light, and lots of laughter in the many years ahead."

She lifted her glass. "To Elaine and Joey."

Everyone in the room echoed the toast and drank before applauding. She took a little bow and smiled broadly in the warmth of their approval until Joey pulled her into a hug, complete with several hard back pats.

"Thanks, Lisa."

"It was my pleasure, and let's be honest, I nailed it."

Joey laughed. "You did. I have to admit, I was prepared for worse."

"I'd be happy to give an encore and tell everyone about that one time I walked in on you and Elaine—"

"Nope." Joey snatched the mic. "Not necessary."

"Really? I'd be happy to—"

"Thank you." Elaine stepped into Joey's place as soon as she spun away with the mic. She wrapped Lisa in a warm embrace, the kind a person couldn't help but sink into. "For everything."

She tried to shrug, but Elaine gave her a tight squeeze. "I mean it. What you did here tonight wasn't a little thing."

"She's family, and now you are too. It was my pleasure, really."

"I believe you, or I wouldn't have let you do it." Elaine stepped back but kept her hands clasped firmly on Lisa's shoulders, her blue eyes intensely focused on her as if searching for something deep inside. Whenever she did that, Lisa realized again how Joey fell so hard, so fast. "Now that the main event is over, how do you feel about the transitions ahead?"

Lisa forced a smile and shook her head. Emotional conversations weren't her thing. Perhaps that's why she'd warmed to every aspect of Elaine's personality except her life-coach voice. She was glad that sort of thing worked for Joey, and she'd come to respect that Elaine's work helped a lot of people, but she had no intention of taking a turn on the couch anytime soon. She'd developed a well-honed ability to get out of anything resembling a coaching situation as quickly as possible. "I feel like I could use a beer. Can I get you anything?"

Elaine's smile didn't reach those killer eyes, but she released her anyway. "No, we've still got plenty of champagne to get through."

"The bubbly's a bit too sweet for me. I need a Labatt's."

Lisa hopped off the low riser their table sat atop and wove her way to the back of the room, accepting compliments on her speech along the way. She slapped high fives to some hockey friends as she passed their table, but didn't slow down. Her official duties were over for the weekend, and she looked forward to the crisp sound of a bottle top being popped. She made eye contact with the bartender when she was still several strides away and smiled, but before she closed the distance, another woman stepped up to order.

She tamped down a hint of annoyance and tried not to make eye contact with anyone else while she waited for the woman to finish drilling the poor Buff State student about his preference for the pinot noir or the cabernet. The kid wrinkled his nose and said, "I'm sorry, I just work here. I don't know anything about the wines."

"I generally do, but I'm not familiar with any of these brands. I like that they're local though. That's a nice touch."

The guy shrugged, but Lisa smiled at her shoes. The local wines had been a nice touch if she did say so herself, even if most of this crowd would go for the beer or the bubbly.

"Do you know if the pinot is young or aged?"

"I'm sorry," the bartender repeated. "I can look at the bottle if you want."

"Oh, for crying out loud," Lisa mumbled. Even if her official responsibilities had been filled, apparently she'd have to take on a couple of unofficial ones if she ever wanted to get a drink around here. "The cab is full-bodied with hints of black cherry and oak. The pinot is a 2008 award winner with an undercurrent of wild berries."

The woman turned and smiled, causing all Lisa's frustration to melt as tendrils of memory got lost in the deep pools of her beautiful brown eyes. "Would you say the pinot is full-bodied?"

"I could say that. I think the winemaker calls it *succulent*."

"Succulent," the woman repeated, and Lisa couldn't drag her eyes off her full lips. "That does sound like something a winemaker would say to make a sale."

"And did the pitch work?" Lisa asked.

"I think it did," she said before turning back toward the bar. "I'll take a glass of the pinot noir."

"Yes ma'am." The bartender grabbed the bottle and poured with about as much grace as one could expect from a college-age male.

"Thank you for your help," the woman said, extending her hand to Lisa. "I'm Marty."

"Marty," she repeated the name. It didn't seem to suit the woman. She looked classy in her little black dress and translucent gray wrap. Marty sounded playful, not elegant like the subtle curve of her neck or the upsweep of her long dark hair against her olive skin.

"It's nice to meet you, Marty. I'm Lisa."

"Yes. Lisa, the maid of ill repute. I caught that. You're dishonest, meddling, and a little loose in your morals."

The temperature in her cheeks rose drastically. She'd thought that speech would help her chances with the ladies tonight, but apparently she'd left a few things open to interpretation. So much for putting her best foot forward. "That's me."

"Apparently, you're also a very good friend." Marty paused to sip the glass of wine the bartender passed her way. She closed her eyes and inhaled through her nose before finishing. "And you're also quite the wine connoisseur. What else did you leave out of your speech?"

"You mean aside from being devilishly good looking?"

"Obviously."

"I'm also shockingly athletic and embarrassingly rich."

"And modest, don't forget modest," Marty added.

"Well, I didn't see the need to pile on everything at once. I thought I might let you figure that one out for yourself."

"And I did. My powers of observation are quite keen. Occupational hazard."

Lisa scanned the woman up and down once more. She was

undoubtedly beautiful from the tips of her high heels all the way up to the almond-shaped eyes that had first caught her attention. She also seemed vaguely familiar, but surely she'd remember if they'd met. Gorgeous, funny, quick-witted women didn't exactly cross her path on a regular basis. "I'm sorry, what occupation is that?"

"I thought you knew," Marty said lightly. "I'm Elaine's life coach."

Lisa's mouth opened, but no words came out, so she closed it again. Then she took a swig of her beer and felt it go down in one hard swallow. Elaine's life coach. The life coach's life coach. Did that make her like the grand pooh-bah of the touchy-feely society?

"Lisa?" Marty finally asked. "Everything okay?"

"Yeah," she finally managed, "everything's great. As expected, actually."

Marty raised her eyebrow.

Of course she'd meet the first woman who'd sparked a genuine interest in her in a long time, and the first woman who seemed at least mildly interested in return in even longer, only to find out she was the epitome of off-limits and incompatible. How did someone tell a beautiful woman her job made her undesirable on the personal, professional, and emotional levels simultaneously?

"Ladies and gentlemen." The DJ interrupted her thoughts. "The floor is open for business, and instead of going the first dance alone, the happy couple has asked that their families join them for the first song."

"Of course they did," Lisa muttered.

"Neither of them are big on being the center of attention, are they?" Marty asked.

"No, but I guess you already knew that, didn't you?"

Marty smiled over the rim of her wineglass.

"You probably know a lot about a lot of relationships in this room, don't you?"

"I can't talk about any conversations I've had within the confidentiality of the coaching relationship."

"I'll take that as a yes."

"I think you were summoned to the dance floor," Marty said gently.

"The DJ said family."

Marty didn't reply. She just waited, her deep brown eyes never leaving Lisa's.

"Joey and I aren't *technically* related."

Marty nodded wordlessly, and Lisa twisted in the silence. She took another heavy swig of her beer and turned toward the dance floor as a slow song started to play. Instead of dancing, Joey and Elaine seemed to be searching the crowd, and she didn't even try to pretend she didn't know who they were looking for. She sighed heavily.

"I told Elaine just a few minutes ago that Joey was my family, and now she was too."

"And?"

"And…" She drew out the word before forcing a smile and turning back to Marty. "Would you like to dance with me?"

❖

Lisa clearly had no formal training as a dancer, but she moved smoothly enough in a slow deliberate circle, one hand holding loosely to Marty's and the other resting lightly on her hip. If only she'd stop watching her own feet, Marty might actually be able to enjoy the closeness of their bodies.

Lisa was not an unattractive woman, with her dark hair and hazel eyes behind a trendy pair of Rachel Maddow-style glasses. Her body was lanky and fit, her smile mischievous, and she'd showcased more than a hint of wittiness before she'd realized who Marty was. For some reason that changed everything about the tone of their interaction. Marty watched the connection roll over Lisa's features like a cloud would cover the sun. Her whole open demeanor faded quickly from confident to closed off. Given what she knew about Lisa, and what she'd given away in her speech, the reaction wasn't unexpected, but she found the shift disappointing.

"I'm sorry I didn't recognize you at first," Lisa finally said, as though she were pondering the same topic.

"It's all right. We've never met, and I didn't make any grand speeches to introduce myself."

"Yeah, but I've heard your name before. Elaine was really excited you were coming to the wedding. I know she mentioned it, but I"—her face flushed—"I sort of glaze over when she talks about life-coaching stuff."

"It's okay."

"It's not that I don't like life coaches. Obviously, I love Elaine and Joey's back to being Joey and that's great."

She wondered what internal sins Lisa was trying to apologize for.

"It's just not my thing, is all."

"Did I give you the impression I was here to fortify my client base?"

"No," Lisa answered quickly. "I just, I'm…"

"Nervous for no apparent reason?"

She laughed. "Maybe."

"I have to admit I enjoyed your company more before you knew I was Elaine's coach."

"Me too."

"Then how about this? I'm here tonight because I'm also Elaine's friend. We work together, but more importantly we like each other. I'm happy to see her happy. Does that sound closer to your comfort level?"

Lisa's brow furrowed, then smoothed. "Yeah, that's fine."

"Fine?"

"Sure. You're a friend and colleague of the bride."

"And you're a long-time friend of the…other bride? The groom? The slightly butcher of the two spouses?" Marty tried in vain to find an accurate term that didn't sound absurd.

"I've been having that problem for months," Lisa admitted with a laugh. "Elaine's definitely the bride, right?"

Marty cast another quick glance at her friend, who looked stunning as usual in a classic cream-colored V-neck dress that stopped just short of sweeping the floor as she moved. "She is."

"But Joey," Lisa said, turning them so she could get a better view, "looks like something out of the Men's WearHouse catalog for prom rentals."

"Yes, classic, but not manly. Softer, younger. I like her short-cut jacket."

"Yeah, since she's short, I suggested that one might make her legs look longer."

"So in addition to a wine connoisseur, you're also her fashion-forward friend?"

"Not really. I just have more experience with tuxes."

"Because you're embarrassingly rich?"

"That's definitely the main reason, yes," Lisa said with mock seriousness, some of her early bravado resurfacing now that they were on more comfortable topics. "But also, I wore them a lot in college."

"Really? I seem to remember wearing pajamas and sweatpants a lot in college. Where did you go to school?"

"MIT."

"You're quite the slacker, aren't you?"

"Pretty much. I'm the underachiever in my family." Lisa's smile seemed tighter, more strained for a second. "But I did an internship for an investment group. They had black-tie events."

"As investment bankers are wont to do?"

"Something like that. I wasn't ever really part of the fast crowd."

"I'm surprised they invited the lowly interns to formal events."

"They didn't usually. I was special."

Marty smiled. She had no doubt of that, but she wanted to hear more. "What made you special?"

"My good looks and abundant charm," Lisa offered quickly enough to make her wonder how many times she'd dodged that question.

"It really is a formidable combination."

"What is?" Elaine asked as they danced closer.

Lisa seemed startled slightly at the interjection, and Marty felt her fingers tightening briefly on the curve of her hip. The increased pressure was not unpleasant.

"Lisa's looks and charm," Marty replied.

"Really?" Elaine asked. "I suppose you're right about that."

"But?" Lisa asked lightly.

"Be careful with this one," Elaine warned in a teasing tone.

"Which one of us are you talking to, darling?" Marty allowed a little of her Southern accent to bleed through.

"I was talking to you about Lisa. Sometimes I still can't tell when she's telling me the truth or setting me up for an elaborate gag." Elaine laughed, then added, "But now that you mention it, you've got a much more finely honed authenticity detector than I do. You might have just met your match, Lisa."

"Seeing as I have no idea what an authenticity detector is, I'll take your word for it."

"You do know what it is," Marty said calmly. "You call it something else in your head, though."

The corner of Lisa's mouth crooked up quickly. "Now you're a mind reader?"

"No, but I'm willing to bet when you hear the term *authenticity detector* you feel like the perpetual schoolboy who snickers every time the teacher accidently walks into the double entendre."

"Maybe."

"Go ahead let out your inner twelve-year-old. I promise I won't be scandalized."

"Fine," Lisa said before turning to Joey. "Just remember, your lovely wife and her mischievous friend were the ones who asked me to label them bullshit detectors in the middle of a formal event."

"Point taken," Joey said, her smile resigned.

"Bullshit detectors?" Elaine repeated. "I am a bullshit detector?"

Joey only smiled and nodded, but Marty laughed outright. "I find that both refreshing and accurate."

"The term? Or the fact that I got the bride to say bullshit during her first official dance as a married woman."

"Both."

Lisa straightened her shoulders a little bit at the affirmation.

Elaine seemed to notice the change too. "Now I really don't know which one of you to worry about more."

"Neither of us," Marty replied. "Go enjoy your wedding reception."

"Yeah, dance away, Mrs. Lang, dance away," Lisa added, and Marty noted the big grin on Joey's face as she spun Elaine out of earshot.

"Is she really taking Joey's last name?"

"I don't think so, but I stay out of their personal business."

"Yes, it certainly sounded like it from your toast earlier."

"Touché, but all I did was throw them together. They figured the rest out for themselves, but I'm sure you know all that."

"Because I'm Elaine's friend and colleague?"

"Right." Lisa nodded. "But I know so little about you."

"What do you want to know?"

"Where did that little lilt of a Southern accent you just used on Elaine come from?"

"Oh, you caught that, did you?" Women usually did. "It's a little muddled, but I grew up in Georgia and then North Carolina before moving to New York in college."

"And you never looked back?"

"Not with any sort of longing. It wasn't the small-town Southern existence you read about in the books."

"So not filled with incest and lynchings?"

"No, thank God, but I just meant we were always transplants. Military brats, if you must."

"I don't think I can ever reconcile this image of you"—Lisa stepped back a little to scan her up and down—"to either the military or brattiness."

"Well I was the first in several generations to break the Maine military line, but only time will give you the opportunity to assess my…brattiness."

"Time? Will I have that or are you just in town for the wedding?"

"I am, actually. I've got a flight back to New York City early tomorrow morning."

Lisa's frown was nearly imperceptible, but it tugged at something in Marty all the same. She wondered again how she'd gotten so much practice hiding her emotions and what had happened to make Lisa feel the need to cultivate the skill in the first place.

"Do you ever make it to the city?"

"Not really. Aside from college, I'm a Buffalo gal, born and bred."

Marty didn't even try to hide her frown, and she didn't care to hide why either. She liked Lisa's sense of humor, her intelligence, the way she didn't seem to take her skills and education too seriously. Many women with her background would've lorded it over everyone in the room, or tried to downplay their accomplishments in an attempt to fish for compliments. Instead, Lisa only projected a refreshing air of amiability.

Suddenly the beat changed from the slow-love-song variety to the thumping bass of a bump-and-grind number as the DJ called for everyone young and old to join the dance party.

Lisa stopped swaying. "Thanks for the dance."

"Thank you."

"I guess I should go check in with the wedding party and make sure everything's running smoothly."

"Sounds very official."

"I'm a very important person at this party. Eventually there will be cake, and you know I'll probably have to taste it first to make sure it's okay for everyone else."

"If that's too much of a burden on you, I've been known to taste a slice of cake or two."

"I'll keep that in mind," Lisa said, "but I'm sure you'd like to get back to the amazing glass of wine I recommended for you."

Marty couldn't tell if Lisa was dismissing her or releasing her. She supposed both options involved saying good-bye here, but the motivation behind the parting mattered to her, possibly more than it should. Still, she couldn't monopolize Lisa all night, so she smiled and said, "Thank you. It truly was a pleasure to meet you, Lisa."

Lisa returned her smile and nodded. "The feeling's very mutual, Marty."

Then she turned quickly and wove her way off the now-crowded dance floor. Marty walked more slowly in the opposite direction, careful to avoid the ring bearer as he busted out some crazy break-dance moves. He was adorable, and even if she hadn't known he was Elaine's five-year-old nephew, she could have easily seen the family resemblance in his mop of blond curls and bright blue eyes. She wondered briefly if his aunt could dance like that and almost laughed at the mental image.

She turned around as if to share the thought with Lisa, certain she would appreciate the humor in that image, but she was already too far away. A pang of emotion pulsed in her chest. Regret? Loneliness? Wistfulness? She wasn't sure, but she didn't leave her emotions unheeded. Was she merely lonely because she didn't know anyone else at the wedding? Or had there been something special about Lisa?

She smiled again, this time just to herself. Of course there was something special about Lisa. She was smart and quick and funny. Who wouldn't enjoy having a little more of those things in her life? Then again, she didn't want to be a one-night-stand or a wedding-night conquest. She also had her coaching relationship with Elaine to consider. She hadn't lied to Lisa in saying she considered Elaine a dear friend and a colleague, but part of their relationship also involved being able to talk freely about the issues—and occasionally the people—in one another's lives. If she got too close to Lisa, she might inadvertently lose her neutrality when it came to future conversations with Elaine, and Elaine was facing some pretty big transitions in the coming months.

She reached the table where she'd left her wine. Taking a sip, she noted the flavors seemed even bolder after having had time to breathe. She inhaled its rich aroma and pulled her thoughts back to the pleasures of being completely in the moment.

Chapter Two

"What do you need?" Lisa asked as Joey wandered back toward the head table.

"Nothing, except to get off my feet for a minute."

"Are you sure? Water? More champagne?" She bounced on her toes in anticipation.

"No, thank you. One was more than enough. I'm afraid a second would wreck me."

"And you want to be able to perform on your wedding night?"

Joey snorted. "Something like that."

Lisa pulled out two chairs, and they flopped into them. "Do you have any questions about that?"

"What?"

"The wedding night." She leaned in conspiratorially. "You know, like what will be expected of you in the bridal chambers?"

Joey shook her head and rolled her eyes. "No, I want to be surprised."

"Good call."

Silence fell between them, and for the first time in a long time, Lisa felt the need to fill it. "What do you think of the DJ?"

Joey looked over the hip young woman with spiked hair and an oversized set of headphones. "She's doing a good job."

"Yeah, but she's cute, right?"

"Did you just ask me to check out another woman at my own wedding?"

"Wedding reception."

"Oh, that's much better." Joey looked over her shoulder again. "Seems a bit young for you."

"Says the woman who just married someone fourteen years older."

"Fair point." Joey nodded. "But aren't you even starting to think about something more long-term?"

"I'm still young."

"We turned thirty this year."

Joey wasn't the first person to point that out recently, but for some reason it annoyed her more. "So, no on the DJ?"

"She's fine. I guess I should just be happy you passed on Marty so quickly."

Her stomach tightened. "Not sure there was anything to pass up there. She was just standing next to me when you sprang that shared first dance thing on us all." They'd had a nice dance, a few laughs, and she'd let her go back to whoever she actually wanted to be with. Surely for a woman like Marty that was a long line.

"I should've known not to worry. She's not your type at all."

"She's not female?"

"No. As far as I know she's a woman-identified woman."

"Then she's pretty much my type. Low bar, remember?"

"Exactly, she's not one to inspire low standards. She's a grown-up. She strikes me as someone who doesn't mess around, and she has a real job."

"Really? I thought she was a life coach."

"I walked right into that one."

"You did. Thanks." But the zing didn't give her as much joy as it usually did. Was Marty really that far out of her league? She'd been fun enough to talk to, and an above-average dancer. And she lived in New York City, so how serious could things really get? Still, the comment about her being a grown-up had stung a little. Why did everyone assume once you reached a certain age you had to start acting different and wanting different things? She liked her life. She liked her job. She liked her friends. Change was overrated.

That thought sent the tightness she'd felt in her stomach spreading up into her chest, and suddenly she felt the urge to move again. Standing quickly, she rubbed her hands together. "Are you sure you don't want a drink or something? Or I could get things set up for the cake cutting. You like cake."

"Everyone likes cake, but really, relax. You've put on a great party here. I want you to enjoy it too."

Lisa looked around the room, from the caterer's table, to the dance floor, to all the people milling around back by the bar. Casual, friendly, fun—everything had come together. "It is a pretty good party, isn't it?"

Joey's eyes softened as she clasped a hand on her shoulder. "It really is, Lisa. I can't thank you enough."

"Happy wedding, friend. I would've done more if you'd let me."

"I don't doubt it, but really, the only thing you can do for me now is go have fun."

"Yeah? Okay." Fun, she could do that. She was known for fun. "I do have some pretty sweet dance moves. Maybe I'll go find Marty again since dancing with her makes you and your bride so nervous."

"I'm not nervous for her," Joey said just a bit too seriously for Lisa's liking. "She's not the kind of woman who will fall for your usual MO."

"She's only in town for one night. How much damage can she really do in twelve hours?"

"Don't tempt fate, my friend. It only took one hour alone with Elaine to break me completely."

"This is so not the same story." She bumped her hip against Joey's shoulder. "Besides, you always were the weaker minded of the two of us."

Joey raised her hands in surrender. "Fine, go on. You've earned your fun, but don't say I didn't warn you. That woman is more than you can handle in one night."

Lisa grabbed her beer and hopped down off the platform before raising the bottle as if toasting her friend. "Challenge accepted."

❖

Marty cradled her second glass of wine in the palm of her hand as she watched Elaine and Joey cut their beautiful three-tier wedding cake. Both of them looked a little flash-burned from all the camera bulbs clicking at them. Joey actually blinked a few times and stepped back, but the moment Elaine placed a hand lightly on her arm, the two of them made eye contact and there wasn't a doubt in her mind everyone else in the room was now just a blur to them.

"God, they look so in love," she said to no one in particular, but a few people around her murmured their agreement.

Joey lifted a piece of cake toward Elaine's mouth with a grin on her face, but Elaine's raised eyebrow and half smile clearly conveyed a message of *Don't you dare*. And despite a few shouts of encouragement from the more boisterous guests, Joey did exactly as expected and behaved like a perfect gentleman. Elaine, on the other hand, embraced her playful side and tapped a light dab of icing on Joey's nose before delivering her slice of cake.

Everyone cheered, causing the happy couple to turn and blush in unison as though they'd just realized a hundred people had watched the sweet exchange. Marty felt like her heart actually had to expand to accompany all her happiness at their happiness. Everyone deserved to be happy. Everyone deserved to be loved, but some people had to work harder to internalize that belief for themselves. Joey and Elaine had worked harder than most to make space for the magnitude of their connection, and tonight proved they'd been duly rewarded. She didn't care if it made her a bleeding-heart sappy romantic to get a little misty on their behalf.

"Are you going to cry because you're at the back of the cake line?"

The voice was close, low, and pleasantly familiar in a room full of strangers. Her smile was full before she even turned to see Lisa beside her.

"No," she said, wiping her eyes softly. "I'm just so happy for them."

Lisa glanced at the newlyweds, her smile sweet but restrained. "Yeah, they're pretty perfect together."

"I wish I knew Joey better, but Elaine is the happiest I've ever seen her, so I know she's found someone special."

"She has, but if true love is all it takes to make you gloriously sappy, then I'll just keep this for myself." With a little flourish, Lisa produced a plate holding three slices of cake from behind her back.

"True love? What true love?"

"True love between two women and three pieces of cake?"

"Yes, exactly that."

Lisa nodded for Marty to follow her, and they wove their way in and out of the crowd to a deserted table off to the side of the wedding party's. Lisa pulled out a chair for Marty, then retrieved two forks from the inside chest pocket of her tuxedo. Marty felt a little butterfly flutter in her stomach. "You do know your way around a tuxedo jacket, don't you?"

"I told you it wasn't my first rodeo," Lisa said, taking a seat next to her and pulling it a little closer. "What's your poison? Chocolate, vanilla, or red velvet."

"Red velvet."

"Predictable."

"Really?" Marty asked, mildly disappointed to be an easy read. "And you like chocolate."

"What can I say? I'm sweet."

"Oh, another piece of the puzzle."

Lisa grinned. "Who gets the vanilla, then?"

"Well, if one of us *has* to eat two pieces, I'd be willing to do that."

"I don't want you to be put out. You're the guest here. If anyone should have to take on extra work, it should be the host."

The host? Marty thought. That was as close as Lisa had come to admitting she'd paid for this party in its entirety, but she got the suspicion she'd close up again if they spoke about it frankly, either because she didn't want to admit to taking something so seriously, or perhaps because Marty had only known such a detail from talking to Elaine in confidence during a session. "It's no hardship really. I'm trained to see the good in everything, even vanilla cake with vanilla icing."

"It's cream-cheese icing," Lisa said as she reached her fork toward the object of their conversation.

Marty countered with her own fork, poking Lisa's hand lightly. "Back off."

"Oh, saucy all of a sudden, are we?"

"Cream-cheese frosting is a game changer."

"Good to know." Lisa laughed.

"Everyone has her boundaries."

"Or triggers," Lisa countered, moving her fork back over to the piece of chocolate cake. "I'm compiling quite a list of yours."

"Oh?" Marty asked, taking a bite of the red velvet and closing her eyes to savor the dense, smooth sweetness.

"Fine wine, cream-cheese frosting, cheesy romantic displays, and dashingly handsome maids of ill repute."

"You went three-for-four there, not bad."

Another flash of a frown crossed Lisa's features before she forced another laugh, this one sounding only slightly less genuine. "Well, in that case I think the dashingly handsome maid of ill repute should at least get the vanilla cake as a consolation prize."

Marty took a piece of the cake on her fork and started to lean toward Lisa before turning it around and directing it back in to her own mouth.

"Hey now."

"No," Marty said, shaking her head. "No consolation prize for you, because the incorrect item on your list was cheesy romantic displays."

Lisa's eyebrow rose as she let that bit of information sink in.

"I don't like kitschy couples. I like genuinely romantic displays. I like seeing my friend's authentic happiness. And while I'm confessing, it's probably worth mentioning that I'm also very much enjoying the company of a dashingly handsome maid of ill repute."

"Bold, I like it."

"Authentic."

"Uh"—Lisa shifted in her seat—"sure, but where were we before the DJ so rudely interrupted our dance by encouraging everyone else to bust a move?"

Nice deflection. What Lisa lacked in willingness for introspection she made up for in social acumen. "I think we were talking about my return to New York tomorrow morning."

"Yes, sadly, that." Lisa didn't seem as sad as she had earlier, her frown clearly staged for effect. "But I was thinking, if you only have one night in Buffalo, it should be a good one."

Marty couldn't help but smile despite her suspicions as to what Lisa was suggesting. "I'm having a lovely trip. The wedding was beautiful, and the reception has been perfect."

"Well there's that," Lisa said, straightening her shoulders a bit either out of pride or an oncoming challenge, "but the clock is ticking, and who knows when you'll be back again, so what if you and I just forgo all the awkward getting-to-know-each-other stuff and get right to the good parts."

"The good parts? Are you suggesting something befitting your formal title or the one you've bestowed on yourself?"

"I like the way you think, but what if we don't think quite so much?"

"Why do I feel like this is all an elaborate come-on?"

"What? From me?" Lisa feigned hurt. "But, no, it can work both ways. Neither one of us banks on any forgone conclusion, not about tomorrow, not even about later tonight."

"No end goal for either of us?"

"None," Lisa said, then crossed her heart with her index finger. "What if we just say, I like you. You seem to like me. For tonight we don't worry about your travel schedule or your job."

"Or the fact that your best friend just married one of my clients?"

"Sure, because that's your job. And your job is in the city, tomorrow. Tonight you're a friend of the bride, remember?"

"So you're suggesting we just be fully present in this moment?"

"Yes, carpe the *noche*."

"Authentically accept the now?"

"YOLO, Marty."

How could she argue with that? Raising her wineglass to clink the side of Lisa's beer bottle, she nodded in agreement. "YOLO, Lisa."

❖

Holy shit, that YOLO thing actually worked. Or maybe Marty really liked her. Probably, though, it was the YOLO thing. Either way she suddenly had a date to the wedding she'd been obsessing over for a year. No more time to freak over things like flower arrangements or bar stock. No time, either, to worry about the new reality of having married best friends and roommates. She'd been granted a stay of execution for a few more hours, and she got to spend that time with a beautiful woman. Oh, and did she mention no strings attached? Because that was a pretty real thing in this scenario too. Life coaching credentials set aside, as they had been, she couldn't conceive a better scenario if she tried. And honestly, she had tried pretty hard in the past with much less fulfilling results.

Now Marty swayed in her arms to the crooning of Sara Bareilles, and for the first time in her life she felt thankful for Joey and Elaine's affinity for emotive women singers. Maybe this was what she'd been missing about the genre all along. Songs like this made women like Marty snuggle closer. Well, it made Marty snuggle closer. She wasn't in a position to make generalizations because she'd never met a woman quite like her before. She wasn't just smart and attentive, she was also damn funny. And fun too. She'd refused to let Lisa leave the floor during the chicken dance, then refused to hide her laughter when she finally relented and joined in.

"What are you thinking about?" Marty asked.

"How you forced me to do the chicken dance, then mocked me for it."

"I didn't mock you so much as I expressed my pure enjoyment at your rendition."

She briefly considered calling that out as life coach mumbo jumbo, but she didn't want to go there. Not tonight. "Fair enough. But if the DJ plays the Macarena, the tables will be turned."

"Because you won't do that one?"

"No, because I'm awesome. You'll stand in awe of my hip cross into booty shake."

"Wow, I've never ached to hear 'Hey, Macarena' pulse through a set of speakers the way I do right now." Marty played along. Another thing to like about her. She didn't have to overanalyze things. She could run with a tangent just as fast and far as Lisa could.

"How do you feel about the Electric Slide?" Lisa asked.

"Of me doing it, or watching you do it?"

"Both."

"I'm a big fan."

"Really? I would've never picked you as a line dance kinda gal."

"It's part of my mystery and intrigue," Marty said in a low, sultry voice before adding lightly, "Also, the whole growing up in the South in the '80s thing."

"Ah, the South, the '80s, such vague concepts to me."

"Right, because you were an embryo in the '80s. Way to point out that I'm a much older woman."

"A cougar, even."

Marty laughed. "Do my big teeth and claws frighten you?"

"No, I'm into danger."

"I like that. What you just did there," Marty said.

"Admitting my attraction to cougars?"

"Well that too, but I meant you didn't feel the need to jump into an elaborate excuse for our age difference. You just owned it and moved on."

"Moving on is one of my finest skills."

Marty's forehead furrowed.

Lisa's heart beat a little faster at the sight of those worry lines. Had she said something wrong? She hadn't meant to imply no strings had to mean no feelings. "I didn't mean to be disrespectful."

"What?"

"The crack about moving on. It made you frown. I didn't mean to imply I go through women easily or often. I'm sorry if I hurt your feelings."

Marty's smile returned, big and brilliant until it crinkled the corners of her eyes. "And I'm sorry if I gave you the impression you upset me. I wasn't put off by the idea of you being an easy-come, easy-go sort of person. I simply didn't believe you."

"Oh, well, there's that. Good," Lisa said, then let the comments sink in. "Except you may have just called me a liar."

"Not at all. I just meant that while you do seem to be able to let little things like my cougar status go with grace and humor, you've had the same best friend since you were a child. That doesn't speak to someone who lets go easily."

Lisa's chest tightened to the extent she wasn't sure she could speak, even if she'd known what to say. Maybe she should've listened a little better to the warning from Joey. But here was Marty, all soft and warm and smelling like bubble bath. What were a few observations compared to all that? And she still hadn't had a single urge to sign up for life coaching, so as far as she was concerned, she was winning on the night. Besides, what had Joey actually said? Something about being completely broken in only an hour?

She lifted Marty's hand in order to look at the watch on her own wrist.

"Have somewhere to be?"

"Not at all. Just checking to confirm I've been hanging out with you for nearly two hours now."

"And have you reached your limit?"

Lisa gently pushed Marty out and gave her a little twirl before pulling her back in again. "Nope, and that best friend of mine might not know me as well as I know her."

"Why's that?"

"Because we're two hours in, and I'm just getting warmed up."

❖

"Want another glass of wine?" Lisa asked as she and Marty exited the dance floor after several upbeat dances.

"You don't have to get me drunk to keep me on your arm tonight," Marty said. Lisa's earlier noting of the time had been a surprise. Hours had eased by like minutes, and the conversation had yet to lag. Staying present was much easier when the present was filled with such enjoyable company. She had to work not to feel like Cinderella at the ball with the clock inching ever closer to midnight.

She couldn't stop time, and she wouldn't waste her energy trying to change something beyond her control, but she also wouldn't deny that she wanted more of this here and now with Lisa.

"So, no on the wine?"

"Actually, yes on the wine, since we're living in the moment."

"Okay." Lisa smiled in the unguarded way that made Marty's stomach flutter. "Come with me this time, though."

Lisa took her hand to lead her toward the bar. The move was casual, confident, and not all that different than the contact they'd shared while dancing, but away from the music, the touch felt softer, more personal, and more public as they wound around tables and chairs filled with Lisa's friends and acquaintances. The crowd had been cut more than half as the night wore on, leaving mostly the young or exuberant to the reverie. The line at the bar was shorter now too, with only one man ahead of them.

He turned and almost collided with Lisa as he collected his ginger ale.

"Hey there, Mr. Bruce, the tux is dry-clean only," she said with a laugh.

"That's why I'm not wearing one," he said, then gestured to Lisa's jacket with his glass. "But yours looks good on you."

"It helps with the ladies—speaking of which, meet Ms. Marty Maine. She's a friend of Elaine's." Lisa turned to face her. "Marty, this is Joey's dad, Mr. Bruce Lang."

"It's nice to meet you, Marty."

He extended his hand, and she felt a twinge of regret at having to break contact with Lisa to accept it.

"It's nice to meet you too, sir."

"Oh, don't call me sir. I already feel old enough tonight. It's not every day your only child gets married." He said it gruffly, but his chest puffed out, and his eyes shone with pride.

"You must've done a wonderful job raising her to have led her to this moment."

"Between her good nature and her mother's guidance, I didn't do much more than enjoy the ride."

Lisa clasped a hand on his shoulder. "We all wish she could've been here tonight."

He nodded stiffly. "She is. In her own way."

Lisa's half smile mirrored his. "I thought so too, when I was tying her bow tie today. Could've sworn I felt a little nudge or two."

Marty felt a little twist in her heart, both at the topic and the unspoken emotion behind it. These two had obviously gone through an ordeal together, one they still carried with them. Lisa did nothing to make light of their loss.

"Well I'm glad she had one of us to guide her," he said. "I still don't know how to tie one of those things. I don't think I've worn one since my own wedding day."

"You're classically handsome, though, so you can get away with it." Lisa brightened. "People like me need to work a little harder."

He chuckled and shook his head, then focused on Marty. "Don't believe a word this one says. She's full of you know what, and slicker too."

Marty laughed. "You're the second person to say so tonight. And with comments like her last one, I'm starting to see why."

"What?" Lisa pretended to be offended. "It's the truth. In normal clothes I'm quite homely, though I have to admit, now that Joey's officially off the market, I hope my stock will rise."

Bruce looked from Lisa to Marty and back again. "I'm not as good at recognizing these things as I used to be, but I think your stock is doing just fine tonight."

Lisa grinned, "What did I tell you about tuxes, Mr. Bruce?"

He shook his head, but the sadness had once again faded from his smile. "Get out of here. Go have fun, and don't get this nice young lady into trouble."

"Yes, sir," Lisa said.

"It was very nice to meet you," Marty added.

"I hope to see more of you, Ms. Maine," he said before wandering off.

"I'd like that too," Marty murmured, surprised at the strength of the sentiment. She often met people she liked, but the sincerity of what had passed between Lisa and Bruce opened a part of herself reserved for deeper introspection than she generally engaged during social situations. "He seems very nice."

"One of the best men I've ever had the privilege of knowing," Lisa said.

"And you were close with Joey's mom too?"

"Sometimes they were more like parents to me than my own parents," Lisa said matter-of-factly, shifting her attention toward the bar. The move was subtle and could easily be explained away, but Marty saw clearly the conversation was closed, and she respected that. Still, her respect for Lisa's boundaries didn't stop her from wondering what lay behind them.

❖

Lisa dropped into a nearby chair, then lifted her glass and took a deep breath, inhaling the robust, aromatic fruit flavors of the wine. She hadn't intended to get too deep with Mr. Bruce in front of Marty, but the memory of Joey's mom had never been far from the surface while planning this wedding. Her absence was felt particularly hard at the service that afternoon, but only to the select few that had really known her. Marty was outside that circle, and right now that was a good thing. Marty had no past and no future. Marty belonged only to tonight, and Lisa wanted to keep her there.

She took a swig of the wine, not nearly as gracefully as Marty, who sipped hers. She hadn't pushed for more information or tried to force conversation, yet another item to add on the already long list of things to like about her. "Tell me something about you no one else knows, not even Elaine."

Marty turned her head to the side and pursed her lips. Lisa worried she might be overanalyzing the request, but after only a few seconds her smile returned, and she said, "And this information stays with you?"

"To the grave."

"I sing in the shower."

"That's not so bad."

"I sing Disney songs."

"Well now, that's a little more surprising." Lisa smiled in spite of her earlier introspection. "What are we talking about here? *Beauty and the Beast*? *Lion King*?"

"Yes, and yes, and so much more, *Cinderella*, *Peter Pan*, *Aristocats*."

"Wow, you're a connoisseur."

"You know wine, I know singing cats and mice," Marty said with mock seriousness.

"But you know wine too, so you're a renaissance woman. I am duly impressed."

"You shouldn't be. I may know all the words, but that doesn't mean I can carry the tune."

"Hence the shower singing."

"Exactly."

"I'd still love to hear your rendition of 'Someday My Prince Will Come.'"

"That would probably require you to be in the shower with me."

"Um…" Lisa's face felt awfully warm all of a sudden. "Well, I think that could possibly—"

"Hey, you two," Joey interrupted.

Lisa and Marty both jumped. Joey and Elaine were standing right behind them.

"Wow. That didn't make you look guilty at all," Joey said, glancing from them to Elaine.

"This is the part where they judge us in their heads and communicate that shared judgment via telepathy," Lisa explained.

"Never," Marty replied. "They're just happy two of their friends found such wonderful company that they didn't even notice their approach."

"I don't buy it for a second."

"I choose to put my faith in our friends' generous natures."

"That's why you're Elaine's friend and colleague, and I'm the maid of ill repute."

Marty laughed heartily in that unrestrained way Lisa had come to crave over the last few hours.

Elaine and Joey exchanged another look, this one clearly filled with more amusement.

"See, they've done it again," Lisa pointed out.

"I take it this happens often?"

"Every day."

"Do we need to be here for this conversation?" Joey finally asked.

"Not really," Marty said, causing Lisa to laugh before she added, "but we'd love to have you join us anyway."

"I'm sorry we haven't had more time to talk." Elaine sat down next to Marty. "I feel like I haven't had a second to breathe today, much less visit."

"Of course not, it's your wedding day. We'll have plenty of time to talk when the dust settles."

"Still, I'm sorry you came all the way to Buffalo and I neglected you."

"Don't be silly. I've not felt the slightest bit neglected."

"I've been very attentive," Lisa offered.

"Yeah, I noticed," Joey said, looking mystified.

Marty seemed to catch the look as well but gracefully brushed it off. "Do we win the odd couple of the wedding award?"

"No, not at all," Elaine said quickly, laying her hand on her wife's shoulder. "Joey and I are clearly that."

"Only odd in that it seems unusual today to find two people so perfectly matched."

Lisa lifted her wineglass, marveling at Marty's ability to say such perfect things.

"I see why Elaine finds you so soothing to talk to," Joey said. "Can't imagine what you've said to keep Lisa so entranced all evening, though."

Lisa snorted. "Who said she was the one doing the entrancing?"

"It's the truth," Marty said seriously. "I've been positively hypnotized. She just had me revealing deep, dark secrets when you walked up."

"Oh?" Joey asked.

"Yes, but I'll never reveal them, not even when tortured." Lisa crossed her heart, then gestured toward Elaine and Marty. "Confidentiality, that's a thing for you people, right?"

"Yes," Elaine said, her smile filled with mirth. "We people do have a thing about confidentially, but I'd have never known you knew that."

"I get the feeling Lisa knows a great many things she won't admit to knowing until she's ready to show her hand."

"I'd say that's pretty accurate," Joey said, a hint of weariness in her voice. "The biggest question is how she intends to use those powers."

Lisa eyed her best friend, those deep brown eyes filled with worry and perhaps warning.

"I'm just glad you two each found someone so wonderful to keep you company tonight," Elaine cut in. "I wish I could keep up with you, really, but I'm exhausted."

"What? The party's just getting started. Nothing has to end," Lisa argued, perhaps a bit too adamantly, then caught herself. "I mean, it's not even midnight."

Joey rose first and offered her hand to Elaine. "But I have to get the missus home before the clock strikes twelve, or she'll turn into a pumpkin."

Elaine kissed Joey lightly on the cheek. "Thank you, Prince Charming."

"What a sweet way of saying you two can't wait to start the honeymoon."

Joey shook her head, but Elaine shrugged. "Maybe that too."

She gave Joey's hand a little squeeze before letting go and turning to face Lisa. "Thank you again, for everything."

"It's nothing, really."

"It is," Elaine said evenly, then she pulled Lisa into a hug. Not the lean-in-and-back-pat kind of hug, but a real full-on body squeeze that always made her feel a little awkward. "I hope you know how happy we are."

"I do," Lisa admitted, finally relaxing into the embrace.

"We want the same for you," Elaine whispered. "So do me one favor tonight, please."

"Anything."

"Be open to the same kind of happiness for yourself." Elaine gave her one more squeeze, then mercifully let go before forcing her to answer. Not that she had an answer. When Elaine went all life coachy, all Lisa felt was mild embarrassment for both of them.

Thankfully the moment was short-lived as Elaine turned to Marty, and Joey caught hold of Lisa's arm. "You rock. You know that, right?"

"Totally."

"Yeah, I thought so."

"Enjoy the honeymoon, Prince Charming. Don't do anything I wouldn't do."

Joey threw her arm around her shoulder, giving her a little shake. "Got it, and you, be careful."

"Me?"

"I mean it." Joey's voice was low. "Don't do anything we'll all regret later."

The hair on Lisa's arms stood on end as she shook Joey off and turned to see if Marty had heard that. She didn't appear to, as she stood back from Elaine's embrace and immediately sought Lisa's eyes. The two of them stood staring, their slow smiles a mirror to one another, as Elaine and Joey slipped away. Finally Lisa held out her hand to Marty once more.

As she took it, her soft fingers sliding smoothly across her open palm, she nodded resolutely and repeated Joey's words, or at least the only part that mattered. "No regrets."

❖

"It's getting pretty late," Marty said as Lisa led her out of the ballroom. "I'm not sure I should be letting a maid of ill repute lead me down dark hallways alone."

"You probably shouldn't," Lisa agreed. "And yet you are."

"I am." Amusement filled her voice. It wasn't so much that she couldn't resist Lisa's charm as she simply didn't want to.

"I bet you have an early flight in the morning."

"I do," she admitted. "I need to go to the airport at seven o'clock in the morning."

"I bet you won't have any time to sightsee either."

"I won't. I've only seen the airport, the church, and now I've seen this building."

"It's called the Marcy Casino," Lisa said, leading her up a flight of dimly lit stairs, feeling along the wall as she went. "And you were only in the Pan Am room, so you haven't even really seen the best part yet."

As they reached a landing atop the staircase, Lisa found and flipped a light switch. It took a moment for Marty's eyes to adjust to both the light and the sight before her. The room's gray stone walls were rimmed in beautiful hardwood finishes and wrought-iron accents. A series of archways encased windows along one side of the room, and the light from the chandeliers danced along the glass before spilling onto a covered terrace.

"Oh, Lisa, it's beautiful."

She smiled broadly. "I've always thought this space was one of the prettiest in Buffalo."

"I'm impressed. I have to admit, I've always sort of thought of Buffalo as a Rust Belt relic."

"It is, in a lot of ways," Lisa said, "but there are still a few jewels in her crown. I wanted to show you some of them before you fly away to the Big Apple again."

Lisa opened one of the glass doors, her hazel eyes containing a spark of magic or mischief.

They stepped onto the stone terrace, away from the light and warmth of the room behind them and into the darker unknown of the night. Lisa's hand found hers once again. The touch was more than comforting, the emotions it carried strong and stirring.

"There," Lisa whispered, looking across a frozen lake toward a skyline filled with light and shadows against the freshly falling snow. "I think it's one of the most beautiful views of the whole city."

Marty's heart gave a little flutter at the assessment. She couldn't disagree. The view from where she stood was quite stunning. A gentle breeze stirred the ends of Lisa's hair and the fractures of light behind them danced across her eyes like candles floating on a reflecting pool. Even in the near dark, her silhouette cut a handsome figure against the snowy backdrop, her tuxedo jacket open and her bow tie unraveled against the stark white of her collar. She looked like a classic photograph in black and white, but so much closer, so much more real than any portrait could ever be.

Marty put her hand on the cold metal railing to steady herself, but Lisa leaned close behind her, pointing out across the winter scene. "See the building across the way, the one with the big Greek columns?"

The warmth of Lisa's body against her back took so much of her mind and physical response she could only nod.

"That's the Historical Society. They've got a museum, and there's a playhouse on the lower level."

It looked like a little touch of Olympic history dropped down on a small city hill in some *Doctor Who*–type time travel gone awry.

Lisa shifted, directing them to the left until they looked out past the end of the lake and up a beautiful set of stone stairs. "The one with the columns over there is the Albright-Knox Art Gallery. It's got over six thousand pieces of art and only two hundred exhibition slots, so every time you go you can see something different."

"Impressive."

"Yeah, this part of town was the hot, happening place to be in America at the turn of the last century. We hosted the Pan-Am Exposition, and the whole hemisphere thought we were mack daddies. Music, art, history, and million-dollar mansions back when a million dollars meant something." The low timbre of her voice floated softly against Marty's ear. "I wish I could've seen it then," she said wistfully.

"I don't know," Marty murmured, leaning back more fully against her. "It seems pretty perfect right now."

"Actually, now that you mention it"—Lisa wrapped her arms around Marty's waist and rested her chin on her shoulder—"I don't think I'd trade right now for all the glory of a hundred years ago."

They watched the snow dance its ballet on the wind. So comfortable, so fitting, so at peace. "Thank you for showing me this."

"Thank you for understanding." Lisa sighed contentedly, her breath warm against Marty's neck, such a beautiful contrast to the cold around them.

The sincerity of the comments tugged at something deep inside her chest. Could it be there was more to Lisa Knapp than her comedic façade? She wished she had more time to find out and wasn't too self-assured to admit the depth of that longing scared her. This evening spent in her company had been surprisingly wonderful, but they'd both promised it ended here. This moment was purely theirs, but it was only the work of the moment. She wasn't naive enough to think they couldn't share a few more hours in more intimate ways, or too pure to admit the idea appealed to her, but she'd already seen enough to realize the dangers in going any further down this path.

Their time together was almost over, and in her calmest, most logical center, she knew those constraints would likely save her. If she saw more of Lisa, she suspected she'd want more of her. More than either of them could really offer or accept.

A shiver ran up her spine at that thought, and she trembled slightly in the circle of Lisa's strong arms.

"Are you cold?" Lisa asked, stepping back. "We can go back in."

"No," Marty whispered, "please, not just yet."

"Okay." She heard the smile in Lisa's voice as she felt the rustle of fabric against her shoulders, followed by the silky warmth of a tuxedo jacket against her bare arms.

"Oh, Lisa, no. Now you'll be—"

"Shh, I'll be fine." She wrapped her arms back around Marty's waist, snuggling in once more. "Trust me. I'm anything but cold."

Marty smiled into the darkness and, running her fingers along the satin lapels, pulled them tighter around herself. She couldn't remember the last time someone had given her their jacket, probably because no one ever had. The tenderness of the gesture confirmed her earlier suspicions that there was something special, something thoughtful and sensitive beneath Lisa's already appealing veneer of playful bravado.

She turned carefully within the circle of Lisa's embrace, trading the gorgeous view of the city behind her for an even more compelling sight. She intended to tell Lisa that, to say she was amazing, to tell her how much she'd enjoyed their time together, to thank her for stirring something wonderful inside her, but when she parted her lips to speak, they somehow connected with Lisa's.

The kiss was both a surprise and surprising. Their mouths came together in such a natural way, not too fast, not too timid, but easy, knowing, perfectly fitting, exploring places they already knew. Marty arched onto her tiptoes to get more, and Lisa held her steady with an arm looped loosely across the small of her back. She tasted the wine on her lips, breathed the crisp frost in the air, and felt the warmth of Lisa wrapped around her.

The kiss deepened, and she relished the warmth of their combined heat. Breaths, shared more than stolen, grew shallow. Marty cupped Lisa's cheek in her hand, running her thumb along the smooth skin. Everything about Lisa was smooth, her skin, her lips, her easy way of being. She could get drunk on her, or even drown. The realization burned deliberate and steady through the haze of perfection. She could get lost in her, in this thing they were edging ever closer to.

She wondered if Lisa realized it too, because slowly, as if by mutual, unspoken agreement, they parted. Marty took a step back and Lisa's arm fell softly to her side. A physical gulf of inches felt like miles as the clock on their time together struck midnight.

"Wow," Lisa said.

Marty smiled, not feeling any need to further describe what had already been so clearly expressed.

"I…I'm…well…" Lisa sighed and smiled, finally giving in to what Marty already knew. There really was nothing left to say. There were plenty of options for next steps, most of them appealing in the short term, but the only real possibility for either of them to get out of this night without committing permanent parts of themselves involved a sweet and simple good-bye.

"I've had a wonderful time with you," Marty finally said.

Lisa nodded.

"I think it's time for me to say good night."

Lisa opened her mouth, and Marty held her breath. Knowing right from wrong didn't prevent her from hoping to be persuaded to choose the latter. If only Lisa would plead her case, she could so easily be convinced not to say good night until the sun painted the horizon.

Instead Lisa nodded again, this time her smile more strained. "You made this a night to remember for all the right reasons. Thank you."

Marty fought the urge to ask for more, but the emotions behind the statement weren't hers to uncover. She'd also heard the invitation that wasn't issued. She wondered if Lisa found it as hard not to say the words as she did. It would be so simple, so natural to speak of a next time, of shared connections, or hopeful happenstance, but they both remained firm in their dedication to leave everything between them in the moment to which it belonged.

Marty began to slip off the tuxedo jacket, but Lisa stopped her, stepping close once more. "Keep it."

"I couldn't."

"It looks better on you than it does on me."

"Don't be silly. It looks amazing on you."

"Trust me," Lisa said, and Marty looked up, meeting her hypnotic eyes.

Now it was her turn to nod, unable to speak for the truth clogging her throat. She did trust her. At least here, at least now, and perhaps that was a much bigger problem than if she didn't.

She quickly arched up on her toes and kissed Lisa on her cheek, then, brushing past her, headed for the door. Lisa turned as if to follow, but Marty froze in the doorway.

"No, now it's your turn to trust me," Marty said softly. "You need to stay here. Right where you are, just exactly how you are. Until I'm gone."

"Deal," Lisa said, looking so beautifully resolute Marty couldn't help but allow her eyes to drag over her one more time.

Yes, if all this night would ever be was a memory, at least it was going to be a damn good one.

Chapter Three

The sun reflected a glaring white off the new layer of snow outside her bedroom window. Lisa covered her eyes against the light, but it was no use trying to fall back to sleep now. She rolled over and cracked one eye open just enough to look at the clock: 9:07.

"That's not enough," she grumbled.

It wasn't enough sleep after the night she'd had, and it wasn't late enough to keep this day from feeling endlessly long. The earlier she got up, the more time she'd have to kill in an already too empty house with too many memories threatening to overtake her. Marty's deep brown eyes seemed to stare back at her from the remnants of a dream, or maybe something deeper.

"No. No time for that." She hopped out of bed and tried to shake some of the wrinkles out of the tuxedo pants she'd been too tired to remove before crashing the night before. Surely she had some work to do. She'd done nothing but work for months, and she'd never run out of projects. Grabbing her iPhone, she swiped open her calendar app and navigated through all the various settings she'd established to organize her time priorities. She flipped past wedding task after wedding task, tuxedo fittings, caterer's meetings, seating charts, DJ catalogs. She also flipped through all her privately contracted programming jobs, only to confirm what she already knew. She'd marked them all completed before the wedding as well.

Well, there was always something interesting to hack somewhere. And by somewhere she meant not in her empty living room. She could go to the coffee house even though she knew Joey wouldn't be there today or any day for a long time to come, since one couldn't student-teach and work the day shift at the coffee house at the same time. A new wife and a new job meant new routines all around.

Still, even if the coffee house didn't have Joey, it had coffee, which so far put it one up on her house. She padded into the bathroom and winced at her own reflection. Her dark hair stood out to one side, and she still had sleep marks from the fold of her pillow across her right temple. She looked like something out of a frat-boy comedy film, and she hadn't even had much to drink last night.

If she was left feeling hungover from anything, it would only be the amazing kiss she'd shared with Marty, who had made the room tilt and spin more than any drink she'd ever consumed. Smart and funny and sexy as hell, and best of all she had low enough standards to go slumming it with her for a few hours. What would've happened if they'd had a few more hours together? She stopped herself there because she knew the answer, the one that had ricocheted through her mind in the seconds following their kiss. She had to get out while she was ahead, and she had.

Hadn't she?

She glanced at the clock again and sighed. Marty would be back in New York City by now.

"And that's a good thing," she said to her reflection.

She splashed water on the parts of her face that had grown pink with the heat of her memories, then set to work trying to brush the fuzz off her teeth.

She threw on some new pants and a hoodie before jogging downstairs and grabbing her MacBook Pro. No time to wander, no time to think, no time to listen to the silence. She was steps from the door when her phone began to play the "Mexican Hat Dance."

She froze. Why would Elaine call her? On her honeymoon?

"Y'ello," Lisa said, lifting the phone to her ear.

"Hi, Lisa." Elaine sounded calm if mildly apologetic.

"Good morning, Elaine. Do you miss me already?"

"Terribly."

"I should've seen that coming, but I didn't expect either of you to be up for air so soon."

"I love your high opinion of our abilities," she said good-naturedly, and Lisa had to admit she wasn't easy to rattle, even if that didn't prevent her from continually trying to.

"Well, the fact that you're talking to me less than twelve hours into your honeymoon tells me you're doing something wrong."

"I'll strive to do better in the coming days, but I have a huge favor to ask you."

"Not sure I can help you at this point in the relationship," Lisa quipped. "I tried to talk to Joey earlier about what to expect on the wedding night, but she wouldn't listen."

"I'll have to get a recap of that conversation later, but right now I just wanted to know if Marty's flight took off this morning."

Lisa's heart did a disturbing little flutter. "How would I know?"

"She didn't answer her phone when I called and I thought maybe…?"

"You thought maybe she was with me?" Lisa didn't want to dwell on the missed opportunity Elaine hinted at. "Don't get me wrong, I'm flattered you think I could work that fast, but a little disappointed you underestimated my gentlemanly qualities."

"I didn't mean to imply anything of the sort."

Liar. The abundance of relief in Elaine's voice gave her away.

"I just thought if she got stuck in Buffalo she might've called you, since I'm out of town and you two hit it off last night."

Elaine didn't even know the half of it. She and Joey left before the best part of the night. She could still feel Marty's lips on hers.

"So?" Elaine asked.

"What?"

"Did she call you?"

"That's a big negative," Lisa said, then before she thought it over, added, "Do you really think she's still in town?"

"You haven't turned on the news today?"

"No." She wondered again why Elaine had seen the news on her honeymoon, but let that go in order to get to the real point of this little conversation. "Why?"

"A big nor'easter just clipped the East Coast. They shut down JFK and LaGuardia."

"Seems like they should've seen that coming."

"You know weather forecasters. Their work seems about as reliable as life coaching, right?"

Lisa snorted. "Admitting it is the first step…or so your counseling colleagues say."

"Well while the meteorologists and I work through our shortcomings, would you check on Marty for me?"

"Um…" Lisa drew out the sound while she tried to ignore the wash of emotions swirling inside her. The thought of spending more time with Marty was both a dream come true and a dream killer. Sure, if she could've extended last night into eternity she would've likely suspended time indefinitely, but in the harsh light of a new day, would the perfection they'd shared prove itself an illusion? They'd left things in a really good place, possibly the highest of heights the two of them would ever experience. Why risk a wonderful memory?

Then again, what if they really could steal a few more hours in paradise?

"What'd she say?" Joey asked in the background.

"Lisa?" Elaine asked. "You still there?"

"Uh-huh."

Silence stretched across the airwaves again. Maybe she and Marty could get along like they had last night for a bit longer. Still, what if they didn't? What if Marty didn't want to see her without the music and the wine and the tux? There was no way she'd be able to keep up the smooth charade long-term. She'd only spoil everything.

"Hey." Elaine's voice was soft, caring, knowing. "I'm sorry. I didn't mean to ask you to do something that might hurt you."

"What?" The tone, those words snapped her back to the present. "I'm not hurt. I've just got a lot going on."

"Of course you do. You've worked so hard on the wedding."

"Did she say she was too busy?" Joey asked.

"No, I didn't say that," Lisa said, trying to be heard through the receiver. "It's just—"

"Don't worry. This is a big transition time for you. You can take all the time you need. I just didn't know—"

"There's nothing to know. Don't coach me. I don't need to be handled."

"Of course not."

She hated how calm Elaine sounded compared to the defensiveness in her own voice. "Just text me her number. I'll call her."

"Lisa," Elaine said her name both with warning and sympathy.

"I told you this was a bad idea," Joey said.

"Oh, for fuck's sake, stop overanalyzing everything. I won't be able to strut around in my skivvies if she comes over. That's all. It's fine, though. What the hell else do I have going on right now?"

The last part of the statement revealed more truth than she cared to admit. She literally had nothing going on in her life now. A little awkward company would probably be better than no company at all, but she didn't have to like that realization.

"You sure?" Elaine asked one more time.

"Yeah. Sure. Just text me, then get back to doing things I don't want to think about, okay?"

The smile was back in Elaine's voice as she offered her thanks, but Lisa disconnected the phone quickly. Maybe she should go change her clothes. Maybe Marty wouldn't even answer her phone. Maybe she was already back in New York. Maybe she'd be thrilled to hear from her and they'd fall into bed for days at a time, then she'd leave feeling sated and indebted to her. Yeah, and maybe pigs would fly by the window.

Her phone buzzed in her hand, causing her to jump.

She needed to chill out. She was known for being chill, for being crass, for having no shits to give about what other people thought. She could handle a simple phone call.

Yes, yes, she could.

Right after she took a shower.

❖

Marty stared at the hotel app on her phone. All the airport hotels were booked, presumably by travelers in a predicament similar to hers. All the East Coast airline hubs had closed. New York, Boston, Philadephia, DC. No one getting in meant none of the planes needed to get people anywhere else could get out. Both the arrival and departure boards had flashed a glaring red for hours. Flights were no longer delayed, but canceled outright. At least she'd been one of the lucky ones. Her flight had been called so early she'd been among the first wave to rebook for tomorrow. Others around her had a two- to three-day wait. The energy in the airport was wretchedly negative, and she didn't want to sit there soaking it up anymore.

If only she could find an open room nearby, she'd gladly pay any reasonable amount to have some quiet time to collect herself. A little time and space to meditate and reflect would be a gift from the universe right now, but she couldn't find any such thing in the vicinity. She widened her search again to include downtown Buffalo as well but found no vacancies. Who knew Buffalo was such a happening place in the dead of winter?

Lisa. Her face floating across Marty's memory again caused her to shiver. Lisa knew Buffalo was a hip place. She knew every part of this city. She'd surely be able to find a place to stay, but at what cost? Would hearing her voice so close and low in her ear weaken her resolve to walk away, or compound her regrets for having done so the first time around? No, she didn't have any regrets so much as a wish that things could've been different, but either way, the result was the same. She felt unsettled about something she couldn't change. She needed to move on, to center herself, and she couldn't do so in an airport filled with frustrated strangers.

She started widening her search parameters to encompass the nearby suburbs when the phone in her hand vibrated with an incoming call. She didn't recognize the number on the screen, which generally meant one of two things—either a telemarketer, or a client calling from a new phone. While she really didn't want to engage the former, the prospect of the call being from the latter made her answer.

"Hello," she said hesitantly.

"Hi." Such a simple word, a syllable really, said so much. Her frustration melted and she smiled in spite of the turmoil around her. "This is, uh, Lisa. Lisa Knapp, from, um, the wedding."

Like she wouldn't recognize the voice of the woman who'd filled her dreams all night. "Hello, Lisa."

"Hi," she said again, her nervousness palpable even across the airwaves. "I just talked to Elaine, and she said you might be stuck in Buffalo."

"I am, actually. It looks like I'm not going home today."

"Oh," Lisa said as though she hadn't planned on that answer. "Do you, I don't know, need some help or something, like a place to stay?"

"I do. Do you know of a hotel with open rooms? The ones close to the airport are all jammed with stranded travelers, and downtown is full for some reason I can't comprehend."

"The World Junior Hockey Championships."

"Is that so?"

"Hockey's kind of a thing around here."

"Interesting."

The small talk punctuated by silence was painful compared to the easy camaraderie they'd shared the night before. Maybe they should've left well enough alone.

"So, it's not a hotel, but it's better than the airport," Lisa said.

"What is?"

"Oh"—she laughed nervously—"my house. I mean, our house. Not yours and mine, but mine and Joey's and Elaine's. We have room, and a fireplace. And food. Well actually, no food right now, but we could get some."

Marty's smile stretched her face until her cheek pressed against the phone at her ear. Never had such a bumbling offer sounded so appealing. Suddenly all the proof she'd seen about the need to let go vanished. Her head might have whispered that allowing things with Lisa to continue unchecked would have serious consequences, but her heart said she'd been granted a gift and the only acceptable response was to accept.

"You don't have to. I mean, if it's weird for you. Because of me or…whatever."

"No," she interjected quickly. "If it's not weird for you."

"No," Lisa said, just a bit too defensively. "I mean, it's cool."

"I don't want to be a burden. I'll try not to get in your way."

Lisa snorted. "There's nothing to get in the way of. It's just…me."

Just her. The way Lisa said the phrase sounded almost apologetic, but Marty couldn't think of anything she wanted to hear more in that moment. "I'd really like that."

❖

Marty was standing on the curb when she pulled up to the airport, and Lisa groaned. Why did she have to look so damn perfect in her jeans and calf-high snow boots, with her matching chocolate-brown coat and gloves? She was just so put together when Lisa felt like a train wreck on a caffeine buzz. She pulled to a stop, reminding herself to play cool, but as soon as she hopped out she realized she had no idea how to greet her. Just say hello? Hug her? Kiss her? She wanted all of the above, but what kind of tone did they need to set? She stopped a few feet away and kind of shrugged awkwardly.

Marty seemed to do the same, though she might have leaned in for a hug, or maybe not. The silence plus awkward leaning-or-not-leaning went on for about ten seconds, which felt like ten seconds too long, before they both laughed nervously.

"This all your luggage?" Lisa asked.

"Yes, I only expected to be here one night."

"Right, well, I like a woman who packs light," she said, feeling a little better to have made her first genuine, if completely inane, comment of the day. "Hop in."

She tossed Marty's one carry-on suitcase into the back of her Subaru Forester and climbed back into the driver's seat.

"Great car," Marty said.

"Thanks, it's good in the winter weather."

"I wasn't sure if I should expect something more ostentatious, what with you being shockingly rich and all."

"You caught that, huh?"

"You mentioned it last night."

Lisa smiled as she pulled out onto the Kensington Expressway. "Did I say that in my out-loud voice?"

"Maybe a time or two."

"Well there's something you should know then, and it's probably best to just get it out there right away."

"What, you're not rich?" Marty teased.

"No, I actually am," Lisa admitted a little bit uncomfortably. "It's just the rest of it, the wine and the tuxedo and the dancing, it was a special occasion, you know?"

"You mean you don't just lounge around your house in a tie and tails all day?"

"No." Lisa gestured to her attire. "I'm more of a jeans and hoodie kind of person."

"What a relief, because if I had to put my little black heels back on this morning, I'm not sure the slipper would actually still fit after the ball."

Lisa relaxed a little bit. She glanced away from the road to see the corner of Marty's mouth quirk up. "What?"

"Nothing, I was just letting it sink in that I have an extra day here. In the airport that seemed like a burden, something to be managed, but now, with you, it seems more like a gift."

The hair on Lisa's arms stood up in anticipation, and she quickly worked to tamp down expectations. "I'm not exactly a shiny-ribbon-and-bow kind of person."

"Hmm."

"What?" Her defenses rose. Was she being judged? Was Marty disappointed in her, or worse, was she overanalyzing the comment?

"I wondered what I said to imply I wanted shiny ribbons and bows. Maybe I gave you the wrong impression."

"Just the thing about extra time together being a gift. I just don't want you to regret that."

"Here's the thing. I don't really do regret. Not over things like extended vacations, especially ones out of my control," Marty said evenly. "I try, though, not always with success, to accept there's a reason for everything and try to take whatever that reason is for whatever it's worth."

Lisa sighed. So there it was. The life-coach speech they'd avoided all last night had finally reared its insanely calm head. "Right, that's Life Coach 101?"

"Sure, it's like first week of classes material," Marty said lightly. "And your tone clearly indicates you're a big fan of basic life-coaching concepts."

"Does that offend you?"

"It amuses me." She did sound genuinely amused, which only added to Lisa's frustration.

"Because you know all about me and I know nothing about you?"

Marty laughed outright. "I hate to break it to you, but Elaine and I don't really spend our sessions talking about you."

Lisa snorted in appreciation of the dig. "Sure you don't."

"I am amused because last night, when we actually were taking every moment as a gift, you were more open and quite frankly more fun, but today when I gave that way of being a name, or the concept behind it, you suddenly clammed up."

"I didn't clam up."

Lisa looked over just in time to see Marty roll her eyes. "Hey, I thought life coaches weren't supposed to roll their eyes at people."

"Okay, I think you need to pull over."

"Now?"

"Yes."

Lisa edged the car over to the shoulder of the road and flipped on the hazard lights.

"I am a life coach," Marty said, matter-of-factly.

"No shit."

"But, and this is a big but, I am not *your* life coach."

Lisa opened her mouth, but Marty cut her off. "I'm not looking to be your life coach. And even if I were, I cannot be your life coach because I'm not neutral toward you in any way."

"No?"

"No. My regard for you isn't abstract. I like you. A lot, actually. Or I did, before you started trying to make me not like you." Marty shook her head. "No, even that's not true. I still like you. I think you're funny and interesting and a good dancer once you relax."

Lisa smiled in spite of the *but* she expected to come at the end of this conversation.

"More than that, though, I cannot be your life coach, nor do I want to be your life coach, because I also think you're a really good kisser."

"Well…okay," Lisa said resolutely. Not a brilliant response to such a wonderful confession, but it was all she had.

"Okay?"

"Yeah. Okay." She smiled both in relief and with the stirrings of real happiness she hadn't let herself indulge until now. "So if this isn't going to turn into an extended life-coach session, what do you want to do today?"

"Well the possibilities are endless now, aren't they?" Marty's smile was playful, coy, and damn tempting. "But I find that when facing the possibility of a big day, it's good to start with the most important things first."

"So…lunch?" Lisa asked.

Marty laughed. "If you continue to think with your stomach, you might actually be a woman after my own heart."

Lisa grinned as she pulled back out into traffic. She wasn't sure she really believed she could come anywhere near Marty's heart, but there wasn't any harm in enjoying the idea a little bit longer.

Chapter Four

"So, I know you come from the big city and all," Lisa said holding open the door to Saigon Café, "but I think this place will rival anything you eat at home."

Marty stopped and pursed her lips. "Because I'm Asian?"

"What?" Lisa froze, all the blood draining from her face.

"Saigon Café? Just like I eat at home? Do you think all Asian people eat pad Thai all day, every day?"

"Oh God, no, I just thought…" Lisa stammered. "I meant New York City. Not home like your house, I didn't mean to imply you were Asian. I mean clearly you are Asian, but I didn't assume…shit."

Marty burst out laughing. She laughed so hard her sides ached.

Lisa stared at her, slack-jawed.

"I knew what you meant. I'm just messing with you."

"Holy shit." Lisa sagged against the bar. "That was pretty awful of you…and awesome."

Marty smiled as the hostess led them to the table. Pride filled her chest at having been the one to punk Lisa. Maybe she wanted to prove she wasn't serious all the time, the way Lisa seemed to expect from life coaches. Or maybe she'd wanted to throw her off her guard, take the wall she'd put up between them down a level or two. More likely, she'd just felt comfortable enough to let loose a little bit. Either way, Lisa's reaction had been priceless.

They sat down, and Lisa sipped her water, eyeing Marty suspiciously as she slipped off her coat. "You're not supposed to joke about racism, you know."

"You're not supposed to lie to life coaches to score your best friend a date, either."

"Oh, I see. Paybacks for Elaine, huh?"

"No, I think you did the right thing there, or maybe not the right thing, but a good thing."

"So you were just messing with me for your own amusement?"

"Absolutely. And I have to admit, you were very amusing." She didn't try to suppress her grin.

"Yeah, well, for a computer programmer, being seen as anti-Asian is kind of the death knell."

"Oh, so now you're saying all Asians are good at computer programming?"

"No." Lisa stayed cool this time. "I think you'd actually be pretty terrible at it."

Marty couldn't even pretend to pout this time. "You're spot-on there. I still have trouble running my iPhone some days. Don't even talk to me about online banking."

"I have to balance Joey's checkbook most of the time."

"She still has a checkbook?"

"I know, right? I'm surrounded by troglodytes."

Marty laughed at Lisa's good-natured insult. "I don't know many people who use the word troglodyte."

"Maybe that's because you don't know many people who are so regularly imposed on by them."

"Or maybe it's because I don't know many computer geniuses. I suppose after MIT, regular people always fall short in that area for you."

"No. MIT was too stuffy. Everyone knew everything, or they thought they did. Most of them only knew a lot about the very tiny world they occupied."

That was awfully insightful. "Is that why you came back to Buffalo?"

Lisa shrugged as the waitress approached. They both ordered, and Marty wondered if Lisa was happy to have dodged her last question. Very little about her demeanor had changed, but the lowering of her eyes and the slight twitch in her smile indicated a momentary lapse in her playfulness. She wondered what hid beneath the façade, but she'd promised not to push.

"I'm not an East Coast kind of person," Lisa finally said. "I'm a Rust Belt kid, at least on the inside."

"Were your parents a lot like Joey's dad?"

She shook her head. "They couldn't be more different, on any level."

Marty waited, spellbound by the flicker of sadness in Lisa's eyes.

"But Joey's family became my family. I spent more time at their house than my own. All the money in the world can't buy a connection like that, you know?" She straightened up and her smile returned. The sadness was gone, or at the very least buried now. "Besides, without me around, Joey would've never gotten a date. Someone has to look after that loveable muck."

"Yes, everyone needs a friend like that."

"What about you?" Lisa asked. "Who gets you into the good kind of trouble?"

Marty thought about the answer. She had friends, a few of them close, a few of them long-term, though no one fell into both categories. "Well, I can't say that anyone in my life is particularly reliable as a troublemaker."

"You know what they say, if you look around the room and can't find the troublemaker, it's probably you."

Marty laughed. "I've never heard that before, but I think you may be right."

"Really? Are you the rabble-rouser in the Marty Maine circle of acquaintances?"

A million memories came back to bombard her at once, from childhood pranks, to bending rules at work, to jaywalking the streets of New York on a daily basis. "Wow, I think I might be. I am the troublemaker!"

"I feel like that's quite a breakthrough," Lisa said smugly.

"I see myself in a whole new light."

"There you go, life-coached!"

"Life-coached?"

"Sure, isn't that what you people say when someone has the lightbulb moment?"

"No." Marty laughed. "I've never used the term life-coached as a catch phrase."

"You should. That's good marketing."

"I'm pretty sure my professional organization would be opposed to using the name of the entire profession as a personal branding tool."

"What do you care?" Lisa said, leaning forward conspiratorially. "You're the rule breaker."

❖

"Okay, I have to tell you something," Marty said as they left the restaurant.

Lisa stopped, her heart hammering in her chest. Those words rarely meant anything good. "Lay it on me."

"You were right, that meal was better than anything I've had at home, Asian heritage or not."

It took a moment for the words to sink in and several more long seconds to realize that was the end of Marty's confession. Food. She sighed heavily. "Wow. Okay. Yeah, it's pretty damn good, right?"

"Wait." Marty rested a hand gently on her arm. "What did you expect me to say?"

Lisa shrugged and started toward the car again. "I don't know. Could've been anything."

"Like what?"

She didn't want to give too much away. "Like, I don't know, maybe you have a contagious disease, or maybe you're looking to score some cocaine, or maybe you changed your mind and would rather stay at the airport instead of with me." Did she say that last part aloud?

Marty shook her head slightly. "That's so silly."

"I thought life coaches weren't supposed to tell people their fears were silly."

"Wait a second." Marty pretended to pull a book out of thin air and flip through it. "Let me check the life-coach handbook."

Lisa stood there, rolling her eyes while Marty played out the gag and closed her imaginary book. "No. Sorry, don't see anything here about me not mocking a non-client's unfounded delusions of me not liking her."

"You're kind of a smart-ass," Lisa finally said, grudgingly.

"I feel like, coming from you, that's a compliment."

"It totally is."

Marty smiled and Lisa returned the expression. Her cheeks felt a little sore from doing that so much. She generally thought of herself as a pretty happy person. If someone had asked her a week ago if she smiled a lot, she would've said yes, but somehow she felt like she'd smiled more with Marty in less than twenty-four hours than she'd smiled in a year. How was that possible?

Sure, they'd spent one pretty amazing evening together, but that was all on fake time. Magical wedding time. Time spent on Joey and Elaine's romantic stage. But she wasn't anything like Joey. And yet, here she was with a smart, funny woman who not only wanted to be with her, she was totally making that point by busting her chops. Hell, if she didn't know better, she'd start to think the magic of this moment might really be theirs alone.

But she did know better. Marty was killing time. She wouldn't be here if not for a canceled flight, and what's more, even if she did stay, could she really find Lisa compelling long-term? No one else had, and not just lovers either. The question about her parents had driven home that message again.

"What's next, Buffalo tour guide?" Marty asked, pulling her out of her internal beat down.

"Well…" Lisa drew out the word. "Here's the thing. I don't know much about you."

"What's on the list so far?"

"You're a life coach."

"As you have established multiple times."

"You like fine wine and the chicken dance."

"Check to the wine, and I do like the way *you* do the chicken dance."

Lisa grinned and started to make another joke, but her breath grew shallow as another memory came sharply into focus. "You like snow-filled balconies in soft light."

Marty's lips curled up in the most beautiful way, and Lisa's heart rate rose with them. Suddenly there were no cars, no buildings, no people passing by. Only Marty and her slow, knowing smile as she whispered, "What else?"

"You like dashingly handsome maids of ill repute who rock a tuxedo jacket."

Marty nodded slowly, her pupils dilating and her lips parting. Lisa's fingers tingled with the urge to touch her, to caress her cheek. To kiss her. The urge struck so sudden and strong, it took a couple more seconds for the knowledge that she could actually do it to materialize.

She could kiss Marty. Right here, on the sidewalk, in the light of day, with nary a drop of wine in their systems. What kind of magic lasted so long past midnight?

She didn't know what to do. Learning magic existed was not the same as learning how to wield it.

"What else do you know?" Marty asked.

"You…" The panic welled up quickly. She couldn't do this. She couldn't feel this, and even though all the reasons were so hazy right now, they were there, and real. As real as the sweat beading on the back of her neck. "You like cake."

"What?"

"Cake." She rubbed her hand over her face and tried to take a deep breath before saying, "I know you like cake."

Marty blinked a few times. "I do. I like cake."

The absurdity of that statement was evident in her tone, but Lisa clung to the words anyway. "Then cake it is."

"Cake? Why not." Marty laughed again. At least it was a genuine laugh. That did a lot to help the sinking feeling in the pit of her stomach.

Lisa kicked herself as she opened the car door for Marty. She'd blown it. But damn it, she'd never felt such a sudden catch of desire and actually had it returned. She needed more time, more practice, but what she wouldn't give to have that moment back.

Still, now she knew the possibility existed. She could at least be ready to act the next time it materialized.

"God," she mumbled as she walked around to the driver's side door, "please let there be a next time."

❖

Marty was still suffering from romantic whiplash when they pulled up in front of a place called Fairy Cakes, but the joy on Lisa's face as she looked from her to the sign was hard not to catch.

"See"—Lisa nodded toward the bakery—"you like cakes. We have cakes. You should eat cakes."

The logic was flawless, really, even if a little bit abrupt. And who argued with someone who wanted to give them cake, but dessert had never felt like such a consolation prize before. Back on the sidewalk she'd been almost certain Lisa would kiss her, and right or wrong she'd wanted her to. Now she just wanted to know what had made her decide not to.

By the time she got unbuckled and opened the door to the car, Lisa was at her side. "The snow's packed a little high there."

"A little?" Marty asked. "More like a foot and a half."

"Haven't you heard, everything's bigger in Buffalo?"

"I thought that was Texas."

"They're overcompensating," Lisa said, offering her hand to help her over the thick crust of snow between the street and the sidewalk. "Every time I see a guy in a big hat and a bigger truck, I think, 'The lady doth protest too much.'"

"You'd probably get shot for that in parts of the state."

"See, Buffalo is safer too. We spend our energy controlling the guns, not our women," Lisa said, letting go of her hand only to hold the door for her.

"Wow, a chivalrous feminist," Marty said, meaning to sound playful, but she clearly heard the hint of flirtation behind it, and from the glint in Lisa's eyes, she had too.

Thankfully, as soon as they stepped fully inside, the smell of fresh-baked cake and a display case of cupcakes drenched in decadent frostings distracted them. Searching for a safer hunger than the one that had nipped at her outside, she perused the menu. From the classic red velvet or German chocolate to the playful pancakes and bacon or root-beer float, every option seemed better than the one before.

"What's your poison?" Lisa asked, low and close behind her.

Goose bumps rose along Marty's arms at the memories that tone sent cresting through her. What little focus she'd had vanished. She fought the urge to turn slowly toward Lisa and did her best to stave off the surge of warmth at the prospect of finding herself once again wrapped in her embrace.

"I, well, I just don't know what the right answer is."

"I don't think there's a right answer here," Lisa said.

"I know that. I really do, but surely one option is better than the others."

"Better for who? You? Me? Better for other people waiting for us to figure out what we want?"

Marty glanced around. There was no one else in line. She sighed heavily. "I feel like the cupcakes just got more important."

"Metaphorically?" Lisa asked.

"Yes and no."

"So important and complicated," Lisa said. "That sounds like a barrel full of monkeys."

"Well let's not get too down about it, because, you know, *cupcakes*."

"In that case, I want one with sprinkles," Lisa said.

Marty nodded resolutely. "I want the salted caramel."

"I want the candy bar one too."

"Oh, if we're admitting to wanting more than we should," Marty jumped in, "I want the one with bacon on it."

"Respect." Lisa held out her fist, and Marty couldn't help but laugh as she tapped it with her own.

Lisa had done it again. She took a totally loaded situation, acknowledged it, smiled through it, and moved on. It was an impressive skill most people would accept graciously, even gratefully, but Marty wondered where that skill had developed. She'd promised not to push or coach, but she'd started to notice a back-and-forth pattern in Lisa's attention and her affections.

Lisa placed their order and had everything boxed up to go while Marty pondered her options. Life coach or not, she wanted to understand this woman, to really know her. Of course that option came with risks. Maybe she wouldn't like what she found behind the social veneer. Who knew how many sweet memories she'd tarnish in the process. Then again, what if Lisa did open up, and underneath that class-clown exterior she was actually as amazing as Marty suspected? The problem then wouldn't be how long she'd have to stay, but rather how she'd be able to force herself to leave.

"You ready now?" Lisa asked, pulling her back into the moment.

"Yes. I think I am."

"Great. Where to next? Winter activities galore? Sledding? Ice skating? Curling?"

"Actually, I'd hoped for something a little more low-key."

"Snowshoeing?"

Marty almost caved to Lisa's exuberance, but something told her if she had any hope of cracking that playful shell, she needed to approach the situation head-on. “Actually, I’d really like to see your place. Would you mind taking me back there now?”

Lisa’s jaw dropped and a quick blush rushed to her face. “Yeah, home is good.”

The honest reaction left Marty feeling more than a little gratified, even if she hadn’t meant for the proposition to sound quite so risqué.

Chapter Five

Home is good? Seriously? A beautiful woman just asked to go back to her place and the best response she could come up with was *Home is good*? Damn. She needed to up her game, but women like Marty didn't generally ask to go back to her place in the middle of the afternoon, or ever.

"Be cool, keep it together, act natural," she muttered as she walked around the back of the car to get Marty's suitcase out. She was making too big a deal of this. She already knew Marty would be staying with her tonight. Did it matter when they ended up there? "She asked to see your house, not to have sex."

"What's that?" Marty asked.

"Nothing."

"Do you often talk to yourself?"

"Yeah," Lisa admitted sheepishly. "I guess I do."

"I find that endearing."

Lisa smiled and grabbed Marty's suitcase. "Endearing. Go figure. Most people would've gone with unsettling, or maybe unstable."

"I'm not like most people," Marty said as she turned and climbed the front steps to the house.

Lisa watched her, particularly enjoying the sway of her hips. *No, I don't suppose you are.*

"Wow, what a beautiful home," Marty said as she walked through the front door.

Lisa let herself feel a little bit of pride. It was a nice place. Not a mansion by any standard, but the old Victorian had abundant charm. The open foyer still had the original hardwood floors and trim, and the hand-carved railing to the staircase was likely original to the house. "You want the full tour?"

"Of course."

"Let's take this upstairs and start there," Lisa said, lifting the suitcase once more. At the top of the staircase she pointed toward a closed door. "That's Elaine's office. I don't go in there, but I'm sure you can."

"It's okay, I've seen it on Skype."

"Right." Lisa fought a wave of nervousness. She didn't need to be reminded that Marty regularly saw the one part of her home she considered to not really be hers anymore.

"And here's Elaine and Joey's room." She opened a door across the hall and set the suitcase down with a little thud. "We can leave your stuff in here for tonight since they won't be home until late tomorrow."

The baby-blue room with white trim and white curtains housed a queen-sized bed covered in what appeared to be a handmade quilt. A small table stood on each side of the bed, and two dressers each topped with photographs were the only other pieces of furniture in the room. Clean and uncluttered, but not sterile either. Everything just fit, causing a little tug in Lisa's chest.

"It's lovely. So very them," Marty said.

She had to agree. Calm, cheerful, and homey. She couldn't help but wonder about the contrast to her own space.

"Yeah. When Elaine moved in, I worried she'd change all of Joey's stuff, and in some ways she did, because all the hockey gear is gone, and so is the TV, but…you know." Lisa shrugged, worried she'd been about to give away too much.

"No," Marty said, her dark eyes attentive and full of questions. "What?"

"Well"—she shifted from one foot to the other before finally saying—"now you can see the quilt Joey's mom made, and the tables we built with her dad in high school. I guess in some ways getting rid of the extra stuff let the things that really matter show through."

Marty lifted her hand as if she intended to touch Lisa's face before letting it fall to her forearm, but the less intimate touch was no less powerful as it sent a tingle through her. "That's such a beautiful sentiment."

Lisa shrugged again, unintentionally causing Marty's hand to fall away. She regretted the move immediately. She hadn't intended to get all heavy in the first place, much less enjoy Marty's reaction to her introspection, but she did, and she had, and then as quickly as she'd sparked that connection, she'd broken it. Maybe it was for the best. Neither one of them should get too comfortable with those kinds of conversations, or they might start to expect them.

She backed out the door before pointing to the next one. "This room is my office, and my bedroom's across the hall. We don't have to go in those. They're boring."

The humor returned to Marty's smile. "I think I should be the judge of that. You can tell a lot about a person by the spaces they choose to occupy."

"That's what I was afraid of," she muttered, but she swung open the door anyway. Maybe that would end the little flirtations that didn't actually feel so little anymore.

Marty paused in the doorway to the office, her smile polite, restrained, hard to read.

Lisa looked from the antique desk to the black ergonomic chair to the bookshelves housing as many tech gadgets and toys as they did books on everything from local history to computer coding. It was a hodgepodge, but it was clean and neat.

"You don't actually work here, do you?"

Lisa looked again. What had she seen to make that completely accurate assumption?

"It's got your touches," Marty said, nodding toward a Lego replica of the Death Star. "But it's not lived in. I can't picture you sitting at a desk like that for very long."

"No." Lisa wasn't sure if the tightness in her chest stemmed from fear at being such an easy read, or pride that Marty had paid enough attention to her over their short time together to make such accurate assumptions. "You're right. I mostly work at the coffee house where Joey works, or worked, but also in bed."

Marty arched her eyebrows. "Bed?"

Lisa didn't know whether to be happy Marty skipped over the part about Joey leaving the coffee house or embarrassed she'd honed in on the bed thing.

Marty seemed oblivious to her conflict, or maybe she just pretended to be as she backed out of the office and reached for the door across the hall. "May I?"

"Sure." She tried to play cool, but a rush of cold sweat pricked her neck. If Marty could tell so many things about her office, what would she learn from her bedroom?

Marty opened the door, and even in profile her smile appeared immediate and genuine. She felt dizzy with relief, like such a kid, showing off her room to a prospective bed friend, but Marty simultaneously meant more and less than that. She didn't know what to say, so she fell back on what she knew and went for the quick joke. "That's where the magic happens. It's okay to stand in awe."

"Thanks," Marty said wryly. "I wouldn't want to disturb the computer-genius mojo."

Lisa peeked over her shoulder to see what she saw. Certainly nothing that bespoke of genius. Rumpled sheets topped with a small mountain of pillows. Pieces of her tuxedo on the floor. An iPad and MacBook both open on the bed. All in all, a mess. And the few things that were in their rightful place, a photo of her and Joey sledding together as kids, an old pond-hockey trophy, an autographed Bills football, were hardly high-end. If anything, looking at the room through Marty's eyes, she would've thought the décor hinted at college dorm meets frat house.

"This is much more you."

"Thanks?"

What if she didn't want it to be her? No, jeez, where did that come from?

Marty laughed her light, easy laugh. "I mean it. This space is lived-in. You're not showing off for anyone. You're not putting up a front. You like sports and comfort and being connected."

"You see all those things from looking at my mess?"

"I see those things from looking at you."

Lisa had no quick comeback, no smart retort. Part of her still wanted to be careful, to avoid getting too close, too fast, but damn it, another part of her, the bigger part right now, liked the way Marty saw her.

So instead of second-guessing, she chose to try something new and just accept a genuine compliment without waiting for the other shoe to drop.

"Thank you," she said. And it felt nice.

❖

Something had changed in Lisa upstairs, just a little thing, but Marty was highly aware of the shift as they headed back downstairs. There'd been no smart remark, no sassy retort, and while Lisa's quick wit had never been anything less than enjoyable, she found her sincerity pretty compelling too. Lisa's insight about Elaine's presence in Joey's space had been surprising, and her pleasure at having her own haphazard style affirmed hinted at deeper insecurity. Still, she offered no sign of insecurity as she swung open a big set of pocket doors, revealing a gorgeous living room.

"This is the showpiece of the house, unless you like kitchens."

"I do love kitchens, but I see something I like even more."

"It's me, isn't it?"

Marty shook her head and chuckled. There was the old Lisa again. "That too, but I meant the fireplace."

Lisa turned toward the beautiful cast-iron fireplace. "Yeah, that's pretty nice too. I guess."

Marty heard the pride she tried to keep in check. The cast-iron insert flared toward a deep blue tile surround, which rippled out to a stunningly finished dark wood mantel.

"Did it come like this?"

"No. It was a mess when we moved in, but I saw the potential, and by potential I mean Joey's potential. She did the restoration and built the mantel, while I kept her fully stocked in supplies and beer."

"Sounds like a good team."

"We were."

"Were?"

"Are." Lisa stiffened. "I said *are*."

Marty stared at her for a moment. Lisa had been crass and sarcastic, with a flair for embellishment, but that was the first outright lie of their short relationship. She should call her on it. Lying was a nonstarter. They couldn't go anywhere authentic from there, and authenticity mattered more than virtually anything else in a relationship.

"You want to see the kitchen now?"

"Sure."

"It's really Joey's domain," Lisa said, walking quickly ahead. "She likes to cook. I mostly just use the microwave. Do you cook?"

"I do." Marty eased back in as best she could while still pondering Lisa's fib and her own willingness to let it pass. "But I only have a small place in the city, so I don't entertain much, and it's not as much fun cooking for one."

"I know, right?"

"On the other hand," Marty said, looking from the six-burner stove to the ample granite counter space, "it does seem a shame to let a kitchen like this go unused. I think I'd learn to cook for one."

"Yeah." Lisa sighed. "Maybe I'll have to."

Marty eyed her seriously. Something had shifted again. This see-sawing between confidence and resignation confused her. Lisa seemed smart, funny, and successful, with a beautiful home and people who loved her. Most of the time she behaved like a woman highly aware of all her blessings to the point of bordering on cocky, but every now and then Marty saw a flash of something beneath her smooth surface. Last night she'd been drawn to the depth, believing it hinted at a powerful reserve of compassion, but the more she glimpsed she also recognized a melancholy, a conflict—hidden hurt or fear, or maybe both.

"So that's the tour of Chateau KnappLangRaitt." Lisa also worked to bounce back quickly. "Unless you want to see the tool shed."

"Actually, I'd like to go back to the highlight reel."

Lisa's smile was slow and mischievous once again. "My bedroom?"

"I was thinking about the fireplace."

"Oh, well, in that case." She pretend pouted. "Go make yourself comfortable, and I'll go grab some firewood, and we'll see if we can heat the place up a bit."

"That," Marty said, "is the best double entendre you've made today."

Lisa once again looked full of herself as she ambled with contrived casualness out the door. God, what about this woman pulled her in so much? Marty pondered the question as she grabbed a few oversized pillows from the couch and spread a large maroon blanket across the wood floor.

Lisa had so many sides battling to reveal or not reveal themselves, and yet everything Marty saw only made her want more. She liked her confident side, her sarcastic side, her humorous side, her irreverent side, but she also felt a connection to the flashes of insecurity, the brief releases of introspection, her sincere desire to please, and even the subtle sadness that surfaced between her quick, easy jokes.

Lisa tromped back into the house and kicked off her boots at the door while carrying a stack of seasoned logs. Marty admitted to herself that their connection wasn't a purely emotional one either. She'd never been one to swoon for unexpected bouts of butchness any more than she did for displays of high femme, but her heart rate accelerated noticeably as Lisa shed her hoodie, revealing a simple gray waffle-weave long sleeve with two of the four buttons at her throat open. There was something alluring about those buttons, though she wasn't sure what she liked more, the open ones or the ones she realized might be hers to undo.

Lisa rolled up her sleeves and set to work stacking the wood just so. There was a comfort in the way she occupied this space, an assuredness about going about the task, so simple, so natural, so competent. No performance.

Striking a single match, she set the kindling ablaze and monitored it intently, until the flames licked the larger pieces, curling their edges orange before coaxing them into the fire as well. There was something hypnotic about the slow spread, the steady crawling consumption, and she felt it slowly tug at her own core.

When it became clear everything was progressing as it should, Lisa turned to her once more. "You warming up?"

"Very much so."

She smiled.

Marty smiled in return. Suddenly they were fully back in the moment, like they'd been on the terrace the night before, only not there. Here, now, together.

"I like the little nest you made," Lisa finally said.

"It's big enough for two." The boldness of the comment no longer surprised her.

Lisa didn't hesitate as she crawled across the blanket, up to the pillow. She relaxed into the cushion, stretching her long legs and resting one hand behind her head. God, she looked so damn languid. Marty couldn't help snuggling down a little closer beside her. The warmth of the fire radiating across her toes wasn't much compared to the heat spreading through her chest.

How had she gone from doubting Lisa's honesty to wanting nothing more than to trace her fingers lightly up the line of buttons along her shirt? And in the space of only a few minutes? Maybe Lisa wasn't the only one doing a dance of two steps forward and one step back. Or was it two steps back and one step forward? She couldn't quite feel sure of anything with the light rise and fall of Lisa's chest so close, so soothing. She could quickly lose all ability to think at all. It would be so easy to just surrender to the physical comfort of the space, and the woman currently sharing it with her.

No, there were too many unknowns, too much uncertainty. She didn't have to pull away completely, but she had to regain some of the balance she always strove for. Rolling onto her side, she propped herself up on one elbow and asked the question she wouldn't have wanted to answer in that moment. "What are you thinking?"

"I can't remember the last time I had a little indoors campout," Lisa said softly.

"No? But you do remember having had them in the past?"

"Joey's house had a woodstove when we were growing up. The living room was always so much warmer than the bedroom. I didn't really realize then, but her parents were probably making some tough decisions about food or heat. I didn't really understand how poor they were." She rolled over to face Marty, the depth of emotion in her eyes holding her as spellbound as the wistfulness in her words. "I thought lying on the floor while her mom played the piano or her dad listened to football games on the radio was the best treat ever."

"That sounds lovely."

"I think it was more than that. I think those moments did a lot to undo my ideas of what it meant to be rich or successful. True comfort goes a long way to combat hollow opulence, you know?"

"Wow. You just got all reflective on me."

"Sorry." Lisa blushed.

"No." Marty put a hand on her shoulder. "Don't be. You shared a beautiful sentiment. You don't hear many shockingly rich thirtysomethings long for days when they were poor."

"How many shockingly rich thirtysomethings who used to be poor do you know?"

"I guess not many." Marty chuckled, then thought harder. "Actually, I guess just you."

"Nope. Not even me. I come from money. I'm actually the failure of the family."

Marty laughed outright. "Oh, I'm sure you're a real disappointment."

Lisa didn't respond, at least not verbally, but the tightened set of her jaw as she stared at the ceiling said plenty.

"Seriously?" Marty asked, unsure whether to feel sad or outraged. "What kind of parents aren't thrilled their kid graduated from MIT?"

"The kind who went to Harvard medical."

Marty took a second to let that sink in, fighting her initial rush to assure Lisa her credentials were no less impressive. She understood the hurt she'd heard there wasn't about acceptance rates or the prestige of an academic program.

In her silent reflection Lisa rushed to fill the void. "My mother's a research biologist, and my dad is a surgical oncologist. My older brother is a pediatric radiation oncologist."

"I know what all those words mean," Marty said slowly, "but I'm parsing them out in my head because I've never heard so many of them strung together before."

"They cure cancer," Lisa said dryly. "Everyone in my family is a top physician or researcher in their respective fields of curing cancer. Everyone but me."

"Okay," Marty said calmly, letting the weight of that understanding settle into her gut and sag against her bones. That sort of legacy was not an unfamiliar burden to her mind or body. If anything, it felt too close to protect her neutrality.

"I help the rich get richer," Lisa continued. "I'm a one percenter who works for other one percenters."

"Do you like what you do?"

"It's not curing cancer."

"But do you enjoy it? Do you find it fulfilling?"

"Yeah, of course I do. I like doing things no one else has ever thought to do before. Coding is like this impossible puzzle. I try and try and try until I hit the right piece in the right spot, and suddenly everyone can see the picture."

Marty lay back and smiled at the celling, glad to hear Lisa articulate some passion. "I'd never really thought about computer coding before."

"And?"

"And it's amazing."

Lisa snorted.

"You don't have to believe me, but I've always taken for granted how everything just appears when I turn on my computer. And my emails zip around the world. I communicate with clients all over the country with my voice and my writing and my video chats. I've always thought I did those things on my own. I wrote the email, I made the calls, I took the classes, but it's not really that simple is it?"

Lisa shook her head.

"Someone like you made all of that possible. Someone spent hours if not years typing in languages I can't understand to make these things work the way I want them to. Why can't you see that's amazing?"

"I didn't invent email or online education or Skype."

"Okay, but you did invent something?"

Lisa shifted.

"Something people needed if it made you enough money to be shockingly rich."

"I'm not shockingly rich, really," Lisa backpedaled.

"Sorry, you give women tuxes on a whim, you owned a four-bedroom Victorian house as little more than an adolescent, you—" She started to say, *You throw lavish parties for your friends' wedding receptions*, but she caught herself. "You're rich by my standards, and I don't know why you won't tell me why, unless the computer business is an elaborate cover for your organized-crime connections."

"Well there's that, but drug kingpins don't make as much as they used to."

"Nice try on the deflection, clever and funny."

"And yet ineffective?"

Marty waited while Lisa shifted her position again. This time she sat up and looked down at her. "I invented a program that links up businesses to investment banks and venture capitalists."

"That sounds positively evil. Does it work like a phone book? 'Cause in my day, we used phone books to find a bank."

"It's not quite that simple."

"So why don't you skip to the sinister part?"

"It's not sinister, really, not in the up-front sense. You know when you shop on a major website or look at movies on Netflix and they have the little suggestion box that says, *If you like the* Beauty and the Beast *soundtrack you might also like the* Little Mermaid *soundtrack*?"

"Yes." Marty smiled at the Disney song allusions. "Thank you for speaking my language."

"Well, instead of assessing singing animals, the program I wrote assesses businesses and gives reports saying things like, *If you enjoyed your hostile takeover of this business, you might enjoy the hostile takeover of this one too.* Or *If you liked raping and pillaging this mom-and-pop operation, you might want to consider raping and pillaging this small company as well.*"

"Wow." Marty was mildly impressed such a program existed and had actually been invented by the person sitting across from her, but she was more interested in how Lisa chose to view her work. "That must've taken a lot of time and intelligence to recognize all the factors involved in a decision like that, then make them all work together to form a coherent picture."

"Oh, it did. I took the expertise of many and used it to put most of them out of a job."

"Like the car?"

"What?"

"You know those nasty things that get people across the country and to work and to hospitals and everywhere. The guy who invented those things put all the horse-buggy makers out of business," Marty said dryly. "That guy was a real asshole."

Lisa's mouth turned up a little bit at the corner. "I see what you did there."

"Good, I don't like to have to beat someone over the head with my metaphors."

Lisa sighed and stretched out her legs again. "I made my decisions. I live with them, quite comfortably really."

"So you still work for those banks?"

"No, not for years now. I sold them the program for a nice chunk of change. It's theirs to wield as they please. Now I do other stuff, contract work mostly."

Something didn't make sense. Lisa's dissonance seemed too

neatly resolved for the amount of conflict she still seemed to feel. She was still holding something back, some part of the story.

"Ready for those cupcakes?" Lisa asked, standing and stretching her arms above her head. When she did, her shirt rode up, revealing a flash of smooth skin at her midriff, and suddenly Marty's desire to keep her close wasn't purely emotional.

And yet, cupcakes always seemed like a good idea. Lisa clearly wanted to put some distance between herself and the subjects they'd broached, and Marty could probably use something to do with her hands in order to keep from reaching out for more than she should really want in this situation.

Cupcakes would pose a delicious and comforting distraction for both of them. And she had no doubt the things they were dodging would still be there long after the sugar rush had faded.

Chapter Six

Lisa took her time getting the cupcakes out of the box and putting them on two plates, grateful to have a few seconds to clear her head and steady her hands. Life coaches were a tricky bunch—they could start what seemed like a totally normal conversation, then end it with you telling them things you didn't tell anyone. Or at least, things she hadn't told anyone in years.

She called bullshit on Marty's unassuming interrogation style with her impromptu floor couch and the seductive way she propped herself up on her elbow to look casually sexy with her curves outlined in the warm glow of the fire. She'd practically set the scene for a damn Hallmark holiday special. And she'd almost fallen for it. She'd let out way more information than she'd intended to, but at least she'd left the biggest of all her cats in the bag o' crazy.

But was it really crazy? She'd made her choices, and she'd made peace with them. She didn't like everything she'd put out into the world, but given the same choice again, she'd make it quickly and gladly. Just because another good-bye was on the horizon didn't mean she had any regrets about what she'd done to try to stop the first one, or what she'd been able to do for the people she loved since then.

"Damn it," she swore, out loud this time. Why was she harping on all this? If she could've been angry at Marty, she would have been. She had no right to meddle, but she looked so damn beautiful while doing it, it hardly felt intrusive at the time. Well two could play that part. She might have been off her game a little bit, but she was aware enough to realize Marty wasn't immune to the situation she'd cultivated. The casual touching wasn't quite so casual anymore, and she'd seen her already dark irises swirl with something deeper as her eyes raked over her body.

If something had to tip the balance between them, she'd much rather land on the physical side of that fence than the emotional outpouring one.

"Did you get lost in your cavernous kitchen?" Marty finally called.

"Nope." She grabbed a bottle of pinot noir and quickly slipped a bottle opener into her back pocket before stacking the cupcake plates waitress style and hooking the stems of two wineglasses between her fingers.

"Voilà, one afternoon picnic of decadence at your service." She presented her cache of treats with a flourish.

"Wow, did you work in food service growing up?"

"No, I'm just a glutton who's learned to juggle her addictions with grace."

Marty took the wineglasses. "I appreciate a woman who doesn't let her vices get in the way of style."

Lisa remembered to take the corkscrew out of her pocket before sitting back down on the blanket and promptly put it to use.

"I also appreciate that we don't mind the social edicts about drinking midday."

"Well the thing is, I was pouring out a lot of personal information there, and you weren't returning the favor quite as much, or even at all."

"So you thought you'd loosen my lips with a little vino?"

"And sugar"—Lisa nodded to the cupcakes—"don't forget the sugar."

"Well, add your valiant effort to the growing list of things I appreciate, but I hate to say it was unwarranted."

"Because you won't spill?"

"No, because I will, even without bribery or buttering up."

Lisa eyed her, hoping she came across as suspicious, but her gaze might have lingered on her beautifully soft lips a bit too long.

"You don't believe me?"

"It just seems like I've done all the talking about my damaged sense of self and my parents' disappointment and selling my soul to the corporate overlords, yada yada." She filled Marty's glass with the deep red wine.

"It's interesting you got that from the conversation. I had a totally different takeaway."

"Nice try, Coacharella," Lisa said, pouring herself a decidedly smaller portion of wine. "I live with a life coach, remember. I know all about the redirect. Now back to you."

Marty laughed as she shook her head. "Maybe I redirect without even realizing it."

"Whatever you have to tell yourself." Lisa curled back into a cross-legged stance and motioned for Marty to continue.

"Okay." Marty sighed heavily as if searching for something to say. "I guess it might be a good time to say my situation's not entirely different from yours, really."

"Really? Or are you just making this cupcake and wine fireside chat all about me again?"

"Both, I suppose, because when you talked about your family, maybe instead of deflecting, I should've said I understood what you meant at least a little bit. Maybe by trying to ask you questions to help you affirm your choice to break the mold, I was making myself feel a little better too."

"But you're classy, and you have a job in a field that helps people. Even if I don't buy into the whole self-help craze myself, I see what it did for Joey. And Elaine's always happier when she gets off Skype with you."

"Well that's awfully magnanimous of you to say. And I do agree, for the most part. I'm prouder of my work than you are of yours, but when you put it up against the family business, it can sometimes look particularly small in scope."

"I thought you were a military brat."

"Yeah, I should've been part of the third generation to serve," Marty said, shifting so she could pick at her cupcake while lying on her side. "My father was actually born in an internment camp during World War Two."

A chill ran the length of her arms. "Are you serious?"

"I am. Sounds like something out of a history book, right?"

"Yeah." Lisa didn't know what to say. An internment camp. Those happened in another world, in another time. Not to real people's parents, at least not people she knew.

"Well it still hangs over our family, most of them, and I guess me too in some ways. My grandparents ran a little corner grocery store in Pasadena. Their parents had been born in America. You have to go back like three more generations to get to the immigrants, but it didn't matter, they all got rounded up. My grandma already had two kids and was pregnant with my dad, but my grandfather, in an attempt to prove his patriotism, joined the army."

Lisa shook her head. "He went to fight for the country that locked up his wife and kids? I'm sorry, but I don't think I'd want anything to do with a military like that."

"Thank you for seeing it that way," Marty said, her relief genuine. "I always feel guilty for those thoughts. He was highly decorated, though. My dad still has all his medals. He brings them out on special occasions and says: *442nd Infantry Regiment, the most decorated unit in US military history.* For a while I thought four hundred forty-two was one of our identifiers, like our last name or our address."

"I can see how something like that could shape a family."

"He was proud to have liberated people from the Nazi camps. I think they felt very personal to him after what happened back home. He lost his right leg in the process. He used to tell us he just left it in Germany. Forgot to pack it in his rucksack on the way back."

She tried to tread as carefully as Marty had with her, but she couldn't hide her amazement. "I guess that's an impressive way to prove you belong in a country you shouldn't have to prove you belong in."

"It would've been enough for most people, but he wanted more. He wanted his sons to always be proud of their American heritage, but I think he was still trying to prove something. The shame of the camps got passed down as much as the pride."

"So your dad joined up too?"

"Yeah. He ran headlong into Vietnam, three times."

"What?" Lisa exclaimed so loudly she grimaced at the sound of her own voice reverberating off the hardwood floors. "Three times? Was that normal?"

"No." Marty laughed. "Most people did only one tour. He says he did all three for love."

"Love?"

"The first two for love of country, the third for love of my mother. She was a military nurse. They met three weeks before she left for

Saigon. He says he volunteered for a post there the day after she left because he'd rather be in a war zone with her than safe at home without her."

"Holy shit. Your dad's a military hero and a romantic rock star." Lisa once again felt wholly unworthy. She'd never live up to a romantic role model of that caliber.

"He really is. They both are. They all are. My brother served in the first Iraq war, and now he's a therapist who focuses on PTSD. My sister works in counterterrorism. They save all the lives."

Lisa fell over dramatically onto one of the pillows. "My family fights death, your family fights the agents of death." Somehow it felt funny. The laughter bubbled up inside her and she couldn't hold it in. It wasn't appropriate to giggle about something so personal, something she'd felt so insecure about, something Marty had shared so openly. A better person would've nodded sympathetically, offered words of affirmation, soothed her fears. Sadly, Lisa was not a better person, because no matter how she clenched her jaw, the laughter still shook her shoulders and hitched her breath.

"I'm sorry. I'm sorry," she finally gasped, but when she pushed herself back up to a sitting position, she found Marty lying on her back, laughing as well. Softly, but with so much abandon that tears streaked down her cheeks, and every time she wiped them she laughed harder, making them flow even more. The vicious cycle sucked Lisa back in, and she flopped to the floor once more.

"Oh my God, we're the most highly functioning underachievers to ever walk the earth," she whispered as she stared at the ceiling and tried to think of things to make her stop laughing. She went through scary clowns, creamed spinach, and sick puppies before she could draw a steady breath.

"We really are," Marty agreed. "Just look at us. Lying around drinking wine and eating cupcakes in the middle of a weekday while our families save the world."

She didn't sound any more disappointed than Lisa felt.

"Do you regret it?"

"No," Marty said quickly. "I can't find it in myself to regret it."

"Me either," Lisa said. "I think that's the hardest part for me sometimes. I don't regret it. I feel like I should. I feel like that makes me a terrible person. Or it did, until you got it. And then suddenly it all felt hilarious!"

"Hysterical is more like it," Marty said, rolling over to face her.

"Yeah, we sort of fell apart there."

Marty ran her fingers lightly across Lisa's cheek. "But in a good way, right?"

Lisa closed her eyes, letting the question seep in like the warmth of Marty's touch. So gentle, and yet so stirring. It had been a long time since she'd felt so secure, so at peace, and yet not quite peaceful. As she opened her eyes to search Marty's darker ones, she saw so much of herself reflected there. Recognition, attraction, and desire all seemed so clear. Her heart rate rose steadily as she lifted Marty's hand in her own and brought it to her lips. She kissed the tip of each finger before smiling at her again.

"Yes," she finally said, "I think we're falling apart in a very good way."

❖

Marty's breath caught in her throat. Lisa was so beautiful, her dark hair falling across her forehead, the mischief in her hazel eyes shifting to something more powerful than playful. She wondered briefly if Lisa could see the same in her. Had she watched the scales tip and their trajectory together alter in the moment when they'd finally fully seen each other? Did Lisa feel it sweep across her skin the way she had? She drew her gaze from Lisa's eyes, dragging it down across the smooth skin of her cheek to the flushed softness of her lips. She gave only a passing thought to the fact that she might never see her again after tomorrow, but somehow the idea that had given her pause earlier only added urgency now.

She hooked an arm around Lisa's waist and pulled them together. Their bodies brushed against each other, hips, legs, chest, and, most thrillingly, lips. Their mouths met in the same way they had the night before, natural, easy, as if they'd been born to kiss one another. They set an unhurried but purposeful pace without hesitation or doubt, not exploring so much as experiencing. Marty worked her fingers under the hem of Lisa's shirt, finding the tantalizing bit of skin she'd caught a glimpse of. It was as soft and warm as she'd expected, but instead of being satisfied, she only craved more.

She slid her hand up the curve of her hip and over the ridges of her rib cage until she found the soft swell of her breasts. Lisa gasped, then caught Marty's lip between her teeth, nibbling just hard enough to send her arousal up another level. It must have had the same effect on Lisa, because her hands began to blaze a mirror path up her body. Marty's attention was divided in the most beautiful way, between touching such beauty and being touched so beautifully.

Lisa pushed her knee between her legs, and Marty found the friction of their clothes all at once arousing and too restrictive, but before she had a chance to act, Lisa rolled her onto her back and kissed a wandering trail down her neck. All other intentions left her mind as she luxuriated in the feel of Lisa's warm breath against sensitive skin. Lisa ran her hands up under Marty's sweater, causing it to ride up as she went. Soon the area of her torso left uncovered was much greater than the part left under the sweater. Lisa kissed her way down along her abs and stomach, then, threading a hand behind her back, urged her up gently enough to slip the fabric off completely.

"You're so beautiful," Lisa whispered, lowering her back to the blanket. The thrill of her voice, so low, so close, pulled at something almost primal in Marty. She didn't want to simply lie back and be admired. The evidence of Lisa's desire fed her own, and she wouldn't be passive on the path to fulfilling it.

Lisa lowered her mouth again, this time to run her tongue along the line where her bra met her skin. Marty raked her hands along her back, pulling the soft cotton up as she went. Lisa paused long enough to help shrug the shirt off before pulling Marty back up and unclasping her bra. She cast it aside quickly, their pace accelerating to match the rhythm of their increasingly shallow breaths.

"Marty, I want…" Lisa stumbled and then, releasing a shuddering breath, smiled. The expression conveyed so much need and still a surprising amount of insecurity.

"Yes." Marty whispered the answer to all the unspoken questions, then, cupping her face in her hands, pulled her back down to reaffirm the word with action.

This kiss was hotter as they melted together again. She loved the weight of Lisa settling against her, skin on skin, heat to heat. The sensations accompanying their closeness were overwhelming and still not enough. She worked her hands between them and unclasped the button on Lisa's jeans, then slipped slowly inside across the smooth plane of muscles hardened with anticipation.

Lisa extended her arms on either side of Marty, lifting her body in push-up position and allowing her jeans and underwear to be pushed down before she kicked them away. Marty reached for her, clutching at bare skin, wanting to be smothered in her, but Lisa had her own ideas. She crawled down, kissing her way along Marty's stomach. As she flipped open the button of her jeans and lowered the zipper, her mouth quickly covered each little bit of skin the second she revealed it.

Marty arched her hips, pressing into the pressure of Lisa's mouth and allowing her to pull her jeans over her hips and down her legs. There were no more thoughts, no more reason beyond their need.

Hands, legs, torsos, mouths all blurred together. How long had it been since she felt like this? Yesterday? Years ago? Never? She couldn't tell. She couldn't focus on anything but Lisa. The sound of her raspy breath in her ear, the scent of her cologne mingled with sweat, the rapid beat of her heart against the skin of her own chest, the insistent press of her hand between her legs, stroking her, urging her higher, closer.

She wanted.

That was all she could process and all she could manage to say through the choking desire. "Please, Lisa. I need…"

Lisa lifted her head. The intensity reflected in her eyes caused Marty to shudder.

"What do you need?"

"You."

The word was all she had, and all the moment required. Everything about the writhing, exploding crush of emotions so neatly summed up in three letters. Lisa hovered above her, disbelief and awe swirling through her hazel gaze, before taking a deep breath and nodding.

"Yes." Another beautiful three letters strung together to encompass so much.

Then lowering her head once more, Lisa slid down the length of her body. With the most beautiful combination of lips, tongue, fingers, and heart, she played their shared need like an instrument or an entire orchestra.

Marty clutched her shoulder, her back, the dark silky fan of hair cascading over her legs and stomach, urging her onward, until in her release she cried out, one more summative word, one name, the only one left for her in that moment. "Lisa."

❖

Her own name echoed through her ears as she lay gasping for breath, but even as her exertion faded, her body refused to settle. The echo of Marty's voice haunted her. The pleading, the need, so raw, asking for more even as it was fulfilled. And the way Marty had looked up at her like she could see straight through to her heart—or her soul, she didn't know. She wasn't prepared for any of the emotions ripping through her. She'd almost broken down, collapsed under the weight of being…wanted? Desired? Needed? She'd never been looked at like she meant so very much to someone. Only her sheer force of will kept her from crumbling under the weight of responsibility.

She'd clung to the physical, the tactile, the tangible. It was what she knew and what she was willing to give. And she did give everything she could. She'd ached to feel Marty's stunning body bend, tighten, and crash beneath her, but that name—her own name, the one she'd heard millions of times—had never sounded so raw to her own ears. She'd never felt so unqualified to answer it.

Marty curled against her side, warm and gorgeous, resting her head on her shoulder, one arm draped lightly across her chest. Lisa stared at her fingers, so slender with elegantly curved nails, accented against her own flushed skin. Whatever made her think she could be the answer to anything for this woman?

"Hey," Marty finally whispered in a way that made it clear she was smiling even though Lisa couldn't see her face.

"Hey." She sounded restrained, forced through false casualness.

"Well, that just happened."

"It did," Lisa admitted with as much coolness as she could muster.

"Quite unexpectedly."

"I'll say."

"But not regrettably," Marty said, letting the doubt creep back in. "Right?"

"No." Lisa kissed the top of her head. "Not for me."

"Me either."

Lisa wondered if she meant that. She didn't seem like the kind to lie or even put on a show for pity's sake, but she was a life coach. She had a certain skill set and ethical sensibility that prevented her from telling someone sex with them was awful.

But it wasn't awful. She'd been present enough to plainly see Marty didn't share any of her doubts. She'd never waivered in her certainty of what she'd wanted. Lisa just wasn't sure how that could be her.

"What are you thinking?"

The question grated on her already-raw nerves. How the hell was she supposed to answer? Who had amazing, unexpected sex with a woman way out of her league and then said, "Do you think maybe that was a bad decision?"

Instead she looked out the front windows, trying to find something else to think about quickly so she could say that instead of what she had been thinking about before. The sun hung low in the sky, casting an orange glow on the houses and snow-covered ground. It reminded her of the firelight across Marty's bare skin. "You're so beautiful."

The words came out before she'd really meant to say them, but at least she'd shared an honest thought.

Marty placed a little kiss on her chest. "So are you, among other things."

Lisa shook her head. She couldn't believe her. Marty was leaving tomorrow. This thing, however awesome it was, couldn't work its way into her heart. It had already worked its way too far into her body, because parts of her were still on high alert, and the tips of Marty's fingernails were inching ever lower down her torso.

"Think we worked up enough of an appetite to put the Anchor Bar out of business?"

"What?"

"It's almost dinnertime, and it wouldn't be a trip to Buffalo without getting some wings, right?"

Marty lifted her head and looked at Lisa as if trying to gauge if she was joking or not. Lisa struggled to keep her expression pleasantly neutral as Marty narrowed her eyes and furrowed her brow. "Wings?"

"It's kind of a thing around here."

Marty stared at her, the silence stretching into the awkward range.

"Buffalo wings, but you know, except here we just call them wings." Lisa tried to laugh, but the joke fell flat even to her own ears.

"What's wrong?" Marty asked softly.

"Nothing, I just thought you'd like to go out to eat at a local historic spot. Dinner and landmark all in one."

Lisa's chest grew tighter as seconds ticked away. Suddenly the weight of Marty against her was almost as unbearable as the weight of her disappointment. She scooted away, gently extracting her arm from underneath Marty, and reached for her pants. Trying to keep the tone light and casual, she went for the easy quip again. "Most of the time a woman wants to be taken out for dinner first, but just because we did things the other way around doesn't mean you shouldn't get a meal out of the deal."

Marty's sharp intake of breath made Lisa wince. She turned to try to do damage control, but Marty was already covering up, both physically and emotionally. The ache in her chest grew to a sharp point. "I'm sorry. I didn't mean to sound crass."

"I know," Marty said, pulling her sweater back on.

"Really. I was just trying to make you laugh."

"No, you were trying to make *you* laugh."

She didn't know what to say. It was true, of course, but a little one-sided. Still, it didn't seem like a good time to split hairs. "I'm sorry."

"I believe you. I just don't understand you."

"Yeah, well, join the club."

"Really?" Marty asked, the hurt evident in her voice. "That's all I get?"

"Look, I said I'm sorry. I made a stupid comment. I make a lot of them. Ask Elaine. Crass remarks are kind of my thing."

"Is it easier for you to tell yourself that?" Marty asked softly.

"What?"

"Does it make you feel better to just write yourself off as someone who says stupid things? Is it easier to cope with than the emotions of what happened between us?"

The heat rose in her cheeks again, and this time not in an enjoyable way. She should've seen this coming. The life coaching shoe dropped and kicked her right in the stomach. She deserved it. She sacrificed herself on the table of overanalysis, and shocker, she'd been found lacking. It was to be expected, but it wasn't something she needed professional help for.

"Lisa…" Marty said softly, laying a hand on her shoulder.

She jerked away. "Don't."

"Don't what?"

She whirled, her insecurity snapping like a caged animal. "Don't coach me."

Marty's eyes widened. "Coach you? Is that really what you think is happening here?"

"It's what you do, isn't it? You see the flash of insecurity, the little hint of weakness, the crack in the dam, and you have to pry it open. Isn't that what a life coach really does when you get down to it?"

"No. But more importantly, I've never coached you. What we just did"—she looked down at the blanket on the floor between them, then closed her eyes like she didn't want to see anymore—"what happened between us was the least coaching thing I've ever done."

"But you said…you said all that stuff about me coping with my emotions, and you said I was…beautiful." The word almost strangled her.

"You *are* beautiful. And you made me feel beautiful too, for a while. Then you pulled away. One minute you made me feel so safe and open and wonderful, like we meant something, then suddenly you're talking to me like you just want a beer buddy to go get wings with."

"That's not how it is." Lisa tried to stay strong, but the edge in her voice had gone soft.

"But that's how you made me *feel*."

Every bit of stone and glass she'd tried to hastily throw up around her fell to shambles at her feet. She pulled Marty close once again, holding her tightly to her chest. "I'm so sorry."

"Well," Marty said shakily, "I'm not going to lie and say I don't feel a little glad for your remorse, but I'd rather have your reasoning. Why the back and forth? It's been going on all day. One minute you're reeling me in with all your charm, and the next you're pushing me away."

"You really think I'm charming?"

"You're doing it again. You're playing this part, this game, and it's fun, but there's more to you. I know it now. Why are you hiding?"

Lisa sighed and loosened her hold on Marty but still kept her arm draped around her shoulder. Even in her turmoil, it was better to have her close. “I like you. And the closer you get, the more I realize I could even fall in love with you.”

The rise and fall of Marty’s chest grew quick and shallow, but she didn’t speak. Lisa both admired and hated her restraint.

“I’m just not very good at emotions. I work with computers. I like black and white. If I mess up, I control-z to back out of it, and no one gets hurt or disappointed. People aren’t like that.”

Marty shook her head. “No, they’re not.”

“I disappoint people.”

“Your parents?”

“Yeah,” Lisa said, a muscle in her jaw twitching. She should leave it there. She always had, but for the first time she didn’t want to, not really. Something about Marty’s heart beating so close to her own made her weaker, or maybe stronger. “I couldn’t save Joey’s mom.”

“What?” Marty leaned back to search her eyes.

“I didn’t save Joey’s mom. She practically raised me. The Langs taught me what love really means, and I let her die of a curable disease. I was too late.”

“Too late for what?”

“I sold the code too late.”

“The code you wrote for the banks? The program you told me about?”

“Yeah. I sold it to help pay for the hospital bills, the treatments, but it was too little, too late.” Her voice caught at the memory. “If I’d done it sooner, if I’d been better, if I’d been more like my parents.”

“Lisa,” Marty kissed her jaw, her cheek, the corner of her mouth. “You did a good thing. You made a tremendous sacrifice. You took on an unbearable burden, and you’ve paid the price for years.”

“For what?” Lisa said, not even recognizing her voice through the anguish. “It didn’t work. In the big moment, I couldn’t do enough. I’m not the person people depend on. I can’t be.”

“That’s not true. Look at what you’ve done for Joey and Elaine.”

“What have I done for Joey and Elaine?” she asked before silently adding, *They’re both leaving.*

“You got them together.”

“Oh, come on.” She laughed. “I almost got Joey branded a manipulative liar for the whole life-coaching appointment, and I could've gotten Elaine in trouble with her job too. It's only because they're both such upstanding, awesome romantic heroes that we can laugh about it now."

"But you all do laugh about it now. Quite openly. And they love you."

"They love me because I'm funny. Don't you see? Funny is what I'm good at, the casual sidestep, the quick joke. I never let them see me sweat, but you"—she shuddered—"you saw me. When you looked up at me with those big brown eyes, you saw so much in me. I saw it in you too."

"And?"

"It terrified me. I'm not the person you can pin hopes and desires on. I'm not a leading lady. I'm the comic relief. If you look to me for grand gestures, I'm only going to let you down, and damn it, I like you too much for that. I don't want to be a fuckup in your eyes."

"You're not. Lisa, how can I convince you you're not?" Marty pleaded. "I see everything in you that you saw in me."

She hung her head, taking a deep breath of Marty's scent, so warm, close and sweet. "Even if you don't see it now, you will eventually, and then I won't be able to live with myself. There's no one in my life I haven't come up short for, no one I haven't lost."

❖

Marty didn't know what to say. She'd coached plenty of clients with dismal self-esteem, and she'd been able to guide them toward an understanding of their worth, but this was different on so many levels. She didn't have time, she didn't have Lisa's faith in the process or even a willingness to try. More importantly, though, she had no neutrality, no professional distance, no distance of any kind. Nor did she want any.

She wanted to be close to her to feel her skin against her once more, to touch her physically and emotionally the way she'd touched her.

She hooked a finger under Lisa's chin and lifted it gently, but she couldn't make her lift her eyes. "Please," she pleaded, "look at me."

When Lisa did, her hazel eyes reminded her of a wounded animal, timid almost to the point of being frantic. Her heart ached to see this strong, charismatic woman reduced to a shell of self-doubt. This wasn't her. This wasn't the real Lisa any more than the comic façade she'd cultivated to protect herself.

"I wish you could see what I see in you," Marty whispered.

"I can't."

"Let me show you."

Lisa tried to shake her head, but Marty caught her face in her hands. "Please. I haven't asked you for anything. No promises, no commitment, nothing you haven't wanted to give, but I'm begging now. Let me show you what I see. Let me make you feel what I feel."

She didn't wait for an answer. She captured Lisa's mouth with her own. It was all she knew to do, the only thing that felt right, but she was still surprised when Lisa responded. She opened up to her, inviting her tongue in, welcoming her exploration like a woman who'd spent entirely too long waiting to be found. Dropping the blanket between them, she clutched at Marty's back, pulling her close.

Between Lisa's jeans and her own sweater, they had only one outfit between them, but it was quickly shed.

"You're beautiful," she said.

Lisa shook her head almost imperceptibly as she whispered, "You."

Lisa clung to her back, pulling her close and closing her eyes as if waiting to be kissed again. She was breathtaking, but Marty wanted more. She didn't want to just take what was being offered, she wanted to return something, to feel it move freely, fluidly between them. She might not have anything else, anything past tonight, but that only made the importance of what she had to accomplish more acute.

Settling her body between Lisa's legs, she let the weight of herself register against her, anchoring them both to the physical before pressing into the emotional. She ran her hand along the soft skin of Lisa's chest and across the smooth surface of her abs, then drew a wide circle back up to cup her cheek. Kissing her once more, deep and fast, she pulled back only enough to see her fully, then, trailing her fingers south once more, she let her caress go lower, down to Lisa's inner thigh before starting to inch up again, this time slowly.

"Lisa," she said, "open your eyes."

Heavy lids fluttered and closed again.

"Don't pull away now. I want you to watch me. I want you to see."

Small hazel slivers grew slowly into a hazy gaze, like a cat awaking to survey her surroundings. The eyes that had held so much mischief earlier now conveyed vulnerability, and a shocking amount of need.

Marty nearly lost her concentration at the sight of her spread out, with her dark hair fanned across their makeshift bed, the firelight casting a warm glow against the white of her skin.

"Do you see it yet?" Marty asked. "Do you see what I see?"

She didn't wait for an answer as she brushed her fingers over Lisa's center. "Watch me. Feel me."

A groan escaped Lisa's lips as the pressure between their bodies grew.

"You're amazing. You feel amazing." She continued as Lisa opened up to her. "You make me feel amazing."

Lisa's hips arched up, her body superseding whatever insecurities warred for control of her mind. Marty intended to vanquish them all. The head was the home of all things critical, all doubt, fear, and disillusion. The body was home to the most basic sense of self, the true form of knowing. She wanted them to exist in that space, at least until she'd made her see what that kind of connection could truly mean.

"Watch me," she whispered. "Watch what you do to me."

Lisa's eyes stayed locked on hers, the haze of arousal replaced by intensity and awe.

"Do you see it yet?" Marty asked. "Do you see yourself reflected in my eyes?"

Lisa nodded, wordlessly.

"Good." She slipped inside, her breath catching at the warmth, the heat, the utter perfection of their separate selves blending.

Lisa's eyes closed, her head rolling back as Marty pushed forward into her all the way.

"Stay with me, baby," Marty said, her voice no longer soft and clear through the arousal coursing through her.

"Yes," Lisa finally said. "Yes."

The word was so sweet, filled with so much more than surrender.

"Yes," Marty echoed. "Do you feel it now?"

"Yes," Lisa called out, pulling her forward.

Darkness had fallen outside, but the fire inside burned hot and strong, fueled by wine, desire, and waning time. She could feel it all now, the pressure, the potential, the urgency, and the need beneath it all. Shadow and light danced across them as their movements grew steadily closer, until finally, tangled together, she felt Lisa shudder and release, not just the tension of their combined need, but all the other wants and desires she'd held at bay.

She didn't cry out so much as gasp, a single clutching sob as she shook, her forehead pressed tight against Marty's shoulder as her breath ripped jagged and hot against her skin.

"I've got you," Marty whispered. "I've got you."

She kissed her hair, her cheeks, her neck, as the trembling subsided.

She pulled the edges of the blanket up around them and snuggled in beside her. They lay together as their heart rates slowed and exhaustion hung thick across their limbs.

"I didn't know," Lisa finally said in a small voice. "I didn't know I could feel like that."

"I did," Marty confided.

"How?"

"You showed me. You've shown me so much in such a short time, your slow smile that gives away so much more than you mean to, the easy way you took my hand and led me up the stairs last night, the insights you let slip when you're relaxed, the softness of your lips, the fire reflected in your eyes."

"I like the way you see me."

"It's not me. I'm just the mirror, showing you what you've shown me all along."

A little noise of contentment hummed through Lisa's throat. "I like that too."

"Good," Marty said, kissing her temple, "because it's the truth."

Or at least part of the truth. As she lay there in the fading glow of the fire, watching the captivating woman before her relax into sleep, she had to admit, if only to herself, that somewhere in the space where they'd come most fully together, she'd shifted from showing Lisa what she was capable of, to trying to convey to her what the two of them were capable of—together.

Chapter Seven

A rush of cold air ran across Lisa's bare skin and she snuggled closer to the warmth of Marty's body. Her awareness teetered on the line between sleep and full consciousness, and she had no doubt which way she wanted to fall. They'd made love well into the night, stopping only to stoke the fire before them, then returning to feed the flames between them. Then, exhausted emotionally and physically, in Marty's arms she'd found rest, peace, and contentment.

From the sense of light in the room and the distant sounds of birds and city traffic, she guessed it must be morning, and not an early one, but she didn't want to open her eyes. She didn't want to face the day or whatever realities it might bring. She wanted to hold on to this woman for as long as she could.

Another burst of cold ran along the floor, sweeping over them like wind through the bare limbs of the trees outside. Only this time the wind was accompanied by the sound of footsteps, and then voices.

"Is she sleeping on the floor?" The familiar tone, full of curiosity and concern, burned the remainder of her sleepy haze.

"Uh, she's not alone." Joey's voice was hushed, but not nearly as amused. "Or clothed."

Marty stirred, arching her back like a sleepy cat before whispering, "Morning."

"Morning," Lisa replied sweetly, her chest tightening at the realization that this might be the last thing she'd say to her before everything came crashing down. She wished she'd uttered something better, more eloquent, something to convey all the things she knew she wouldn't be able to put into words, but she was out of emotions, and they were out of time. "We've got company."

"Hmm?" Marty rolled over, and Lisa held the blanket tightly so she wouldn't expose herself any more than she already had.

"Uh, Elaine, Joey," Lisa said, her voice more steady than she'd expected. "Could you two give us a moment?"

"Of course," Elaine said quickly.

Marty stiffened beside her, as if freezing could somehow prevent them from being seen.

"We'll go get the luggage," Joey added, and the click of the door closing behind them signaled their departure.

"Holy shit," Marty said.

"Yeah. The honeymoon is over, literally."

"Were they supposed to be back so soon?"

"Not until tonight, but I think that's sort of beside the point now."

"I guess you're right." Marty laughed.

She loved that sound, but she couldn't join in. Reaching for her jeans, she said, "We'd better get dressed."

"Probably right about that too."

How was she so calm? She'd just had a client walk in on her naked on the floor. Wasn't she embarrassed? Or, more likely, angry with her?

Marty collected her clothes and put them on in short order, but not with any outward signs of the panic starting to well up in Lisa. She was Elaine's coach, and she'd just had a one-night stand with her roommate. That had to break some kind of rule, didn't it?

"What time is it?" Marty asked.

Lisa glanced at her watch. "Almost eleven."

"Oh no. My flight. It leaves in two hours. I should call the airline."

"No, you can make it."

Marty froze and looked at her.

"We're only twenty minutes from the airport," Lisa explained.

And still Marty regarded her with the same unreadable gaze, eyes wide, lips slightly parted, hands hanging loose by her side. "Okay, then," she finally said. "I'll run upstairs and change, then I'll go."

For some reason the last part of the statement stuck in Lisa's chest, and that little jolt only spread as Marty jogged quickly up the steps.

But, before she could process anything else, there was a knock at the front door.

"Everyone decent in there?" Joey called.

"Yeah, come on in."

Joey peeked her head around the door slowly as though she didn't quite trust her, but upon seeing Lisa fully covered, she stepped all the way into the room, letting Elaine in behind her.

"So, you guys are home early. Didn't ever get that honeymoon thing figured out, did you?"

"We thought if we left early we could beat the bridge traffic and maybe get to see Marty a little more before she left," Elaine explained.

"Well, I guess you were right on both counts." Lisa smiled awkwardly. "A little more than you expected on the latter, though, huh?"

"A lot more," Elaine said.

"Lisa," Joey cut in. "What the hell?"

"That was one of my first thoughts when I heard you two walk in."

"Do you really think this is funny?"

Lisa shrugged. She didn't know, honestly. The whole situation felt like a lot of things all mixed together, but funny had to be in there somewhere, didn't it?

"We asked you to take care of Elaine's life coach, and you end up taking her to bed."

"Well, we never actually made it to the bed."

"Jesus." Joey pushed her hands through her chestnut hair, and Elaine suddenly found something very interesting to look at out the window.

"I don't know what to say," Lisa blurted. "We obviously didn't expect you home so soon."

"And that makes it okay?" Joey snapped. "Did you think something like this would just be all over by the time we got home? Did you think this wouldn't end up affecting us? You slept with my wife's life coach! Did you think that wouldn't make things awkward for everyone eventually?"

"I didn't really think it through."

"Of course you didn't. You were having fun."

Lisa hung her head.

"What about Marty?" Joey finally asked.

"What about her?"

"Are you serious about her? 'Cause things looked pretty serious there when we walked in."

Lisa's stomach clenched. Serious. That's probably a good word for what passed between them, but what chance did she have of keeping that up? Hell, did she even want to?

"Please tell me you at least thought about your intentions with Marty before you—"

"I think that's my cue to enter, stage right," Marty said, coming down the stairs. She was still in yesterday's jeans, but she'd put on a new sweater, this one cream colored with a high neck. It clung tightly to the curves Lisa had so recently caressed. Her hair fell down, dark and flowing, across her shoulder. She looked so beautifully put together Lisa had to fight the urge to cling to her as a way of settling her own spinning turmoil. "Did you two have a nice trip?"

"We did," Elaine said calmly, but her smile was forced and her cheeks flushed. "I take it you had a good time here?"

"I did," Marty said. "Lisa was a wonderful host, but contrary to what I heard a moment ago, I wasn't her responsibility."

Joey's jaw was set and she said nothing.

"I was a guest in her home, and any decisions we made, thoughtfully or otherwise, were shared jointly," Marty continued. "It's not anyone else's job to protect my honor or my emotions."

"Of course not," Elaine said. "You're wonderful and capable people, and we care about both of you. I'm sorry if either one of us suggested otherwise."

"And we both care about both of you," Marty said. "I'm sorry if we put you in an awkward situation."

"It's not," Elaine assured her.

"It is a little bit," Joey said.

"Honey," Elaine warned, her hand lightly on Joey's back.

"No, it's okay," Marty said. "She has a right to her feelings."

"But we don't have a right to moralize," Elaine said, "and we of all people should understand that no amount of professionalism can stand in the way of two people who belong together."

At least Joey looked properly chagrined now. "So are you guys together? Or was this just a one-time thing?"

Marty and Lisa both opened their mouths at the same time, but no words came from either of them. Instead they stared at each other. What had Marty intended to say? Had she intended to leave the door open between them, but then doubted herself? Or was she closing it and simply didn't want to say so in front of the others? Probably the latter. Who would willingly sign up for this kind of awkwardness, especially after Lisa had simultaneously disappointed every person in the room?

Finally Joey spoke. "I'm sorry. Clearly I stepped into something else we probably all should've just stayed out of."

"No, I'm sorry," Marty said. "That's not a question that should've fallen to you to ask."

"Stop apologizing," Lisa snapped.

Everyone turned to stare at her as if the sound of her voice, so long gone from the conversation, had stunned them all, at least momentarily.

"We're both grown-ups," Lisa said as a throbbing pain started to pulse between her eyes, but she pushed through, eager to be done with it all. "Marty and I had some fun, maybe more fun than you're comfortable with, but it's our damn business. There's no need to turn it into a full-fledged life-coaching drama."

Joey rolled her eyes. "'Cause life coaching is all a bunch of hippie voodoo, right? Classy, Lisa."

"Actually, I agree with her," Elaine said matter-of-factly.

"You do?" everyone asked at once.

"Yes." Elaine smiled one of those genuine smiles that always put everyone at ease. "Your relationship, whatever it entails, is within your purview. Joey and I love you both very much, and that's the extent of our involvement. So if you'd like the two of us to get lost for a while and let you two have the conversation we prevented from happening, we'll gladly do so."

Marty looked to Lisa again, clearly deferring to her, but her beautifully neutral expression gave no clue as to what she wanted her to do. Once more, the emotional pressure rested on her. Everyone hung on her decision, which would no doubt be the wrong one. Marty probably just wanted to be excused from all this awkwardness, and if she didn't, what the hell was wrong with her? This entire debacle only proved what she'd tried to tell her last night. Every time she opened up or put herself out there, every single time she went for the grand gesture, she came up embarrassingly short. At least now, Marty couldn't deny anymore what a massive screwup she really was.

"I think we're all talked out," Lisa finally said. "And Marty has a plane to catch."

Marty pursed her lips and clenched her fists quickly, then forced a smile. "I guess I do. Have a plane to catch, that is."

Silence once again stretched out, and Lisa realized everyone was looking everywhere but at her. She felt the disappointment radiating off them. What did they expect her to say? To do? Didn't they realize by now what she was made of, or at least what she lacked?"

"Maybe I could drive you to the airport," Elaine offered. "Since we haven't had any time together."

Marty stared at Lisa a second longer, her eyes seeming to plead for something Lisa couldn't understand, much less give, before turning to Elaine. "That would be wonderful, darling. Thank you."

"I'll get your bag," Joey said, jogging up the stairs.

"I'll go warm up the car," Elaine added, heading out the door.

They were alone together again.

"I guess this is good-bye," Lisa said.

"It could be," Marty agreed.

"I tried to warn you, you know," Lisa said. "Multiple times."

"You did. Funny how that worked out just the way you expected it to."

"What's that supposed to mean?"

Marty shook her head sadly. "You know exactly what it means, but I don't need you to admit it to me. You don't have to pretend either, though. I'm sorry if I failed to make that clear last night. God knows I tried."

Part of her resolve cracked. "I really am sorry about what happened."

"Don't be," Marty said. "I'm not. I have no regrets, at least not any regrets about anything that's happened up until now. I hope you feel the same way."

She wasn't sure she did, but before she could say so, Joey came back down the stairs with Marty's suitcase. It was too late to undo anything. All she could do for Marty now was let her go.

"Ready?" Joey asked.

"I guess so," Marty said.

"Travel safe." Lisa internally kicked herself for not coming up with something more original.

Marty smiled sadly and leaned up to kiss her lightly on the cheek. "Thank you."

Lisa caught her hand, and Marty froze, her eyes pleading and Lisa's chest aching, both of them begging for something more, but she could only whisper, "You too."

Chapter Eight

"To the airport?" Elaine asked as Marty got in the car.

"I guess I should probably catch my flight."

"You guess you should?"

Marty laughed mirthlessly at Elaine's repetition of words that sent up red flags in their line of work. "Are you holding up the metaphorical mirror for me?"

"Occupational hazard," Elaine said as she shifted the car into reverse and backed away from the beautiful old Victorian house.

It looked so stable from here, but Marty'd felt as though all the world had tilted when she'd been inside. As the house grew smaller in the rearview mirror, the pain in her chest only grew bigger. Shouldn't it have been the other way around?

"So," Elaine said, her smile awkwardly sympathetic.

"So," Marty repeated, knowing she needed to follow up with something assuring, or introspective, something to help right the scales at least between the two of them, but she had nothing to offer in that vein.

"It's strange to not feel comfortable talking to you," Elaine finally said.

"I'm sorry."

"Don't be, please," Elaine said. "It's just suddenly all very one-sided, you know?"

"One-sided?" That was a good word for so many of the things she'd experienced over the last twenty-four hours.

"I've talked to you about every single conflict in my life, personally and professionally, for the past five years, and now that I have a chance to return the favor, I'm not at all sure about my role. I want to be a coach, I want to be a friend, I want to be a confidant for you, and an apologist for Lisa."

"There's no need to make explanations for Lisa."

"I guess not. She's an adult, but she's more complicated than she seems."

Marty snorted. "I got that."

"I won't pretend to know what happened between when I left and when I came back, but the Lisa I saw this morning…she was different, and somehow the same, all at once."

"I think that's part of the problem," Marty admitted. She wasn't blind. She saw the conflict, the fear, the need in Lisa almost as clearly this morning as she had last night, but despite the internal war, she came down on the same side she always had.

"How do you feel?"

"I feel sad, exhausted, and a little silly."

"Why silly?"

"Because it's been two days." She laughed again. "Two days with her, and you know what? She's right. She never misled me. I heard what Joey said to her earlier, but please, Elaine, Lisa tried to push me away several times."

Elaine didn't respond. Was she waiting to see what bubbled up after that emotional outburst, or did she disagree with her assessment of Lisa's responsibility?

"I asked her to give something she couldn't give. Or maybe I didn't ask her outright, or maybe it's not that she *couldn't*, so much as—I don't know." She covered her face with her hands and took a few deep breaths. "I don't even know how it happened, but I think somewhere along the line I started to want something she didn't really want."

"Something she didn't want, or something she doesn't know how to give?"

"I don't know if the difference means much to me. I like her. A lot. I know it's not very becoming for someone who's supposed to be calm and reflective, but I fell for her, hard and fast."

"You'll not find judgment from me for that," Elaine said. "Don't forget why you came to Buffalo in the first place."

A gentle wave of warmth spread through her chest. Elaine and

Joey, living proof that true love could overcome anyone's better judgment. "Maybe that's what's most frustrating in all of this. None of the obstacles between us, the long distance, our jobs, our outlooks on life, none of those things ever really factored in for me. None of those things were ever more than a passing thought. Maybe they should've been."

"But they weren't. Maybe that's a sign."

"Maybe they were signs we ignored. Or at least I ignored them. I have no idea what Lisa thought about them. Maybe that's another sign."

"Lisa's not one for heavy conversations," Elaine admitted.

Marty started to disagree. She thought of all the personal subjects they'd broached in their short time together, but even the most serious of them had ended up being laughed at, or kissed away. Had they ever really gotten serious? Even in those moments? If they had, they hadn't let themselves stay there very long.

"It took me a long time to get to know Lisa," Elaine continued. "I think sometimes I still don't know what drives her, but I've learned that she jokes to cover a lot of really strong feelings. It's just easier to do amazing things behind the scenes."

Marty nodded. That made sense with everything she'd learned. "I believe you."

"She can come across as really crass. She pretends not to understand things that make her uncomfortable, but she does. She feels those things, maybe even deeper than those of us who've learned to process through them." Elaine bumped her shoulder lightly. "She's never had a life coach."

"No." Marty smiled in spite of her pain. "She made that abundantly clear…multiple times."

"I bet she did. I know how she comes across, but I also know she's one of the most genuinely good people I've ever met. There's nothing she wouldn't do for the people she loves."

"Believe it or not, I know that. I knew it from the beginning. It didn't take me any time to see, really. You don't have to convince me she's worth all the struggles ahead. I want to try, at least give us a chance to see what we can be, but I can't make the decision for both of us."

"What if she wants to make that decision too?"

"I can't pressure her into it. Honestly, I've probably already pushed too hard. I thought I could show her what I could see for us, and this is where I got us."

"Where is this?" Elaine said, pulling the car to a stop in the airport parking lot.

"It's nowhere. And that hurts," she admitted, sadness blurring her eyes and clogging her throat. "It hurts to let go, but in the long run it'll hurt a lot more to hold on to someone who doesn't want to be held."

"What if she wants the same things you do but she's been typecast for so long she can't admit it? Surely, you've seen similar things with clients. So many people miss out because they're afraid to break the mold."

"There's one major difference here. I can't coach Lisa. Even if I wanted to, I can't. I hope you don't think less of me, but I am very much a human being, flawed and needy, emotional and weak. I want to be wanted, I want to be sought after, not hidden from and pushed away."

Elaine took her hand and squeezed it tightly. "Of course I don't think less of you. I understand."

"Good." She wiped her eyes before the tears had a chance to fall. "It's not that I don't want to try. It's that I don't want to try alone. As crazy as it sounds, I'd still be willing to put my whole heart on the line for her, but I need the same kind of investment from her. I more than need it. I deserve it."

Elaine pulled her into as much of a hug as the seat belt would allow. "You're right. You deserve that, and so much more."

Marty hugged her back, grateful for the soothing affirmation for the first time all morning. She wished she could carry the hug with her through the airport, onto the plane, and all the way back home, because even knowing what she deserved didn't offer much solace when it came with the knowledge that she wouldn't get it.

❖

Lisa gathered the blankets from the living room, trying to avoid the sensory memories now associated with that spot. Would she ever sit in front of the fireplace again without feeling Marty, or her absence? That thought was entirely too maudlin for her. She'd lost worse and felt less in the past. Why should she doubt her ability to let go of a woman she'd only known a couple of days? Maybe she was still too close.

Marty had been gone only half an hour. She probably wasn't even through security yet. There was still time to go after her. She could speed through Buffalo, buy a ticket to anywhere, chase her down in the terminal, and…what? Her stomach clenched so tightly it hurt.

She'd seen the movies. She knew how these things were supposed to end, but her life had never been like the movies. At least not like the romantic ones. She was more of a slapstick, screwball kind of character. She'd never pulled off the grand gesture before. There was no reason to think she could do so now, or that Marty even wanted her to. Her disappointment this morning had been palpable. Surely Marty saw by now what she'd tried to tell her all along. Only now, for the first time in her life, she wished she'd been the one to be wrong, instead of Marty.

"Shit," she muttered, dropping the blankets into a laundry basket.

"All right, dude," Joey said, coming in from the kitchen. "Spill."

"Actually," Lisa sighed heavily, "I didn't get much sleep last night. I think I'm going to bed."

She tried to sidestep her, but Joey put a hand flat on her chest. "What the hell? I come in and find you naked on the floor with my wife's life coach, and you're not even going to talk to me?"

"Yeah, maybe that's it."

"What?"

"I don't want to talk to you about your wife's life coach."

"What's that supposed to mean?"

"Nothing." Lisa rubbed her face. "It means nothing."

Joey stared at her, her dark eyes expressive and swirling with too many emotions not to remind her of Marty's. "I don't believe you."

"Have I lied to you, Jo? I mean like about something major? Ever?"

"No."

"Okay, then."

"But you lie to yourself."

She rolled her eyes.

"You're doing it right now. You're pretending you're not upset about this, whatever this is."

"It's nothing. I mean, it was a thing, but it's over."

Joey eyed her seriously. "It doesn't feel over."

No, maybe not yet, but it would be as soon as Marty got on the plane. She just needed to stay calm until then, even if doing so hurt a little bit. "It was just a one-night stand."

"Except you're going to see her again."

"I'm not."

"Yeah, you are," Joey pushed. "And so am I, and so is Elaine. They work together. You're going to hear her voice coming from the upstairs office, she's going to come visit occasionally, Elaine and I are both going to count on her to help us get through the transitions ahead. If you wanted to screw around, no strings attached, you could've picked a better option."

"I'm sorry my sex life is inconvenient for you."

"You don't get it, do you?" Joey snapped. "We're not talking about your sex life. We're talking about human beings, real people and real emotions. I know you think life coaching is a bunch of crap, but the people you live with, the people you care about, don't. And we're facing some of the biggest changes of our lives right now."

The front door opened and Elaine stepped in, causing both Joey and Lisa to fall silent and freeze.

"Well that wasn't suspicious at all," Elaine said, taking off her coat. "Can I assume you didn't just clam up because you're planning a wonderful surprise party for me?"

Lisa laughed harder than the comment warranted, and even she heard the hysterical edge in her voice.

"How are you doing, Lisa?" Elaine asked.

"Fine."

Elaine nodded thoughtfully but didn't say anything. Did she not believe her? Did she expect her to break down?

"I can handle this," she added.

"Of course you can," Elaine said calmly. "You're a strong, capable woman. A good friend. A thoughtful individual."

Lisa snorted. Now she knew she was being played. "I'm not thoughtful."

"You always work so hard to make us feel comfortable. You supported Joey and me through all the trials of our relationship. And you hosted the most beautiful wedding reception I've ever been to."

"No." She shook her head. Those weren't important things. Those were little things.

"No?" Elaine asked softly. "You didn't know Joey well enough to push her toward me? You didn't help me see her value? Or you didn't plan the reception all on your own, handling every detail intuitively?"

"No. I'm not intuitive."

"You are," Joey said. "You knew exactly what was best for us all along. You read people really well. You always know how to make everyone laugh."

"Yeah, I go for the cheap joke. I don't take anything seriously enough."

"That's not true." Joey defended her against herself. "You don't take the potshot. That would never work. You can make anyone smile, no matter what. You couldn't do that if you didn't understand people's feelings."

"You make people feel comfortable," Elaine added. "It's a gift."

"Yeah, but I'm already losing you both"—her voice shook—"and I just made it worse for all of us."

Joey opened her mouth, but Elaine laid a hand gently on her arm, and she closed it again.

"There are a lot of transitions ahead," Elaine said thoughtfully.

"No shit." Lisa sighed. "And I'm sorry, I messed them all up again."

"Like last time?" Elaine asked.

"Yeah. First I fucked up saving Joey's mom. Then I damn near wrecked you guys with that stupid life-coaching-appointment scheme. Now I blew things with Marty. I tried to warn her. Ask her. I told her I always let people down, but I can't stop. I always come up short, and now I'm going to be alone too."

"You're not." Joey's eyes filled with tears. "You're not a screwup, and you're not alone."

"Yeah, I am," she said. "You've got this amazing life. You pulled everything together. You've got a wife, and you're about to become a teacher. You're going to buy a house and start a family, and you deserve that. But I'm still in the same place I've been for years, only now I'll be alone. Maybe I deserve that."

"Damn it, Lisa." Joey pushed her hands through her hair. "I mean, you never said anything. You've been my best friend for more than twenty years. I tell you *everything*. You know every doubt and insecurity I've ever had."

Lisa smirked. "Yeah, you were a real downer for a while."

"Well you could've returned the favor." Joey punched her in the arm a little harder than usual."

"Ouch."

"I thought you were a cocky smart-ass because you knew how awesome you were. That's why it didn't bother me. I was glad you saw what you're worth, and all this time…" She shook her head sadly. "All these years you never told me anything, did you?"

Lisa heard the hurt in her voice. Another betrayal. Another way she'd let her down. "I never told anyone," she said, then hesitated. "I mean not until…"

"Until when?" Elaine asked softly.

The tight grip of emotion squeezed her chest again. "Until last night."

Joey and Elaine both stared at her, wide eyed and waiting. Were they putting the pieces together? Did they see what she was only beginning to understand?

"I didn't know," Joey finally said.

"There's nothing to know." The words sounded weak, even to herself, and from the look that passed between Joey and Elaine they obviously didn't believe her, either.

"You couldn't tell me how you felt. Me, the person who knows you better than anyone in the world, but after two nights with Marty you told her about every hidden insecurity."

When put that way, she had no defense.

"And she didn't run away?"

Lisa shook her head. Marty had listened. She'd stayed. She'd made love to her. Lisa had laid all her fears—all her insecurities about letting down the people she loved, all the things she couldn't even tell the people who loved her most—at her feet, and Marty wanted her anyway.

"I'm so sorry." Joey hugged her so tightly she nearly cracked her back.

"Why? What do you have to be sorry for?"

"I didn't know you'd fallen in love with her."

"No." She pushed her away. "I'm not in love with her. I've only known her a couple days."

Joey and Elaine both laughed.

"What?"

"What a silly excuse from you of all people," Joey said. "You gave a speech two nights ago about how you knew from the moment I saw Elaine that she was the one for me. You knew before we'd even spoken to each other."

"That's different."

"How's it different?" Elaine asked.

"Because you guys are you, and I'm me," she stammered. "If I ever let her down, I couldn't take it."

"You already did let her down," Elaine said bluntly, "but there's time to fix it."

She shook her head again. She couldn't get her hopes up. She couldn't stand the way it swelled her chest and pushed at her rib cage. "What if I mess up? What if I put everything on the line and she doesn't want me."

"Then you'll be exactly where you are right now," Joey said.

"No," Elaine said, "you'll never be right here, right now, again. You either go backward or forward. You can't just let things happen to you anymore. You have to make a choice."

She was right. Damn her, she was always right. The choice had been hers all along, and for too many years she'd chosen regret.

Regret. What had Marty said about regrets? She didn't have any? At least not until the moment they'd said good-bye. The pesky push of hope pressed against her muscles again. If she was wrong, if Marty didn't want her, if she'd missed her chance, if she fell short again, at least she'd know for sure.

"Can you guys drive me to the airport?"

"Are you serious?" Joey asked.

Lisa grinned nervously. "Yeah, I'm getting there."

Chapter Nine

Marty stood in the long line at the check-in counter. The East Coast backup from the day before was far from clear. At least she didn't stand out in the throng of tired and downtrodden travelers. Everyone shuffled forward every couple of minutes as if moving up, even enough to take the place of the person in front of them, took great effort. Still, she was envious of her traveling companions. The burdens they carried were temporary. Today they'd go home. Tomorrow all would be made new again. Today would only take her farther from where she wanted to be.

The line shuffled ahead again. She counted the people in front of her. Ten more to go. Then she'd have a boarding pass to take her away from Buffalo. Wouldn't it be nice if the plane could also take her away from the turmoil, away from the conflict, away from the memories of Lisa? No, she didn't want to lose the memories, just the confusion and sadness surrounding them.

She closed her eyes and inhaled, slow and deep, in through her nose and out through her mouth. She thought of Lisa in the firelight, her arm across her chest, the scent of her filling every breath. She heard her laugh and saw her smile, full and bright, as they danced. She felt the breeze as it wove around them on the balcony and tousled Lisa's dark hair. She felt her lips part against her own. Those were the memories she could cling to. She felt the line move around her, and she fought the urge to let it pass her by. She wanted to stay in that space a little longer.

"Um, ma'am," someone behind her said. "Ma'am, I think that woman is trying to get your attention."

She grimaced and opened her eyes, afraid she'd missed a cue from an airline employee, but when she looked around she saw several people still in front of her.

"Over there." The man behind her pointed toward the back of the line.

Nice try. There was no way she would lose her place in the line.

Then she heard a familiar voice, clear and strong, closer than any memory. "Excuse me. Pardon me. I'm not cutting. I just need to—Sorry, sir, can I get through here?" Lisa came into view, half-elbowing, half-begging her way through the crowd.

She was so beautifully disheveled and flustered, her cheeks rosy, her jaw set, her eyes searching frantically.

"Lisa," Marty called out. "What are you doing?"

"I'm coming to stop you."

"Stop me from what?"

"From leaving," she said, pushing past the last few people between them.

"You could've called me."

"I didn't really think of that," she said, flustered. "This is my first time tracking someone down at the airport."

"Yeah?" Marty asked, amused by her consternation, and beyond thrilled that she'd made the effort. "How's it going so far?"

"It's not as easy as it looks in chick flicks. I didn't have anywhere to buy flowers, and parking's a mess. Elaine let me off at the curb, and you know, the crowds don't just part."

"But you found me anyway."

"I did." Lisa finally smiled. "Only now that you're here, or I'm here, I feel like getting here might've been the easy part."

Marty fought the urge to kiss her, to soothe her. The fact that she'd come, that she put herself out there meant so much, and at the same time so little. If Lisa only wanted a little more time to drag out good-bye, manage expectations, or, even worse, if she'd come out of some misplaced fear of disappointing her, it would only add to their torment.

"Look," Lisa started again. "I don't know how to do this."

"Do what?"

"Profess my feelings for someone. I don't know how to sweep someone off her feet. I'm probably not going to be very good at it."

Not a promising start.

"I've always left the emotional stuff to people who are better at it. I've seen so many great love stories, but I never thought I could live one of them. I'm the class clown, the tension breaker, the comic relief. I'm good at being funny, I'm good at keeping things light, and people liked me for that. I was okay with just being liked, until you came along."

"But I liked you too," Marty said. "I still do."

"I know, and that scared me because I knew you deserved better than I'd ever given before. The night we met, Joey tried to warn me off you. She asked if I was ready to settle down."

"And you said no?" Marty already knew the answer.

"I did, but that was only partially true. It wasn't so much that I wasn't ready to, so much as I wasn't sure I could."

"And now?" Marty asked and then held her breath.

"I still don't know if I can. I've never had a serious relationship in my life, but you make me want to try." She took Marty's hand. "I can't promise I'll be perfect, but I do promise to try with everything I have in me to be the kind of partner you deserve. One who's open and honest and thoughtful, and who will always do everything I can to make you smile every single day you'll let me."

"Wow," Marty whispered, squeezing Lisa's hand. "For someone who's never done this before, you sure did a good job."

Lisa beamed. "Really?"

"You set the bar pretty damn high for the rest of us," the guy behind them grumbled.

Marty looked up to see several of the people around them watching the exchange expectantly before she turned back to Lisa. "I know you're afraid you'll disappoint me if you don't say or do the right thing, but what you just did, what you just said, it was perfect for me."

"Seriously?"

"Seriously." Marty laughed. "And you did it all with an audience."

Lisa turned a bright shade of red before whispering. "I'm glad to hear it, but…"

"But what?"

"What do I do next?"

"I don't know," Marty admitted. "You're the romantic lead of this story. You just had your big moment. You've got the girl. What do you want to do about it?"

Lisa's sheepish grin grew into a full-fledged smile as she slipped her hand behind Marty's back, pulled her close, and kissed her.

As their lips met, she knew they still had plenty left to work out. This was not the end of the story. It was merely the prelude to their happily every after.

Life coach Elaine Raitt and blue-collar boi Joey Lang fall in love in LoveLife.

RISK FACTOR

Karis Walsh

Chapter One

Myra Owens returned to the feed room and set two buckets on the cement floor near her friend Kate Brown, who was stooped over a wooden bin. She continued her pitch for a new student body for the stable. "The program even has family days, so the soldiers can spend time grooming or walking the horses with their kids and spouses." Myra leaned against the door frame while Kate measured scoops of grain into each bucket. Even though Kate was the owner of Portland's Cedar Grove Equestrian Center and could afford to hire stable help, she chose to do most of the hands-on work with the horses herself. Myra shared the barn chores as often as she could, mostly because she loved being around the horses, but also because it gave her more time with Kate, who was often busy with her new girlfriend, Jamie, and Jamie's niece, Anna. Some of Myra and Kate's best conversations took place while they mixed feed or cleaned tack together.

"Riding gives them a topic of conversation," Myra continued. "A quiet way to reconnect with their loved ones, with the horse as a sort of mediator. Rebuilding relationships."

Kate nodded and emptied a pouch of herbal joint supplement into one of the buckets. She added a scoop of vitamins to each, and Myra grabbed the metal handles and left the room. She walked down the aisle to a chorus of neighs from the horses that hadn't been fed yet. Frosty, an older school horse, got the supplemented feed, and one of the boarders got the regular mix. Myra dropped the buckets near Kate again.

"Some of the wounded vets need more support while riding, but the ones who are dealing with emotional issues like PTSD are usually able to ride on their own, so we won't need as many volunteers as we do for our regular therapeutic lessons."

Myra paused in the middle of her speech while she took feed to the next two hungry horses. She was accustomed to carrying on conversations with Kate in this disjointed manner while they did barn chores—whether they paused to empty a full wheelbarrow of manure or to return a cleaned bridle to a tack-room hook. When she had been planning how to broach the subject of a new riding program to Kate, she had automatically memorized the facts in separate sound bites. Kate was paying attention to the rations she doled out, making sure each animal got supplements and grain in the proper amounts, but Myra had no doubt that Kate was also listening to every word she said.

Myra dumped feed into her own horse's bucket and paused briefly before her next trip to the feed room. She leaned against Dragon's neck and felt the rhythmic tensing of his muscles as he chewed the grain. The sound of his contented munching was soothing, but Kate's horse Topper banged a hoof against the adjoining wall, reminding her that the other horses were still impatiently waiting for dinner. She gave Dragon another pat and left his stall. The last part of her talk was the impassioned plea for them to make this program work here at Cedar Grove. Myra had discovered the Bright Stars riding program when she was at a conference in Washington State last week, and she had been struck by her overwhelming need to help establish another like it as an adjunct to Kate's already thriving therapeutic riding school. Myra knew why she needed to make this happen, and she also was acutely aware of how difficult it would be for her to work with the returning soldiers who came there to ride. Still, she couldn't let her own discomfort keep her from doing what she felt compelled to do.

A loud whinny accompanied by the sound of a metal horseshoe striking a wooden stall door broke Myra free from the weight of her memories. She walked down the aisle with determination and started talking as soon as she came through the door.

"We have to do this, Kate. We have the infrastructure in place, we have volunteers, and we have enough horses to fill the extra classes. Not only would it be a great opportunity to help more people, but it's a chance to give back to our community and support our local troops."

"And a way to honor Jeffrey's memory," Kate added in a quiet voice. She and Myra each picked up two buckets and returned to the stall-lined aisle.

They fed the last four in silence. Myra inhaled the scent of horses and fresh cedar shavings, but her breath came in shallow and rapid gulps as she felt the constricting fist of sorrow tighten her throat. The barn and horses had been a safe haven for her, and she needed to repay the favor somehow. Assuage the guilt because she had survived and had found some peace here while her brother Jeffrey hadn't. Possibly keep another family from facing the stupefying shock of welcoming back a loved one, only to lose them at home. Myra had witnessed plenty of miracles while working with Kate and her therapy program. Maybe they could squeeze out a few more.

Kate closed the latch on Topper's stall, and she draped her arm over Myra's shoulders as they took the empty buckets back to the feed room.

"I think it's a great idea," she said. "Jamie will be out of town next weekend, so why don't we take Anna for a drive and visit this Bright Stars program together? You've wanted to take on more lessons since you got certified, and this would be a good place to start. You can do the lesson plans from scratch instead of just taking over the ones I've already created. Really make the program your own."

Myra—still reeling from the onslaught of memories she felt whenever Jeffrey's name was mentioned—took a few moments to realize what Kate was saying. She stopped walking and turned to face Kate, breaking the contact with her to get a little distance.

"I don't want to be the teacher. I thought I could help out if you need me. I'll take on some of your regular lessons so you have the time to do these."

Kate frowned. "If this will be too difficult for you…"

Myra shook her head. She felt her brow tighten in an answering frown as she searched for a way to express the conflicting emotions she felt. "I want the program to happen. It matters to me more than I can say. But I don't know if I can be the instructor and interact with the riders. I couldn't help the way you could."

"You can help them in ways I *can't*." Kate said. She stopped in front of the white boards that covered the walls where they stood, just outside the feed room. Both barns were full of boarders and lesson horses, and Myra and Kate had detailed charts listing when horses had training sessions and turnout time in the paddocks, when students had lessons, and what horses required veterinary or farrier care. Splotches and smears covered the boards as old schedules were erased and new ones added almost daily, but the one constant was the amount of work required to run a training barn this size, plus a full-time therapeutic program.

"I have a full load of classes right now," Kate continued, gesturing toward the boards with a green dry-erase marker. "If we expand, it will need to be with you as the instructor, but I'll understand if you don't want the extra responsibility. The barn as it is couldn't survive without your help, let alone if we added an entirely new therapy protocol. You're always here for classes, you do all the insurance billing, and you take over when I'm at shows or traveling. I don't know when you find time for your regular job. Why don't we wait until next summer for this project?"

Myra sighed. Kate might be exaggerating when she talked about Myra's indispensability, but she wasn't overstating her own workload. Kate taught the therapy classes, traveled to shows with her training horses and students, and served as barn manager and chief stall cleaner. Add Jamie and Anna, and Kate barely had time to take a breath of her own. Myra juggled full-time school teaching with barn work, and she had recently qualified to teach in the barn's therapeutic program. Her goal had been to lighten Kate's responsibilities, and here she was suggesting they expand with a different kind of program. Kate was willing to add the classes for service members—she was always willing to help someone in need—but Myra recognized the signs of strain on her longtime friend's face. If Myra wanted the military program, she'd have to take charge of it herself.

Myra's attention shifted around the barn while she considered whether she could go forward with the project. Could she teach the lessons? Face the constant reminder of what Jeffrey was like when he returned from his second deployment to the Middle East? Keep going forward when it was too late to go back and help him like she should have done? She had won the right to start the program using Kate's resources and arena, but she felt as if she'd lost the tight grip she always held on her memories. Her work with the therapy students was unwaveringly personal. She got attached to them and celebrated small victories and defeats as if they were her own. But with these new riders—the veterans and active-duty military members who would come to the program with both mental and physical wounds—she'd need to remain detached.

She watched as Kate wrote out the next day's agenda. Perhaps the distance Myra would need to maintain would help her be more effective as the program's teacher. She'd be able to observe as an outsider, not allowing her personal pain to get in the way of the students' progress. Myra sighed. She wasn't fully convinced of her logic, but she had to hold on to the shaky confidence it gave her.

"I'll do it," she said.

Kate grinned and pulled her into a tight hug. "I knew you would. Come up to the house and we'll start doing some research. I'll contact the Bright Stars people so we can observe some lessons and get more details about the structure of the program."

Myra unresistingly followed as Kate pulled her toward the house, but her mind was shouting at her to run. To escape. Kate—in her usual enthusiastic way—had taken hold of the new idea and was running with it, conversely energized by the idea of more work. She chatted about the equipment they might need for the lessons, and the modifications they'd make to the existing arena space, seemingly happy to have a new project to plan and organize. Myra tried to focus on the details and facts rather than her own gnawing misgivings. She only had herself to blame for bringing up the idea in the first place.

"Remember when we took Jeffrey on the trail ride?" Kate stopped on the gravel driveway and gave Myra a smile that seemed as tinged with sadness as with humor at the funny memory. "He jumped off when his horse started trotting, and then thought she was chasing him around a tree."

Myra choked back a laugh that threatened to turn into a sob. Her brother, three years younger than she was, had begged for weeks to be invited to ride with them. He'd been enamored of beautiful, blond Kate—who hadn't been?—and Myra had finally relented and let him come on one of their weekend trail rides. He'd panicked at Snoopy's bouncy but sedate trot and had jumped off the little mare. She'd been confused by his abrupt dismount but had obediently followed her rider as he ran around a sapling, convinced the horse was chasing him with malicious intentions. Jeffrey had given up on riding after that experience. He gave up on Kate after he found out that she and Myra were caught kissing beneath the school bleachers.

"He didn't want to ride again, but he still enjoyed being around horses. He'd hang out at the barn with me even when he realized he didn't have a chance of dating you."

Kate laughed. "He had your touch with animals. I remember coming to your aunt's barn when you first got Dragon. Jeffrey would be sitting on the grass with all the barn cats draped over him while Dragon grazed nearby."

Myra nodded, easily able to picture the exact scene Kate was describing as if it had happened just this afternoon. It seemed to define her brother, who had been able to charm animals and humans with equal ease. If only she had been better able to see the pain beneath his charm. If only she had known how to reach him when he had disappeared so deep inside his memories. If only…She wiped the back of her hand across her cheek and brushed the wetness away on her worn denim jeans.

"I love that about you," Kate said quietly. "You take your own sadness and use it as a way to help other people."

Myra shook her head wordlessly, unable to speak. She hooked her arm through Kate's and started walking toward Kate's house again. She wasn't a saint, wasn't someone as altruistic as Kate believed her to be. She pushed her grief back inside, deep in her heart, and changed the topic of conversation from Jeffrey to which horses would be best suited to her new program.

Chapter Two

Myra!" Kate called from the main barn's aisleway. "They're here."

Myra checked the grooming area one last time to make sure everything was in place before she greeted her new students. The three horses were standing quietly in the crossties, and a wooden tote full of brushes and combs was sitting on a shelf at each station. Everything was tidy and ready for the lesson, but Myra knew what really mattered. Before every lesson, she fussed over her lesson plans and the equipment each student would need, even though none of it was as important as the horses themselves. They were the true miracle workers. They were the ones who would be able to reach past barriers and touch human hearts. She gave old Spot a quick scratch on his neck and walked down the aisle.

She saw her small group of riders clustered around the entrance to the barn, standing just inside the large sliding door where a sharp line separated the bright spring sunshine from the shadowy interior of the barn. To an outsider, they were an unremarkable group, but Myra had access to their private lives. She had read their files and knew the darker secrets behind their homecomings. The damaged lives and shattered relationships. The pain—mental, physical, and emotional. The burden to help them was overwhelming, and she reminded herself yet again that she was only the facilitator in the process. The horses would heal more scars than she'd even realize were present and hidden. She paused for a deep breath while she matched each person with the information she'd learned about them.

Drew leaned against the barn wall, facing out and away from her. His crutches were propped against the wall behind him, as if he took every opportunity to tuck them out of sight. Myra had read about the muscle damage he'd sustained when he was hit by shrapnel, but she knew she was only getting the bare bones of his story. He wouldn't have been recommended for this program for physical therapy alone, although Myra hoped riding would help in that area as well. He wouldn't be here if he only needed healing on a muscular level. Unlike Drew, Blake didn't have any outward signs of damage but had been suffering from PTSD and was having difficulties coping with the return to his old life. Only his proud and shuttered expression showed the barriers he had erected to protect his pain.

That left Ainslee Cooper. Myra could only see her silhouette, but the slender outline of her prosthetic was easy to spot. Myra had been intrigued by her file, partly because her story was similar in some ways to Jeffrey's and partly because of the photo attached to it. Ainslee was beautiful. Dark hair pulled back in a tight bun and little makeup only emphasized her elegant bone structure and large chocolate eyes. Dark, angular eyebrows framed those eyes and gave an impression of someone with a strong and stubborn personality—no softly arched brows or diverted gaze, but one of directness and openness. Her smiling mouth and full bottom lip quirked up in one corner, like she was ready to break into hearty laughter. She looked impish and younger than her age of twenty-six, but the photo had been taken before she'd been deployed. What changes would Myra see in her now?

The three people in her lesson had much in common but they stood in silence, not speaking to one another. Would anyone notice if Myra escaped out the back door of the barn?

"Hey," Kate said, appearing by her side and dashing Myra's plan to run away. Kate nudged her with an elbow. "You'll be great. You've taught plenty of lessons before, and once you get started you'll see that this one isn't any different."

Myra didn't quite believe her, but she stepped forward anyway. She cleared her throat to get the attention of her students and inhaled sharply when Ainslee turned and looked at her.

Myra slowly exhaled. She had expected Ainslee to appear older than in her picture after all she had been through, but there was something young and vulnerable in her expression that hadn't been in the photo. No smile this time, and her skin was paler, but the faint laugh lines near her eyes and curving to the corners of her lips were evidence of a lost propensity to an easy grin.

"Welcome to Cedar Grove. I'm Myra and I'll be your instructor for the next eight weeks. Do any of you have experience with horses?" Three brief and silent head shakes were her answer. Myra was relieved since they could all start from scratch. She tried to ignore her awareness of Ainslee while she talked—disconcerted when her body's response to the actual woman was even stronger than to her picture—and concentrated instead on the information she needed to share and on a cursory appraisal of the three students. Blake was tall and slender, focused slightly to the left of Myra's face, never holding direct eye contact. Drew, on the other hand, met her gaze with an almost belligerent expression, as if daring her to challenge him somehow. He still had the muscular build of someone who had spent hours a day in a gym, but Myra knew his injury would have severely curtailed his workouts. All three were wearing long pants and heeled, tread-less boots. The right leg of Ainslee's jeans was cut off at the knee, and the metal of her curved prosthesis was as shiny as the brand-new looking cowboy boot on her left foot.

"I see all of you are wearing the appropriate clothes," Myra continued. "We'll provide safety helmets, and that's our first rule. No riding without one. Rule Two: until you get familiar with our horses and we get to know you, no one is allowed to ride or enter a horse's stall without permission and supervision. Three: ask for help if you need it. I know you're accustomed to being in control, but allow yourselves to be beginners here. Finally, Rule Four, keep your anger and frustration out of the barn and away from the animals. If you need to blow off some steam, do it outside. Any questions so far?"

At this point in her lessons, new students would either be excitedly clamoring for attention as they threw question after question at her, or they'd be nervous and silent. This group was simply quiet, expressionless. Myra felt an urge to apologize for giving them rules as if they were children, but she didn't. She had learned from her first days working with Kate that the riders often craved structure and guidelines. The framework gave them a sense of security in a new and sometimes frightening situation. These three riders, although they had the outward appearance of confidence and calm, were probably feeling some trepidation—invisible as it was—about riding for the first time, especially with physical and psychological limitations that were still foreign to them.

"Today we're going to learn how to groom and tack the horses." Myra talked as she led the group toward the crossties. Their silence was still unnerving, but Kate had been correct—once Myra had started the lesson, the familiarity of the words comforted her. She seemed hyperaware of the uneven sound of Ainslee's gait on the cement floor of the aisle, but she knew she'd survive the lesson. Jeffrey was always present in her mind, and Ainslee had insinuated herself there as well, but Myra would survive. She'd manage to keep the threats to her emotions at bay as long as she kept most of herself in teaching mode. "We'll start the actual riding next week, and you'll have the same horse throughout the entire eight-week session."

Myra stopped when they were close to the horses. She had already decided which human to pair with which horse, and her quick evaluation when she first saw the students confirmed her original choices. She felt the weight of this responsibility almost more than any other she'd face while teaching this group. The success or failure of the program might depend on her ability to connect the right horse to each rider since the bond they'd form with their new partners would be such an important factor in their healing and their engagement with riding. If her judgment was off…She took a deep breath and gestured at a dozing pinto. "Drew, you'll be paired with Spot."

Spot wasn't the prettiest horse, but he was solid and reliable and would be the safest mount for Drew, with his back injuries. Myra paused for a moment, expecting the dark and brooding Drew to say something derogatory about the horse, but he just shrugged slightly, tightened his grip on his crutches, and limped over to Spot.

"Blake, you and Frosty will be partners. Ainslee"—Myra paused as even the act of saying Ainslee's name for the first time seemed too intimate—"you're with Deacon."

Once the three were standing in their places next to the horses, Myra gave a quick demonstration of the various grooming tools. She kept it short because she wanted them to get in contact with the horses as soon as possible. During the riding sessions, she'd have volunteers leading the horses and supporting the riders, but today she would be on her own.

"We'll start with the rubber currycomb to loosen mud and dirt on the horse's body. Use this in a circular motion, but only on the muscular parts of the horse, not on their legs or face." Myra curried Spot's shoulder while she explained what she was doing. "Go ahead and try this yourselves."

Myra handed the currycomb to Drew, and he and the other two wordlessly began to imitate her actions. Myra blinked back unexpected tears as she remembered seeing the same passivity in Jeffrey the last time she had brought him to visit Dragon after he had come home. She had to break through, somehow.

"Why don't you keep just one crutch while you're grooming," she said after watching Drew work for a few minutes. "You can rest your free hand on Spot's neck for balance."

"Okay." He handed her the metal crutch and she leaned it against the wall, near enough for him to reach if he needed it.

"Better?" she asked.

He shuffled several steps, keeping his hand braced on Spot's sturdy neck, and began grooming the horse's back. "Much. Maybe someday I can get rid of both the damned things."

His voice was toneless, but Myra felt his frustration. She herself felt a wave of relief that he had acknowledged his situation. Would Jeffrey have been as communicative if she had spent more time with him? Or asked the right questions?

She couldn't keep second-guessing herself. She and her parents had tried everything they could think of to help Jeffrey. It hadn't been enough.

"Riding is an excellent way to work your core and spinal muscles," she said. Focus on the facts, not the emotions. Heal the physical, and hopefully the emotional will follow. "I'll bet you notice a marked improvement in your range of motion and strength by the end of the eight weeks."

He gave another noncommittal shrug. Skeptical? Or afraid to hope? Myra patted Spot on the shoulder and went to check on Blake and Frosty. She had paired them because the mare was a good physical match for Blake's height and slim build, but she had also thought they might fit well in other ways, too. Blake was healthy and would probably progress quickly. Frosty was well-behaved, but she had a stubborn and spirited streak that made her more suitable for advanced riders. Maybe the movement and freedom he'd experience while riding would help dissipate the aura of tension Myra felt when she got close to him. Yet another reminder of Jeffrey. He had been outwardly placid and detached, but an agitated energy had practically rippled the air around him.

"You seem very comfortable around her," Myra said, after watching Blake confidently sweep a stiff-bristled brush over the mare's coat. She was shedding the last of her winter fur and gray hairs already covered Blake's jeans and dark polo shirt. "Have you ridden before?"

"Once or twice on family vacations," he said, not looking at her but instead staring at the horse as if grooming her was a vital mission. His brush strokes got more determined. "My daughter loves horses."

Myra remembered his file. A son and daughter, ages six and eight. He was currently separated from them and his young wife while he went through class after class in anger management. Myra thought some good gallops along the trails behind Kate's barn would do more to help than all the therapy, and she hoped he'd stick with the program long enough to try out her theory.

"After a few weeks, we'll schedule some times when you can bring your family to the barn. By then you'll be able to show your daughter how to groom and ride Frosty." Something positive to offer them, instead of pain.

Blake paused with his arm in midstroke. "I'd like that," he said, resuming his resolute grooming.

Myra turned finally toward Ainslee. She had been avoiding personal contact because she wasn't certain how to handle her obvious interest. She had been hoping to get through the lesson with minimal resurfacing of sad memories—and that hadn't worked—but now she was drawn to one of her students. Ainslee was beautiful, and based on Myra's reading of her file, she had intelligence and integrity. In a normal situation, Myra wouldn't have fought her attraction, but Ainslee came with more tangled strings than a game of cat's cradle. She had been having trouble coping with her injury, and the subsequent problems were more than Myra was willing to handle. Ainslee had abandoned every attempt to help her—from physical therapy to a variety of counseling methods. Myra worried she'd quit this program, too, before the horses had a chance to break her out of her protective shell. So many professionals had tried to help Ainslee—what could Myra hope to do? Get close enough so she'd be destroyed if Ainslee decided to take the way out that Jeffrey had chosen? Not a chance.

Ainslee was standing as far from Deacon as she could, reaching out so the currycomb barely skimmed his body. Deacon's dark, liver-chestnut coat was flecked with gray, but he had the proud, arched neck typical in a Morgan, and a proud spirit to match. Myra had picked him for Ainslee the moment she saw her picture.

"He likes to be scratched here," Myra said. She lifted Deacon's heavy mane and found an itchy spot along the crest of his neck, near his withers. She held his mane out of the way and Ainslee tentatively used her currycomb on his neck. "Use a firmer motion," Myra suggested. "You don't have to be afraid of hurting him."

Ainslee had to step closer to follow Myra's suggestion, and Myra had a feeling that any fear Ainslee had was self-directed. She kept her body positioned so her right leg was farthest from the horse, and she seemed ready to jump to safety if necessary. She increased the pressure with her brush, however, and Deacon responded by curving his neck toward her and curling his upper lip in pleasure.

Ainslee laughed, and Myra realized it was the first sound she'd heard from her. A brief but musical glimpse of the vivacious person she used to be. The humor and joy were still there, however deeply buried.

"He likes it," Ainslee said. Her voice was huskier than Myra had expected, a contrast to the facial expressions that fleetingly altered her mouth and eyes before disappearing and leaving her with a calm mask again.

"Yes. If you watch his ears and posture, you'll be able to recognize when he's nervous or relaxed or interested. See his left ear, how it's tipped toward you? He's paying attention to you and most likely hoping you'll scratch him some more."

Myra stepped back and watched Ainslee's stance change slightly. She was still protecting her right side, but she was now paying attention to her horse, not just herself. One short laugh and three tiny words from Ainslee, and Myra found her even more appealing than before. She walked back to Drew for another round with each of her riders, even though she wanted to stagger into the barn's lounge and lie on the comfy old sofa. She hadn't done more than give a few instructions and carry on short conversations, but she felt a heavy weariness settle on her neck and shoulders. She had known them for only an hour, but she already cared about these people. She had been fooling herself to think she could escape from these sessions with her heart unscathed. Or shattered completely, she added, as she looked back at Ainslee.

Chapter Three

Two weeks later, Myra hoisted a sixty-pound bag of grain over her shoulder and carried it toward the feed room. The first four bags had been relatively easy to carry, but she was sagging under the weight of this one and they still had a dozen left before the truck was empty. She shifted to find a more comfortable position, and her muscles protested the extra movement. The summer day was mild, typical of an Oregon June, and she was dressed lightly in jeans and a red cotton tank, but she already felt a trickle of sweat between her breasts and down her spine.

Myra had spent most of her free time riding and working at barns, and she always reminded herself that the bright side of hauling bales of hay, bags of feed, and heavy wooden jumps meant she didn't need to waste any time at the gym. Her hobby gave her plenty of exercise and kept her body in great shape. She felt her biceps flex as she repositioned the shifting bag. More muscle than your average woman, perhaps, but Myra liked the confidence her strength gave her. Today, however, with the stress of teaching harried teenagers during the last weeks of high school and working with her military students here at the barn, Myra felt depleted. She needed to find some way to energize herself again, before the three soldiers arrived for their lesson. Last week's lesson had rushed by, as usual for the first time her students got to mount their horses. By the time they'd learned how to mount, had gotten their stirrups adjusted, and had been instructed in the basics of stop-go-steer, the lesson had been nearly over. Myra had been happy when the two hours rushed by with little time for any personal interaction. Now when she passed Kate—who was on a return trip to the full pickup truck—

in the doorway, they playfully jostled each other as each tried to get through the door first.

"Ouch! My shoulder!" Myra winced when Kate was about to push past her, and then sped through the opening as Kate hesitated with a look of concern on her face. "Ha! You are too easy."

"I'll get you next time," Kate said, sprinting toward the truck.

Myra hurried to drop the bag of grain on the ground next to the feed bin and jog back to the door. She had deliberately provoked Kate's competitive side, and she wanted to keep her split-second time advantage. Turning the unloading process into a game would make it more strenuous, but also more fun. Myra would be even happier if she beat Kate through the door every time.

She saw Kate's shadow and rushed to cross the threshold first. She braced her hands on either side of the door to keep from propelling herself into a collision with Kate. "I win again," she said. Her laughter ended with a sharp exhale when she realized she was face-to-face with Ainslee instead of Kate. Ainslee, visibly startled by Myra's sudden appearance, stepped back too quickly onto her right foot and lost her balance. Myra reflexively reached out and steadied her.

"Sorry about that. Are you hurt?" Myra felt as if a current passed between her and Ainslee where their skin was in contact, vibrations of the unreadable emotions behind the frown on Ainslee's face. Myra wanted to let go, to regain her own equilibrium after the simple, yet intimate connection, but she kept her hand around Ainslee's upper arm until she was certain she wasn't going to fall. She still seemed uncertain on her prosthesis, even when walking a straight line, let alone during such an abrupt change of direction.

"I'm fine." Ainslee shrugged away from Myra's touch. "I saw you come in here and I…you said I should use a different saddle this week."

"Right." Myra motioned for Ainslee to follow her. She went into the adjoining tack room, walking slowly for Ainslee's benefit.

"You don't need to crawl."

"This is my normal—" Myra turned and saw a scowl on Ainslee's face. The same expression she had used during the entire lesson last week when the students rode for the first time. Ainslee had just witnessed her rapid exit from the feed room, so Myra's false protests were meaningless. If she were in Ainslee's position, she'd want to be treated as a capable adult, not a baby. "You have good mobility and don't need to be coddled. I apologize."

"Well. Okay, then," Ainslee said. She seemed flustered by Myra's words, as if she'd been hoping for a fight and hadn't been expecting Myra to yield. She seemed more irritated by Myra's acquiescence than she had been by her condescendingly slow walk.

Myra stepped back when she felt a sudden urge to hold Ainslee, to ease the raw emotions she saw on Ainslee's face. She resisted the desire, partly because she needed to keep her distance, but mostly because she knew Ainslee would reject any sign of compassion or pity. Myra guessed that Ainslee's family and friends had tried to comfort her the same way Myra wanted to, but the gesture was one *they* needed, not what was best for Ainslee.

What she and Ainslee both needed was distance and detachment. Myra walked quickly over to one of the tack lockers and slid a heavy black saddle off the rack.

"This is my dressage saddle. It has a deep seat, but it still allows you to feel contact with your horse. I think it will fit you better than the Western one you used last week."

Myra brushed her hand over the saddle, rubbing away a thin film of dust that had settled on the well-oiled, soft leather. She tried—unsuccessfully—not to picture Ainslee's crotch and thighs in contact with the saddle. She shifted the stirrups forward and wiped off the long flaps, and her hand tingled with the imagined caress of Ainslee's thighs.

She decided against her original plan of carrying the saddle into the barn for Ainslee. She didn't need a groom toting things around for her—better to let her do the work herself. Besides, Myra needed some time to yank her mind out of its delusional fantasies about Ainslee's body and get her focus back onto the business at hand today. Maybe flinging a few more bags of grain around the feed room would help her exorcise the pressure building in her own body. She draped the saddle over Ainslee's forearm, careful to keep touch to a minimum.

"I'll be out in a few minutes," she said, holding the tack room door open as Ainslee limped through it. "Chris is in the barn if you need help with anything."

Ainslee only nodded, not making eye contact. Myra stood still for a moment and watched Ainslee walk away from her. She moved slowly, awkwardly, but something seemed to tremble through the air around her. A need to run? To find some sort of release from the restrictions of her new physique?

Myra wasn't sure how to help, and she needed to allay her own physical tension before the lesson. She jogged to the truck and grabbed one of the few remaining feed sacks. Kate had put a big dent in the load of grain, and Myra hurried to make up for the time she'd missed.

She finished the last trip and slammed the tailgate shut just as Blake's car pulled into the parking lot. She waited for him near the barn entrance.

"Hey, Myra," he said, offering a more genuine smile than she'd seen from him so far.

"Hi, Blake. How are you feeling after last week's lesson?"

He grimaced and then laughed, pushing blond bangs out of his eyes as they walked together down the barn aisle. "I didn't believe you when you said we might be sore after only a few minutes on a horse. I guess I hadn't realized how inactive I've been since…lately."

Myra grinned. Trying new things, challenging their bodies and minds. The program was already beginning to fulfill its purpose. "Just wait until I start teaching you the posting trot. You'll discover muscles you never knew you had."

"I can't wait." Blake gave an exaggerated sigh. He stopped and faced her. "Seriously, though, I want to thank you for asking me to join this program. You know I've been separated from my family while I work some things out?"

Myra nodded. The details from her students' applications and the letters from their therapists and doctors were so familiar to her they seemed part of her now.

"Well, visits have been strained, to say the least. All I wanted to do was apologize, and all Tracy seemed able to do was cry. We'd ask about each other's lives, the same awkward conversations over and over."

He paused and looked over her shoulder for a long moment. Myra sensed some of the frustration he must have felt during those meetings, while everyone walked on eggshells.

He looked at her again. "For the past two weeks, though, we've had something different to talk about. Heidi, my daughter, can't get enough horse talk, and somehow we all seemed more at ease when she became her normal chatty self again. She'll call tonight, wanting to hear every detail of my lesson. It feels good."

Myra stayed in place, but she was jumping up and down like an excited child inside her head. She was familiar with small achievements like these after working with Kate's program for so long, but they never failed to thrill her. The program wasn't changing the world, but for Blake the simple joy of sharing a riding story with his daughter was a small miracle. She felt privileged to be part of it.

"The barn is closed to regular lessons and riders on Mondays. If you want, you can bring your family out here next week and your kids can meet Frosty. Around four thirty?"

"Yeah," he said. "We'll be here."

He went over to the gray mare and started his grooming routine. Drew and Ainslee were already working on their horses, with Chris and Vanessa—two of Myra's volunteers—helping them. Myra tugged on her tank top, loosening it where it had stuck against her chest while she had hauled grain bags at a punishing speed. She felt good. Exhausted enough from work so her mind stopped fretting about her attraction to Ainslee and her worries about the military program. Buoyed back to life by Blake's progress here and with his family. For the first time in weeks, she felt she was capable of handling the lessons and the memories of Jeffrey without—

The thud of a metal hoof pick hitting the wall jarred her out of her smug reverie.

"Stop pushing me! I told you I was as close as I was going to get," Ainslee shouted. She was facing Vanessa with a defiant and scowling expression on her face and her arms crossed tightly over her chest. Teenaged Vanessa stepped between Ainslee and Deacon, her hands held out either to placate Ainslee or to protect the horse in case she threw something at him. Probably both, Myra decided. She rubbed the bridge of her nose. One small victory had made her forget how far the students still had to go in the healing process, and how many challenges she'd yet to face while she helped them.

Although she wanted to rush into the scene and fix everything, she made herself walk slowly over to Deacon. Ainslee didn't seem inclined to continue throwing things, and neither Vanessa nor Deacon appeared to be in danger. The horse was so accustomed to people and noises that he had done little more than prick his ears toward the sound of the hoof pick against the side of the barn.

Myra shook her head at Chris, who had come over to help, and he nodded in silent acknowledgment of her gesture. He went instead to where Drew and Blake were watching Ainslee and got them back to work on their own horses. Myra appreciated the easy communication with him, at least. The lanky, bearded young man had been working with her and Kate for years, and she could count on him to distract the other students and keep them safe so the disruption in the lesson didn't escalate.

"What's going on?" she asked, directing her question at Ainslee. Let her take responsibility for her actions instead of being discussed like a child by Myra and Vanessa.

"She kept harping at me to stand closer, but I can't. She should have backed off when I told her to." Ainslee's cheeks had turned from pale olive to a blotchy red, and she was frowning so deeply that her full lower lip made her appear as petulant as a child. There was something heartbreakingly unguarded in her expression. Her pain was showing to the world, and she seemed incapable of controlling its expression and protecting herself. "Why does it matter anyway? Cleaning stupid horse hooves won't change anything."

"I'd never ask her to do something unsafe," Vanessa said. "I only wanted her to move toward him a little to make it easier for her to hold his hoof, but I should have—"

Myra held up her hand before Vanessa could apologize. The girl was experienced, and Myra trusted she knew what she was doing with her students. "I understand, Vanessa. Please take Deacon back to his stall for me."

Myra stepped closer to Ainslee as Vanessa led Deacon away from them. She suddenly remembered standing over the heater vents in her grandmother's house when she was young. Ainslee's anger blew at her with nearly as tangible a force. Myra wanted to reach beyond it, to see the wounds Ainslee was fiercely protecting. She wanted to join Ainslee's battle against the unfairness of her injury. She wanted and wanted, but she wasn't capable of fighting or cajoling her way through to Ainslee. And as much as she longed to forget everything else around her and focus on the beautiful, touchy, and hurting person in front of her, she had to do her job. That meant providing a safe place for her horses, her volunteers, and the class as a whole.

"Rule number four. Don't bring your anger into the barn or around the horses."

"I didn't throw the hoof pick at Deacon. I'd never…I was just…" Ainslee's words sputtered to a halt.

"I know. If you had, I'd tell you to leave and never come back. Instead I'm telling you to take a break from riding today. Find another way to vent your anger, and we'll be happy to have you join us again next week."

Ainslee raised her hands in a gesture of disbelief. "You're actually kicking me out of the lesson? The horse didn't even flinch!"

"Deacon is very calm, but another horse might have been frightened by what you did. And Vanessa gives her time as a volunteer. She doesn't deserve to be yelled at when she's only trying to help."

Ainslee stared at Myra before shaking her head in disbelief and walking away without another word. Her halting gait kept her from storming out of the barn like she probably wanted to do. Instead, the irregular clack of her leg against the concrete of the barn aisle seemed to echo for ages.

Drew, Blake, and Chris had been watching the interchange in silence, but now they broke into an overly cheerful-sounding conversation about bridles. Myra needed to get her attention back to them and continue the lesson, but instead she watched Ainslee limp down the aisle, pause briefly by Deacon's stall to exchange a few words with Vanessa, and then disappear out the barn door. Myra was about to go after her—common sense and duty be damned—but Kate appeared through the side door of the barn and put a firm hand on Myra's arm.

"You handled that well. Don't doubt yourself. Let her go."

"And if she doesn't come back?" Myra asked. She knew the answer. It would be *her* fault. Her silent words mimicked the ones she had stopped Vanessa from saying. *I should have…*

"If she chooses not to come back, it's up to her. You did the right thing." Kate's low voice was soothing, although not entirely convincing. "I have a feeling she'll make the right decision and continue with lessons. Give her time to calm down, and time to heal."

"You're right. Thanks." Myra gave Kate's hand a pat and moved away from her and toward the other students. She wanted to help every rider who came through the barn, and she was sad each time one of them gave up and left. But she had never before felt as if part of herself was walking out the door.

Chapter Four

As quickly as Ainslee's temper flared, it disappeared again, leaving her weak and confused. She kept to the shadows and leaned against the outer door to the barn with her eyes tightly closed while she tried to figure out what had just happened and where she should go now. She wanted to jump in her car and fly down the driveway with a spray of gravel, but she wasn't even able to drive herself anywhere yet. Her neighbor Sasha would be back to pick her up after the lesson was over. Until then, since Myra had rudely kicked her out of the lesson, Ainslee would have to lie low and deal with her unpredictable range of emotions on her own, without any physical release from the frustration she felt.

She had tried to leave the barn with some dignity intact, but she had been hampered by her stiff gait and her need to stop and apologize to Vanessa. Even in Ainslee's haze of temper, she had realized how uncharacteristically nasty she had been, and she had needed to make things right with Vanessa before she dealt with her own issues. Now, her fists were clenched so tightly she felt her short fingernails digging into the softened skin of her palms. She used to have calluses there, from her M16 and from regular visits to the obstacle course. She'd always had ways to burn off excess energy or emotion—run, jump, fight. What could she do now? Duck behind the barn. Hide behind a tree.

"Hello."

Ainslee's eyes flew open in surprise. A young girl with a strawberry blond ponytail was sitting close beside her in a wheelchair. Ainslee hadn't even heard her approach. If she'd let her guard down so much on the battlefield, she'd be dead now. She calmed her breathing with a huge effort. She wasn't there anymore. She was home.

"Hi," she said shortly. She didn't trust herself to carry on a civil conversation while she was still fighting to get control.

"I'm Anna. I know you're Ainslee because I saw your name on the lesson board. Shouldn't you be in the barn getting ready to ride?"

Ainslee looked away. She felt like she was living in a stranger's body. She had always been strong and disciplined. She'd been aware of her feelings, not controlled by them. Now she couldn't even identify her emotions anymore. She was weak. Jealousy, anger, despair. They seemed to rise out of nowhere, triggered by unidentifiable factors. Before she could figure out why she was throwing a hoof pick or yelling at someone, her mind was flung to another extreme. She couldn't name her emotions or fight against them, but instead she was helplessly molded by them into someone she didn't recognize. How could she explain any of this to Anna when she didn't understand it herself?

"I…um, Myra decided I shouldn't ride today."

Anna's laughter made Ainslee smile in spite of her foul mood. The sound was musical and carefree—exactly like a child's laughter should be. Finally, something that made sense and seemed right to Ainslee. She couldn't share Anna's youthful joy, but she liked witnessing it for a brief moment.

"Aunt Myra doesn't let you get away with *anything*," Anna said.

Aunt Myra? Was she really a relative, or was this Kate's daughter? Ainslee thought of Kate and Myra and the way they laughed and joked together. She felt her face flush and her fists screw tight again. What the hell was wrong with her?

"You look like you want to be alone," Anna said. She pointed at a large open-sided building on the far edge of the parking lot. "The hay barn is the best place to hide out. Your new leg looks cool. Can you climb with it?"

"Well, thank you." Ainslee heard her voice stutter a bit. People usually asked awkward questions about her leg, or—most often—they desperately tried to keep their gazes from wandering lower than her neck, as if ignoring her injury made it go away. She'd never had anyone compliment her limb, aside from the prosthetist who'd designed it for her. "I guess I could climb. That's more upper body strength than legs, I suppose."

"Then go to the top of the stack. I'm not allowed up there unless someone helps me, but it's great. The hay smells good, and you can see the whole property. It's a good place to think."

Anna gave her a quick wave, and then she moved away. Ainslee stood still for a moment, feeling the residual sense of peace Anna had left with her. Anna had seemed to understand Ainslee's turmoil and her need to find a private space where she could regain control. Ainslee didn't know how Anna had come to need a wheelchair, but she had a feeling she had also dealt with some difficult emotions in her past. Somehow, the brief connection helped Ainslee feel a little less distressed and alone.

She glanced down the aisle and saw the other riders in her class starting to walk her way, so she skirted the parking lot in a series of quick hops on her sound leg and made it to the hay barn before the riders emerged. Ainslee peered around a wooden post, feeling like a guilty delinquent who was skipping class. Myra followed behind the riders and volunteers, glancing to her left and right every once in a while. Was she looking for Ainslee?

Ainslee turned away. Myra stirred up too many feelings inside her. She was having enough trouble with the chaos of her emotions after the accident and amputation of her leg. Myra seemed to be destroying what little equilibrium Ainslee had left.

She leaned against the post and stared at the imposing stack of hay bales. She'd sounded confident when she'd told Anna she was sure she could climb, but actually facing the obstacle, she felt anxious. There were a few bales scattered on the ground. Maybe she could just sit on one of those for an hour.

Ainslee sighed and walked over to the wall of hay. She reached high and slid her hands between two bales before lifting her right leg and wedging the edge of the prosthesis into a small gap. She pulled herself up and groped blindly for a place to fit her left foot. Her breath came in short gasps, more from panic than exertion, and she had to look down and remind herself she was only a couple feet off the ground. Still, when she finally found purchase with her left leg, she clung to the hay for several minutes, afraid to move higher. Gritting her teeth, she reached overhead and started the process over again.

Ainslee's fear escalated with each step higher, and her anger rose to match it. She hated being afraid. Afraid of Deacon—who was so gentle, but so big. Afraid of living without a leg. Afraid of facing this alien with extreme mood swings who seemed to have taken up residence in her mind and heart after the accident. Afraid of saying good-bye to the person she used to be.

Damn Myra. Hay dust clung to Ainslee's face as her tears and the sweat of exertion wet her cheeks. Myra should have been more understanding. She should have felt sorry for Ainslee and calmed her down—like most people did these days—instead of booting her out of the lesson. Then Ainslee would be in the arena, walking calmly on Deacon while volunteers helped keep her steady in the saddle, instead of scaling this mountain of hay. Her biceps quivered as she strained to haul herself up another inch. She couldn't stop now, even though she wanted to call for help, for someone to come rescue her, since she couldn't seem to take care of herself anymore.

She moved her right leg to the next foothold, and then her left followed. Suddenly, instead of the consuming fear that had been controlling her, she felt the rhythm of the climb. Right hand, left hand, right leg, left leg. The physical strain was still difficult, but Ainslee kept pushing through it. With each contraction and effort, she felt some of her wild emotions getting squeezed out of her pores. Inch by inch, she moved up the mountain.

Finally, her right hand grasped the top bale. She grunted as she used all her remaining strength to pull herself up. She draped her upper body over the hay, with her legs still dangling off the side, and lay still while she tried to catch her breath. She felt the sharp pricks of hay blades against her breasts and stomach as her lungs fought for air. She hadn't pushed herself this hard since she'd lost her leg. Sometimes PT was tough, but she never put her whole effort into it. Today she had. Every muscle in her arms burned, and it felt damned good.

Once she could breathe without panting, she scooted across the top layer of hay. She lay on her stomach near the edge and propped her chin on her crossed arms. Anna was right—she could see the whole farm from here. The door to the indoor arena was open, and every once in a while she saw Myra walk past inside, gesturing and talking as she taught her two students. Ainslee wanted to be out there with them, but she'd needed the climb more than she needed the riding lesson.

The physical effort gave her a clarity she'd been lacking for a long time. She had traced the thread of her outburst in the grooming stall back to its source. She was relieved to finally understand the trigger and the course her emotions had taken, as if she finally figured out the logic behind tides instead of simply being tossed about by waves. Unfortunately, the revelations she was reaching were uncomfortable ones.

Myra was at the heart of it. Ainslee could only see distant glimpses of her now, as she walked by the arena door, but her mind conjured up the picture of Myra carrying bags of grain as she and Kate playfully raced each other to empty the truck. Ainslee saw every detail. Myra's brown hair bleached gold by the sun, her strong forearms and elegant, work-roughened hands. She was everything Ainslee used to be. Everything Ainslee *wanted.* Not wanted to be, but wanted to have. She'd started to follow Myra on instinct, drawn to her beauty and her strength, before she remembered who she was now. Ainslee no longer had things to offer Myra like Kate did. She couldn't play the same games or run the same races.

Ainslee clearly saw the progression of her emotions for the first time in ages. Watching Myra, brushing her skin when she took the saddle from her, walking out of the tack room and hearing doors slam on every aspect of her life. Ainslee understood why she had gotten to the point of throwing the hoof pick. She wasn't proud of how she had reacted, and the memory of Myra smiling in the sunshine would taunt her for a long time, but at least she understood. She shifted on the hay, stretching muscles that were already beginning to tighten, and felt a small part of her old strength returning as she finally faced some of her new weaknesses.

Chapter Five

Myra jogged out of the barn after Drew and Blake had finished untacking and grooming their horses. Blake had trotted Frosty for several circuits around the ring, and she knew he'd be happy to share the exciting news with his daughter when she called tonight. Drew was still moving at Spot's slow walk, relying on the support of sidewalkers until he regained more strength and mobility, but he had followed her instructions with a palpable intensity. She had originally thought he might be defiant and reluctant to listen to her, but she was quickly realizing that she'd need to rein him in instead. She admired his determination to improve, and it was up to her to temper it so he didn't aggravate his injury instead of healing it. She had managed to lose herself in the lesson for the most part, drawn as she was to her students and their progress, but she had also been acutely aware of every car she could see driving in or out of the parking lot. Ainslee hadn't left yet.

She skidded to a halt in the middle of the gravel lot and tried to decide where to look first. Kate, returning with a full wheelbarrow from the huge pile of shavings, tilted her head toward the hay barn. Myra waved her thanks and headed over there.

She slowed down once she was in the large, open-air structure. A mountain of flaked golden shavings towered over her on her left side. Behind the retaining wall that kept the bedding contained was a storage area for the tractor and miscellaneous equipment. Trunks containing winter blankets, extra poles and jump standards, and pots full of brightly colored plastic flowers that decorated the arena when Cedar Grove hosted horse shows were strewn about on the packed-dirt floor. Myra scanned the area. No sign of Ainslee. The right side of the barn was filled with bales of hay—timothy in the front and alfalfa in the back. Kate had just received a shipment of alfalfa, and the bales were piled twenty high. The timothy section was less full and looked more climbable, so Myra started there.

She reached up and tucked her fingers between two bales, scrambling for a foothold as she hoisted herself up. Some loose hay fell onto her face and hair when she pulled her hands out to climb higher, and she sneezed at the dusty smell. The woodsy scent of cedar shavings and the crisp, floral smell of grass hay were as familiar as her coconut shampoo and lavender soap. She couldn't count how many hours she had spent in hay barns like this one, from teenaged years when she needed solitude to later when she had wanted privacy with a girlfriend or a lonely place to weep after losing Jeffrey. Just last week, she had been sitting up here near the rafters on a woolen saddle pad while she graded chemistry assignments.

Myra crawled over the topmost bale, careful not to pull too hard on it and send both herself and the hay to the ground. The thought of Ainslee maneuvering up here with her new leg and her uncertain balance made Myra squeamish. She exhaled in relief when she saw Ainslee sitting on the top of the hay pile with her back propped against a bale. She had bits of hay stuck in her dark hair, and Myra wanted to pull it free from its rubber band and run her fingers through it, removing the green stems. She imagined what the wavy strands would feel like against her sensitive wrist and palm as the hair brushed her skin, curled away, and touched her again. A curving helix with intermittent contact. Myra swallowed and sat on a bale several yards away from Ainslee.

"I'm glad you're still here," Myra said. She sniffed as the dust stirred up by her arrival settled around them. "I'm so—"

"Don't. Don't apologize. I deserved it and I'm the one who should say sorry." Ainslee shrugged and turned away. Her eyes were red rimmed, but dry. "I can't believe I acted like such a baby!"

Her exclamation ended on a high note, and Myra covered her mouth to hide a laugh at the match between words and tone. She was so relieved to have found Ainslee still at the barn—and had been proud when Vanessa told her Ainslee had stopped to apologize even in the midst of her sullen exit. She'd been convinced that Ainslee would walk out the door, out of the program and out of Myra's life. The worry had overwhelmed her, and she had tried to dismiss it as a normal reaction she'd have with any of her students. Even if she hadn't truly known better, she'd have realized it when she climbed up the stack of hay bales and felt unaccountably giddy at the sight of Ainslee sitting here.

Ainslee glared at Myra, but her mouth turned up in a smile and the rest of her sour expression cracked bit by bit, like dominoes falling, until she was laughing along with Myra. The release was as potent as the earlier tension had been.

Myra wiped her eyes with the back of her hand and sighed as her laughter died down. "Do you want to talk about it?"

Ainslee had flopped into a prone position while laughing, and she tucked one elbow behind her head. "It was you," she said, her voice serious and quiet now.

"Something I said?" Myra asked, replaying their conversation in the tack room. "Or because I was walking slowly?"

"No." Ainslee waved her free hand. She paused. "I saw you outside, carrying grain, and you were…"

Her gaze skimmed over Myra's chest and up to her face and Myra felt it like a rough caress. She inhaled with a barely audible gasp and self-consciously tucked her hair behind her ear. Ainslee looked up at the ceiling of the barn.

"You were strong, playful. You made me think about the woman I used to be."

Did Ainslee mean she used to be like Myra? Or that she'd have been interested in someone like her? Myra let the silence stretch between them like a rubber band, ready to snap. Finally Ainslee started talking again.

"Before…*this*"—she gestured toward her right leg, the metal gleaming incongruously against the dull green hay—"I was different. I'd have been the first to jump on a horse and gallop into the woods, even if I didn't know what I was doing. Crazy. Now I can't get close enough to brush a sweet old guy like Deacon. I'm not used to being afraid."

"So it comes out as anger," Myra said. She gave in to some of her yearning and moved across the hay to sit by Ainslee's feet. She put her hand on Ainslee's left ankle.

"Right. I don't know how to be me anymore. I'm scared of the horse, scared of hurting my leg more even though it's gone. Scared of being attracted to someone because I have nothing left to offer."

The last sentence was spoken so softly Myra barely heard it. Ainslee's admission frightened her, too, but for the opposite reason. What did *she* have to offer someone like Ainslee? Myra would always be afraid, always expect Ainslee to make the decision that life without a leg yet with so many painful memories was too much to bear.

They stayed there, unmoving, with only the tentative connection of Myra's hand and Ainslee's confession between them, until a blue Ford drove past the hay barn and parked under a stand of fir trees.

"That's my ride," Ainslee said. She put her hand on the hay bale she'd been using as a backrest and pulled herself to her feet. "Sasha. A neighbor who's been chauffeuring me around. I didn't want to call and tell her to come early because I'd been booted out of class like a delinquent."

She smiled, and the arch of her lower lip gave her a rueful air. Myra was happy she and Ainslee could joke about the incident. She followed her to the edge of the bales.

"Can I help you get down?"

"Seriously?"

Myra held up her hands in surrender. The instinct to take care of Ainslee was a stubborn one. "Sorry. I'm sure you're fine on your own."

Ainslee lowered herself over the edge of the bales without another word, and Myra took a parallel path. She reached the ground first but let Ainslee jump the last few feet on her own.

"I'm glad you stuck around," Myra said as they walked to the parking lot.

"Me, too. I'm sorry about the lesson, and I hope you'll let me back next week."

Next week. When they'd be surrounded by the other riders and the volunteers. A regularly scheduled lesson, with Myra as the professional instructor. That'd be the best way for them to meet.

"Of course. As long as you promise to behave."

"Not a chance," Ainslee said as she opened the passenger door.

Myra grinned, even as warning signals coursed through her mind. The lesson today—as usual in this program—had aroused too many conflicting emotions in her. She'd be a fool and hold on to the moments of happiness and laughter she'd felt for a short while, even if they didn't have a chance of lasting.

Chapter Six

Myra buckled Dragon's girth loosely around his belly. She'd tighten it once she and Ainslee were ready to ride. She gave her bright bay gelding a pat and went over to where Deacon stood in the crossties, groomed and ready for his tack.

She had planned family rides for all her students this week, and so far she had been proud of the headway they'd made in such a short time. She had put Blake's children on two of the barn's ponies and had led them along a tree-lined bridle path while Blake and Tracy walked behind. The weather had been perfect—warm, but breezy—and everyone seemed relaxed during the visit. Blake was improving remarkably after only six lessons, but Myra was even more pleased to see progress on the ground, with his family. She scratched Deacon's neck while she remembered Blake and his daughter laughing together while they groomed Frosty. The horses were doing their good work again, providing a conduit for conversation and a connection with nature.

Drew's mother and girlfriend had come by after lessons on Wednesday. His stout, shy mom and willowy girlfriend, in her cutoff jean shorts and midriff-baring tank, had seemed to share little in common, but they had stood side by side and cheered him on while he rode Spot. Chris had stayed late to lead the pinto while Myra supported Drew, who was relying less on his sidewalker every week. His attitude had steadily improved, and he'd formed an unlikely friendship with hippy throwback Chris. Myra was glad to see him more at ease and patient as he hung out with Chris or groomed Spot, but his physical accomplishments were greater than either Blake's or Ainslee's. He could walk using only a cane and he supported himself for short times with just a hand on Spot's shoulder for balance.

Ainslee was another story. She'd had neither emotional breakthroughs like Blake nor physical ones like Drew. She had come to each lesson since the day she'd thrown her hoof pick, and she was unfailingly polite and compliant. Myra had come out of the hayloft determined to keep her distance from Ainslee. She'd be polite but professional, and avoid being alone with her. She hadn't needed to bother, though, since they never were caught in private without either one of the other students or a volunteer nearby. Was this merely the result of chance, or was Ainslee avoiding her, too? Myra wasn't certain. She should have been relieved at the lack of intimacy, but she instead had offered to take Ainslee on a secluded trail ride this week since she didn't have any family close enough to offer her support in person.

Myra couldn't deny her attraction to Ainslee no matter how much she tried, but her suggestion about today's ride had as much to do with her role as Ainslee's instructor in a therapy program as it did with her personal desire to spend more time with her. Ainslee was in her lessons but not really *present* in them. She did what was asked of her, but without the addition of a true drive to get better, she was stagnant. Myra was torn between hoping she could break through Ainslee's passive resistance and a reluctance to approach her because she saw shadows of Jeffrey in Ainslee's detachment from the bustle of the world around her.

Belief in her obligation as Ainslee's teacher had won. Or rather, the belief that this new program wouldn't work without the full commitment of the students, the volunteers, and Myra herself. She smoothed the green saddle pad over Deacon's back and gently placed her dressage saddle on top. She'd keep the conversation focused on Ainslee today. What she needed from the program and how Myra could help her. Maybe they could tailor a new set of goals that would serve her better. Light a fire in her to reconnect with life, missing leg or not.

Or, perhaps Myra could set the goal of ripping Ainslee's shirt off her. She sighed as Ainslee came through the side door of the barn, wearing a red-and-black checked top and faded jeans. Gorgeous. Her sleeves were rolled up to her elbows, and her forearms—though pale—showed a beautiful curve of muscle. The deep red emphasized her angular, dark brows and gave her the impression of humor and intelligence. Myra had only been privileged to see flashes of Ainslee's wit—at unguarded moments—but every time they talked she was struck by the contrast between Ainslee's sharp mind and her dulled participation in her own recovery.

"Hey, Deacon, I'm behind you. Hi, Myra," Ainslee said before walking into the grooming stall. She had taken to entering and leaving the barn by the walkthrough situated halfway down the aisle. It brought her directly into the crosstie area, but Myra had a suspicion that Ainslee chose this entrance because then she had to do less walking on the concrete inside the barn. Her hesitant gait was aural, not just visual, on the cement floor.

"Hi, Ainslee. Are you ready to ride?"

"Sure." Her short response was the same as the one she used each time Myra asked her to do something in class. An affirmative answer, but one carrying in its tone a mental shrug, as if Ainslee didn't really care. Myra, anxious to get Ainslee on the horse and out on the trails, hurried with Deacon's bridle. She knew all too well how crucial her job was right now. Ainslee *had* to care. As much as Myra knew the feeling had to come from Ainslee herself, she felt responsible for triggering it.

Myra—not daring to slow her pace to accommodate Ainslee—led Deacon to the mounting block inside the arena and tightened his girth while they waited for Ainslee to catch up to them. He stood quietly as Ainslee used the handrail to climb the ramp, and then mounted him from the right side. Tradition dictated riders mount from the left side of the horse, but Kate and Myra didn't let a custom from medieval times interfere with the differing abilities of their students. Ainslee balanced on her right leg, with her hands braced on Deacon's withers, and swung her left leg over the saddle. Deacon was too well-trained to care which side his rider used, and he stood still until Ainslee asked him to walk.

"Stay in here, and I'll be right back," Myra said. She sprinted back to the barn and got Dragon, swinging easily into the saddle from the ground even though her draft horse cross gelding was over seventeen hands high. Ainslee had been riding on her own for two weeks now, but Myra didn't relax until she was back in the arena where Deacon and Ainslee were sedately circling the ring.

"Come on, Ains," she called. Ainslee guided Deacon over to her, and they walked across the parking lot toward the trail system that circled and crisscrossed the Cedar Grove housing development. "Some of the trails are wide enough for us to walk side by side, but we'll have to go single file most of the time. When you're behind us, be sure you're far enough back to be able to see Dragon's back hooves when you look between your horse's ears. Dragon isn't a kicker, but it's better to be safe and have plenty of room between us."

"Okay," Ainslee said. Yet another one-word answer. This time, though, Myra heard a tinge of worry in Ainslee's voice. Even though they'd be walking on calm horses, the move outside of the arena held more risk than an indoor lesson. Myra never wanted Ainslee to feel fear with her, but she was almost relieved to sense Ainslee's awareness of the new situation instead of her usual non-caring attitude.

Once they crossed the tree line and were separated from the barn by a row of slender pines, all four of them seemed to relax. Myra was accustomed to her own sigh of relief every time she rode deep enough to be surrounded by nature and away from any sign of civilization beyond the manicured path and the small jumps she and Kate had built. The horses changed as well, pricking their ears as they looked around and walking with more energy. Even Ainslee relaxed somewhat. She looked around the small clearing they were crossing on the way to the deeper woods.

"Looks like a busy area," she remarked, gesturing at the ground. The dirt had been churned by horse hooves after the last rain and had dried in uneven clumps.

"Lots of the kids bring their horses here. They'll say they're bringing them here to graze, but they'll climb on bareback over there." She gestured at a tree stump on the side of the trail. "No one's supposed to ride with only a halter and a lead rope, but they do it anyway."

"And you let them do it?" Ainslee looked at Myra with her eyebrows raised in a surprised expression. "You seem so attached to your beloved safety rules."

Myra laughed. "Throwing tantrums in the barn is inexcusable."

"You think that was a tantrum? You have no idea..." Ainslee laughed along with her, and Myra was glad to hear her respond to teasing so easily.

"You're right, though, that we're relaxing the safety rules when we let the kids ride bareback. I guess Kate and I both know from experience that they're going to break the rules and get on the horses no matter what we do. We can yell at them for doing it here, and they'll find another place or time to play their games. Or, we can give them this safe space where we keep an eye on them even though they seem to believe they're invisible back here. Besides, they're actually learning better balance and connection to their horses when they ride bareback. They think they're only playing, but they're building a foundation. Like little centaurs."

"That must be why you look so good on a horse. I'll bet you were a hellion when you were young," Ainslee said as they left the clearing and moved to single file along a grass-lined path. "It's always the rebels who turn into the strictest disciplinarians when they get old."

Myra shook her head at Ainslee's emphasis on the last word. She ignored her flush of pleasure at Ainslee's compliment—and her awareness of Ainslee walking so close behind her and watching her backside—and responded only to Ainslee's exaggerated reference to the difference in their ages. "Then I guess in six years you'll be even worse than I am."

"I'm not exactly a rebel now," Ainslee said, all laughter gone from her voice. "Not anymore."

Myra wanted to reassure Ainslee—about what, she wasn't exactly sure—but she chose instead to keep her tone teasing. She'd rather Ainslee had rapid mood changes than no emotional response at all.

"At least try to behave for the next two weeks. Kate and I are planning a party for the last day of class, and I'd hate to have you miss it."

"You and Kate…You seem very close."

Ainslee's intonation changed her statement into a question. Myra turned and looked back at her, wondering how interested Ainslee would be in her answer. Ainslee gave her a small and enigmatic smile.

Myra faced forward again and ducked under a low-hanging limb of a Douglas fir. "Watch out for that branch. Kate and I have been friends since high school. I played softball on my public school's varsity team, and I met her when I played a game at her private school. She was a cheerleader and very pretty, of course. We kissed under the bleachers—a first kiss for both of us. We got caught and had to face the humiliation of having our parents called to the school, but it was worth it." Myra grinned over her shoulder.

"I'm sure Kate agrees that a kiss from you was worth getting in trouble. Sooo…" Ainslee drew the syllable out for several seconds while she looked off to the side, a faint flush of pink coloring her pale cheeks. "What happened after?"

Myra shrugged. "Nothing much, really. We had an instant connection, and I know we both were interested in discovering what a real kiss would be like. It was more a shared experiment than a romantic encounter. We stayed friends through high school, trail riding together on weekends at either my aunt's barn or the fancy stables where Kate rode. We lost touch in college but reconnected again after we graduated."

"No regrets? No lingering what-ifs?"

Myra glanced back again. This time, Ainslee was looking directly at her, waiting for an answer. She seemed relaxed in the saddle—more at ease than Myra had seen her yet. Nature and conversation were agreeing with her, apparently. Myra pushed aside her concern about her personal divulgences. She had vowed not to let Ainslee get close, but she also wanted her to benefit from the ride and their time together. Ainslee was just being curious, wasn't she? She had intimated an attraction to Myra, but she probably hadn't meant anything serious by it.

"Not at all." Myra chose to answer honestly. "I value her friendship, but we'd never have been a good fit as a couple. On paper, maybe, but who can predict love? And now she has Jamie. You haven't met her yet, but she and Kate are perfect together. Very different, but perfect."

"And you haven't found perfect yet?"

Myra laughed. "I'm too busy to look these days. With teaching high school, helping Kate, and riding my two horses, I barely have time to grab fast food for dinner, let alone go on an actual date. What about you? Have you found someone with the surname Right yet?"

"It'd be a Ms. if I found one, but no. It seems pointless to even hope now."

"That's ridiculous," Myra said, more sharply than she intended. She couldn't bear to hear Ainslee dismissing herself and her future because of her accident. "You're just as capable of love as anyone with two legs."

"I guess, although I haven't felt much of anything until…I mean, for a long time, especially love. I know it's possible for me to be in love, but I don't have much hope in the feelings being reciprocated."

Myra turned Dragon onto a wide trail that circled the edge of the development and slowed down enough for Ainslee and Deacon to catch up to her. She wanted to convince Ainslee that she was attractive and appealing no matter what her physical condition made her believe. She hesitated, though, not daring to speak until she was sure she wouldn't reveal the extent of her own confusing feelings.

"Your horse is huge," Ainslee said once they were abreast of each other. She looked up at Myra even though they were close to the same height when standing. "He looks like one of the horses from the beer commercials."

Myra stroked Dragon's neck. She welcomed the change in subject. "He is, partly. He's a Clydesdale-Thoroughbred cross. He has the easygoing temperament of a draft horse and the athleticism of a hot-blooded racer."

"Have you had him long?"

"Almost twelve years. Since he was about seven months old." About the time Jeffrey had been deployed. Myra put both reins in her left hand and rested her right on her hip, feeling the sway of Dragon's big-striding yet contained walk. He had been on plenty of trail rides with students, and he automatically matched his pace with Deacon's. "He's a PMU rescue."

"A what?"

"PMU. Pregnant Mare Urine. It's used to manufacture hormones for women, but not as much anymore. When I got him, it was big business."

Ainslee grimaced. "Yuk. People inject that into themselves? Gross."

"I agree," Myra said. She remembered the sick feeling she'd had when she first read about the horses on the collection farms. Not so much about the end product, but about the treatment of the animals. "The mares would be bred, and then they'd spend the eleven months of their pregnancies in narrow stalls while their urine was collected. They'd have a short break to have their foals and nurse them, and then they'd be bred again. The babies were by-products, especially the males that couldn't be used for breeding, and a lot were simply…discarded."

"So you saved him," Ainslee said in a quiet voice.

Myra nodded, although she had been saved herself by the gentle horse. His comforting and undemanding presence had been what she needed while she recovered from the first shock of Jeffrey's death.

In the months following, while she sought to regain her equilibrium and come to terms with her loss, long rides on Dragon had been her salvation. She wanted to talk to Ainslee about Jeffrey, but she kept her private sorrow to herself. Because it was too private to share? Or because she worried Ainslee might identify too closely with Jeffrey's pain and his final decision?

"Dragon was the reason I got in touch with Kate again," she said instead. "There were some wonderful foals at the farm where I got Dragon, and I wanted to rescue more of them. I contacted Kate, and she agreed to help. We managed to find new homes for over forty horses before the product got less popular and we weren't needed as much."

"Awesome. What are you doing now? I can't imagine you stopped rescuing just because the situation changed for those particular animals."

"Kate and I help where we can," Myra said with a shrug. She wanted to deflect the attention off herself and not sound like she thought she was an incarnation of Saint Francis. She didn't mention the rehabilitation and rehoming program she managed for ex-racehorses—many of which had become lesson horses or beloved mounts for Kate's students. "Do you want to trot a few yards? Just to the cedar up ahead?"

Ainslee grimaced. "I feel like I'm going to fall off when I trot."

Myra pulled Dragon to a halt, and Deacon obediently stopped beside them. "You never mentioned that when I asked how you felt in the trot over the last three weeks." She emphasized the words and sighed with frustration. How could she know how Ainslee was doing if she blandly answered *fine* to every inquiry? "You look great in the arena, so how was I supposed to know you had a problem?"

Ainslee shrugged. "Everything is harder or more painful with this thing." She waved toward her right leg. "How was I supposed to know I had a problem?"

"We need to stop repeating what the other person says," Myra said. She had enjoyed the banter at first, but now she got nervous when Ainslee focused more on her injury and what she believed was lacking in her rather than when she seemed engaged in the present and future. "As a reference point, you know you have a riding problem when you feel like you're about to fall off. What was Rule Three?"

"Ask for help," Ainslee said with a barely concealed roll of her eyes.

"You can remember them, but you can't follow them," Myra said. She had to grin at Ainslee's exaggerated sigh. "When you feel out of balance, do you feel like you're going to fall off the right or left side of the horse?"

"Left."

"What do you do to compensate?" Myra scanned Ainslee's position while they talked. She felt much more comfortable discussing the mechanics of riding and trying to solve Ainslee's problem than discussing her personal life. The need to help Ainslee achieve a more secure seat in the saddle *almost* kept Myra from dwelling too long on the sight of the lovely curves of Ainslee's lower back and ass.

Ainslee bit her lower lip while she considered the question and Myra shook her head to dispel the fantasy of using her own teeth on Ainslee's mouth.

"I guess I lean to the right."

Myra dismounted and draped Dragon's reins over her arm. She walked over to Deacon and put one hand on Ainslee's right knee and the other under the heel of her metal leg. Myra sensed Ainslee's recoil when her leg was touched, and she understood the vulnerability Ainslee must be feeling.

"It's okay," she said, rubbing Ainslee's knee with her hand. She hoped the touch was soothing to Ainslee, because it sure as hell wasn't calming her at all. She often touched students when she explained position changes to them, but she'd never had such an unprofessional—and exciting—response to anyone else. *Focus on teaching, not on sex.* "Pretend you're off balance and about to fall off to the left. Push harder into this stirrup to counterbalance."

Ainslee stiffened her right leg and pressed against Myra's hand where it rested under her prosthesis. Myra couldn't see the change in Ainslee's position like she'd have been able to notice stiffness in a natural leg, but she felt the muscles tense and Ainslee's weight shift.

"When you push like that, where does your weight go? Is it balanced on both seat bones?"

"No," Ainslee said. Awareness spread visibly over her features. "I'm just pushing myself farther to the left. No wonder I was getting worse instead of better."

"We'll make you better," Myra said. She paused as she realized she'd do just about anything to make that happen. And if she failed?

What would happen to her then? She adjusted Ainslee's leg position and slid the hand that was under Ainslee's knee up a few inches. "Try using your thighs for balance instead of shoving your feet harder into the stirrups. Squeeze against my hand. How does that feel?"

"Works for me," Ainslee said. Myra was staring at Ainslee's leg, her whole body zeroed in on the feeling of Ainslee's thigh muscles against her palm, but the husky tone in Ainslee's voice made her look up in surprise. Maybe she wasn't the only one who felt this lesson growing more intimate than it should be. She removed her hands as quickly as if she'd been given an electric shock, busying herself with mounting Dragon and readjusting her reins.

"Let's try a short, slow trot now," she said. She squeezed her legs gently against Dragon's sides and he jogged quietly along the dirt path. Deacon stayed close to his side, and Myra watched Ainslee's look of concentration as she put Myra's instructions into practice.

"Hey, now I feel it," Ainslee said. She kept staring straight ahead as if she were driving herself toward a finish line, but a smile softened the edges of her mouth. Myra kept Dragon in a trot for several yards after Ainslee seemed to get the correct feel for the trot, and then she slowed back to a walk before Ainslee's muscles could protest the change in position.

"Whew," Ainslee said when she and Deacon were walking again. "I'm going to feel that in my thighs tomorrow, but it was worth it." She reached over and playfully poked Myra in the ribs. "You're a pretty good teacher. I should have told you what was wrong before this."

"Yeah, you think?" Myra laughed and swatted at Ainslee's hand. "If I were really a good teacher, I'd have noticed something was wrong sooner than this, but…"

Ainslee frowned when Myra left her sentence unfinished. "Go on, say it. But…?"

Myra sighed. Their conversation kept moving from joking to irritable seriousness and back. She could barely keep up. She tried to remain positive with her therapy group, approaching their issues obliquely instead of dealing with them head on. She'd never really mentioned Ainslee's leg and today was the first time she'd felt the sun-warmed metal against her skin. What did she expect? That Ainslee would one day become emotionally whole with a rosy outlook? That she'd forget about her leg and return to her pre-accident self, whoever she'd been before Myra had met her? No, her missing leg defined her now in a way her real one probably never had.

"*But* you always look uncomfortable, whether you're walking or riding. I couldn't tell when it was an issue with your riding position or the adjustments you regularly have to make with your leg."

Ainslee's cheeks flushed the way they did when she got mad. Myra was beginning to recognize the sign of frustration and anger all too well. "I *am* uncomfortable and I always will be. Like I told you in the hayloft, I don't even know who I am anymore. I'm living in a body I hate. I'm scared most of the time. I'll never be back to normal, able to do what I want."

Myra felt her own anger in response. Not because she couldn't sympathize with Ainslee, but because the words *never* and *always* made her scared, too. Ainslee was seeing herself and her future in the worst possible way. No hope, no way out.

She knew she was letting her fear speak for her, but she couldn't stop the words, or even temper them. "You're missing part of your leg, but the rest of you is whole and healthy. Your body, your mind, your emotions—those will all work if you let them. You can't let this change who you are or destroy your life. Your soul wasn't located in your shin, you know."

Ainslee glared at her. "And you think *you* could do better in my situation? If you couldn't ride like you do now, or haul bags of grain, or run yourself ragged on your mission to save every human and animal you can find?"

"I don't…I would still…" Myra stopped. Would she be any different from Ainslee, or would she, too, limp through the rest of her life with a chip on her shoulder? "I don't know," she said. "I can't say I'd handle the situation any differently and I shouldn't have implied that I would. I'm sorry."

"Of course you'd do better than I am." Ainslee shook her head with a cross look on her face. Myra wasn't sure how to read the expression. Disgust, or a grudging respect? She suspected the former. "You'd be leading amputee parades on horseback through the streets of Portland when you weren't organizing one-legged charity races to buy crutches for all the lame horses in America."

Myra had to laugh at the images Ainslee put in her mind, even as she acknowledged the truth behind her silly words. Myra knew she'd always find a way to be around the animals she loved, whether she was able to compete and train or had to be led around an arena on a therapy horse. And she'd probably find a way to turn her own disability into a way to help others through similar challenges. Ainslee had captured the person she was, and Myra felt a warm glow inside when she realized how clearly Ainslee saw her after such a short—but intense—acquaintance.

"Being around you makes me want to be a better person," Ainslee said. "But I'm not ready yet. I'm still feeling sorry for myself. Don't push me to heal more quickly than I can."

"I didn't realize I was pushing," Myra said. She understood Ainslee needed time to process her transformation in her own way, but Myra wasn't sure she could control her sense of urgency. What if Ainslee wallowed in frustration and helplessness too long? What if she never recovered any optimism for the future?

"I'm angry with you right now," Ainslee said. Her frown appeared forced, though, as if she were pushing her beautiful lips into a downturned arch to keep herself from laughing. "Can you teach me how to ride a gallop? I'd like to run off and leave you in the dust."

Myra laughed. "You'd be sitting on your ass in the dust, more like it, if you tried. How about settling for a ride home in brooding silence instead? It's safer."

"Deal," said Ainslee.

A break from conversation would do her good as well, Myra decided. She was worn out by the ups and downs they'd taken in a short hour of riding, and altogether too aroused by their brief moments of touch. She let Dragon's rhythmic walk relax her muscles, but she couldn't find a way to calm her mind and heart.

Chapter Seven

Ainslee felt sweat fusing her to the hard plastic seat on the MAX the day after her trail ride with Myra. She'd had to walk a quarter mile from her apartment to catch the train and she was dreading the two blocks from the station to her physical therapist's office. The temperature was pushing ninety on a cloudless summer day, and the heat, combined with her sore muscles, made Ainslee cranky. She had refused to sit in one of the handicapped seats near the door, so she stood in line with a crowd of people who were disembarking at her stop and slowly filed through the door.

She stood near the brick wall of a department store and considered her choices. Head north to the therapist's office, or cross the street and rest in an air-conditioned café? She had already dropped out of three different PT programs. None had been failures—she'd seen improvements along the way, but she'd always found some reason to stop going. She didn't get the point of endless sessions. No therapist would ever make her whole again.

This therapist, however, was the link between her and Myra's riding program. He had filled out an application for her and had encouraged her to try the lessons. He'd be certain to tell Myra if Ainslee went AWOL and didn't make her appointment. The imagined look of disappointment on Myra's face was enough to make Ainslee push away from the building and start walking north.

Her thighs protested her accustomed way of walking with her prosthesis. She usually tried to keep tension in her hips, controlling the swing of her walk to make her limp as unobtrusive as possible, but yesterday's trot on Deacon had turned her muscles to mush. She stepped out of the flow of people and rested near the curb. She thought about Myra's words to her, and the way she had been pushing herself off balance by trying too hard to restrict movement. The memory of Myra's hands on her leg and under her thigh made her uncomfortably aware of every sensation in her legs. The friction of denim and the warmth of the sun seemed to set her nerve endings on fire, but she tried to ignore her arousal and focus on the concept Myra had been teaching.

Ainslee started walking again, but she stopped fighting her prosthesis and let her leg find a new, natural way of moving. Instead of trying to hide her limp and move like she used to before her surgery, she relaxed her hips and swung her leg forward. She wasn't sure how she looked from a bystander's point of view, but she felt some relief in her aching muscles. Once she was inside the office and on the treadmill warming up for her appointment, she kept the same loose stride.

"What did you change?" Dr. Campbell asked, coming over to where Ainslee was exercising. "Your gait is better. Range of motion, smoothness. What are you doing differently?"

Ainslee told him about her experience with Deacon's trot and the way she'd incorporated the lesson into her walk. She was able to balance without the handrails while he increased her speed. "I feel more inside myself," she said, struggling to find the right way to express what she was feeling. She'd never had to think about her body before. She'd walked, jogged, sparred, and made love without giving the processes much thought—her body had simply done what she wanted it to do. Not anymore. "I guess I was detached in a way, like I was moving the legs of a puppet."

"Perfectly normal," Dr. Campbell said. "At first, the prosthesis is a foreign object. Something to be manipulated and controlled, not a part of you."

What if I don't want it to be a part of me? Ainslee didn't ask the question out loud. What was the point? She didn't have any choice now.

Dr. Campbell raised the incline on the treadmill and Ainslee had to work too hard at keeping her balance to let her thoughts dwell on her misfortune. Her respiration increased, and she reveled in the feeling of balance and strength even though she was nowhere near her former fitness level.

"Riding is improving your core strength and your upper body control," Dr. Campbell said, with a hint of satisfaction in his voice. He'd never be unprofessional enough to say *I told you so*, but Ainslee had a feeling he was thinking about the conversation they had when he'd first brought up the possibility of lessons. Ainslee had been reluctant, and he had listed the benefits she'd likely experience. She'd been afraid of the idea—she had been afraid of almost everything at first—and she'd much rather have exercised on a safe treadmill than on an unpredictable horse. He was right about the physical aspects of riding, and she was seeing the results more clearly today than she had so far.

When they moved to the parallel bars for a single-limb standing exercise, Ainslee could feel an even more pronounced improvement. She held one of the bars with her right hand while she balanced on her prosthesis and slowly lifted her sound foot onto a box in front of her. When she'd first had to perform this exercise, she had gripped the bars with both hands and had rushed to get her left foot on the solid box. Now, she repeated the movement several times while she told Dr. Campbell about the way she balanced on her right leg to mount Deacon.

"I also had to keep my weight on my right leg when I climbed in the hay barn one day while I was waiting for my ride to pick me up," she said, omitting the part about Myra kicking her out of the lesson. She took her hand off the parallel bar and stepped onto the box without any assistance. "The bales were stacked about twenty high and I got all the way to the top. It felt good to accomplish something tangible, even though it wasn't a big deal. I'm sure the teenagers at the barn climb up and down those bales like monkeys."

"I'm proud of you, Ainslee," he said. "I don't care if the climb would be easy for anyone else. I know what it took for *you* to get to the top."

Ainslee smiled at his words. She was proud of herself, too, but it felt nice to hear from someone who understood her situation. She was accustomed to having him and her other doctors look at her with worried expressions, their concern for her clearly evident on their faces. She had felt a little guilty about her own lack of engagement in her healing process when everyone else—including Myra—seemed to care so much more than she did. Still, she had been too wrapped up in her own mind, where she needed to hide and heal. She hadn't had any energy left over to reassure them.

Today, though, she felt able to move past her own thoughts and pay attention to someone else's. She wasn't sure if it was because she was physically stronger or if it was due to the trail ride with Myra when she'd felt her world expand a little as they moved outside of the arena and in the woods. Dr. Campbell was obviously pleased with her riding experiences, and she felt good about making a doctor smile instead of frown with worry.

By the time she finished her exercises and got back on the train, she felt as if every muscle in her body was going on strike. She sagged in her seat and watched the buildings rush by as the MAX took her back toward her apartment. She felt physically bruised, but she'd become even stronger because of the exertion. She only wished her emotional, fearful, angry parts could heal as quickly. Those parts of her still recognized how comparatively weak she was.

She sighed and leaned her head against the window. She was grateful to Myra for helping her get some of her strength back. The exercises she did on Deacon during lessons were obviously making her stronger and more flexible, and Myra's advice and astute observations had made Ainslee rethink how she walked and moved. Ainslee had to be very careful not to confuse her gratitude with real attraction, even though she didn't seem to need the same distinction with her other doctors and therapists.

Ainslee stretched her legs in front of her and kneaded a tight knot in her thigh. She felt Myra's hands on her again, as if the sensation had been burned into her mind. Ainslee had been poked and prodded by numerous people since her accident and surgery. She usually recoiled from their touch because it was symbolic of her weakness. But she craved Myra's hands on her. When Myra had held her leg and helped her learn to balance in the saddle, Ainslee had felt safe and supported. But the burden was too much to place on anyone else. Ainslee needed to find a way to stand on her own.

Still, harboring a small, secret dream of the future seemed healthy enough. Ainslee couldn't fool herself forever—her interest in Myra wasn't some sort of transference or misinterpreted gratitude. She would have felt the same attraction to her if they'd met before the accident. The only difference was that Ainslee wouldn't have been afraid to act on her feelings when she was whole.

Chapter Eight

Myra paced around the outdoor arena, leaving uneven circles of footprints in the sand. She watched Jamie canter toward the next small post-and-rail fence on the course Myra had set for her. The jump was under two feet high, but Kate's girlfriend Jamie made so many adjustments to Dragon's stride, Myra would have thought she was riding a Grand Prix course. Myra's relationship with Kate had always been smooth and easy. Even their minor disagreements were mere bumps in the road. But Jamie? She and Myra had been at odds since their first meeting, when investment banker Jamie had come to the barn to observe Kate's riding and evaluate her as a potential client. Myra had risen to her friend's defense against Jamie's badgering, but they'd since formed a rocky friendship. Most of their head-butting was in fun, some of it wasn't, and Myra couldn't help but enjoy the challenge of knowing someone with Jamie's strength and brilliance. Most of the time…

"Relax your hands," she called. "You're pulling too hard on the reins."

Jamie slowed the big bay's stride out of the corner, and then nudged him with her heels at the last minute. Dragon chipped at the fence by adding a short, choppy stride right before he popped stiffly over the jump.

"Why won't he take off when I ask him?" Jamie trotted to where Myra stood in the center of the ring. Her face was red from exertion under the brim of Kate's black safety helmet, and she had her usual look of obsessed determination Myra knew all too well. "He keeps getting too close and practically hopping straight in the air to get over it."

Myra crossed her arms over her chest. When Jamie had first told her about the surprise horseback riding trip across Ireland she was planning for Kate and Anna, Myra had been excited to be in on the secret. As part of the surprise, Jamie wanted to learn how to jump well enough to manage the cross-country obstacles they'd encounter on the intermediate level ride. After three months of frustrating lessons, Myra was having serious second thoughts about her initial offer to help. And third and fourth thoughts.

"He's doing exactly what you're asking," she explained for the umpteenth time with what she hoped sounded like patience. "You're making too many adjustments on the approach, so by the time you get to the fence he doesn't have enough length of stride to take off from that long distance."

"Of course you'd take his side," Jamie muttered. She unbuckled the helmet and pulled it off, running a hand through her damp red-blond hair. She gave an exasperated sigh and fanned herself with the hard hat. "Horse people."

Myra bent at the waist and put her hands on her knees, stretching her lower back while she searched for a way to phrase her instructions so Jamie would understand. She'd rushed through rides on three horses just so she'd be able to teach Jamie while Kate hauled a horse to the vet for X-rays. She wanted to tell Jamie to give up. Plan a cruise vacation instead and never ride again.

"You turn everything into a competition," she said. She straightened up and stuck her hands in her pockets. Anything to keep from throttling her best friend's girlfriend.

Myra put a hand on her belly and realized she felt the same tension as when she was talking to Ainslee. Another woman who challenged her well-being and made her feel the urge to stretch and grow. But Ainslee's presence brought up other urges than Jamie's did. Myra wanted to punch Jamie sometimes, but Ainslee? She'd prefer to kiss her. All the time. She curbed her sudden desire—as strong as if Ainslee was standing right next to her—and concentrated on teaching. "You seem to believe we're all out to get you. Dragon and I are in cahoots—he's trying to mess up the jumps on purpose. You're learning a new hobby, not marching off to battle."

"Do you know me *at all*?" Jamie asked. She jammed the helmet on her head so it sat low over her brow. "When I want to do something, I attack it. I'm not going to be one of your flower-child students, cantering around in a Zen-like state and communing with nature. *Be the jump. Lift your heart over the fence with butterfly wings.*"

Myra had to laugh. "Where the hell did you come up with that?"

"Some book Anna's reading. She keeps reciting passages about breathing with the horse and forming a beautiful partnership. I'm paraphrasing."

"Yeah, I assumed as much." Myra was still laughing at the picture in her mind of Jamie galloping bareback along a beach, like a scene in a movie, with her eyes closed and her arms spread wide.

"My point, Myra, is that you need to teach *me* how to ride. I'm not going to change who I am just because I'm sitting in a saddle and not a boardroom chair."

Myra shook her head. Again, Ainslee was filling her mind. *Don't expect me to heal more quickly than I can.* "And the student teaches the teacher," she said. "Okay. You're in a competition here, but you're not seeing the real adversary. You're trying to conquer and control the horse instead of focusing on the actual enemy. The jump."

Jamie looked at the tiny obstacle with a skeptical expression. "Hardly a worthy adversary."

"Please. It's been tripping you up for an hour. Humiliating you. Do you know how funny you looked the time you landed halfway up Dragon's neck? I thought I was going to pee, I was laughing so hard."

"Your point?" Jamie asked, frowning.

"My point is that Dragon and I are your partners. Like your assistant Jenn and your research department. We're gathering information for you, to help you overcome your foe. You trust Jenn when she gives you advice, don't you? Or do you try to control what she says? You need to trust Dragon the same way. He's more experienced and knowledgeable than you are right now, but he can't help you beat that damned pile of poles unless you stop micromanaging and let him do his job."

"That was a painful metaphor, but it makes more sense than most of your other advice," Jamie said with a wicked grin as she quickly moved Dragon before Myra could sock her in the leg. She urged the horse into a canter and aimed toward the jump again. She couldn't seem to completely stop picking at the reins and changing Dragon's stride, but she fussed with him less and the jump was smoother because of it.

Myra whooped and clapped. "Better!" she called as Jamie circled around her. "Try again, and this time make sure you have the pace you want before you turn the corner. Once you do, don't make any more changes before the jump."

Fifteen minutes—and at least as many jumps—later, Myra finally felt confident that Jamie had internalized the lesson. "Let him walk and cool out," she said, falling into step beside the pair. Jamie let her reins slide through her fingers and Dragon stretched his neck toward Myra. She rubbed his nose. She felt the quiet elation she experienced after particularly good lessons, when she was able to communicate more clearly and her students achieved breakthroughs, no matter how small.

"Good job," she said to Dragon. She patted Jamie's knee. "You, too."

"Thanks, Teach," Jamie said, tugging off one of her black riding gloves. "I'm not saying I achieved nirvana out there, but I think I got a taste of the whole partnership-with-the-horse thing."

"Careful," Myra said, peering around as if looking for eavesdroppers. "If anyone hears you, they might think you're getting soft. Even downright cuddly."

Jamie playfully slapped the top of Myra's head with her glove. "If you repeat anything I said today, I'll have to make you disappear."

Myra held up one hand. "I swear I won't. Except maybe the part about butterfly wings."

"You'd be wise to take my threats more seriously," Jamie said. "I'm sure Kate would miss you."

Myra laughed and draped her arm over Dragon's neck. They walked in silence halfway around the ring before Jamie spoke again, in a more serious tone this time. "How are you doing with your soldier therapy program?"

"They're doing well," Myra said. With only one lesson left in the initial eight-week session, Myra felt confident in her statement. Blake seemed more open, and Drew was already moving better on the ground because of the stretching and strengthening work he was doing in the saddle. And Ainslee? She'd improved physically, at least while on the horse. During last week's lesson, she'd trotted around the arena several times without noticeable tension or fatigue. She showed flashes of humor and the briefest of smiles. Had she really made definite progress, either physically or emotionally? Myra couldn't determine the answer, although she spent long hours trying to decide whether she thought Ainslee was getting healthier in the ways that mattered. She wanted to know for certain, since not only Ainslee's future happiness, but possibly also her own were at stake.

"Of course your students are doing well. You're a great teacher," Jamie said, waving her hand dismissively. "What I'm asking is how *you* are. I never met Jeffrey, but Kate's told me a lot about him. He sounds like he was a really special guy, and I'm betting you've been dealing with some difficult memories over the past seven weeks. I can't claim to know exactly how you feel, but I do have some experience in living with regrets and guilt."

Oddly enough, Jamie was probably the only person who really did understand what Myra had gone through. Jamie's sister hadn't committed suicide, but she'd pursued a dangerous life of addiction that had culminated with her death in a car crash. Myra knew Jamie had been left with memories of their last fight, as well as her injured niece Anna. They'd found a place of healing and love here at Kate's barn, but the scars never faded completely. Jamie and Kate had just started dating when Myra had lost Jeffrey, and Jamie had offered quiet and steadfast support without forcing Myra to rehash her story or rush through her grief. The shared experience had helped the two very different women establish an unexpected friendship.

"I see part of him in each of the riders," she said. She was still feeling a connection with Jamie because of their accomplishments in the lesson, and somehow that made it easier to talk about the emotions she'd been keeping locked inside. "Every time I celebrate a step forward for one of them, I wish I had been able to help him the same way. I swing back and forth between happiness and mourning so often I'm wrung out after only an hour with them."

"And it's even more intense when you add attraction to the mood swings. I know that firsthand."

"How did you..." Myra halted and Dragon stopped as well without any cues from Jamie.

"Kate told me," Jamie said with a fond smile. "She's been scheming."

"Tell her to stop." Myra's voice held more force than she'd intended. "I might admire qualities in Ainslee, but I won't take a chance on anything more than a student-teacher relationship."

"Why not? You're all flushed and pissed, so you must really like her."

Myra fumed silently for a moment, until she was sure she could speak without stammering. She wanted to vehemently deny any desire for Ainslee, but her voice and apparently her face would prove her a liar. She opted instead for honesty. "I can't go through losing someone like I lost Jeffrey. Never again. Ainslee seems so strong at times, but then she's as fragile as a stunned bird that just smacked into a window she didn't see coming. She doesn't know who she is anymore, and I can't…"

She stumbled to a halt after her spate of truth, and Jamie finished the thought for her. "You can't invest your heart without being sure she's here to stay."

"Exactly."

"Have you done a risk assessment? Have you told her about Jeffrey and asked her whether she can identify with what he did?"

Myra gave a bitter laugh. Leave it to Jamie to reduce love to numbers. Love? No—attraction. "Do you have a specific percentage of certainty you recommend?"

Jamie shrugged. "Sixty-three. If a proposal has a feasibility score of sixty-three percent or more, according to my personal scale, then I'll recommend my bosses invest in it."

Myra shook her head in disbelief. "What was Kate's score?"

A slow smile spread across Jamie's face, so full of love that Myra had to look away from the brightness of it. "Much lower," she said. "But it could have been zero percent, and I'd still have taken a chance on her. On us."

Myra stared at her hand where it rested on Dragon's neck. She wished she could be as brave where her heart was concerned, but the risk of loss seemed much too high. Intact and lonely had to be better than being shattered by love.

Chapter Nine

Myra set a bowl of apple and carrot slices on the table next to a bag of chips. She fanned out a pile of green paper napkins and fussed with the arrangement of a tray of hoagies. The treats for humans and horses were in the shade of the barn's awning, and a stainless steel water tub full of ice and drinks sat next to it.

Myra looked around, searching for something else to occupy her time until the students arrived, but there was nothing more to do. She and Kate had hosted countless end-of-session parties and they had the routine down to a science. Food, extra volunteers so some of the guests could ride, and a lesson plan consisting of mostly games and fun activities.

She perched on the edge of a large wooden planter brimming with pink, white, and red geraniums. She had more to celebrate than usual this time. Not only had her three students shown considerable growth over the past eight weeks, but she'd also gotten through her first military riding program without succumbing to the pain of her memories. Even though Jeffrey had been on her mind, she had felt comfort in the belief that she was giving his memory meaning as she helped other soldiers through the transition back to life at home.

Ainslee was a different matter altogether. She'd burrowed into Myra's life in a wholly unexpected way. Proud, yet vulnerable. Bright and sharp, yet dimmed—hopefully temporarily—by her wounded leg and soul. At times, Myra had wanted to speed the weeks along and reach the respite after the program's end, but sometimes she had wanted to hold on to certain moments forever.

"Everything looks great," Kate said. She made room on the table for a box of doughnuts and then sat next to Myra. "This program was even more of a hit than I expected, thanks to you. We already have a waiting list for every class."

"Any repeats from this group?" Myra asked with what she hoped was a casual air. She and Kate had already made plans to expand the program over the summer session, when Myra was free from her high school obligations. She'd have three beginner classes and one for intermediate riders. She'd already started the lesson plans for that one, and she'd pictured Ainslee doing every stretching and strengthening exercise she added to her list.

Kate bumped her shoulder into Myra's. "Blake and Drew are both signed up for the summer. Ainslee hasn't sent her form yet, and I don't know if she's planning to continue. I'm sorry."

Myra shrugged. After all the turmoil she'd felt when around Ainslee, she should be heaving a sigh of relief. Instead she felt empty inside. Would she ever see Ainslee again if she didn't come to the barn for lessons? Hadn't Ainslee noticed how much she'd improved in bearing and balance since she'd been riding here? Didn't she *want* to improve? "No big deal," she said, keeping her unanswerable questions to herself. "Two out of three is a good return rate."

"It is." Kate looked at her with those mossy green, knowing eyes. "And you still have today to talk Ainslee into coming back, too."

"It's her choice," Myra said. She felt a confusing mix of hurt and resignation. She stood up. "They'll be here soon, so I'll make sure the volunteers know the order of events for the day."

"I'll get the tack ready." Kate rose as well and put her hand on Myra's shoulder. "You should be proud of what you accomplished here, Myra. I know Jeffrey would be." She squeezed Myra's shoulder and walked into the barn.

Myra wasn't sure how she felt. Luckily, the time before the students arrived was busy with preparations for the lesson and party. She had just finished hiding the last set of stickers for the scavenger hunt when Blake and his family drove into the lot. Ainslee and Drew weren't far behind.

Myra welcomed the group which included Drew's parents and girlfriend, and Sasha, who had been driving Ainslee to and from lessons. She stood back and watched as the students groomed their horses. They chatted with each other and with the guests and volunteers, laughing and getting ready for the lesson with minimal help. She thought back to their first day at Cedar Grove, when they'd stood in distant and passive silence during their intro lesson. Hesitation and recalcitrance had been replaced by friendships and confidence around the animals.

"Remember the first time you did that?" Myra gave in to her clamoring need and walked over to Ainslee. She was balancing Deacon's hoof on her right knee while she cleaned it with a metal pick.

Ainslee laughed—a more and more frequent occurrence. "I seem to remember getting into all sorts of trouble with this hoof pick."

She gently lowered Deacon's hoof to the ground and straightened up. Myra handed her a fluffy white saddle pad and Ainslee settled it on Deacon's back.

"You did fine once you started using it for its intended purpose and not like a barroom dart," Myra said. She stepped back so Ainslee could reach her saddle. She wanted to stay beside her, to keep talking about the class. Their teasing only underscored how far Ainslee had come over the past weeks. But Chris called out a question about Spot's bridle, and soon Myra was immersed in the group.

The riders' moods were significantly lighter than they'd been on their first day. Even though Myra always planned a series of mounted games at the end of each session—and she hadn't yet met a group of adults that didn't have as much fun as children did—she'd figured this program would be different. When she'd met these three students, she'd thought they were much too serious to play, but she'd been wrong.

"Told you so," Kate said when she joined Myra in the center of the ring after a heated egg-and-spoon race. She handed Drew his ribbon with a flourish and they slowly followed the riders to the door of the arena. "What a blast. I've never laughed so much during a game day."

Myra's face was sore from grinning so much. Seeing the riders and their guests having so much lighthearted fun had made the effort of planning and implementing the program totally worthwhile. She wanted to bask in the success of the day, but she had one more event planned. She assigned volunteers to help Blake's kids with their ponies, and the rest were sent to various hiding spots around the barn to hand out clues for the scavenger hunt.

Myra jogged to her spot behind the hay barn. She sat on the roll top, a large rounded wooden jump that was covered with plastic grass. She and Kate hauled the heavy beast to the outdoor arena when they hosted horse shows at the barn, but today it sat in its usual place behind the tractor and the pile of shavings. Myra turned her face to the sun and closed her eyes, waiting for someone to figure out her clue and come find her.

"Ha!" Ainslee's triumphant shout startled her. "*Look for grass that doesn't grow. It hides away and comes out for shows*. You're quite the poet."

"You didn't sign up for another session," Myra said. She hadn't intended to blurt it out like that, with a hint of hurt in her voice, but she spoke before she could stop herself. She was supposed to put a sticker next to the clue and send Ainslee off to find the next hider, but if she didn't take advantage of this moment of privacy, Ainslee would leave and Myra would never have another chance to ask. "I just…I was wondering why."

"Can I dismount for a few minutes?" Myra held Deacon and helped Ainslee slide to the ground. Her hands lingered on Ainslee's hips to help her balance, and Ainslee didn't push her away. Myra sighed. The touch calmed her, even though her mind and heart had been in turmoil since Kate told her Ainslee wouldn't be returning.

Ainslee turned out of Myra's hands. She rested her arm along Deacon's back and looked at Myra. "I'm not sure. I was planning to, because I really did get a lot out of this experience. I was very self-focused when I came here. Angry and in pain. You helped me get my mind off myself and my situation for a while, to pay attention to the people and animals around me. I also was scared, and not used to feeling that way. I still don't understand why I was trying so hard to protect this leg when I'd already lost my real one." She tapped the toe of her prosthesis against the ground.

"You made us take riding seriously. You never assured us we'd be perfectly safe, you always reminded us that being around and on horses can be risky. I think I needed to be pushed past my new comfort zone. To take those risks again."

"Then why won't you continue?" Myra was grateful for Ainslee's words, but sad, too. There was something of good-bye in them.

"It's complicated," Ainslee said.

"Try me." Myra started in surprise as Ainslee—instead of answering—stepped forward and kissed her. Myra felt her heart thud as their lips pressed together without moving for a moment until the sensation of a deep exhale released the passion she had been keeping inside. Myra slid one hand along the nape of Ainslee's neck, tangled it in her dark hair, and curved the other over Ainslee's hip, pulling her closer. She nibbled gently on Ainslee's full lower lip and gasped in pleasure when Ainslee opened to her and met her tongue with her own.

Myra's world exploded into textures. The suede-soft flannel under her hand and the scratch of Ainslee's fingers where they twisted in Myra's T-shirt. The rasping brush of Ainslee's tongue and the mesmerizing suppleness of her satin lips. Myra's skin was electric with the feel of Ainslee in her arms. Jeans—she'd felt jeans before, nearly every day of her life. But the resistance of fabric where their hips rubbed together, the small catch of rivets and buttons, nearly drove Myra to orgasm.

Only the awareness seeping into her consciousness of other people nearby—and possibly headed right toward them—kept Myra from ripping off Ainslee's pants right there. She put a few millimeters of space between them, staying close enough to feel the caress of Ainslee's gasping breath against her face.

"Someone's coming," Ainslee said. The sound of laughter and hoofbeats pushed them apart like a tangible force.

Vanessa and Blake's daughter Heidi came around the corner of the hay barn just as Myra was helping Ainslee climb onto Deacon using the rolltop as a mounting block. She kept her hand on Ainslee's knee. Myra already felt a sense of loss with only the tenuous contact between them. She had to prolong it somehow, to keep a connection until she decided what she'd do about this attraction that had quickly grown into full-blown lust. "Will you have breakfast with me Saturday? Angel's Bagels at eight?"

Ainslee nodded, her face flushed and her eyes bright with the same desire Myra knew was shining from her own. She gave Ainslee's knee one last rub, and then turned away.

Chapter Ten

Early Saturday morning, Myra sat at a gray plastic table, enveloped in the scent of yeast and onions, and doodled on a paper napkin while she waited. She'd been nervous about this morning's meeting, but still she was able to immerse herself in her scrawled notes. A tap on the plate-glass window next to her made her jump, and she felt her face stretch into an automatic smile when she saw Ainslee on the sidewalk.

Ainslee came into the deli and over to Myra's table. Her limp seemed less noticeable, and Myra thought the sound of her right leg was more rhythmic than it had been when they first met. Or was she being overly optimistic and seeing progress where there really wasn't much?

"Thanks for meeting me here," Myra said. After sharing such a powerful kiss, Myra had decided to try the Jamie approach and give Ainslee a chance to either alleviate or confirm her worst fears. Maybe she'd be comfortable giving in to her interest in Ainslee if she had an honest conversation with her. She didn't have much choice—her desire was growing too strong to be ignored, and her common sense seemed to be diminishing in proportion. The reality of Ainslee's kiss had far surpassed even Myra's fantasies.

"I'm glad you asked me," Ainslee said. She sat down and looked around. "I haven't been here before, but it smells wonderful."

"You won't be disappointed in the taste, either," Myra said. Ainslee raised her eyebrows and laughed at the words, and Myra felt her face heat. She stood up and motioned at the counter. "What would you like?"

"What would I like, or what should I order off the menu?" Ainslee asked with a devilish smile. She scanned the chalkboard menu quickly. “A blueberry bagel with cream cheese and a white chocolate mocha, please.”

“Wow,” Myra said with a grimace. “Sweet tooth?”

“Guilty.” Ainslee shifted and rested her left heel on the rung of her chair.

“What were you writing so intently when I came to the window?” Ainslee asked after Myra had placed their order.

“Oh, nothing. Just scribbling.”

Ainslee leaned forward. “Come on, you can tell me. Were you writing your memoirs? Haiku? The complete list of Myra’s Barn Rules?”

Myra fished the crumpled napkin out of her pocket and tossed it at Ainslee’s head. “None of the above. I was balancing chemical equations.”

“For your high school classes?” Ainslee unfurled the napkin and smoothed it out on the table top. She pointed at one of the compounds. “What’s this one?”

“Phosphorous pentachloride. And no, it’s not for class, it’s just a habit of mine.” Myra usually brushed off questions about her game of equations, but she wanted to be completely honest with Ainslee today, and this was as good a way as any to start.

“For fun? Chemistry?”

Myra laughed at Ainslee’s pained expression. “I take it you didn’t enjoy chemistry classes in school. I find it comforting, I suppose. The beauty of these equations reminds me that the universe is orderly, even if it doesn’t seem like it in my life.”

“Huh,” Ainslee said with a brief nod. She folded the napkin carefully and put it in the pocket of her jeans. “I can see how that would be soothing. A little strange, though.”

Myra’s name was called, and she went to the counter for their tray of food. She tried to come up with a subtle way to broach the subject of Jeffrey while she and Ainslee silently glopped cream cheese on their bagels, but nothing came to mind. She decided to ease into the conversation after she had a chance to learn more about Ainslee. She’d read her service record and she knew some aspects of her character, but she wanted to understand her better.

“Now you know my secret hobby, tell me about yours. What do

you like to do? What subjects *did* you enjoy in school, if not my poor maligned chemistry?"

Ainslee didn't frown, but her smile disappeared and left a neutral void. Even her voice became monotone. "I ran track and was a damned good soccer player." She gestured at her leg. "Can't anymore. I liked studying biology and anatomy, and my goal was to be an EMT someday. Can't anymore."

And that concludes the getting-to-know-you portion of our morning. Myra's first reaction was to change away from the painful subject and find an easier topic for Ainslee to discuss, but she stopped herself.

"Tell me what happened when you injured your leg," she said instead.

Ainslee bit her lip and looked around the restaurant—anywhere but at Myra. She seemed about to refuse to answer, but she started talking in a hesitating voice.

"We were in a Jeep, driving back to base through what was supposed to be a safe part of the city." She shook her head. "Like any place was truly safe. But someone tossed a grenade, and the Jeep flipped over and landed on my leg. Gunfire broke out with us in the middle. I was…I was pinned there for almost an hour, before two soldiers could get to me."

Ainslee sat quietly, perfectly still, and Myra saw the same expression of inward vision that Jeffrey wore the few times he'd talk about the worst things he'd experienced. She needed to pull Ainslee back to her. She reached across the table and squeezed Ainslee's chilled hand. She sighed when she felt a tentative pressure in response.

"What was it like, while you waited?"

"Loud. I'd never realized how many different sounds a gunshot could make. A ping against the metal of the Jeep. Thuds when the bullets hit the ground." Ainslee looked at her, and Myra recognized that Ainslee was allowing her to see the anguish in her eyes. "I was with two other people from my unit. My friends. They were in the front seat when the grenade hit, and they were killed instantly. I couldn't do anything to help."

Myra wrapped Ainslee's hand in both of hers and raised it to her mouth. "I'm sorry," she said against Ainslee's skin, quietly and inadequately.

Ainslee inhaled audibly at the touch of Myra's lips, and she appeared to physically step from the world of her memory into the present. She gave a small shudder and brushed her palm against Myra's cheek before pulling away.

Myra wondered how such a cold hand could leave a trail of heat on her face. "My brother served in the Middle East," she said. "He deployed twice."

"I didn't know you had a brother," Ainslee said. She took a drink of her mocha. "Are the two of you close?"

Myra wanted out of the conversation as soon as she'd gotten in it, but she couldn't leave Ainslee's question unanswered. She had talked about Jeffrey's death with Kate and her family—always people who knew what had happened. She couldn't remember the last time she'd said the words out loud.

"We were," she said.

Ainslee set her mug on the table. "I'm so sorry, Myra. What happened? Was he killed over there?"

"No. He came home to us almost two years ago." Myra paused. "He committed suicide soon after."

"Jesus," Ainslee swore under her breath. "Why didn't you tell me sooner?"

"I don't talk about Jeffrey much, unless it's with people who knew him. And I didn't want my own sorrow to intrude on the program."

"Sharing your story would never have been an intrusion. I think we might have realized how much you understood what we were going through. What was Jeffrey like?"

Hearing his name coming from Ainslee gave Myra a sense of comfort. Jamie had been right—although Myra wasn't about to admit it to her—and she should have told Ainslee about her brother sooner than this.

"He was three years younger than I am, my kid brother. He was sensitive…not in a flaky, daydreamy way, but empathetic, I guess. Intuitive might be a better word." Few people had seen the side of Jeffrey that Myra knew so well, and she struggled to capture who he was for Ainslee. "He was popular in school, with teachers and the other kids. Athletic. He was on the varsity football and baseball teams. But he felt things more deeply than most teenagers. Animals of any kind adored him, and he'd be devastated if he saw one hurt."

She paused and blinked away the threat of tears. "My parents fought a lot when we were in school. They never got along well, and they finally got a divorce once Jeffrey had graduated from high school. He'd get so upset when we were young and they fought, so we spent a lot of time together, trying to distract each other."

Myra's speech halted again, and Ainslee gave her time to gather her thoughts. "I don't want you to think he was weak or cowardly because of how I'm describing him. He was a decorated hero. I have his medals at home. He just never got over what he experienced over there. He wouldn't talk about it much, even though I tried everything I could think of to help him. It wasn't enough. *I* wasn't enough."

Myra felt her eyes sting and she stared at her breakfast. She hadn't removed the tea bag from her mug yet, and the liquid was dark and murky. Her bagel was untouched. Ainslee lifted her hand to Myra's face again, cupping her chin and making her look up. "You sound like a great sister, and now I understand your drive to help everyone and every animal you meet. But sometimes there's a dark sadness inside, and no one can help a person out of it."

"You understand how he felt, don't you." Myra was stating a fact, not asking a question. She saw the sympathy in Ainslee's eyes and had the answer she'd been searching for—Ainslee knew the same darkness Jeffrey had felt. Myra felt numb. Resigned.

Ainslee brushed her thumb over Myra's cheek, leaving the same trail of fire her palm had left earlier. Why couldn't Myra's physical response to Ainslee follow the same rules of common sense and self-protection her mind had set?

Ainslee let go of Myra's chin and sat back in her chair. "In a way, I do. There were so many emotions to sort through, so much anguish. I get buried in self-pity because I lost my leg and my future, but then I feel guilty because I should be grateful I survived when I had to watch my friends die. I'm still struggling to break that cycle."

"But would you ever…could you…hurt yourself like he did?"

Ainslee frowned. "I won't lie and say the thought never occurred to me, especially when I first got to the hospital. I hurt so badly, and all my goals in life seemed to have vanished when they removed my leg. But it was fleeting and faded once the intensity of my memories and my pain eased a little. Why do you ask? Are you worried about me?"

"No. I mean, of course I care about you and want you to be healthy and well. But I needed to know for me, too." Myra wanted to reach for Ainslee's hand again, but her own were shaking and she kept them on her lap, fingers entwined. "I like you, Ainslee. You're beautiful and I was attracted to you from the moment I saw your photo. Meeting you in person just made those feelings stronger. More than just that, I love how complex you are. Funny and smart and challenging and sometimes frustrating."

Ainslee smiled a little at the end of Myra's sentence. "I like you, too, Myra. You stuck by me when I was having a hard time, but you treated me like a person and not an invalid. The day I saw you carrying those sacks of grain." She shook her head. "You were so sexy I couldn't stand it. I didn't think you'd want someone like me, someone…partial."

Myra had to remain resolved, had to explain why she needed to regain some distance between them. She couldn't help but protest about the way Ainslee described herself, though. "You're a whole person, Ainslee. You aren't lacking anything, and I hope someday you realize how much you still have to offer, and how much life has to offer you. I wish I could prove it to you, but I can't do it, Ainslee. I wasn't able to bring Jeffrey back from the edge. I'd never survive if I failed you, too."

Ainslee's smile faded, and her eyebrows pulled together in a frown. When she spoke, her voice was as icy as her hands had been earlier. "What are you saying, Myra?"

"I was hoping we could date, but—"

"That's funny," Ainslee said, leaning her forearms on the table. Her tone didn't sound at all amused. "I thought we were on a date right now. You asked me here for breakfast to, what, *interview* me for a date? And because I answered you honestly about the despair I felt after my accident, the pain I still feel, you're dumping me already?"

"God, no," Myra protested. She couldn't seem to make Ainslee understand that the reason she couldn't pursue a relationship was because she cared too much for her, not because she could easily dismiss her feelings. "You're not the one falling short here. I am. I'm not strong enough to keep you from that kind of pain—"

Ainslee stood up, interrupting Myra's words. "No one, no relationship comes with a guarantee, Myra. You either accept me as I am—broken but healing—or you don't. You've made your choice, so it's time we both move on."

Myra rose to her feet and put a hand on Ainslee's arm, trying to keep her from walking out. "I came close to self-destructing when I found Jeffrey and for months after, while I tried to recover. I'm sorry. I never wanted to hurt you."

"Myra, since the day we met, you've been trying to get me to have some hope for the future again. To believe I could still have a worthwhile life. Well, you accomplished your goal. When you asked me here, I was happy. I came here and took a chance on the future I've fantasized about since we met. Congratulations—you can add me to your list of successful rescue stories. Too bad you won't stick around to see how this one turns out."

Myra let go of Ainslee's arm and sat down, overwhelmed by the anger she felt from Ainslee and by her own gnawing regret. Ainslee turned and walked slowly but resolutely out of the café, with barely any trace of a limp.

Chapter Eleven

Ainslee moved through her days like a robot, scarcely feeling or noticing anything around her. She should feel some relief from her usual jumble of anger and fear and sadness, but instead the emptiness of apathy threatened to overwhelm her. She had numbly forced herself to eat a protein bar in the morning and get on the MAX to go to her therapy session. She would have canceled, but she had put off calling Dr. Campbell until it was too late to avoid going.

She looked at the directions he had given her over the phone a few days earlier when he had called to change the meeting place for today. She stared at the paper, unseeing, and nearly missed the stop. She made it off the train seconds before the doors closed and headed toward the gym.

She thought she had felt hopeless after her injury, but nothing compared to the sense of loss she experienced after walking out of the bagel shop and leaving Myra behind. She wanted to feel *something*. She should cry or scream or throw grooming equipment. Instead, she seemed to fold in on herself.

The problem was, she didn't blame Myra at all. She had been indignant and hurt at first, of course, but those feelings had turned into resignation. How could she expect Myra to be strong enough to take on this situation when Ainslee wasn't sure *she* was strong enough to bear this herself?

Ainslee pushed through the door into the gym and looked around. What did Dr. Campbell have in mind for today? Weight lifting? Ainslee didn't need to lift dumbbells. She was getting enough of a workout carrying around a load of what might have been.

Ainslee gave her name at the front desk and was sent through a door at the back of the large room. She caught a glimpse of herself in the floor-to-ceiling mirrors as she walked past. She barely noticed her limp, but what she did see were slumped shoulders, a lowered head, and a vacant expression on her face. She stopped and stared at herself. So this was what self-pity actually looked like.

She straightened her posture and glared at the mirror. A smile might have been preferable, but any emotion seemed to be an improvement.

"Shape up," she whispered. She was a survivor, if nothing else. She had lived, and she was getting stronger. One day she might thrive. She'd felt elated when Myra told her she liked her, and deflated when Myra changed her mind and said she couldn't handle Ainslee's baggage. Ainslee wouldn't let herself be broken. She would mourn the loss of a short-lived and barely believed-in dream, but she wouldn't allow this to destroy her.

She had been getting stronger than she'd realized, in more ways than she'd anticipated, but when she went through the back door and saw the rock climbing wall with its brightly colored holds, she felt panic squeeze her lungs until they were empty. She inhaled with effort and waved when Dr. Campbell spotted her and called her over.

"After you told me about climbing the hay bales, I thought this might be a sport you'd like to try. It's a great workout for your upper body, and a good way to practice more precise manipulation of your prosthesis."

"Sounds like clinically approved fun," Ainslee said. She frowned as she looked up at a climber who dangled above her.

"We'll take one of the easier routes today," he said as he stepped into a nylon harness one of the gym employees was holding for him. "Trust me, you'll love it."

"I'm not sure I—"

"I'm Sandy and I'll be supporting your climb today." A woman with shoulder-length black hair and a bright yellow polo shirt with the gym logo on it interrupted her. "Put your leg right through here." She buckled Ainslee into her harness and handed her a plastic helmet.

Ainslee put it on and tightened the strap with trembling fingers. No one was giving her any time to back out of the exercise. Before she could come up with a plausible excuse to run away, she was standing next to one of the easier walls and Sandy was behind her holding her rope.

Dr. Campbell grinned at her and grabbed a handhold. "Race you to the top."

He had a head start, but the words brought something to life inside of Ainslee. She reached for a green hold and began to climb. She found the rhythm of movement faster this time, and her sharp exhales matched the tempo set by her hands and legs. She'd been spurred on by Dr. Campbell's dare, but once she was moving, she only saw the next hold and the next pull upward. She heard Myra's voice in her head, cheering her on, and for a brief moment Ainslee felt what Myra and her doctors had been wanting her to feel. A connection to the moment. A reason to be present and a desire to move forward. The tears she hadn't yet shed for Myra threatened to come now, but she blinked them back. Later she'd allow herself to feel the pain of loss, but right now she had to climb.

She reached up and smacked the bell at the top of the wall, earning her some claps and shouts from the people who weren't doing their own climbs. Dr. Campbell got to her side moments after.

"Thanks for letting me win, Doc," she said, clinging to the wall.

"Yeah…you're…welcome. Thought I'd…take it easy on you."

She grinned at his wheezed words and his flushed face. Maybe she'd been faster than she thought. "Can we go again? I'd like to try one of the higher walls."

"Sure," he said with a weak wave before he started his descent. "But no more racing."

Ainslee carefully picked her way down the wall. She'd always had goals in life. Winning races, advancing in her career. Specific and visual. She'd lost sight of her old way of planning her life when she got hurt. Suddenly the vague notion of survival had been her only ambition. She balanced on her prosthesis and felt for the next foothold with her left toes. She needed to make some changes. Set some new goals for herself—some new walls to climb. She could create new visions and dreams.

Would Myra be part of them? Ainslee wasn't ready to take a chance on such a slim hope. She was getting stronger, though. Maybe someday she'd be strong enough for love.

❖

Myra squeezed the nozzle and directed a spray of water over the back of the pony. The mare shook vigorously and managed to get Myra wetter than she was. Myra sighed and pushed damp strands of hair out of her eyes. She was a sweaty mess anyway. A cold shower would do her more good than harm.

She'd been pushing herself like a fiend in the two weeks since her fight with Ainslee, but the long hours of riding, teaching, and mucking stalls hadn't put a dent in the blend of desire and sadness that had settled over her like a thick woolen blanket. Her mind felt fuzzy and sluggish, and her body seemed determined to recall every detail of Ainslee's touch and kiss. She went through her days on autopilot, hoping merely to get herself tired enough to be able to sleep at night.

She put down the hose and brought a bucket of sudsy water closer to the pony. She handed one sponge to Jamie's niece, Anna, and she took the other. Anna started on Calliope's legs and belly—the parts she could easily reach from her wheelchair—and Myra slathered the diluted shampoo in the palomino's creamy white mane and on her deep gold, nearly bronze neck.

"We'll need to thin her mane to make it easier to braid," she said, working lather through the thick hair. Anna was going to her first big show with her new pony this weekend, and Myra had taken charge of helping her get ready. Kate and Jamie were even more nervous than Anna seemed to be, so Myra had shooed them away, giving them a rare afternoon together while she and Anna did last-minute bathing and tack cleaning.

Calliope stood quietly as Anna wheeled closer and scrubbed her shoulder. The mare was worth the gold she resembled, taking perfect care of her young owner. Myra could barely recognize this Anna as the same girl who had shyly come to Kate's barn for her first lesson nearly two years ago. Now she handled her pony with confidence and growing skill. She'd never walk again, but she got to fly when she was on Calliope.

Myra soaped the mare's back and hindquarters, her eyes hot with tears. She got emotional thinking about Anna's journey at the barn, and she couldn't help but compare her with Ainslee. She had hoped Ainslee would experience the same transformation Anna had.

Myra paused while the sponge dripped soapy water down her arm. Was she being fair? Anna had always been horse crazy, and she'd had the advantage of living here with Kate and riding every day. Ainslee had only had a handful of lessons, but she'd improved nonetheless. Better balance, an easier smile, more laughter and teasing. Why couldn't Myra accept the small changes she'd experienced instead of expecting Ainslee to miraculously become whole overnight?

Because Myra *needed* someone whole and unshaken by life. She dunked Calliope's tail in the bucket of suds until it was saturated and reminded herself that no one stayed that way forever. Any human being would eventually face challenges that shook them to the core. Ainslee had met hers while still young. She was handling it in her own way, at her own pace—not Myra's.

"Won't she just get dirty again by Saturday?" Anna asked as she bent over to reach her pony's lower legs.

"We'll keep a light blanket on her until then," Myra said. "If we wash her the day before, her mane will be too slick to braid. Ready to rinse?"

"Yes."

Anna wheeled herself back several yards, and Myra got the hose again. She thoroughly rinsed the pony, getting every last drop of shampoo out of her coat, before flicking the water in Anna's direction.

Anna squealed with laughter and threw her sudsy sponge at Myra. "You're supposed to be washing Calliope, not me."

"You got as much soap in your hair as you got on the pony," Myra said. She shut off the hose and scraped the excess water off Calliope. "Can you put this conditioner on her hooves?"

"Sure," Anna said. She came closer and stretched nearly out of her chair without a hint of fear.

Myra could vividly picture Anna's first time at the barn. Jamie had hovered near the arena door—like a shark, Myra had suggested to Kate, but a scared one. She'd been used to protecting her niece by keeping her away from new activities.

"I can't believe I'm really here sometimes," Anna confided, as if her thoughts had been following the same path as Myra's. "If you'd come to me before I met Kate and told me I'd have my very own pony and be getting ready for a show, I'd have said you were crazy. I'd never have believed it in a million years."

"You've worked hard for this, Anna. You listen to me in our lessons, you practice every day, and you take very good care of Calliope. You made this happen as much as Kate and Jamie did, and no matter what happens at the show this weekend, I hope you feel proud of how far you've come."

"Thanks, Aunt Myra."

Myra, always touched when Anna treated her like family, smiled at her glowing expression. She thought of Ainslee's disparaging remarks about her missing leg. Would she look back one day with surprise and pleasure over how far she'd come? Would she be as surprised by happiness as Anna was? Ainslee had so much ahead of her, if she only tried to—

Myra stopped in midthought. What about her own happiness? She had put effort and love and her very soul into healing Jeffrey, but she hadn't been able to fix him. Now, she was expecting a relationship, a partner, to arrive fully realized and without flaw, when she herself was damaged. The cheerful, fun-loving woman she had been had nearly disappeared. When she looked back from the future to this moment, would she be able to say—like Anna had—that she couldn't believe how far she'd gotten because she took a risk and gave happiness a try? Or would she be the same Myra she was right now, alone and afraid to love and possibly lose?

"Are you okay?" Anna asked. "You look sad."

"I am, a little," Myra said. She went over to Anna and kissed the top of her head. "But I might know a way to make it better."

Chapter Twelve

Ainslee got a beer out of her fridge and carried it into the living room. She sat on the couch and took a drink while she looked around her. Living room didn't seem to be an apt description of the space. Temporary way station was more like it. Or storage locker. She had a sofa, a television, and some unpacked cardboard boxes she was using as makeshift tables. She shoved a pile of college catalogs out of the way and set her beer down. At least she didn't need to bother with coasters since most of her furniture was absorbent.

She picked up a yellow legal pad and added *decorate apartment* to her list. Once she had started to look for them, she had been surprised by the number of possibilities for her future. The germ of hope had been planted the day she and Myra were on their trail ride, when she had challenged Myra to imagine what she would do if she were in Ainslee's position. Ainslee had initially intended to prove her point—that she was right to wallow in self-pity and shouldn't be pushed out of it. Instead, though, she had realized that Myra would continue to be Myra, whether or not she had all her limbs attached. She would *do* things and *be* things, and not let her disability dictate what options she had. Ainslee hadn't believed she could be the same way at first, but she'd been surrounded by people who were convinced otherwise. Dr. Campbell had seen the same spirit in her, and he had brought her dormant competitive, goal-setting side to life. Since their wall climbing session, the two of them had spent time brainstorming physical challenges she could strive toward. Running a marathon, playing with a soccer league. Definitely continuing her favorite new hobby of rock climbing. Dreams she'd thought were lost forever suddenly seemed attainable.

Ainslee appreciated Dr. Campbell's belief in her, but other therapists had tried to bring out her will to fight and had failed. Ainslee knew what was different about this time. Myra. Her lessons had helped Ainslee gain strength. Her expectations had forced Ainslee to identify and control her rampant emotions. And her touch and kiss had awakened Ainslee's hope for the future.

Myra. Her name was printed in large letters at the top of Ainslee's page of goals. Maybe someday Myra would take a chance on love again. Ainslee hoped so. She was developing these aspirations for herself—she understood now how much she needed both concrete objectives and budding fantasies to give meaning to her life.

Ainslee tossed the pad aside and picked up her beer and the half-filled in form for the next riding session at Cedar Grove. She had lost her way for a long time after her accident. She had felt carried along by a tsunami of emotions and change, helpless in the hands of her doctors and her fate. She was starting to claw her way back to dry land, back to the woman she recognized as herself. Her, and not her. Changed, but familiar. As much as she wanted another chance with Myra, she felt betrayed because Myra hadn't accepted her with all her insecurities and messiness. Myra had helped her heal. She had pushed Ainslee to grow and challenge her new body. She had encouraged and supported her even when Ainslee was blinded by anger. But Myra had stopped short of loving her. Ainslee had been hurt, but she realized Myra was wounded too, had her own healing to do.

Ainslee heard a knock at her door. Probably Sasha with some of Ainslee's mail—the postal carrier was forever putting letters in the wrong boxes. Ainslee opened the door and just about slammed it again when she saw Myra standing on her porch. She looked gorgeous. Suntanned and healthy, in a sleeveless turquoise Western shirt that was tied in a knot at her waist. Ainslee could see muscular definition under the skin between Myra's top and her faded jeans, and the sight brought out the usual confusing turmoil of emotions she was coming to expect when she was around Myra. Lust, regret, anger.

"You were wrong," Myra said without preamble.

"Did you learn that conversation opener in charm school?" Ainslee asked. She leaned against the doorframe and struggled to fuel her anger at Myra, hoping it would overpower her desire. "Enlighten me. How was I wrong?"

"You said no one came with a guarantee, but I do. If you give me another chance, I guarantee that I'll accept you for who you are right now. Not the person you were before your injury, and not some unknown future version. You. Frightened, brave, uncertain *you*."

"Hmm, that's not what you said at the bagel shop," Ainslee said. Myra's words gave her hope, but she wasn't confident enough to grasp at it yet. Hopes and dreams had disappeared from her radar. Her changed outlook on the future was still too new to trust, even though she desperately wanted to believe Myra. "How could you change your mind in so short a time?"

Myra reached out and brushed the back of her knuckles over Ainslee's cheekbone. "I remember exactly what I said. And I believed it, too, until I was faced with losing you forever, Ainslee. Can I come in, please? Just to talk and try to explain myself?"

Ainslee wasn't sure whether or not to believe Myra's words. They were exactly the ones she had wanted to hear, but could Myra honor what she was saying? Would she walk away when the memories of her brother rose to the surface again? Finally, she stood back and made room for Myra to enter her apartment.

She'd been here since the beginning of summer, but she hadn't bothered to settle in her new home. She had just put decorating on her to-do list, but she hadn't fully realized how bare and sad the place looked until she looked at it the way she imagined Myra was seeing it now.

"I like what you've done with the place," Myra said. "It's homey."

The hint of humor in Myra's voice broke some of the rock-hard anger Ainslee was using to shelter her heart. Ainslee gave her a playful push. "What were you just saying about accepting me as I am?"

Myra laughed and grabbed Ainslee's hand. "I meant every word. Even if you get all your decorating tips from U-Haul. I just..." She sighed and her voice lost its laughter. She sat on the sofa and tugged until Ainslee sat next to her. "I just want to be with you. I've missed you so much, Ainslee. I didn't think I could bear being with you because you reminded me of what happened with Jeffrey. But I found out I can't bear to *not* be with you."

Ainslee stayed silent while Myra stroked her palm with trembling fingers. The combination of Myra's tender touch with the slight roughness of her fingers from hours spent at the barn was mesmerizing.

Ainslee's attention was wholly centered on the place where their skin was in contact, and she barely heard Myra's voice.

"I have a friend…well, she's Kate's girlfriend. She's an investment banker and is exactly the sort of person you'd want handling your money. She's savvy and brilliant—although please don't ever tell her I admitted those things to you—and she chooses the kind of investments that make millions. She told me the other day how she'd have taken a chance on Kate even if she had believed their relationship had zero chance of lasting. I didn't understand what she meant at the time, but I do now. I wasn't ready to invest in you or in us because I thought the chance of me getting hurt was too great. Even worse, I knew the chance of me hurting you, of not being enough for you, was even higher. But the alternative, as safe as it is, is unacceptable."

Myra inched closer until Ainslee felt the soft brush of Myra's breath against her neck. "I was a fool to let you go and I'm sorry."

Ainslee leaned her forehead against Myra's. She'd seen firsthand how much Myra cared about horses and people. Myra doubted her ability to help, but she proved again and again how able and willing she was to put someone in need before herself. Ainslee loved that about Myra, but she needed more than a protector. "I don't want to be just another of your charity cases. I don't want to be pitied or to be made to feel worthless if I can't pick myself up and conquer the world after what happened to me."

"I don't expect you to. I won't push you to be in a different place than where you are right now." Myra leaned back against the arm of the couch and Ainslee curled up next to her, her head resting on Myra's breast. The steady and comforting beat of Myra's heart finally broke through the last of Ainslee's defenses. When Myra kissed the top of her head, Ainslee felt the resulting increase in Myra's pulse rate. She felt wanted and accepted, and she kept still while the warmth of those feelings washed over her.

She felt Myra shift and looked up to see her holding one of the brochures Ainslee had set on the box beside the couch.

"What's this?" Myra asked. Ainslee smiled to hear the barely suppressed enthusiasm in Myra's voice.

"Don't get excited yet," she warned Myra. Her fledgling idea was still fragile, but Myra had helped Ainslee conceive it and she wanted to share her plans with her. "I've been researching other careers I could pursue using my interest in anatomy and also my own experience of being an amputee to help other people. I sent away for some information on occupational therapy programs in Portland. I haven't decided anything, so wipe the proud mother hen smile off your face."

"What are you talking about?" Myra straightened her expression into an unconvincingly neutral one. Ainslee tickled her in the side and Myra laughed, kissing her on the mouth. "Whether or not this pans out, I'm truly happy to see you looking for opportunities instead of blockades. I'll support you no matter what you decide to do," she said. "I think you'd have something very valuable to bring to that career, or to any one you choose."

Ainslee's hand was still resting against Myra's rib cage. She slid it lower and rubbed her palm against the exposed skin at Myra's waist. "And what will I be able to offer you in return?"

Myra shook her head with a look of wonder on her face. "How can you not realize what you've already given me? You brought me back to life, Ainslee. I had friends, horses, teaching, but I was alone. I thought I was safer that way, but something inside me has been dormant for too long. When we kiss, when I touch you, it's like the volume for my senses is turned up. You've changed the whole world for me."

Ainslee felt a slow smile spread across her face. "I feel the same way about you. I've spent so much time mourning what I lost, but I've found so much more in you."

Ainslee leaned forward and captured Myra's mouth in a lingering kiss. Slow and giving, grateful and full of promise. Myra wrapped her arms around Ainslee's waist, leaning back until Ainslee was lying on top of her. Ainslee raised herself up and propped an elbow on either side of Myra's waist. She slowly unbuttoned the turquoise plaid shirt while she kept eye contact with Myra.

"Before we go any further, I need to make sure you understand Ainslee's Apartment Rules, inspired in part by your barn rules."

Myra grinned. "What happens if I break one of them? Will you send me to the hay barn?"

Ainslee captured Myra's mouth in a kiss, sliding her tongue against Myra's until she felt Myra's hips twitch and shift under her. She raised her head again. "If you break one, I'll send you directly to bed."

"That's not much incentive to behave, but I'll try. What are these rules of yours?"

"Rule One, no inappropriate clothing. We'll need to get this shirt off you." Ainslee pushed the thin cotton over Myra's shoulders, baring her breasts. Ainslee licked her lips as she watched Myra's nipples tighten once exposed to the cool apartment air. She lowered her mouth and sucked one firmly against her teeth. Myra arched and gasped, and Ainslee switched to the other nipple. She circled it with her tongue as Myra's hands pulled her closer.

Ainslee came up for air. "Rule Two," she said, out of breath. "We're still getting to know each other, and I'll respect your space. I won't touch you without your permission. Please let me know when you want me to slow down or move forward."

Myra shook her head. Ainslee saw desire glistening in her expression. "Forward," Myra said, her voice rough. "Please. Touch me."

Ainslee moved her hips to the left and slid her hand between Myra's legs. She cupped her gently, and the damp heat she felt under her palm was surely echoed in her own body. She curled her fingers and kissed Myra simultaneously, both hearing Myra's moan and feeling it vibrate against her own lips.

Ainslee brought her hand back to Myra's hipbone. She didn't want to stop touching her, but she was rapidly losing coherent thought. She needed to tell Myra her next rule before her control was vanquished completely. This one mattered.

"Rule Three. I will ask for help when I need it."

Myra lifted her head and softly kissed Ainslee's lips. She pulled back and met Ainslee's eyes. "I understand. I won't take away your choices or try to rush you into anything. But I will be here if you need me."

Ainslee nodded, feeling the warmth of tears in her eyes. Even in the haze of desire and in the midst of playful touching, Myra understood when Ainslee was saying something truly important. She heard the promise in Myra's voice—the pace of Ainslee's healing would be respected and honored. She sighed and nibbled Myra's neck.

"Rule Four," Ainslee whispered against Myra's ear. "If you need to let off steam, get in my bed."

Myra laughed. "Deal," she said. She put her hands on Ainslee's cheeks and brought their lips together for a deep kiss. "Maybe we should go there now. I've been feeling a little tense lately."

"I can help with that," Ainslee said. Suddenly, even the short walk to the bedroom seemed much too long. "Right here and right now." She slid her hands lower and let her desire have free rein.

Investment analyst Jamie Callahan and Grand Prix show jumper Kate Brown take a chance on love in Worth the Risk.

About the Authors

Melissa Brayden (melissabrayden.com) is a multi-award-winning author of six novels published with Bold Strokes Books and currently hard at work on her seventh. Alongside her writing, she is in pursuit of her Master of Fine Arts in directing in San Antonio, Texas.

Melissa is married and working really hard at remembering to do the dishes. For personal enjoyment, she spends time with her Jack Russell terrier, Bailey, and checks out the NYC theater scene several times a year. She considers herself a reluctant patron of the treadmill, but enjoys hitting a tennis ball around in nice weather. Coffee is her very best friend.

Rachel Spangler never set out to be an award-winning author. She was just so poor and easily bored during her college years that she had to come up with creative ways to entertain herself, and her first novel, *Learning Curve*, was born out of one such attempt. She was sincerely surprised when it was accepted for publication and even more shocked when it won the Golden Crown Literary Award for Debut Author. She also won a Goldie for her second novel, *Trails Merge*. Since writing is more fun than a real job and so much cheaper than therapy, Rachel continued to type away, leading to the publication of *The Long Way Home*, *LoveLife*, *Spanish Heart*, *Does She Love You*, *Timeless*, and *Heart of the Game*. She plans to continue writing as long as anyone anywhere will keep reading.

Rachel and her partner, Susan, are raising their young son in western New York, where during the winter they make the most of the lake effect snow on local ski slopes. In the summer, they love to travel and watch their beloved St. Louis Cardinals. Regardless of the season, she always makes time for a good romance, whether she's reading it, writing it, or living it.

Visit Rachel online at rachelspangler.com or on Facebook.

Karis Walsh is the author of the Rainbow Award–winning romances *Harmony* and *Sea Glass Inn*, as well as a romantic intrigue series about a mounted police unit that begins with *Mounting Danger*. A Pacific Northwest native, she recently relocated herself and her goats to Texas, where she lives with her partner and their four-legged kids. When she isn't writing, she's playing with her animals, cooking, reading, playing the violin or viola, or hiking through the state park.

Books Available From Bold Strokes Books

Cold to the Touch by Cari Hunter. A drug addict's murder is the start of a dangerous investigation for Detective Sanne Jensen and Dr. Meg Fielding, as they try to stop a killer with no conscience. (978-1-62639-526-8)

Forsaken by Laydin Michaels. The hunt for a killer teaches one woman that she must overcome her fear in order to love, and another that success is meaningless without happiness. (978-1-62639-481-0)

Infiltration by Jackie D. When a CIA breach is imminent, a Marine instructor must stop the attack while protecting her heart from being disarmed by a recruit. (978-1-62639-521-3)

Midnight at the Orpheus by Alyssa Linn Palmer. Two women desperate to make their way in the world, a man hell-bent on revenge, and a cop risking his career: all in a day's work in Capone's Chicago. (978-1-62639-607-4)

Spirit of the Dance by Mardi Alexander. Major Sorla Reardon's return to her family farm to heal threatens Riley Johnson's safe life when small-town secrets are revealed, and love may not conquer all. (978-1-62639-583-1)

Sweet Hearts by Melissa Brayden, Rachel Spangler, and Karis Walsh. Do you ever wonder *Whatever happened to...*? Find out when you reconnect with your favorite characters from Melissa Brayden's *Heart Block*, Rachel Spangler's *LoveLife*, and Karis Walsh's *Worth the Risk*. (978-1-62639-475-9)

Totally Worth It by Maggie Cummings. Who knew there's an all-lesbian condo community in the NYC suburbs? Join twentysomething BFFs Meg and Lexi at Bay West as they navigate friendships, love, and everything in between. (978-1-62639-512-1)

Illicit Artifacts by Stevie Mikayne. Her foster mother's death cracked open a secret world Jil never wanted to see...and now she has to pick up the stolen pieces. (978-1-62639-472-8)

Pathfinder by Gun Brooke. Heading for their new homeworld, Exodus's chief engineer Adina Vantressa and nurse Briar Lindemay carry game-changing secrets that may well cause them to lose everything when disaster strikes. (978-1-62639-444-5)

Prescription for Love by Radclyffe. Dr. Flannery Rivers finds herself attracted to the new ER chief, city girl Abigail Remy, and the incendiary mix of city and country, fire and ice, tradition and change is combustible. (978-1-62639-570-1)

Ready or Not by Melissa Brayden. Uptight Mallory Spencer finds relinquishing control to bartender Hope Sanders too tall an order in fast-paced New York City. (978-1-62639-443-8)

Summer Passion by MJ Williamz. Women loving women is forbidden in 1946 Hollywood, yet Jean and Maggie strive to keep their love alive and away from prying eyes. (978-1-62639-540-4)

The Princess and the Prix by Nell Stark. "Ugly duckling" Princess Alix of Monaco was resigned to loneliness until she met racecar driver Thalia d'Angelis. (978-1-62639-474-2)

Winter's Harbor by Aurora Rey. Lia Brooks isn't looking for love in Provincetown, but when she discovers chocolate croissants and pastry chef Alex McKinnon, her winter retreat quickly starts heating up. (978-1-62639-498-8)

The Time Before Now by Missouri Vaun. Vivian flees a disastrous affair, embarking on an epic, transformative journey to escape her past, until destiny introduces her to Ida, who helps her rediscover trust, love, and hope. (978-1-62639-446-9)

Twisted Whispers by Sheri Lewis Wohl. Betrayal, lies, and secrets—whispers of a friend lost to darkness. Can a reluctant psychic set things right or will an evil soul destroy those she loves? (978-1-62639-439-1)

The Courage to Try by C.A. Popovich. Finding love is worth getting past the fear of trying. (978-1-62639-528-2)

Break Point by Yolanda Wallace. In a world readying for war, can love find a way? (978-1-62639-568-8)

Countdown by Julie Cannon. Can two strong-willed, powerful women overcome their differences to save the lives of seven others and begin a life they never imagined together? (978-1-62639-471-1)

Keep Hold by Michelle Grubb. Claire knew some things should be left alone and some rules should never be broken, but the most forbidden, well, they are the most tempting. (978-1-62639-502-2)

Deadly Medicine by Jaime Maddox. Dr. Ward Thrasher's life is in turmoil. Her partner Jess left her, and her job puts her in the path of a murderous physician who has Jess in his sights. (978-1-62639-424-7)

New Beginnings by KC Richardson. Can the connection and attraction between Jordan Roberts and Kirsten Murphy be enough for Jordan to trust Kirsten with her heart? (978-1-62639-450-6)

Officer Down by Erin Dutton. Can two women who've made careers out of being there for others in crisis find the strength to need each other? (978-1-62639-423-0)

Reasonable Doubt by Carsen Taite. Just when Sarah and Ellery think they've left dangerous careers behind, a new case sets them—and their hearts—on a collision course. (978-1-62639-442-1)

Tarnished Gold by Ann Aptaker. Cantor Gold must outsmart the Law, outrun New York's dockside gangsters, outplay a shady art dealer, his lover, and a beautiful curator, and stay out of a killer's gun sights. (978-1-62639-426-1)

White Horse in Winter by Franci McMahon. Love between two women collides with the inner poison of a closeted horse trainer in the green hills of Vermont. (978-1-62639-429-2)

Autumn Spring by Shelley Thrasher. Can Bree and Linda, two women in the autumn of their lives, put their hearts first and find the love they've never dared seize? (978-1-62639-365-3)